STRUCK BY HER

THE REFLECTION SERIES
BOOK 3

BY BRIANA MICHAELS

COPYRIGHT

OTHER BOOKS
BY THIS AUTHOR

THE REFLECTION SERIES:
BURN FOR HER
LURED BY HER
STRUCK BY HER

HELL HOUNDS HAREM SERIES:
RESTLESS SPIRIT
THE DARK TRUTH
THE DEVIL'S DARLING
HARD TO FIND
HARD TO LOVE
HARD TO KILL
RAISE HELL
RAISE THE DEAD
RULER OF THE RIGHTEOUS

SINS OF THE SIDHE SERIES:
SHATTER
SHINE
PASSION
BARGAINS
IGNITE
AWAKEN
RISE
EXILE
DISCORD

DEDICATION

For Jen and Carrie – Long live the dog walker.

CHAPTER 1

Sometimes violence clawed its way out of Bane's throat and damn near choked him. Other times, that side of him slept. Today, he unleashed his viciousness, and it felt so damn good, he could almost burst into fur. Chest heaving while his lungs sawed air, blood dripping down his face from the cut over his eyebrow, he'd never felt so alive. Dukes up, he circled his opponent—a fellow Lycan he should have never taken on. Locked in the cage together, neither held back with their strikes.

Bane took another swing. Missed. His opponent ducked down and ran at him, slamming into Bane's chest, driving him backwards in the fight cage. *Nice try.* When his back hit the fence, Bane used the barrier to his advantage by shoving his foot against it, climbing back and up. Hands on the fucker's shoulders, Bane flipped and landed behind the Lycan. Before his opponent could spin around and swing, Bane jabbed him in the side, sending him stumbling into the fence. Then Bane spun him around and clocked him with a perfectly placed undercut.

Cheers erupted all around them. It was static in Bane's ears. The Lycan sucked in air. Bane stepped back to give him a minute to collect his balls and strap them back where they belonged. Never one to end a fight quickly, he loved drawing battles out for as long as possible. Stamina had more than one meaning for Lycan. They loved a long hard fight almost as much as they relished a long hard fuck. Bane's energy had stayed bottled for far too long this time, and now that he uncorked his aggression, there was no stopping him.

He needed this. Bane hadn't made it to a fight club night in weeks. Circling a Lycan that had a good fifty pounds on him, Bane's adrenaline pumped fire in his veins. His mouth watered for flesh to bite down on. His cock ached for a something hot and tight. But this Lycan throwing hands with him wouldn't cut it for Bane.

No one did lately.

Good thing this was a Lycan-only fight tonight or he'd suffer with his self-control. Usually, Bane tested his skills in underground fight rings that were a mix of humans, Lycan, and the occasional vampire. There, fighters were forbidden to use their heightened supernatural skills. Don't want to scare the sensitive humans and all that jazz.

But tonight? It was anything goes.

So, when his opponent—a wolf named Cedar from the Vermont pack—challenged him, there was no denying the MMA trained shifter.

Cedar caught his breath, found some fury, and rushed at Bane. *Time to go next level*. Bane twisted at the last second and slipped under the brute's body. Cedar hadn't expected the move and ended up with his arms pinwheeling as he slammed against the cage. The crowd of jeering, barking, foaming-at-the-mouth Lycan rattled the fencing from the other side, growing more aggressive by the minute.

Such a newbie, Bane thought. *This was hardly worth breaking into a sweat for.*

Furious and embarrassed, Cedar turned around to face Bane and roared, "You cock sucking piece of shit!"

Bane blew him a kiss from across the cage.

This Lycan bit off more than he could chew with an opponent like Bane. Smarter, faster, and more cutthroat, Bane didn't give a shit about anything other than the endgame. Plus, he was definitely better looking. "Better fix your face," Bane teased. "You look like you fell out of an ugly tree and hit every branch on the way down, man."

Cedar growled low, his split lip peeling back to reveal his white teeth. He crouched down ready to attack.

Bane wasn't impressed. He sure as hell wasn't intimidated.

"Come on, Bane! Finish him so we can get out of here and have some real fun!"

Bowen, Bane's identical twin, always was an impatient

2

motherfucker. He had a point though. Bane needed to get this over with because the fight wasn't satisfying him the way he'd hoped. Usually, he hopped into one of these rings, pummeled a few guys, and got some righteous bruising himself. He usually went home feeling like he'd expelled a decent amount of pent-up energy. This bullshit tonight was barely a cardio workout.

So disappointing, considering how badly Bane needed a release. *Damnit.*

He poked and teased, goaded and pissed Cedar off, hoping to incite a more vicious reaction from the shifter. Even ragged on the shifter's mother—a dirty blow that should have Cedar coming for Bane's throat. No such luck. Bane gave up about five minutes later and cold-cocked the sonofabitch, knocking him out completely.

The crowd roared. Bane groaned. This sucked donkey balls. The entire night was disappointing as hell, considering he'd held back the entire time. This was supposed to be Bane's opportunity to go wild, not teach fighting 101 to newbies. Cedar had zero skill. Where was the MMA training? Boxing lessons?

What a waste of time.

The match ended. Bane felt anything but triumphant as he exited the cage. Dissatisfied, he stormed away, biting back a frustrated growl as he shoved his way through the crowd. The sooner he left, the better. Tonight's fight was an epic fail on so many levels.

"Come on, brother!" Bowen draped his arm around Bane's sweaty shoulders and guided him through the exit doors. "My cock needs a female's hot mouth, and yours does too."

"I need a shower first." He wanted to wash the stink off him before he tried to have any fun. "I'll meet you there."

Bowen arched his brow, a menacing smile crawling across his face. "The females will love that 'stink' on you."

So, his twin wanted to hit a Lycan club. Yawn. "I'm still showering." And maybe he wouldn't go back out at all afterwards. The night seemed to drain, instead of energize, him.

"What the Hell is your problem lately, Bane?"

"Same shit, different day," he grumbled. The muggy air did little to cool down his body. Lycan ran hot. Bane ran extra hot.

Bowen climbed into his truck while Bane slammed the passenger side door shut. They headed down the road in silence.

"Cedar was too fresh for tonight."

"Waste of time." Bane scratched his jaw. He needed to shave. "I can't believe his alpha even considered him up to my standards."

Bowen huffed a laugh. Hanging a right onto the highway, he gave Bane the side-eye. "I doubt anyone is up to your standards."

It wasn't a compliment.

"What's that supposed to mean?"

"You're edgy as Hell lately, bro. And you're setting the bar too high for everyone."

"So, I should lower it to make everyone else feel adequate?" Not going to happen. Not with fights, food, or females.

"Cedar tried his best. He's a new shifter."

"Then he should have been paired with a new shifter." Honestly, why was Bowen arguing about this?

Oh... wait... because Bowen kept trying to fill the role of Alpha and the good ones didn't tear shifters down, they built them up. Well, fuck that. Bowen wasn't Bane's alpha, nor was he Cedar's. "You forget your place, brother."

"My place is by your side." Again, Bowen's tone wasn't kind.

The tension between them had intensified recently. Bane suspected Bowen wanted to break away from the family and start his own pack, which he had every right to do. But that didn't mean Bane would trail along with his tail between his legs and follow him. He also didn't want to *not* trail behind his brother either. To be separated felt like he'd lose a vital piece of himself.

But Bowen's desire to be Alpha of his own pack was only half the threat that could tear the twins apart for good.

Bane was holding a secret tight to his chest. He didn't have the balls to tell his brother what he was considering—not until he made a final decision.

Hell, maybe not even then.

Bowen pulled onto the road that morphed from asphalt, to gravel, to dirt. The cabin they lived in was a modest size and well maintained. It once served their family as a vacation home, used by their father when making rounds up and down the Appalachian Mountains to visit other packs, but once the Woods family split off, Bowen and Bane claimed the cabin for their own and kept an eye on pack issues in this section of northern Georgia. It was close enough to family in case of emergencies, but far enough away to have space

4

and their own lives.

"You *are* coming out later, right?" Bowen hadn't turned the engine off.

"Probably."

"That means no." His grip tightened on the wheel as he blew out a breath. "Damnit, Bane, what's gotten into you lately?"

He didn't want to say. He wasn't ready to yet. "I'll be there. Just give me an hour to get pretty."

That earned him a small laugh. "An hour won't be long enough to improve your ugly mug. I doubt a year would either. You'll never hit my level of beauty brother, stop trying."

They were identical twins.

"I'll see you later, okay?" Bane really didn't want to go out again, but whatever.

Clenching his jaw, Bowen nodded once and put his truck in drive. Bane cringed a little at how fast his twin rolled down the driveway. Bowen was pissed. Okay, fine, totally warranted. But Bane wasn't in the mood to go out and get laid. Bowen was never not in the mood for a sweet piece of ass.

Sometimes it's best to go their own separate ways.

Scrubbing his face with both hands, Bane trudged up the creaky wooden steps and onto the porch. Unlocking the door, he exhaled loudly once he stepped inside. Leaning against the door after closing it, he stared around the cabin. The first floor made up the kitchen, den, dining area and laundry room. Upstairs used to have four bedrooms and one bath. Now it was two bigger bedrooms and two baths.

For being twins, Bane and Bowen stopped sharing things when they came out of the womb. The uncompromising need for their own space and things was something they both agreed on.

Once, they tried to share a woman. It ended badly. Both were too aggressive and dominant when it came to fucking—Bowen more than Bane—and they ended up calling it quits with their date before they even walked into the restaurant.

Damn near ripped the hinges off the door trying to hold it open for her. That was clue number one. Clue number two came when they both tried to pull the chair out for her. They meant well, but it came off as possessive. They actually broke the chair, pulling it apart. It was atrocious.

5

But what else would one expect from two shifters like them?

Bane couldn't imagine what they were thinking that night, trying to share a woman. Jesus, think of what might have happened had they gotten as far as the bedroom! Foreplay would have probably turned into a battle of wills.

Look, everyone had their limits. Their downfalls. *Oh well.*

Heading upstairs, Bane stripped as he went, all too grateful for a hot shower and a fresh pair of sweatpants. Those two things didn't disappoint. Twenty minutes later, in his steam-infused bathroom, he ran a hand through his short, wet hair, and stared at himself in the mirror. *Damn.* Bane barely recognized who he was anymore. The blood curse on his kind made the longing ache in his chest sometimes unbearable. Rubbing his sternum, he sucked in a ragged breath and swallowed through the tightness in his chest.

Every day, the ache intensified. Every night he howled in longing. It was an endless cycle that worsened as years passed. He was reaching his limit.

"Damnit." He walked out of the bathroom to sit on the edge of his bed. Mindlessly—because at this point it was habit—Bane pulled open the drawer of his nightstand and plucked the vial hidden in the back corner. Running his thumb across the glass bottle of silver water, he chewed on his bottom lip.

Should he do it?

His heart rate kicked up and put him in stroke territory at the thought of going through with this plan.

If he drank the liquid silver, he'd find his mate. If he found his mate, his curse would break. If his curse broke, he'd finally be able to live without this horrendous weight in his chest and hollowness in his soul.

But... if he did this, Bowen would be hurt. If he did this... Bane would see his mate in a vision, but might not be able to find her in time. If he didn't find her in time, his curse would drop kick his ass into the final stage and he would succumb to his animal side and be lost to his wolf form forever. No more man. All animal.

Was finding a mate worth that risk?

Judging by the ache in his chest, his constant restlessness, high standards that were never met, and increased aggression, yeah. Yeah, it fucking was.

Bane popped the top on the vial.

6

CHAPTER 2

"This better be good," Kennedy growled. What was her brother doing, calling her in the middle of the night like this?

"Meet me at the clinic."

She sat up and rubbed her eyes. "Are you okay?"

"Yeah, just fucking meet me there, alright? *Now.*"

Kennedy's heart hammered in her chest. "Tell me what's going on?" Jake already hung up. *Sonofabitch.* Her brother really pissed her off sometimes.

Why on earth would he want her to go to the vet clinic at this hour? He wasn't an animal lover, nor did he own a pet. There could only be one other reason, and the possibility made her queasy. He was hurt. Hurt enough to need medical attention... *annnnd unable to get it because it would raise questions.*

Holy Hell, Jake joining that motorcycle club would be his undoing. She told him it was a bad idea three years ago. She told him every time they saw each other that he should get out.

But there was no getting out.

Jake was locked in for life. Now he might be hurt.

Kennedy snatched her shorts and a t-shirt and quickly got dressed. One in the goddamn morning and she was running out of the house like this. Their parents were probably rolling in their graves right now.

With laughter.

It took her ten minutes to reach the clinic. Hand-to-the-Creator, if she got caught and lost her job over this, she was going to

7

kill Jake.

Unlocking the backdoor, her mind scrambled to come up with excuses in case her boss caught wind of this. Pushing things open, the scents of orange, animal-friendly cleaner, cold steel, and dog fur hit her nose. It took about three inhales before she went nose blind with it. She'd worked here for two years and now the smell of dog piss, shit, fur, and slobber barely registered.

Keeping her ears open for the sound of Jake's bike, she wasn't sure what to prep for. Maybe he needed stitches? If so, he could have just gone to her house for that. No, it had to be something way worse. *Damnit, Jake!* Biting her lip, she prepped one of the tables and pulled out a few instruments. Her palms were already sweating. This was a bad idea. A really bad motherfucking idea.

I'm going to kill him for this. Kennedy might do anything for her brother, but she had her limits and him dragging her into something dangerous was dancing too close to her hard line. Her gut twisted with bad vibes. This wasn't going to be good.

"Kennedy." Jake kicked in the back door, nearly scaring her out of her skin. "Help me."

It took her a beat to make sense of what Jake had with him. "Oh my god, what happened?" She ran over to help him with the Cane Corso in his arms. Or, shit, it looked like it might be a Cane Corso. It was hard to tell. This poor animal looked like it had come close to being eaten alive.

"Jesus, Jake."

"Just see if you can save him, okay?"

Kicking into save-the-animal mode, Kennedy helped Jake lower the dog onto a sterile table. Her adrenaline kicked in and she started evaluating what, exactly, she was dealing with. Bites, gashes, ripped out fur and flesh. Her anger burned a hole in her belly. "Another animal did this?" *Please say it was a bear. Please say it was a mountain lion. Please say it was a —*

"A Pitbull Mastiff."

God. Damnit. Kennedy wanted to scream. "So, *you* did this?" She held pressure to the dog's neck, which was the worst of the wounds. Never mind that he was missing an ear and most likely would never see out of his left eye again. *This poor animal.*

"I didn't do anything!" Jake barked at her.

"You brought this dog into a dogfight. *You* did this to him."

God, of all the shit things her brother's done over the years, she shouldn't be surprised he got involved in something like this. But she was. Like her, Jake also had limits. Apparently, those hard lines had changed for him recently.

"I wasn't part of it, Kennedy." Jake grabbed her arm and spun her to face him. "I swear it. I wasn't part of the dogfights. But I got there after it was over and this one," he said, nodding towards the dying dog, "was left lying in a pen."

To suffer. To die alone.

And some people wondered why Kennedy hated humans so much? They were the only animals she ever met who could constantly remain cruel and heartless towards others. Even rats showed empathy and compassion for each other. Hell, dolphins could go out of their way to save a whale left stranded. But humans? They screwed over whatever was in their way and used anyone or anything to gain something from it.

Despicable.

She wanted to believe Jake was innocent, but... "This is too far," she snarled. "*Too far*, Jake."

"Just see if you can fix him."

"So you can throw him back into another fight for your precious club? Kiss my ass." She hadn't told him the dog didn't look savable. She didn't want to believe it herself. So yeah, she was still going to try, even knowing it was a lost cause. Hey, miracles happened, right? She wouldn't be able to rest, knowing she hadn't at least tried to help this poor creature. But she'd be damned if she was going to give it back to her brother afterwards.

She jabbed her finger in the direction of the supplies. "Go into that cabinet and get me exactly what I say. You're getting your hands bloody too."

She could have sworn he mumbled something about having too much blood on his hands already, but chose to ignore it. The less she knew about her brother's actions, the better. That was always the rule between them. As she rattled off everything for Jake to retrieve, Kennedy prepped the dog for surgery.

They hadn't even hooked him to an IV before the animal passed away on the stainless-steel table.

"He's gone," she grumbled.

"Shit."

Looking up at her brother, she barely recognized him anymore. He had new ink on his neck. His hair was longer. Even though they saw each other every month, he'd changed drastically in a short amount of time. Thinned out. Got darker circles under his eyes. She'd seen the transformation over the past couple of years, but it wasn't until this very moment that he'd become unrecognizable to her.

Jake was all she had. And now...

The sound of engines roared from out back.

"Shit!" Jake completely panicked. "Stay in here," he snarled. "Don't say a goddamn word, no matter what you hear. Got it?"

What the ever-loving Hell had her brother just dragged her into?

Before slipping out the back door, he snagged a scalpel from her tray and sliced his bicep with it. Kennedy's heart stopped at the sight. "B—"

He pointed the bloodied instrument at her and shook his head, his lips a thin line. Then he dropped the scalpel and grabbed a towel. "Get the dog out of here. *Quick.* And don't come outside no matter what. I mean it."

Where was she supposed to drag a hundred-and-forty-pound dog by herself?

Jake slipped out through the backdoor, and as the heavy steel clicked shut, Kennedy's panic kicked into overdrive. But she did as her brother told her. Grabbing the dog's legs, she squatted down and tried to lift the animal over her shoulders. She wasn't sure where to put the poor thing though. Grunting with the effort of keeping upright, she pivoted and slipped on the blood that smeared the floor. She crashed down with a holler and lost her grip on the dog.

"Ouch! Damnit!" Heart pounding, ass aching, she sat stunned on the floor and couldn't get up in time. Not before the backdoor opened again, and she heard several pairs of boots stomp across the floor. *Shit, shit, shit!*

A huge man with a thick beard meandered around the operating table, towards her side of the room. "What do we have here?"

Kennedy was too flustered to move out of his way. She just stared at her brother, who'd come back in with two other guys

10

flanking him. If looks could kill, Jake would be on the floor like that poor dog.

"I thought you said she was here to patch you up, Diesel?"

"She is, Blade."

Blade. What a stupid name for a stupid-looking asshole. And Diesel? Come on. Who was Jake fooling with that bullshit? Kennedy kept her opinions to herself. The beast of a biker kept his eyes locked on Kennedy as he squatted down and placed his hand on the dog. Licking his lips, he gave Kennedy a once over before lasering his focus to the animal. "How did Ox get here?" He canted his head towards Jake. "Speak before I cut your tongue out, Diesel. Why is this dog here?"

But Jake didn't say a word. Kennedy stared at her brother, willing him to make all this go away, but when he froze up, she knew it was no use. Jake wasn't in charge here. With that, her anger kicked in and made stupid things fly out of her mouth like, "Leave."

Blade, the one who ran the show, half chuckled at her. "Not until you finish the job Diesel here came to you for." He grabbed Kennedy by the throat and hauled her to her feet. "Get your sutures, cunt."

"*Blade.*" Jake stepped forward, as if he was actually going to do something. The other two men made fast work of holding him back.

"You better rethink yourself," warned the one on the right.

Jake didn't budge, nor did he look over at Kennedy.

Her hackles raised. Jake never let someone else talk to him or treat him like that. How bad were these guys that he'd submit so fast?

Blade was a tank of a man who stunk like cigarettes, stale laundry, and whisky. He put his middle finger up and lifted it high enough for Jake to see. "See this? It's a warning. Next time you open your fat trap, actin' like you're gonna come at me, I'll make it a promise and split your tight ass wide open."

He was talking to Jake, but his threat was aimed at Kennedy. It made her stomach clench. She tried jerking away from the bastard when he brought his middle finger down between her legs and grabbed her there. "Sweet little thing like you," he said, licking his lips, "bet you scream real pretty when a man's railing you."

11

Jake lost his shit. Grabbing Blade by the shoulders, he—

Stopped dead in his tracks. Kennedy didn't even see what happened until Jake's face drained of color and a shiny new object protruded from his arm.

"You never learn, do you?" Blade grinned without turning to look at him. "Hog, Acid, one of you teach him a little lesson while I talk to the doc here."

Kennedy had no idea who any of these people were. Acid twisted the knife into Jake's flesh, making her brother shake even as he kept his lips sealed. Blood stained his shirt. Kennedy's gaze darted around to each of the men, then it flicked back to Jake. She wanted to reach out and save him somehow. Punch this asshole, Blade, in the throat. Stab the other two in the eyes. But she kept those fantasies to herself and watched as Jake twitched while locking the lid on his explosive side.

Her brother had a terrible temper, one that got him in a lot of trouble growing up. If he wasn't tearing these men in half, they must be way worse than Kennedy ever imagined. What a terrifying realization. She had to do something. Figure out how to get out of this and make sure her brother did too.

"Well?" Blade tipped his head to the side, drinking her terror in.

Well? Well, *what*? She didn't know how to react in a way that wouldn't get them both hurt or killed.

"You wanted to help." Blade let go of her throat. "So, help."

Kennedy shook her head, unable to make sense of what Blade was telling her to do. "The dog's dead."

"I thought Blade came here for you to help *him*. Ox was just in the back of his truck for disposal. Isn't that right, Diesel?"

Kennedy fought to swallow. Her throat hurt and was getting tighter by the second. When Jake didn't answer, Blade turned his fury on her. "Better answer for him, sugar. Seems our boy's a little preoccupied."

Yeah, with having a knife inserted into his arm, twisting and making his wound way worse.

"Yes," Kennedy said as she rolled her shoulders back. Lies were better told with as much confidence as one could muster. "I was just putting the dog in the freezer when you all pulled up."

Blade must know she was lying and let it slide. Thank God.

12

"So, help our boy, sugar. Looks like he's injured." Blade still hadn't spared Jake a glance yet. He flashed her a challenging smile, as if seeing how much nerve she actually had. If he thought she was a lamb amidst wolves, he was wrong. Kennedy dealt with plenty of assholes like this one before. They needed to up their intimidation game. Still, she didn't want to be hurt or make things worse for Jake. That's the only thing she kept thinking—*Don't make it worse. Get this over with and get out of here.*

Kennedy blew out a shaky exhale. "Hop on up, *Diesel*."

Maybe they didn't know she was his sister? If so, she wanted to keep it that way. Better to keep as much distance as possible between herself and Jake's shady life. She loved him, always would, but this was too far. Once she sewed him up, she was cutting ties and would tell him that as long as he was in this MC; he had to stay away from her.

Kennedy refused to look at him as she inspected the stab wound. The guy with the knife made a spectacular mess of Jake's arm. *Asshole.* "Can you make yourselves useful and put the dog in the freezer in the back?"

When they laughed, Kennedy got mad. "It's not funny. That thing stinks and is in my way." She hoped she sounded bitchy enough. "Do something with it while I fix your latest problem."

Someone whistled. "Ohhh, she's feisty. Diesel, where'd you find this bitch?"

Kennedy felt her brother stiffen. She wanted so badly to look him in the eyes but remained fixated on the shank in his shoulder. Damned thing was buried deep enough to hit bone.

"She's just cheap labor," Jake gritted out.

Pissed, she yanked the small knife out of his muscle and swiftly applied pressure to the wound. Was she being nasty about it? Yeah. Look, her heart bled for animals, not humans. And her brother was barely either of those things. Jake was diabolical.

Adrenaline made her hyper focused. Kennedy worked in silence and had to block out the sounds of his grunts and protests while she sewed him up with only localized numbing meds.

"Nice," Blade said from the far side of the room. Leaning against a floor-to-ceiling cabinet with his arms across his chest, he didn't look impressed though. He looked amused. Giving a signal to the man who'd stabbed Jake, he said, "Acid, give her some gratitude."

She immediately took a step back, not knowing what his gratitude would be.

Acid reached into his back pocket and slapped a few hundred-dollar bills on the table. "You're on retainer now. Your services are much appreciated."

"What?" Kennedy dropped her needle and suture. "No."

Blade whistled, and everyone fell into line. "Just so you know," he said as the men began filing out the backdoor, "I have zero respect for that word."

God, Jake wouldn't even look at her as he left the vet clinic with the others.

Kennedy shook her head. *Unbelievable.* "I'm not working for you, and I definitely don't want your money."

"See you soon." Acid blew her a kiss. "Better do something with that dog before someone asks questions. Oh, and thanks for your help. I'm sure Diesel appreciates it."

Shit.

CHAPTER 3

Too restless to get any shut eye, Bane gave up at around two in the morning. Roasting and nauseous, he kicked his sheets off and stared at the ceiling. Holy shit. Sucking down that vial of silver water earlier was possibly the most damaging thing he'd ever done in his life. He'd sealed his fate.

Signed his own death warrant.

Invited total destruction to upend his perfectly peaceful life, and for what? A chance at true happiness and love?

Seemed foolish now. But it was too late to go back. Puking the substance up wouldn't change a damned thing either. Once the silver elixir hit a Lycan's system, it was a one-way ticket to... where? Doomsville? Yeah, that sounded right. Doom was the perfect word because no matter what happened, the end was either become a wolf forever or rip a human out of their life, their world, their safe-zone, and literally throw them to the wolves.

Shit, he couldn't breathe. Sitting up, Bane swung his legs over the edge of the bed and rubbed his chest. Was he stroking out? Lycan didn't have cardiac issues, but there was a first for everything, right? The pain worsened. He winced and rubbed his chest harder. His wolf was suffering.

See, this was why it was good to have a support system. Usually, Lycan joined together for a huge ceremony and those ready to find their mate drank the liquid silver together, both for moral support and to enhance their shifter energy. Lycan thrived in packs for many reasons, energy exchanges being one of them. That was something they had in common with vampires. The vibes they radiated could help others around them.

15

And when you tip back a tiny bottle of fate-might-fuck-me juice, you needed all the support you could get.

But being the asshole, Bane went solo.

Was this what regret felt like?

Shoving onto his feet, Bane paced in his room. The walls closed in on him. Okay, time to move, be productive, do anything that required more than the pace-in-a-cage schtick. He went downstairs and made breakfast for a late-night snack—complete with pancakes, sausage, bacon, French toast, eggs, beans, hash browns and oatmeal. Almost called his twin six times between flipping the toast and burning the sausage. Then he debated on calling his eldest brother, Emerick, and his dad while stirring his hashbrowns. By the time he sat down with a loaded plate of feel-good-food, he couldn't stand the sight of it, much less the smell. Holy shit, he never expected the guilt of going out on his own, and taking the silver water in secret, to hit this damn hard. The urge to confess and regurgitate the elixir was unrelenting.

Time to go out for a run.

Between his fate and the waste-of-time fight earlier in the underground fight club, Bane was ready to explode. Too much energy and no outlet made Bane a ticking timebomb. Now he was also on borrowed time.

Lycan who drank the silver elixir only had until the next full moon to find, turn, and mate with their *Deesha*—their soul mate. If they didn't do those things in time, they were lost to their wolf forever and would end up being hunted and put down before they hurt others. How did one find their mate? In a fever dream. *I wonder what she'll look like.* He almost smiled while his imagination started building a sensual image. But... shit... what if his mate turned out to be a guy? He pumped the brakes on that one, because it stood to reason if he was into women now, fate would gift him a woman in the end. Bane had never been with a dude before, no reason to think fate would set him up with one for all eternity. Actually, it didn't even matter. Whoever his soul mate was, he'd be madly in love with them. It was *fate*, for fuck's sake. Who was he to argue or complain?

But was it a dick move to wish for a woman? He loved women. Never picky about shapes or sizes, he adored everything about a female. Their scent. Their softness. He was a total sucker for

16

thick thighs and that amazing little extra squish around their middle. *Oh yeah...* shit, his dick got hard just thinking about it. So yeah, hopefully fate gifted him with a curvy beauty with a set of thighs to smother him with and an attitude that kept him on his toes.

Talk about high standards. One might think women like that were a dime a dozen. They weren't. Not built with Bane's preferences, at least. He liked his women kind, smartassy, brilliant with an inappropriate sense of humor, and who loved simple things like naps and cuddling. But also fishing and fighting. Like him, but more feminine.

Wait. No. That wasn't right. *Gross.*

Damnit, he just wanted a good woman who made him melt in her hands but also let him dominate when the mood called for it. Or... could she at least like tacos?

Whoa, okay, was he actually making a wish list? Like the universe was going to jot that shit down and come through on his specifications for the perfect mate? He was ridiculous. Time to get out of here and go for a run.

Stripping out of his clothes, Bane stomped onto the front porch and sucked in the evening air. The full moon was last night, which meant he had as much time as possible to dream about and find his *Deesha*.

He also needed to tell his twin about all this.

Yeah, not going there right now. Time to run. Shifting into his wolf, Bane leapt off the porch and shot straight into the woods. The soft ground felt wet against his paws. His crisp vision remained sharp as he dashed deeper into the forest. Being in wolf form was freeing in a way no human could understand. It was as though every thread tying him to responsibility and morality got cut and left behind.

As a wolf, Bane cared only about freedom. For an animal, nothing else existed beyond those primal, base needs of wilderness, sleep, and the hunt and chase. Within minutes of shifting, his mind cleared, and he submerged into wolf-mentality. The scent of animals, dirt, grass, and fresh water filled him to the brim with delight. The cut of sticks and thorns on his paws kept him grounded. The wind in his fur gave his heartbeat an extra kick. Nothing compared to this.

17

He stopped halfway down a trail and looked around. *Threats, threats, threats. None.* Pushing off with his hind legs, he ran further into the woods as if he could truly outrun the consequences of his actions. Hours later, Bane was still running, only now he felt the joy of it less and less. The clear-headedness that came from being in wolf form weighed heavy with human thoughts. *This a first.* Was it caused by the magic from the liquid silver? It made sense–the wolf and man were both in need of a mate. A blend of minds would be part of that. Bane was a full-blooded Lycan. Separation of man and wolf didn't last long past his third birthday, so he was too young to remember what it was like. Even as a wolf, he could think at a higher level, as if still in human form. His instincts and needs, however, remained simpler. Until now.

He'd never asked another Lycan what it was like to take the liquid silver. It seemed too personal of a question, and terrifying too. This shit wasn't for the weak-hearted romantics. It was do or die.

Bane's claws dug into hard earth. He ran for so long he'd lost track of where he was.

What if I'm a wolf forever? What if I fail and I can never be with my family and friends again?

The weight of his actions slowed him down. His ears twitched. As if the entire state park had cleared out when they sensed him enter, the area seemed void of heartbeats. Such stillness came with a collection of held breaths. A bracing for impact. Or that was his paranoia and guilt getting the better of him. He looked around to gain his bearings. Wait, was he still in the State Park? His property bordered game lands, and with his head a mess, he'd managed to get lost. Disoriented, he dashed to the right.

Bane's sense of smell was off. *It just gets better and better.* His mind jumbled with animal and human emotions, which clashed against each other. He yipped, reared back, and bolted in a different direction. Lost, lost, lost. He couldn't shake the urge to keep moving, but had no clue which direction to go. This had never happened to him before.

Panic's grip tightened around his throat like a choke collar.

Home. He needed to get home. Dodging around a dead tree, he half-ran, half-slid down a steep slope. In order to not lose balance, he committed to the run and stayed low to the ground, picking up pace. The ground shifted, morphing from dirt, to grass, to rock, to asphalt. Bane's ears perked up, and a roaring noise coming from his left. Turning his head, Bane froze as a pair of headlights came straight at him.

The impact was so fast, he barely felt a thing.

Crying her eyes out, Kennedy drove home with more rage packed into her than she'd felt in a long goddamn time. Alone, pissed, and scared, she cleaned up the vet clinic and got rid of all evidence. The more she scrubbed and put shit away, the angrier she grew too. This was bullshit. Every fucking bit of it.

How dare Jake get her roped into his shitshow. How dare those assholes use poor dogs in a fight!

Kennedy didn't know what she was most upset about—the fate of the dogs, or that Jake's choices and actions had, once again, bled into her quiet life to stain and wreck it.

Ever since they were kids, Jake always landed in trouble. He came by it honestly—trouble ran in their genes. Their parents were menaces to society, and the fact that Kennedy didn't follow in their footsteps made them bully her to no end. To put it mildly, the parent/child dynamic in their household had been unhealthy.

Her parents took turns belittling Kennedy because she got good grades, never took them up on their offers to have a beer—even at the age of eleven—and the fact that she preferred books and animals to people, drugs, and TV made her a disgrace to their family name. They hated everything about her.

You think you're too good for us, huh? You think because you get good grades, you're better than us, smarter than us? Yeah, she was. But she never said it. Even when it got too hard to live under their falling down roof, she stayed, if only to make sure they didn't let the house fall down around their ears and collapse with Jake in the center of their sorry ass lives. He was older, but she was wiser.

Jake slept on the couch of their two-bedroom mobile home and gave her the tiny bedroom that served as a safe space for her and closet for him. It wasn't ideal, but it worked. So long as they had each other, every less-than-ideal situation seemed doable.

Meanwhile, her parents knocked her down, called her names,

made fun of her, and once her dad even set fire to all her schoolwork. She spent less and less time at home when they were there, and more time in libraries and pet stores. Jake covered for her all the time, making excuses for why she wasn't around during their big parties with enough weed to choke out the neighborhood and pills of the mix-and-match variety in a dish once used to serve mints by Kennedy's grandmother's house.

While they praised Jake for being their pride and joy, Kennedy remained in the shadows or gone from sight all together. She often wondered if Jake liked her gone sometimes just for the chance to get all the praise without the guilt of her hurt feelings.

In their house, Jake was a golden child. Kennedy was the outsider.

Now look. He'd followed in mom and dad's footsteps and joined the worst motorcycle club possible and now Kennedy was linked to them.

She stared at the wadded-up cash on her passenger seat. The icing on this shit-tastic cake? She needed the money.

That's probably where the rage was really coming from. The old Kennedy would have tossed that shit in the trash and refused to take it on principal. But the old Kennedy didn't have substantial debt. And let's face it, whether she took the money or not, Blade, Hog, Acid, and whoever else was in that MC with "Diesel" would still consider her on retainer. She might as well put the money to good use and pay off more of her bills while she could. The sooner she could become untraceable, the better.

"Damnit, Jake!" A fresh wave of disappointment washed over her, and she slammed her palms on the steering wheel. She couldn't even see the road; she was crying so hard. Hitting it once didn't help. Two, three more times, barely did a thing. Gripping it half to death also did nothing to make her feel better. There was no outlet for this level of anger. She ugly cried even harder and stepped on the gas pedal. Maybe speed down an open road in the middle of the night would bring relief.

She didn't see the animal up ahead. Not until she was directly upon it.

"Oh God!" She hit it. The impact was sickening. As was the *bum-bump* of her rear tires rolling over whatever it was.

Kennedy screamed, slammed on the brakes, and nearly spun

out. Sucking in air, she panted with eyes wide in terror once her car finally slammed to a stop. Fumbling with her seatbelt, she got the damned thing unlocked and opened her door.

"Oh god, oh god." She scanned the road, desperate to find what she had hit. Was it dead already? Jesus, where was it? *What* was it? A bear? A deer? A —

She sucked in a sharp breath. Twenty feet away, on the side of the road, was a... a *wolf*?

"Oh no," she whispered as she approached the wounded animal cautiously. It was still breathing, but its hind leg was badly injured. The wolf laid on its side, panting and whimpering. "Hey, buddy." Kennedy kept her voice nice and soft. "Don't bite me, okay? Let me just —"

The wolf gnashed his teeth at her and tried to scramble away. The effort caused him more pain, and he rolled back, unable to use his back legs. Shouldn't there be more damage done to him? At a quick glance, he didn't look nearly as injured as she expected him to be. Then again, it was dark, and it's not like she could get too close to him yet.

"Easy, boy. *Easy.*"

She couldn't just leave him here to suffer. And she couldn't very well pick up a wild, wounded wolf off the side of the road and not expect to get attacked by it. Wolves were skittish, but no animal went without putting up a fight. Especially scared, hurt ones.

"This night just keeps getting better and better."

Fortunately, she had a field bag in her trunk. "Hang on, boy."

The wolf tried to get up again but failed. It made her heart clench. She'd caused this. In throwing a fit over her brother while driving, she'd endangered an innocent creature. Kennedy's chest tightened as she ran back to her car, popped the trunk, and dug around for the right stuff. Staring at the syringe, she bit her lip as reality hit her. Was she really going to drug a wolf? Then what? Carry him back to the vet and fix him?

You bet your ass she was. No other alternative registered. Her instinct was to save him.

"Okay," she said to the wolf, now baring all his teeth and snarling at her. "This is gonna sting." The closer she got, the more agitated he became. Holding the syringe in one hand, she got down on her knees, leaned forward and froze. This wasn't going to work.

21

He was too scared and hurt, defending himself the only way he could. No way did she want to get bit by this thing.

Damnit.

Sitting down at a safe distance, Kennedy waited it out. It killed her to do it. Made her sick to sit there while an animal suffered in front of her. To calm her nerves, and hopefully the animal's, she talked to him instead. Treated that beast like he was a person, not a wolf. All the while hoping like hell the poor thing wasn't suffering from internal bleeding. "I've had the worst night," she said. "But I gotta say, you might have topped mine. Sorry about that."

The wolf stopped snarling and stared at her with his tongue lolling to the side. He must be in serious distress, which was entirely her fault. "What were you doing tonight, huh? Getting some rabbit?" When was the last time she'd had something to eat herself? Shit, she couldn't remember. Annnd now her stomach growled. The wolf's ears twitched. "It must be fun being a wolf," she inched a little bit closer. "Life's so simple for animals, right? Eat, hunt, sleep, play. I mean, it helps if you're at the top of the food chain, but still... I think even being a muskrat would be a better deal than being human."

He whimpered in response. His pants getting shorter and faster. She needed to make her move before it was too late to save him. No way was she losing two canines in one evening. Her heart couldn't take more failure. "I'm really sorry," she said, inching closer to him. "I didn't mean to hit you. And I hate that I've waited this long to help you, but I'm not trying to get eaten, ya know?" Kennedy finally made her way over to him and risked putting her knuckles at his nose for him to sniff.

The wolf was huge. Healthy. His fur, a thick blend of light and dark browns. He looked magnificent in the moonlight. His ears had black tufts. Kennedy patiently waited as the wolf sniffed her. She could only imagine what was going through his head. Figured it wasn't good once when he jerked back and snorted.

"Yeah, that's sanitizing chemicals leftover from a clean-up job I just did. Strong stuff, right?" She smiled and kept her hand still for him to come back to. He eventually did, and as she reached up to scratch behind his ear, her heart sank. "I'm so sorry, big guy." Kennedy jabbed the needle in his hind leg and sprang into action.

22

CHAPTER 4

Look, this was a big wolf. Getting him into her car was no small feat. Kennedy pulled a few muscles hoisting the beast into the back seat of her car. His back leg was gruesome, but there weren't many other serious injuries. Again, she wondered how that was possible. It was a miracle and a half, for sure. Shifting gears, she started down the street again, gritting her teeth at the sound of something grinding underneath her car. She could only imagine the damage done to her vehicle. Not that she'd looked at it yet, or that it really mattered in comparison to the unconscious wolf in her back seat.

At least her air bags hadn't gone off. Small silver linings were pretty sweet.

Constantly checking on him, Kennedy kept reaching back there to stroke the wolf's head while talking to him. It was pointless because the chances of him hearing, much less understanding what she was saying, were zilch. Those meds had knocked him out completely. "Almost there," she said in an exhausted tone.

What on earth was she going to do with this animal once she patched him up? For the tenth time, Kennedy prayed there wasn't any internal bleeding. What if he needed a lot more care than she could give him? Should she report this? Have someone take him to a sanctuary?

Her lips curled downwards at the thought.

Maybe it was sleep deprivation, or maybe she was finally at her mental limit, but she didn't want to release this wolf to anyone.

She struck him, so she'd care for him and set him free herself. Wolves were smart. He'd know where to go once unleashed.

And then what? Would he get hit by another car again someday?

"Pull your shit together, Kennedy." She gritted her teeth and managed to get the beast inside through the back door. Sometimes it felt like she lived at work. In the wee hours of the morning, kicking that damned door open and flicking on the lights, she felt like she'd never left. It was exhausting on so many levels.

This place, she silently groaned. She was torn between gratefulness and resentment. Kennedy put in more hours than anyone else on payroll and had very little to show for it. Always trying to prove herself, always seeking her boss's approval, always preferring animals as company over humans, she was a workaholic for too many reasons.

No wonder she was still single. *Oy.*

"Come on, big guy." She got him all the way onto the surgical table and propped his head. Man, the gash was sizeable on his hind leg, but other than that, he was in fairly good shape. X-rays confirmed nothing was broken. Hallelujah.

She talked to him the entire time she sewed him up. Checking his teeth, gums, and paws, she was beyond impressed with him. He was probably the healthiest animal in the woods. If his size had anything to say about it, this wolf was at least fit and well fed. It made her wonder how many more like him there were. And why had she never seen one before now?

As his breathing slowed and strengthened, Kennedy wrapped his leg and ended up talking to him about everything and anything. God, she needed to get out and socialize more.

But one of the best things about animals was they listened. Although, granted, this one was still light's out. Looking up at the clock, she had about an hour before the first shift of vets and techs rolled in. One more time, she lifted the wolf up and got him into one of the large kennels to recuperate. Some small voice in the back of her head wanted Kennedy to put the wolf in her car and take him home. But if he had any complications from the sedatives, or there was something internally wrong that she'd missed, it was best to keep him here for now.

"Okay, you sleep and I'll figure out what to do with you as

24

soon as I can. I'll be back later to check on you, okay?" she rubbed his head before pulling back and locking the cage door.

Bane groaned, his head throbbed so hard his teeth had a pulse. Jesus, had he gone on another moonshine binge with his brothers again and not even remember it?

Worst. Hangover. Ever.

Groaning, he tried to stretch out and a shock of pain zipped up his leg and straight out of his mouth in a yelp. What the—

He was still in wolf form. And… he was in a cage.

Oh, hell to the no.

Gritting his teeth, he shifted back into human form and nearly puked with the pain wracking through him. A bitter, chemical taste filled his mouth, making him gag. This wasn't a hangover. He'd been drugged. The taste in his mouth made his stomach roll and as he sat up and rubbed his eyes, it took way too long for things to clear up.

Bars. The scent anesthetic. Animals. Piss. He shifted his hulking body and hissed at the pain biting into his leg. Shit, there was a massive bandage over his thigh. And his stitches had ripped during his shift. Fuck him sideways. What the hell happened?

The events of last night took their good ol' time to piece together. Liquid silver, running, woods, panic, confusion, *headlights*.

He'd been hit by a car.

Just his luck. At least Lycan were sturdy creatures. The car probably suffered more injury than he did. But still, he'd been drugged, sewn up, and locked into a fucking kennel. *Oh, the humiliation.* He needed to get out of here. It was a miracle he hadn't reverted to his human form when the car slammed into him. But then again, Lycan magic worked in a way that one shifted into their stronger form when their health was threatened. Bane's wolf was stronger than his human side.

What a kick in the balls.

Nausea worked him into a mouthwatering, swaying, half-drunk lug of a man. Naked, bruised, and bleeding, Bane looked around the kennel. Most of the cages he could see were empty. He smelled citrus-scented cleaning products, antiseptic spray, cold metal, wet concrete, and a lot of animal. Clenching his teeth, he kicked the door with the heel of his foot, springing it from the hinges.

Two dogs in kennels further down cowered in the corner of their cages and didn't make a sound. Bane didn't take offense. The aggression rolling off him was pungent. And....

He took a whiff under his armpit. What... What the hell was that? *Pheromones?*

That silver magic was kicking in big time. Holy shit, he should have done more homework on that stuff to have been better prepared. Fine time for his body to go into mate-mode when he was jacked up and bound in bandages.

Voices rose from the room beyond the kennel, springing Bane into action. He better get out of here before he got caught. Limping, he hit the back door with his bare ass and stumbled into the morning light.

Shit, shit, shit, where was he?

His eyes watered at the brightness of the morning sun. Hobbling forward, eyes streaming with sunrise tears, he doubled over, vomiting the drugs out of his system. Lycan were sensitive to manmade sedatives. It fucked their magic up. Staggering around to hide behind a large bin at the back of the clinic, he sucked in air and puked two more times.

Bane's gaze locked on a car with both the front and back doors wide open. Well, if that wasn't an invitation, he didn't know what was. Bane rushed forward, sweat pouring down his temples and back, and slid into the driver's side. The key was still in the ignition! Could this get any better? Bane started it up, slammed down on the gas pedal, forcing the car to lurch forward just as the back door to the clinic swung open. A woman ran after him, hollering, "Stop!" while he tore out of the back parking lot.

He made it ten miles up the road before guilt set in. He stole a car. It probably belonged to that woman. And going off the scent of the blood in the backseat, and the way the wheels were wobbling, this was the vehicle that smashed into him like a wrecking ball earlier.

With no phone, no clothes, and no cash, he had no choice but to keep the pedal to the metal until he made it home. He was running on fumes by the time he made it there.

26

Stumbling out of the car, he hollered for his twin. Shit, he couldn't see straight. And the ground... who decided to rip it out from under his feet? The sky turned upside down as he fell onto his back, knocking the wind out of himself.

Breathing through a fresh set of what-the-hell's-happening-to-me, Bane clutched his thigh and snarled.

"What happened?" Bowen's voice struck Bane's ears with a resounding thud. Or maybe that was his heart rate slowing down? Or his headache getting worse?

"Car. Hit. Sedative." He blacked out.

"Wakey, wakey, eggs and bakey." Bowen waved a bacon, egg, and cheese sandwich in Bane's face. "Come on, brother. Wake up."

Bane's wolf-side growled, even as he reached up and took the sandwich. Grease and meat would help. "You put extra cheese on it?"

"Of course." Bowen's brow furrowed. "You want to explain to me what's going on?"

"Got hit by a car. I don't remember much past that."

"You mentioned sedatives."

"Mmmph." Damn, this sandwich was good. "You got more of this?"

"Six more on the counter."

Bane was on the couch. He didn't remember getting this far. He barely remembered the trip home. "The cops might come."

Bowen stiffened. "What did you do?"

"Stole a car."

"That hunk of metal is called a car? You must have really hit your head hard."

"Call around and see if you can't get new parts to replace the damaged ones. I'll pop the smaller dents out, but she'll need a new bumper and fender. Jack it up to see what damage was done underneath."

"You can't be serious," Bowen argued. "What are you going to do, fix the thing and return it?"

That's exactly what he planned. "It's the right thing to do."

Sitting down next to him on the couch, Bowen scrubbed his face with a heavy sigh. "What happened? And I don't want to hear you can't remember. Put your wolf to the test if you can't man up."

"I went for a run. Ended up on the south part of the game lands."

"You ran a long distance."

Much longer than he'd realized. "I had a lot of energy to expel."

"You sure that's all it was?"

"Yeah." *No.*

Bowen leaned forward to rest his elbows on his knees. Turning his head, he deadpanned Bane. "What have you done, brother?"

"Nothing." *Liar, liar, fur on fire.*

"Okay." Bowen smiled all toothy and angrily. "Fine. Then I'll go first." Straightened his posture and rubbed his palms up and down his thighs. "I'm moving."

Bane's face tingled. "You're moving?" *Why? How? When? With who?* "Where?"

"Maine." Bowen looked away and sighed. "I've been trying to find a way to tell you this, and every time I attempt it, I panic and don't follow through."

"But you can tell me *now*?" While he's all broken, bloody, and half-out of his head?

"I came home last night to tell you, but you were gone." Bowen's jaw clenched as he reached into his pocket. "And before you get shitty about me keeping secrets from you… remember, this goes both ways." He dropped the empty vial of liquid silver into Bane's lap.

Well shit.

In true Bane and Bowen fashion, they didn't speak as the guilt between them grew thick enough to cut with a chainsaw. "I'm going to sleep off the meds," Bane grumbled, and headed upstairs.

"I'll get started on the car then."

The disdain in his twin's voice made Bane's chest tighten. He didn't want Bowen cleaning up his mess. "I'll take care of it myself."

"Better get used to it."

The implications of those five words hit Bane like a bullet

through his heart. *Just kick a wolf while he's down, asshole.* Holy shit. Bane knew they were on rocky ground, but it hurt like hell to realize there was no coming back from this.

Because once fate was set into motion, it became unstoppable.

CHAPTER 5

"That's it. Good girl. Take my cock. Fuck yeah, you're so tight." Bane took his female slowly. Pulling his massive cock out of her until only the tip of his fat head remained, he shoved back into her pussy with a punishing thrust. "So good. So damn perfect," he growled. Even in his dreams, his voice was more wolf than man. It was gravelly and slow, deep enough to rattle his ribcage.

He always dreamed of fucking women. Though they were different every time, their position never was. Always on their knees, facing away from him, ass up and hips back, he fucked them all hard and endlessly. The repetitive dream came so often, Bane could tell he was dreaming. It took away some of the fun. If only he could manipulate it. Make them say something. Look at him. Suck him off.

But no. It was always some female with her face turned away from him, ass up as he railed her from behind.

"That's a good girl." He spanked her ass to make her yip. "You like my cock stretching you out?"

The women never answered him in his dreams. No hollering, begging, moaning, or screaming his name like in real life. These ladies were as silent as the grave, no matter how hard he pounded into them. No matter what he said or asked. No matter how he pleaded for them to at least look at him just once.

Maybe this was because of his wolf. Animals didn't need a connection to fuck. No staring into their lover's eyes and kissing them. They mounted, came, and moved on until the mood struck again.

Bane needed connection. Craved it like the cursed Lycan he'd been his entire life. And just like his curse made him suffer in constant longing, this dream would leave him hard and unfinished until he took matters into his own hands after waking.

Still, he thrusted. The hunger for her body couldn't be helped. She was built beautifully. The small of her back flared into a spectacular set of wide hips. Her ass jiggled as he pounded into her from behind. Her pussy was tight, gripping his shaft as he retreated and plunged, retreated and plunged. "Such a good girl."

Bane grabbed all her dark hair into his hands. Winding his fist around her deep brown locks, he growled with possessiveness. God damn, even her hair was thick like the rest of her. It made his mouth water and hands itch to touch every square inch of her body. "Take it."

Take my cock. Take my touch. Take all of me.

She gasped when Bane tugged her hair harder than he meant to. "Did that hurt?" He wasn't sure if he wanted it to or not. If it did, it meant she just responded more than anyone else ever had in a dream of his. He liked the idea too much to not try again. He tugged her hair harder, aching for a response. "Answer me."

She gasped again, her head tipping back, spine arching. The shift in position stunned him, and he dropped her hair. It fanned across her back in thick waves. He froze, dick still buried in her wet heat when she looked over her shoulder and said, "Don't stop, Bane."

Bane jolted awake with a holler, the vision of that woman fading out as his room became crystal clear. Sweat dripped down his temples and chest, soaking his bedsheets, and he—

He was mid orgasm.

White jets of cum spurted out of his thick, hard cock, in white ropes all over his abs and thighs. He wasn't even touching himself. And yet… he couldn't stop orgasming. As if still buried balls deep in that gorgeous woman's body, he could still feel her pussy clench down around him, pulling his pleasure out.

"Don't stop, Bane." Her voice echoed in his brain, bouncing around like a ping-pong ball. But it was her face that had him

31

reeling. He saw her. He. *Saw. Her*. She turned around and looked him dead in the eyes. *"Don't stop, Bane."*

As if his body obeyed her commands, he couldn't stop. Not his orgasm, and not the possessive growl ripping out of his throat. His abs flexed painfully as he gripped his cock and stroked it harder than he ever had before. Torrents of electric fire spiked down his limbs. His heels dug into the mattress as his hips kicked upwards, while another orgasm claimed his thoughts. He saw white light. Pretty sure his soul just left his body on that one.

Pumping himself faster, faster, faster... A cold sensation slithered down his spine, drawing his balls in tighter. With a bark, he came harder than the first time. He came all over his abs and thighs with no end in sight.

It was the most violent, head-spinning, ravaging climax Bane ever experienced in his fucking life.

Holy shit, even his ears were ringing. Gasping for breath, he tried to sit up. "Mmmph," he gripped the side of his head and squeezed his eyes closed. Who put the marching band back in his skull? Ripping the sheets off his hot, sticky body, he stumbled out of bed, headed for the bathroom, and nearly missed the toilet when he puked again.

Little stars danced in his vision. His wolf stirred, swiping his claws from the inside as if to scrape the remnants of the drugs out of their system.

A dull ache in his upper thigh made Bane reach down to rub the bandages. Pulling them away, he hissed at the tenderness of his skin. It was bruised from his calf up to his hipbone. The stitches were still busted, and the wound hadn't healed.

Shit.

"Bowen!" He needed his twin to bring up the first aid kit so he could resew his wound shut before it got infected. The drugs must have slowed his healing process down. "Bowen!"

"What?" he snapped back from the bottom of the steps.

"I need the kit and water!"

Bowen stomped across the foyer and went into the kitchen. With their keen hearing, every footstep sounded like an elephant stomping through the house. And with Bane's sensitivity rocking his system right now, along with a hellacious migraine, those noises made him more nauseous.

He leaned over the toilet and yacked again.

"Jesus," Bowen growled from the doorway. "What did she give you?"

"No idea, but it's not metabolizing at all." Neither of them said what they were thinking, which was that it wasn't the drugs from the vet, but the effects of the silver he drank. Magic would explain a lot of this trouble.

"You're not healing?"

Bane shook his head and stared at his brother through hooded eyes. Everything felt heavy—his limbs, eyelids, thoughts. It was like a weighted blanket covered him, lulling his ass into a thick brain fog. "Can you stitch it back up?"

Bowen sighed and with it came a lot of pity. "Yeah."

They remained silent and Bowen patiently waited each time he had to stop suturing so Bane could puke again.

"I didn't plan to do it," Bane finally confessed. "I mean, I did, but not like I did."

"I hate it when you don't make sense. Speak fully and clearly."

See? That was the thing with Bane and Bowen. They weren't like typical twins who could sense each other or understand each other on a different spiritual level. Sharing a womb was all they'd ever shared. Where Bowen was rigid and controlled, Bane was chaos and impulsive.

"I planned to take the silver." Bane hissed as Bowen punctured his skin with the needle and thread again. "But I never thought it would be last night. I just did it on a whim. I'm.... I'm lost, brother. And desperate."

"Aren't we all?" Bowen continued working on Bane's thigh, not sparing him a glance. "I knew you'd gotten a vial. I just thought..." he clenched his jaw and shook his head. He didn't speak again.

"I wanted to tell you, but it scared me."

"I'm the last person you should be scared of, Bane."

"Says the alpha to his disappointing beta twin."

Bowen bit the end of the suture off with his teeth and grabbed the gauze next. The silence between them made the air evaporate.

"You're not disappointing," Bowen finally grumbled. "You're just not living up to your fullest potential."

"Well, you're more than making up for my downfalls." Damnit, he shouldn't have said that. What was wrong with him? Bowen had every right to be an alpha. The worse part about being in their family was the number of alphas in it. As kids, they spent a ton of time together laughing and playing, but when maturity hit each Lycan in the Woods family, they got territorial quickly.

All worked beautifully as a unit—under their father's reign. But Emerick, Bowen, and Killian were natural-born alphas, which meant they sometimes got into serious fights about the dumbest shit. Emily and Bane were more docile. Deadly and gutsy, but not nearly as aggressive as their brothers. It always made Bane feel like there was a flaw in his code or something.

The jealousy he harbored over Bowen's dominance, and how easily he could command an entire pack, was uncalled for. He should be grateful and happy for Bowen. But Bane wasn't happy or grateful for a goddamn thing. He was too miserable for joy. Too lonely.

Twins were supposed to stick together. Wasn't that an unwritten law? But Bowen was searching for his own pack... in Maine. Bane had only found out about it at the last ceremony when he overheard another pack discussing it. "Were you going to tell me before or after you packed your shit and headed north?"

Bowen's jaw clenched as he secured the bandage around Bane's thigh. "I was going to discuss it during the next family dinner."

Oh, right. Family dinner was just a few days away. "Why bother? It's not like you need permission to go."

His brother didn't say anything else about it. He just stood, grabbed the first aid kit, and handed Bane a bottle of water. "I've put in a call," he changed the subject. *Bastard.* "The vet's getting taken care of."

Bane's blood turned to ice in his veins. *"Don't stop, Bane."* That voice. That face... it was....

Bane scrambled to get up and slipped on the tile floor littered with his old, bloodied bandages. "No!"

No? No what? *No*, don't "take care of her"? *No*, that couldn't be the same woman from his dreams? Or *No... NO...* his wolf's clock just started ticking.

The hunt and chase with fate had begun.

34

CHAPTER 6

Maybe Bane just needed to get laid. Perhaps that dream wasn't his silver fated fuckage triggering, but just a simple erotic dream due to a long dry spell. Seriously, what were the chances of such perfect timing? None. That's what. No way did he chug the liquid silver and get struck by a car driven by his own fated mate, then dream about her. Series of events like that didn't happen anywhere except in b-rated movies with a pathetic budget.

Okay, yeah, it was just a coincidence. Totally. Had to be.

Better be.

Holy shit, what if he was wrong? What if that glorious bombshell was his mate? *"Don't stop, Bane."* Her husky, molten lava voice still haunted him. Still rocked him. Damnit, he was getting a boner again. Bane was a headcase and a half. While his brother made the call to have a Lycan with specific manipulating powers "handle the vet" Bane sat at the kitchen table with his head in his hands and a hard-on tenting his sweatpants.

"I can call Derek and have him handle it. We'd owe the asshole, but it is what it is."

Bane growled at the thought of that asshole anywhere near his woman.

Nope… he meant that vet lady person. Yeah. No. She was not his woman. She was the…

Prettiest, sexiest, sweetest creature on this green earth.

Bane shot up from his chair, hellbent on doing something. Trouble was, he didn't know what the hell to do. "I don't want him near her." The thought of any other Lycan near that woman made

35

him see red. Was that a sign? Someone should have warned him about this level of aggression. Liquid Silver — also known as silver water — should come with a goddamn manual. And a warning label.

"Don't stop, Bane." Her voice slithered down his spine and rang his bells. Once more, protectiveness surged through his system, nearly making his knees buckle. He couldn't let Derek near her.

"You were hit by a car, bro. That's probably knocked you and your wolf off kilter." Bowen slammed two plates down on the table. "Eat, it'll help."

Bane glowered at the club sandwiches and chips on his plate. He couldn't eat that. He... he needed to —

"I gotta go for a run."

"Not with that leg still injured."

See, this was the thing about his twin. Bowen was a bossy sonofabitch. Most alphas were. But Bowen wasn't Bane's motherfucking alpha. "I'm going for a run." Defiant and furious, he pulled off his clothes and ignored his raging hard-on bobbing like a divination rod as he headed for the front door. Swinging it open, he stepped out into the fresh air and shifted. Or, he tried to shift. "Shit."

Bowen watched cautiously from his seat at the kitchen table. "The silver will fuck with your wolf's mind too."

"How do you know all this?"

"I've asked around. Dad's got enough knowledge, brother. Surely you asked him before you went on your own and made this decision?"

Nope. Bane didn't want to know the details because quite frankly, he might have chickened out if he knew what he was getting into beyond the whole *find your mate before the next full moon or you'll be lost to your wolf forever* part. Bane saw, firsthand, what that did to his baby brother, Killian. The Woods family hadn't been the same since the day they lost the youngest of their family.

"You always do things half-cocked," Bowen bit into his sandwich while Bane stood naked at the front door like a dipshit. "You could have at least come to me for guidance."

Bane grit his teeth. "Because you did a helluva job guiding Killian, right?"

Bowen shot out of his chair so fast it crashed to the floor. He

36

was at Bane in two seconds flat, snarling in his face. "We tried *everything*."

The twins glared at each other with a mix of hurt and rage. Killian was a terribly sensitive topic. The bottom line was, Bowen was right—Bane went in half-cocked with everything. Fear did that to him. Fear of failure, rejection, expectations. Where Bowen was meticulous and mindful, Bane was free-spirited and spontaneous. They both had their reasons. One was a control freak, the other was go-with-the-flow.

The list could go on and on.

Bane couldn't afford to go with the flow anymore. His life depended on him having order and direction for the next twenty-seven days. Fuuuuck. Grabbing his twin's shoulder, his chest heaved with rising panic. "Help me."

Immediately, Bowen's features softened and the dynamic between them morphed from hostile to compassionate. "Always."

The universe needed to stop screwing Kennedy over. First, she got roped into dealing with a motorcycle club, then she hit an innocent animal with her car, then some asshole *stole* her car. Seriously, could this day get any worse?

Yeah, it could, since she wasn't able to tell anyone about any of it. She should have reported the accident and the theft, however, involving the police invited extra trouble. If Jake's crew saw cops around her, they might suspect she was reporting their dog fights. It would serve them right, assholes. But if that assumption was made, they might retaliate and punish Jake for hiring a snitch. She might hate her brother now, but he was still her brother. No way was she going to risk getting him into deeper trouble than he already was. Call her paranoid, but Acid, Blade, and whoever else was in the club, probably killed first and asked questions later. Besides, at the very least, an accident report would result in her insurance going up and she couldn't afford another big bill.

"What a mess," she grumbled while walking down to the corner store. Now there was a wolf on the loose too. How on earth that animal kicked the kennel door down was beyond her. He'd been sedated when she put him in there before cleaning up the mess, then going out to the lobby area once she heard the receptionist come in to open things up.

Where had that guy even come from?

She wished she could have gotten a better look at him. Not that she was about to go on a solo hunt to find him or anything. Still, it hurt her feelings that some dirtbag would take her car. Seemed stupid, but there you have it. She felt insulted and vulnerable and pissed.

Punching in the only person she could call, Kennedy gritted her teeth and said, "Come get me." She'd left the vet's before the techs and her boss showed up. There was too much to explain and keep hidden and Kennedy sucked at lying. Better to just sneak out through the back.

"Where are you?"

"The corner between Sullivan and Conley."

"Where's your car?"

"JUST COME GET ME, ASSHOLE!" She hung up on Jake and crossed her arms over her chest. Tired, fed up, hungry, and frustrated, her chin trembled with the effort it took to hold her tears back. This was the worst day ever. Considering her life, that really said something.

Stomach rumbling, she went into a convenience store on a mission. A tub of ice cream would do. And chips. Chocolate, most definitely. She balanced all her goodies in her arms and dumped them on the counter, letting them tumble out of her arms, only to realize she'd left her purse in her car.

Fuck. Me.

Bursting into tears, she grabbed everything to put it back when the cashier said, "Just take it."

Kennedy blinked twice and gawked. "What?"

"Just take it, dumplin'. You look like you've had a hard time."

Sniffling, Kennedy let loose a fresh set of tears. "Thank you. I promise to come back and pay you for all of this."

"No need, just get yourself right." The old woman flashed her a sympathetic smile and Kennedy almost couldn't bear the kindness. "Go on now, before that ice cream melts. Don't forget to grab a spoon from over there."

Kennedy ugly cried over to the napkin/utensil/cup station and grabbed all she needed. With one more "Thank you so much," she bumped the door with her ass and headed back outside to wait for her brother. He showed up forty-five minutes later, looking as shitty as she felt. Dumping her empty ice cream container in a bin, she stuffed half of a candy bar in her mouth and hopped into his truck. They drove home in dead silence. Once safely in her driveway, she slammed the door hard enough to make his windows shake and stormed up to her front porch.

Jake wound his window down. "I'm really sorry, Kennedy."

She flipped him the bird and grabbed her spare key from under her chipped flowerpot. Not giving him a second glance, she went inside and kicked her door shut.

Kennedy expected Jake to drive off. Clearly, she wasn't in the mood for company. But when he came inside just seconds later, she hated how some part of her felt happy about it. Jake was trouble, but he was her brother, her only family, and that blurred a line between toxic and tolerable.

"What happened to your car?"

She didn't want to tell him the truth. He'd likely hunt down whoever stole it and kill them. No way could she carry that on her shoulders for the rest of her life. "It's getting serviced."

Not a lie. It was probably getting chopped for parts, which could loosely be considered a service.

Jake seemed satisfied with her answer by the way he dropped his ass down on her couch and stretched his arms across the back. One look at her and he crumbled. Leaning forward, he buried his head in his hands, sighing heavily. "Look, Kennedy..."

"What were you thinking?" she hissed at him. Unwrapping her second candy bar, she broke a chunk off and shoved it in her mouth. Talking while she chewed, she shoved her finger at him, "How could you drag me into your shitshow like this?"

"I didn't mean to!" he hollered. "I swear. I just didn't know what else to do."

"Dog fights, Jake? *Seriously*?"

"I'm not part of that."

"Well, you became part of it the instant you grabbed that half-dead animal and tried to save it." But that was the part of Jake she loved. The only part, honestly. Deep down, he cared about things—especially innocent things—and Kennedy made excuses for his bad behavior because of it. That, and he was protective as hell over her, which made her reciprocate the favor.

"I'll get you out of it," he promised. "I'll set you up some place new. I've got the money to do it."

She didn't want to consider where he got that money from. The possibilities made her nearly lose her ice cream and chocolate bars. "I don't want to move. My life is here. My work is here."

"You can be a vet anywhere."

"I'm sick of running," she stomped her foot. "I'm done, Jake."

"If you stay—" he scrubbed his face with both hands, like it could reset his attitude.

Kennedy noticed new ink on his forearm. "Oh my god, you're not a prospect anymore, are you?"

Jake clenched his jaw, his lips thinning as he refused to answer.

"You sonofabitch. Did you learn *nothing* from Mom and Dad?"

He shoved up from the couch and screamed, "What did you think I was doing, Kennedy? Playing house over there? Networking for a business opportunity? Jesus!" He tossed his hands up and prowled around her coffee table. "This is all I am." He swept his hands down his torso. "This is me."

"That is bullshit." But it wasn't. This was absolutely him. Jake was built for a dangerous life. Exactly how dangerous, however, was yet to be seen. That didn't mean she had to like or support it. "You didn't have to join *that* club, *Diesel*."

He cringed at her. "You don't understand."

She was beyond understanding and smack dab into I-don't-give-a-fuck territory. "Where'd the name come from, huh? I didn't miss the part where you're all named a certain way." Acid, Blade, Hog, Diesel… "Tell me, Jake."

"No."

"Then leave and don't come back." She marched over and swung open her front door for him. "Now."

"Kennedy, I can't tell you."

"Fuck your code. You got me involved, and I want to know exactly what I'm into now."

"I swear I'll get you out of it. Just give me time."

Yeah, right. "And in that time, your boys will be back with more injuries I'll have to fix. If they come to my work, I'll lose my

40

job, Jake. And if they come here, I want to know what danger I'm allowing into my damn house." Now rage replaced her self-pity. "And if I am dragged to your club, I'll be thrown to the wolves."

Jake's face turned red and the veins in his temples started throbbing. *Good.* She wanted him pissed. She wanted him rattled. She wanted him to understand exactly what he did with that stunt he pulled last night.

"I tried to save a dog, that's all," he growled.

"You tried to save a dog *and* your own ass." She jabbed her finger towards the front porch. "Get. Out."

He met her halfway across the floor before stopping. "I..."

She cocked her brow. "You have one last chance to tell me the truth about everything, or so help me God, I'll blow whistles until every cop in the ten surrounding counties tear your club apart."

Jake's anger surged. He stormed over and almost wrapped his hands around her neck, but stopped himself. She'd long ago lost her fear of him. He always threatened. Never delivered. Kennedy never even flinched when he got like this. But Jake was different than the other men he rode with. "Last chance, Jake."

"If I tell you about my name..."

"I'll never say a word. Even if the cops catch you for whatever you're doing."

This was a major breach in MC protocol. She knew it. He knew it. But it was also a test. A final chance to prove where his ultimate loyalties lie. If he didn't tell her, fine. She'd move forward knowing his allegiance was to the club. If he did tell her, she'd never tell a soul and would trust that he would get her out of this mess somehow. Holding her breath, she waited for him to say something.

"First kill," he said quietly, his gaze cast to the floor.

Kennedy's eyes widened in disbelief. *Oh god, no, Jake. First kill. First. Kill?*

Hog... Blade... Acid... Diesel. It wasn't what they'd killed; it was *how*. Her stomach twisted, and she fought back tears. "Leave," she said with a shaky breath.

"Kennedy, I can ex—"

"*Leave!*"

Blowing out an exasperated breath, he obeyed. "I'll make this right," he said just as she slammed and locked her door in his face.

41

CHAPTER 7

While Bane redressed, he talked through his last dream with Bowen, who agreed it could mean nothing or everything.

"Funny you only see the back of their heads." Bowen leaned against the wall with his arms crossed. "I only see them faceless."

"That's—"

"Creepy," they said at the same time. Bane beamed the first smile he'd made in ages. "We should start by searching her car. Maybe we can get her info off her registration card or something." It was that or adopt a dog and make an emergency visit to her vet and pray she was the one who dealt with them. Searching her car was far better.

"Did you call Derek yet?"

"No."

Bane blew out a long-held breath. "Good. Don't."

"We don't have a lot of time to figure out if she's your *Deesha* or not. You know the rules, Bane. If she isn't and she's seen you shift, or if there's even a chance of it, her memory will need to be swiped."

Annnnd now his chest hurt again. Yeah, he knew the rules, but hated messing with human minds. No matter how necessary it might be to ensure the safety of Lycan, it didn't seem fair. What if something went wrong during the swipe? Derek might be one of the few Lycan born with mind manipulation magic, but Bane had zero confidence in the bastard. Even if this woman turned out to be just a human and not his fated mate, he wasn't willing to risk her mind. A vet needed all her wits to save animals. Derek wasn't an option, no matter what. A possessive growl slipped up his throat at the mere thought of that Lycan getting near his maybe-might-be-hopefully-is *Deesha*.

"If you lose yourself," Bowen said, cutting into Bane's possessive thoughts, "I'll shift with you and remain by your side until the end."

Dread landed in his gut with a thud. "Not on your life."

"Not your call, brother." Bowen didn't even seem scared about it.

"*Bowe.*" Bane turned to face him. "No. This is my fate, not ours."

"You're wrong."

Had Bowen dreamed of the same woman? Was it possible they were fated for the same mate? That would be... shit, he didn't know if that would be weird or amazing. But why else would Bowen say this if that wasn't a possibility. Bane's mind ran wild. As far as he knew, Bowen declined the opportunity to drink the silver with the other Lycan at the last ceremony a couple days ago. He could have nipped a vial just like Bane had. The possibility was there, but...

No, Bowen's goals were different lately. Finding love wasn't his top priority, and he'd never do things out of order. First, secure his own pack. Second, find love. He'd want to be able to offer the world to his *Deesha*, and in his mind, that required climbing ranks and securing one of the highest positions in the Lycan world first.

"What's your endgame, Bowe?" Bane swallowed the lump in his throat. "What's the catch? If I fail, you come with me. And if I succeed?"

"I want you as my beta in Maine. If," he rubbed the bridge of his nose and toed the ruined bumper. "If I beat the current alpha."

"You're going to challenge *Kain*?" Was he insane? Kain was ruthless and unreasonably violent.

Bowen only shrugged his shoulders. "I keep thinking about it. It's a good move."

"It's suicide." The instant the words left his mouth, he wished he could suck them back in and choke. "I mean..." *time for damage control*, "He would fight to the death, Bowen. You wouldn't."

"You don't know what I might do."

43

"I know you're not a ruthless killer." Unless something had changed in Bowen over the past couple of years that Bane didn't know about. "Why not just challenge our father? He'd step down for you in a heartbeat."

"And get laughed at by everyone because the title was handed to me? Not a chance. Besides, Emerick's taking over the Woods territory when Dad steps down. It's already set."

True. And Emerick had a lot to learn before then. Bowen was leaps and bounds ahead of the rest of them in the alpha department.

"I want to earn it," Bowen said.

"Your pride will be the death of you."

"And your stupidity might be the death of you," he opened the passenger side door and popped the glove box open. "The sooner we learn about this woman, the faster we can figure out our next move. No sense in talking about being alpha of a new pack if I'll be chasing my tail with you for the rest of our days."

Bane refused to let Bowen make that kind of sacrifice. And yet... some part of his aching heart soared that even if his curse kicked in and took over his existence, he wouldn't be alone. Damn him for even thinking such a horrible, selfish thing.

And as for being Bowen's beta in the Maine pack—if he actually went through with it—that would require some serious ass kicking on Bane's part too. The beta position wasn't by appointment, it too was earned. No problem, there. Bane was one of the best fighters among their kind.

So much to think about...

As Bowen rummaged through the glovebox, Bane surveyed the damage to the car. Her frame was bent. Plenty of body damage, both superficial and dismal. Bane's guilt went through the roof. "I don't know how the air bags didn't go off."

"Might be faulty wiring," Bowen frowned.

In which case, Bane would replace this car with a brand new one.

"Can we fix it all?" It was the least he could do. He wasn't a mechanic by trade, but knew enough to pop, tighten, rewire, and replace most stuff on a car. "Can we get the parts on a rush delivery?"

"One thing at a time, brother," Bowen growled. "Fixing her car isn't a priority."

Yeah. Okay. He knew that, but it was something he could remedy fast. Nothing said *Mate Me* like returning your *Deesha's* stolen vehicle all fixed and shiny, right?

Shit, he was totally going to botch this.

Bane's mind ran a mile a minute until Bowen slapped him in the gut with a registration holder. "You want to do the honors, or should I?"

Bane held it like it was a precious national treasure. Even ran his thumb across the smooth, cheap plastic surface before flipping it open and getting to the info inside. "Registration says her name's Kennedy Taylor." And wasn't that the prettiest name under the sun? "Got her address here too."

"Wow," Bowen teased. "Name *and* address. You're winning the day so far."

Bane flipped him off, the insult negated by the cheesy grin on his face. "Let's roll!" He was too close to finding out if this woman was his or not to waste another second staring at her busted up car. They both hopped into his truck and took off again. Bane tucked the registration in his back pocket for safekeeping, all the while wondering a million things about this woman. What kind of house did she have? Had she lived in town long? What was her favorite flower? Did she like tacos?

"Look at you." Bowen flashed a toothy grin. "You're picking out paint colors already."

Bane didn't confirm or deny. They both knew the truth.

Punching the addressing into the GPS, Bane's heart thudded hard in his chest. The possibility of finding his *Deesha* so easily was too good to be true. He couldn't afford to think she was just some woman who hit him with her car and nothing more. The timing was so perfect.

Yeah... *too* perfect.

Did he dream of the vet, or was his memory fuzzy? His wolf might have hit his head too hard to capture a true image of this woman. Or maybe his wolf and man minds were too murky from the silver?

"What are you doing, bro?"

Slowing down and contemplating making a U-turn.

"Don't stop, Bane!" Bowen tossed his hands up.

"Don't stop, Bane." The woman's voice echoed in his mind.

Her face was clear as day too. Gorgeous brown eyes, dark mahogany hair, and plump lips and plumper ass. Fuuuuuck.

Bane stomped on the gas and gunned it again. His head and heart split. He didn't want his curse to come full circle, but he also didn't know how to get Kennedy on board. There was more to his curse than simply finding his mate.

He also had to turn her into a Lycan and...

Holy Blood Hounds, how was he going to do that without tearing his, and her, soul apart?

The act of turning someone else Lycan was typically violent. Her body would crack and break until she reconfigured into another creature entirely. It wasn't just painful. Sometimes a *Deesha* didn't survive their first shift.

Could he live with himself for damning and maybe killing her? Could he live with himself if he didn't at least try?

Holy. Fucking. *Fuuuuuck.*

"Think of Killian." Bowen's deep bass snagged Bane's focus. "Think of Emerick and Emily. Mom and Dad. Think of Dorian."

Dorian. Bane's grip tightened on the wheel. The GPS gave directions, but Bane didn't pay attention. It was all *blah, blah, in one mile turn, blah, blah.* Bane's heart thudded into his throat. Dorian was their foster brother. A vampire at that. He'd battled his own fate and conscience about his mate, too.

Turning someone vampire wasn't as violent as turning someone Lycan. Those creatures had tricks—a form of hypnosis to make the transition from human to vampire almost euphoric. Lucky bastards.

For two species to get hit with the same curse at the same time, thanks to a set of twins sired by two different men, the blood curse for Lycan and vampires were vastly different. Same for turning their mates. Same for the endgame should they fail.

Vampires died if they didn't find their *alakhai* in time.

Lycan were forever lost to their wolf, never to be human again if they didn't find their *Deesha* before the next full moon. They lost their family, friends, life, and human mentality completely. Then they turned feral.

"Smoke's coming out of your ears," Bowen huffed.

"I'm just thinking about what's worse, dying fast or losing yourself slowly."

"You mean incinerating from the inside out or running free until you're feral? No comparison, they both suck balls."

Their thoughts must have turned to their little brother, Killian, at the same time. "You think he's out there still?"

"Maybe." Bowen ran his thumb between his eyes. "I can't let myself think about it or I die a little with every breath."

Bane tensed. "I'm sorry I did this," he blurted.

"No reason to be sorry for wanting love, brother."

"I should have waited for the next ceremony."

"That's not staying true to your nature."

Bowen's right. Still, "I should have at least told you about it before I did it."

"I'll kick your ass for it later. You just missed your turn."

Damnit. Bane hit the brakes and put the truck in reverse to turn left. The GPS dinged with, "Your destination is three hundred feet on the right."

His entire body felt electrified. The hairs on his arms and the back of his neck stood on end. Turned out Kennedy lived in a rundown house at the end of a long dirt road. Secluded. Vulnerable. It made him immediately want to put a fence around her property, complete with security system and tripwires. What kind of woman lived in the middle of nothing like this? Was it by choice or misfortune? Not saying there was anything wrong with having seclusion and all—hey, he lived in the middle of the woods with his twin, so he got the lifestyle—but this felt different.

The little flowerpots out front were the only bright thing about the place, and they were definitely a piss poor attempt at curb appeal. Her grass needed to be mowed. There were bare patches everywhere. Her porch steps were crooked, the wood rotting.

But a bright, shiny new pickup truck sat in her overgrown driveway.

Bane's hackles raised. Was she married?

On cue, a tall male stormed out of the house and headed right for the truck. Bane and Bowen leaned forward at the exact same time, watching the guy like two predators. "Interesting ink," Bowen growled.

"Interesting cut." They both noticed his MC cut.

"Wolf Pack MC," Bowen said with an almost laugh. "Bless his heart."

"So precious."

The guy looked positively furious as he stormed to his truck and hopped in. Bane vaguely registered Bowen taking a picture of the truck with his cell phone as the guy pulled out and headed in the opposite direction. He paid the Lycan no mind as he flew down the dirt road, leaving them, and the house, in his dust.

"Can you run the plates?"

"That's my intention." Bowen leaned back with a sigh. "Think that's her husband?"

Bane fought for breath. "I hope not."

Because like it or not, if Kennedy was Bane's *Deesha*, he would kill that cocksucker to get her if he had to.

CHAPTER 8

After Jake left, Kennedy took a hot shower, chugged some water, screamed into a pillow, and attempted to fall asleep. Thankfully, she was off today and tomorrow. Her cat, Molly, hopped up on the bed with her, purring loudly.

"Come here," she said, pulling Molly into her arms, grateful for the company. "I'm in another bind. Can you believe that?" The calico bumped her head to Kennedy's chin. "Jake's really done it this time."

What the hell was she going to do now? Damn Jake and his bullshit. Damn herself for caring so much.

Curling up, she cried herself to sleep and lost the entire day to tossing and turning in her bed with the curtains closed and Molly curled up on the corner of the bed. When she finally did manage to get some decent rest, she woke up having no clue what time it was or even what day.

"Shit." She scrambled out of bed in search of her cell phone.

Finding it in the kitchen, Kennedy listened to her voicemails while chugging more water. Man, she was thirsty. Refilling her glass, she eyerolled at the first message.

"Hey, it's me. I'm sorry. I just," Jake stopped talking and sighed heavily. *"I owe them, okay? You know that."*

Yeah, yeah, so he kept saying. Ever since he got out of jail, Jake practically hunted that Wolf Pack MC down and joined immediately. He told her it was because some of them had protected him in prison. He was indebted to them now. For life.

"*Anyway,*" Jake said with a softer voice. "*I'll figure this out. Just...
go along with it until I do, okay? And don't answer the door for Acid.
Ever.*" He hung up.

Really? Don't answer the door for Acid? She wasn't
answering the door for any of them. Just because Jake owed them
something didn't mean Kennedy was part of that debt. The shittiest
part of this wasn't that Jake roped her into his mess. It was that she
was going to have to get out of it on her own. Jake wasn't reliable
enough. No matter how devoted he wished to be to her, his self-
preservation instincts ran too thick to put anyone before himself.

The second voicemail was from her boss. Kennedy's heart
kicked into overdrive the second she heard his voice. "*Hi Kennedy,
it's Mark. I came into work earlier than usual this morning and noticed a
cage door was busted. No paperwork on the kennel, so I'm not sure if there
was an animal in there or not. I've asked the techs and they don't know
anything. Figured you were the last one here, so if you know anything
about it, can you call me back? Thanks. Oh, and I'm going to need you to
work a double this weekend. Alright, bye.*"

Grrrrrr. Why was she always the one who got stuck with the
doubles? It wasn't fair. There were four other vets at the clinic and
Kennedy always got stuck working more than her fair share.
Usually it didn't bother her, and that's probably why Mark didn't
even ask. It wasn't like Kennedy had a life outside of work. But still,
she was exhausted and needed a hot minute to herself and away
from responsibility. Was that too much to ask?

The third voicemail made her stomach drop. "*Kennedy, it's
Risa. Girl, don't you dare try to back out on us tonight. I'll be at your
house at six to pick you up. Wear something fire.*"

Kennedy's gaze swung to the clock on her oven. It was
already five-thirty. Shit!

Going out with Risa from work, and some of her friends,
wasn't the worst thing she could be doing, but it was close.
Kennedy only agreed this time because Risa always invited her and
she never went, which started to make her feel like a bitch. Soon,
she figured Risa would stop trying and Kennedy wasn't ready to let
that happen.

But tonight wasn't the best time to go out and people.

Staying at home wallowing in her woes wasn't any better.

Maybe she needed to get out and be a person for a night. Like,

50

smack on some lipstick, wear clothes instead of scrubs, and actually have a conversation with another human.

Nope. Just the thought of it sounded like too much.

She texted Risa and told her she couldn't make it, but hoped she and the other girls had fun.

Making a bowl of soup and sitting back to watch TV, Kennedy couldn't shake the feeling that doom was looming over her. It wasn't until she heard someone bang on her door a half hour later when fear truly set in. Quietly putting her empty bowl on the coffee table, she muted the TV and crept to the front door. Living in the sticks wasn't always the safest, so she grabbed the baseball bat from its resting post against the wall and peered through the curtain on the side of the door.

You've got to be kidding me. Kennedy unlocked the door and swung it open. "Risa!"

"I know, I know, it's not my fault. Carrie took forever to get her makeup on." Risa stepped inside and her eyebrows shot into her hairline when she saw Kennedy holding a bat. "Damn, girl. Paranoid much?"

"I texted you saying I wasn't coming tonight."

"I must have missed it." She had the audacity to wink. "Maybe you should get a dog? That might be better than a bat."

"Can't do dogs. I work too much and can't leave one alone that long." Kennedy blew out a breath. After putting her bat away, she crossed her arms. "For real, Risa. I'm not going out tonight."

"Yes, you are. You never do, and this has been planned for a month. Two months, if you include the three times we had to reschedule before this. Fucking Mark, always rearranging the shifts." She turned with a frown. "He didn't get you to work the double this weekend, did he?"

Kennedy's non answer was answer enough.

"Damn, K. You gotta speak up. He's just going to keep doing it unless you do something that lets him know you can't be taken advantage of like that all the time."

Risa was right. But Kennedy didn't have much of a social life, so she could easily take the shifts. She also didn't want to piss Mark off and risk losing her job.

"Come on. Let's pick something out for you to wear. Unless you wanna go out in that?" Risa wiggled her fingers at Kennedy's sushi print pj set. "I mean, you do you, booboo."

Should she go? Ugh. Her gaze swung from her pajama pants to the baseball bat. If she stayed, what would be the point? She'd likely go crazy with paranoia, thinking Acid or Hog or Blade or some other dipshit biker would pull up to terrorize her. Or her brother, who she didn't want to see or talk to for a while.

For the first time in a while, Kennedy didn't feel safe in her own home. Anger at Jake boiled in her veins because of it.

"Hang on." Damned if she was going to be a sitting duck at a self-pity party. "Let me get fired up."

"Yes, girl! That's what I'm talking about!" Risa clapped and followed her into the bedroom.

It took more time to put on her lipstick and braid back her hair than it did to pick out jeans and a tank top, because really, Kennedy didn't have much else. Okay, she was doing it. She was going to people.

"Let's go."

How long do you follow someone before you unlock a new stalker achievement? After burning a half tank of gas sitting in idle on Kennedy's road, watching a bunch of nothing go on and then all her lights turn out because she'd likely gone to bed, Bane had gone home and fucked Kennedy in his dreams again last night. Then he rolled out of bed, showered, shaved, dressed, and found himself down the road from her house again.

This was beyond pathetic. It was creepy.

He canted forward when he saw a car pull into Kennedy's house and a woman run up to the front door. Not even fifteen minutes later, Kennedy and the girl were leaving.

Yeah, he followed. What the hell else was he supposed to do, go home and resume life? Not a chance. Playing it cool, he checked to make sure he didn't have anything stuck in his teeth and then straightened his shirt a bit before walking into the bar.

Loud country music blasted and the dimly lit dance floor was already packed.

He scanned the perimeter, looking for threats—vampires, territorial Lycan, and most importantly, *Savag-Ri*. Of all the dangers to look out for, *Savag-Ri* were the worst. Those assholes stopped at nothing to take Lycan and vampires down. Shit, they'd even use innocents as bait if they had to. Cocksuckers.

The coast was clear. Bane weaved through the crowd and growled behind some human sitting at the bar. The scrawny dude paled when he saw Bane eyeing him and got up immediately.

Look his manners burned to ashes the instant he saw Kennedy. That man sat too close to her. Bane didn't like it. Neither did his wolf. Dressed in a tight navy-blue tank top and jeans clinging to her like a second skin, Kennedy was a wet dream. Any man who looked at her would have Bane's inner wolf snapping its jaws. That could lead to a bar fight. Which would land the human in the hospital.

So really, getting rid of the guy was a courtesy, not a dick move.

Bane took a seat and flipped his finger up, snagging the bartender's attention. "Water, please. And a menu."

He noticed Kennedy was also drinking water. Annnnd actively not participating in the conversation the girls on the other side of her were having. One of them, the girl who Bane saw run into Kennedy's house earlier, gave him a look that said he was on her radar.

He didn't return the gesture.

"Let's dance!" she chirped, grabbing Kennedy's hand to try and yank her off the stool.

"No thanks. I'm not much of a dancer."

"So what! Come on!"

"No, Risa. I'm good."

Risa pouted while getting lured away by another one of the girls to the dance floor. Kennedy laughed as she watched them for all of three seconds before she turned around and took a sip of her water.

The bartender returned with a menu and drink for Bane. Then he placed a huge plate of food in front of Kennedy. "Let me know when you're ready to order," he said to Bane, then set off to pour a beer for someone else.

He looked at the menu, not reading a damn bit of it. "What's good here?"

No one answered. It got awkward.

Kennedy tucked some hair behind her ear, and the tip of it was red. "The burger's decent."

Bane worked hard to tame his smile. "Decent, huh? Not mind-blowing, mouthwateringly scrumptious?" Because mark his words, what he was looking at fit that very description.

Spoiler alert: He wasn't looking at the burger she just took a bite of.

"Hmm." She chewed slowly, thoughtfully. "Mind-blowing, mouth-wateringly scrumptious..." she wiped her mouth with a napkin. "Nothing in this town matches that description."

"Ohhh ouch." He chuckled and set the menu down.

Kennedy bit her lip just before taking another sip of her water. She kept her gaze straight ahead, as if the lineup of rail alcohol was the single most interesting thing she'd ever seen.

Then he realized she was staring at him in the reflection of the mirror behind all that booze.

The bartender came back. "You decide what you want?"

"I'll have what she's having."

"Burger, medium with bacon, jalapenos, and BBQ sauce?"

Bane salivated immediately. That's what she was having? Maybe he should have looked past her eyes to notice before he'd said that. What a bonus that she had incredible taste in snacks. "I want everything she's got."

Kennedy cough-snorted her water and set the glass down again.

"Fries or chips?"

"Both," he told the bartender. "Make it a double order."

Kennedy took another bite of her burger, chewed it in three bites, and swallowed. Was it normal for a woman to look hot eating a messy burger? Wiping her mouth with a napkin, she grabbed her water and drained the glass.

"Can you bring her another water when you get a chance, too?"

"No problem." The bartender got on it immediately.

This dude was getting a massive tip.

Twenty minutes of no talking and Bane was ready to crawl out of his skin. In that time, he'd sucked down his drink, and watched Kennedy turn different shades of red and pale white. The woman was thinking so hard he expected smoke to billow out of her ears.

Her friends came back and ordered another round of shots. Kennedy, he noticed, didn't drink hers.

The bartender placed Bane's order down. "Thanks, man."

"No prob. Can I get you anything else?"

"Just two more waters."

"On it."

Bane slid the plate of double fries over towards her. "It's yours if you want it."

Kennedy pointed at her plate. "I have my own, thanks."

She was down to three fries. If she was primed to be a *Deesha*, it would take more than on order of food to fill her up. It was a shot in the dark, but if she didn't want it, he'd happily eat it. Hell, Bane could eat four of these and still have room for pizza in an hour.

"No rule against having more of what you like." He made it a point to shove the plate of fries towards her.

She stared at him, then the fries. Whatever she was thinking, raised her blood pressure and turned her cheeks pink. Adorable.

Cocking his brow playfully, he attempted to drag the plate back. She quickly gripped the other side of it and stopped him. He let go with a big, fat smile.

"Thank you." She slid the fries over to herself and ate a fresh, hot one. "I swear they sprinkle crack on these things. This seasoning is to die for." She grabbed another and shoved it between her plump lips. "I'd eat anything if it was dipped in this BBQ sauce too."

He'd have to remember that for later.

Bane watched her go to town on the fries. Seemed trivial, but it wasn't. Male Lycan took immense joy in providing for their mate. Bane felt a shift of his wolf when she went in for another French fry. Would she eat the second burger too?

They fell into silence again. He couldn't figure out if it was awkward or comfortable. Still working on that second plate of fries, Kennedy kept her gaze straight ahead, but was now staring at the bar's edge.

"You're right," he said in a friendly tone, after taking a bite of his burger. "It's decent."

She laughed and wiped the corner of her mouth again, catching the little bit of BBQ sauce she had there. He wished he could have licked it off instead. Oh well. He finished off his burger in five bites. Then took care of the fries and, lastly, the chips.

Kennedy didn't speak another word.

What do I do? What do I do? What do I do?

What's the protocol for something like this? The guy next to her was insanely hot. Too hot for this town, that's for sure. No way could he be single, right? It took her three tries to catch his left hand and look for a wedding ring without getting caught.

Kennedy had zero chill.

In order to not look like a complete awkward noodle, she stared straight ahead, and both actively ignored the gaggle of women she was here with and also studied the man's reflection—or what she could see around the bottles—in the mirror behind the bar.

This man was stunning. Buff. Broad shoulders, chestnut brown hair that was just enough to run her fingers through. His eyes were a ridiculous shade of amber. Even his teeth were stupidly perfect. He'd devoured his entire meal in the time it took her to eat a quarter of her burger and all the fries.

A man with a hefty appetite always appealed to her. Somehow, that voraciousness always seemed like it would spill into other activities.

She'd been sitting like a Dodo bird this entire time. She should say something. Make a move. She might be shit with people skills, but she did have manners for crying out loud. All night long she kept mentally revisiting her shitshow—rehashing things, scheming, worrying, getting mad.

Kennedy came out tonight to get away from all that. To escape her life for a few measly hours.

This man would make a great temporary distraction.

Look, she had needs like everyone else. And fantasies. This guy looked like he could check off plenty of her boxes and leave her satisfied way more than a decent burger and awkward conversation ever could.

"I'm Kennedy." She held her hand out.

"Bane."

Wow, his hand was huge. And warm. And strong. And…

She pulled away and tucked her hair behind her ear again. *Stop playing with your hair, idiot!* "So, you from around here?" Good grief, could she be more lame?

"Few towns away. Just stopping through on my way home."

"Oh." She looked down at his empty plate. "Did you even taste that burger? You inhaled it."

Shoot. Me. Now. Holy shit, she was bad at this.

Bane's grin went a mile wide. "Not the worst thing I've put in my mouth." He raked his gaze down her body. "I can think of juicier bits to sink my teeth into though."

Her cheesy smile matched his. It was exhilarating and awful at the same time. "Nice," she teased. "Does that line work on most women?"

"No idea," Bane leaned his elbow casually on the bar. "I'll let you know tomorrow."

"Ugh," she said loudly, making sure to give a dramatic eye roll.

"No good? How about, Dayem girl, did it hurt?"

"When I fell out of heaven?" She finished where his pathetic pickup line left off. "No, but I—"

"—Chipped a nail crawling out of hell," they said at the same time.

It was almost too perfect.

Oh, this guy was good. Really good.

Super good.

Holy hell, her cheeks were burning so hot right now. Grabbing her water, she took a drink, only to realize her glass was empty again. Flustered, she tried to snag the bartender's attention, but he was too busy serving the other patrons to notice her yet.

"Wanna get out of here?" Bane suddenly asked.

Yes, she did, but not necessarily with him. Kennedy wasn't much on one-night stands, but every girl found an exception. Bane looked sexy enough to break code for. Speaking of code… "I came with friends," she said, jacking her thumb over her shoulder at Risa and the other girls.

"Well…" Bane didn't look detracted at all by the mention of her friends. "We can walk two doors down and be someplace a little quieter. They can scoop you up when they're ready to leave. Or I can walk you back here. Or..." his mouth lifted into a wicked smile, "I could take you home."

Kennedy swallowed all the saliva building in her mouth. Seriously, what was wrong with her? She should say yes. She was a grown ass woman with needs, and Bane was too beautiful to sidestep. He was also way out of her league. Surely Bane must have one-night standards and Kennedy doubted she met them.

Or maybe she did? Shit, she must if he was hitting on her. Wait. Was he hitting on her or was this all just in fun?

For crying out loud, she really needed to get out more. Kennedy didn't have a clue how to handle even the simplest situations with another person.

"Hey girl!" Risa showed up just in time to save her from answering Bane. "We're thinking about hitting the strip club in the city. You down for that?"

No. Kennedy wasn't in the mood for a cowboy inspired Magic Mike show. God bless Risa, but Kennedy had to take her in small doses. Not that she was one to throw stones or anything, but Risa had some bad habits that made her fun and reckless, and terribly annoying. Even with the dim bar lights, she could tell Risa had taken something to "enhance her evening" at some point. She knew from a lifetime of experience the night was too young for Risa to stop now. That meant it was going to get worse. Now she wished she hadn't come at all.

Her gaze swung back to Bane. He was staring straight ahead, making it obvious he was listening in. He clenched his jaw and took a sip of his water.

How can a man look sexy while drinking water?

She swallowed again. "I, uh, think I'll pass." Her gaze remained locked on Bane, even though he wasn't returning the favor.

Risa got the message loud and clear and whispered in her ear, "If you aren't queening that man's face tonight, we're no longer friends."

Queening? "Huh?"

"Ride that man every which way you can." Risa giggled in her ear. "And I want details later. Boy looks like he could make a woman scream till her throat's raw."

Kennedy's face went up in flames. Her heart thudded too

loud to be healthy. Risa had a point though. "I'll call you later, okay? Have fun at the strip club."

Once Risa and the girls left, Kennedy turned to Bane and said, "So, what now?"

His smile nearly knocked her off the stool. "Let's get out of here."

CHAPTER 9

Victory felt like paying a bar tab and escorting the finest woman on earth into an ice cream parlor. Not gonna lie, he struggled to keep it together back there when that girl asked Kennedy if she wanted to go to the strip club.

This possessiveness roaring in his veins was new. Unlike Bowen, who was possessive of everything, Bane liked exploring and never thought women should be held back from doing anything. But the thought of Kennedy handing over dollar bills to some half-naked cowboy fucktwat dancing on stage made him murderous.

Uncalled for and wrong, he knew it. Didn't care.

Kennedy enjoying herself would be one thing, but what if one of the men tried to get more from her? She was spectacular. Tits and ass for days. Hips wide enough to make a grown man weak. And considering there was only one strip club in town, and it was run and owned by vampires, that shit was definitely a cocktrap for women.

The vampires in this area were part of the House of Blood. Each vampire House—Death, Blood, and Bone—had smaller communities scattered all over the world. It was part of their network. And although Lycan had their fair share of territories too, the two species rarely crossed businesses.

Bane's family was friendly with most vampires only because of Bane's adopted brother, Dorian. But that wasn't enough to get Bane happy about the prospect of Kennedy going to a strip club filled with bloodsuckers. Vamps were gorgeous, cunning, beguiling, and they made bank off their prey in clubs.

Not to mention, the House of Blood vampires were always

looking for donors, aka courtesans. Bane had no clue what he would have done if Kennedy agreed to go there instead of hanging back with him.

And guess what else he was overthinking about?

Her thirst.

Kennedy drank six glasses of water in less than two hours at the bar. Either she was serious about hydration or...

Okay, he had a bad habit of getting ahead of himself, but Bane couldn't help but wonder if her thirst came from her body priming.

"Here we are," he said, smiling as he held the door for her. Kennedy's awkwardness was adorable. And her ass looked as juicy as a peach. She slipped by him and headed towards the counter of the ice cream parlor, eager to order. Bane hung back just to appreciate the view.

Dayem.

He was getting hard, and that wasn't okay. His dick was massive, and there'd be no way to hide his arousal. They were in a public place. Not that it mattered to him, but it would to her. And if he had to take a guess, he'd say she spooked easy.

Closing his eyes, he stood at the door, holding it open as a gaggle of grandmas came in. Their mothball scent and wintergreen chewing gum did the trick on tapping down his lust. Phew. "Good evening, ladies."

They filed in, one-by-one, as Bane held the door for them. Kennedy watched from the counter, her eyes bright with humor. When he approached her, her smile broadened, and the tips of her ears turned red again. "So..." He clapped his hands and rubbed his palms together. "What are we getting? Banana split? Milkshakes? The Big Bucket?"

He could eat all three and still have room for more. Lycan had fast metabolisms since they were basically eating for two. Although his wolf side didn't care for dairy, Bane loved a thick chocolate shake.

He liked lots of thick desserts.

Again, his gaze roamed down Kennedy's body. His eyes couldn't help themselves. A growl of approval tried to slip from his throat, but he had the sense to catch it before it unleashed. Acutely aware that he must look like a predator assessing its prey, Bane forced his attention to go elsewhere. Like... the ice cream choices.

Yeah, so many big, deep, tubs of goodness.

"What's the bucket?" Kennedy asked.

She stuffed her hands into her back pockets, which made her back arch a little, which made her tits more prominent. Damn, what he wouldn't give to rip that tank top off her. Split the fabric right down the middle, snag her bra with his teeth and rip it just to get a lick of her nipples.

His wolf side approved.

Forget ice cream. He wanted Kennedy for dessert.

Easy boy. Easy. Bane cleared his throat and pointed at the chalkboard menu. "Five scoops of anything with all the toppings."

"Let's do it."

Color him surprised. "One or two?"

"Buckets?" Her brow furrowed. "Two, obviously. I don't share ice cream."

Be. Still. His. Heart. If this woman packed away a big ass bucket of ice cream in one sitting, he was marrying her whether she was his *Deesha* or not.

They ordered, he insisted on paying and tacked on three large ice waters with the intention of giving all three to her if she needed or wanted them. Once they got their buckets, he carried everything over to the table and kicked the chair out for her as he set the hefty tray down.

Look, he wasn't spectacular at being a gentleman, but he had a few manners. Like, not only did he wait for her to dive in first, he made sure to sit across from her and not smother her too much. For a Lycan, that took effort. They liked closeness. Had they been mated, he'd likely ask her to sit on his lap so he could feed her himself.

There went his dick again. A second of imagining her on his lap and he went rock hard.

"So, what do you do?" he asked, then wanted to facepalm himself because his timing was off. Kennedy had just put one of the seven cherries in her mouth. She ripped the stem off and dropped it onto a napkin.

"I'm a veterinarian."

"Really?" He dug into his bucket and stuffed a spoonful of double chocolate chunk into his face. "I like animals. They're easier than people."

62

Kennedy perked right up. Everything about her lightened — her eyes, cheeks, smile. Shit, she even sat up straighter. "Right? I think the same thing. Animals are way better."

"Mmm hmm." He ate another spoonful. "I'm a dog guy."

"I'd be a dog girl, but I work long hours and would feel horrible leaving a dog alone all day or night. I have a cat though."

"Oh yeah? Just one?" He hated cats.

"Yeah, she chose me, and I couldn't refuse." Kennedy grabbed one of the three cups of water he'd added to their order and started chugging. "God, I'm so thirsty. I swear I've had ten glasses of water tonight."

Seven, actually. Not that he was going to point it out. "Maybe you're dehydrated."

"Maybe." She dug into her cookie dough scoop first. "So, what do you do for a living?"

"My brother and I have a landscaping business." Partly true. They rehabbed houses and sold them to low income Lycan, and by landscaping, he meant working on pack land. Bowen rarely contracted human jobs. It was hard to explain their significant strength when moving massive boulders without equipment and to use trucks was a waste of time because they worked better and faster without them. Lycan needed to expend a lot of energy. If they weren't fucking or running, they were lifting heavy shit. Or fighting, in Bane's case.

"Do you have any animals?"

"I wish, but no."

Cue awkward silence again. The smell of freezer burnt cardboard, sugary sprinkles, and maraschino cherries filled his nose. "Soooo, have you always lived here?"

"No," she said, her ears getting red again. The constant color change was remarkable. Did she realize that happened? "I moved here with my brother a couple years ago."

Brother. Was it too much to hope that the man he saw come out of her house the other day was her brother and not a boyfriend? Probably.

"What brought you guys down to Georgia?"

She shrugged and tensed a little. "Change of scenery."

They must be close if they moved together. Did her brother live with her? Bane wasn't about to risk going into a full-blown

63

interrogation. Instead, he pointed at the ice cream, "What do you think of the bucket?"

Her features relaxed, and she shot him a playful smile. "It's decent."

Bane barked a laugh that had his shoulders bunching. She started laughing with him and the mood shifted again.

The door opened. Out of habit, Bane looked up to see who came in because he was never not on guard. And what do you know, a *Savag-Ri* stepped inside with his family of five. Fuck. Fuck. Fuuuuck.

Bane tracked the *Savag-Ri* as the piece of shit ushered his kids to the counter and ordered each a kiddie cone. Either he hadn't noticed Bane was a Lycan, or he was deliberately ignoring him because he had his wife and kids in tow. From this distance, it was hard to discern if the wife was a *Savag-Ri* too. But the kids would be. Any children sired by a *Savag-Ri* would become one once they were old enough to handle the magic load. This was one of the many sticky situations Lycan and vampire found themselves in with *Savag-Ri*. They needed to die. Bane had every right to follow them out and kill that male. But he couldn't. Not with his kids and wife around. Even if the kids would one day grow to be their enemy, Bane never could raise a hand and end their life so early.

He was one of the few who held onto hope that the next generation of *Savag-Ri* would calm down and stop hunting his kind.

The family took their cones and left without paying Bane any notice.

" — here long?"

Shit. He'd missed what Kennedy asked. Clearing his throat, he shook his head, "I'm sorry?"

"Have you lived here long?" She was halfway through her bucket. Grabbing another cherry, she held it between her teeth and ripped the stem off again.

"Yeah, no. I uhhh," Shit, his wolf was clawing at him, desperate to chase the *Savag-Ri*. It made his thoughts slower to form. "We've lived here a while. I like it. It's quiet. My brother and I have a cabin in the middle of about fifty acres of untouched woods."

"Nice!" She wiggled in her seat and chugged the second cup of water. "I'd love to have property like that. I bought this shithole

64

of a house on about four acres, which sadly proved to be more than I can take care of since I'm hardly home. The place is a dump."

"I doubt that." He smiled. "Does it have good bones?"

"No idea. It was affordable and small."

They went back to eating and fell into another weird silence. "We're really bad at this," Bane said, half-chuckling.

"Bad at what?" Kennedy's cheeks reddened again.

"Peopling."

She almost snarfed her ice cream, which made them both laugh. "I think it's mostly my fault. I'm not good with people. Like I said."

"Nah, you're great. It's me. I'm not the best at keeping conversation rolling."

"Silence isn't terrible," she said with a shrug. "And besides, the company's still decent."

He held his chest like she'd just struck him. "Ooph. Decent burgers, decent ice cream, and decent company. I gotta up my game a little if I'm going to ask if I can see you again after tonight."

She wiped her mouth with a napkin. "Yeah, you probably should."

He barked another laugh, and she started giggling. It made her tits jiggle. "Well," he said, slamming his hand down on the table, "How about a do over. Tomorrow afternoon? Picnic?"

The color drained from her face, and she suddenly looked nervous as Hell. Outside, the sound of motorcycles riding by was loud enough to make Bane's ears ring. Lycan were sensitive like that. "Yeah," she said finally. "Yeah, that would be nice."

He flashed her a toothy smile. "What's your favorite food?"

"I'm not picky."

"Any allergies?"

"Nope."

"Any preferences?"

"Surprise me."

Bane took that as a challenge. "Can I pick you up at your place?"

Her facial expression changed again. "Shit. Umm." Kennedy tucked her hair behind her ear again. "Yeah, I think you're going to have to. I don't have my car. Actually, I... my car was stolen and..." She shook her head. "Sorry, I don't want to ruin this night by bitching. I'll shut up now." She took another cherry and ate it.

"No, tell me." Bane hoped he could pull this off and not give himself away. "When did this happen?"

"Yesterday." She slumped in her chair. "I hit a..." her lips tightened as she frowned. "I accidentally hit an animal, brought it in to fix him, and then some guy took off with my car while I was at the clinic."

"Shit," he said. "That's terrible. Did you call the cops and report it?"

Kennedy slowly looked over at him and studied his face. Shit. Was it was dawning on her? Was she recognizing that he was the one who'd stolen her vehicle? Her mouth parted a little. Her eyebrows pinched together. She stared at him for so long he squirmed in his chair. "Is everything okay?"

She bristled. "Yeah, sorry." Gripping her head, she leaned against the table and groaned, "I think I'm losing my damn mind."

"Happens to the best of us."

"I think I'd like to go home now."

"Yeah, sure. I'll take you." He collected their trash and threw it away. When Kennedy didn't get up from the table, he stopped and kneeled down by her chair. "You sure you're okay?"

"I don't feel well."

She looked pale.

"Come on." He gently grabbed her hand and lifted her out of her seat. Bane held onto her all the way back to his truck, both to support her and keep her safe in case that *Savag-Ri* was still around. "Here you go," he unlocked his truck and opened the door for her.

Kennedy got in and he noticed her hands were shaking. And her face was a sickly greenish gray color.

Was she going to puke? Shit, he shouldn't have suggested they go out for ice cream. Not after the burger and fries they ate. Maybe she'd overstuffed herself? Stupid, stupid, stupid. Kennedy didn't have a Lycan's metabolism. Was it costing her now? Damnit!

"I feel dizzy," she said, hunching over as he climbed into the driver's seat. "Can you get me home fast?"

"Absolutely."

She rattled off her address, and it caught him off guard. He was about to drive to her house without asking. And what would that have looked like?

66

Exactly.

Pulling up to her house, he swiftly got out of the truck and was just about to get the door for her when she tumbled out on her own. "I'm... oh no..." Kennedy was so shaken, Bane's hackles raised.

"I got you." He scooped her up as if she weighed ten pounds and carried her up the creaky porch. "Got a key?"

She didn't answer. The stray strands of hair around her face stuck to her forehead and cheeks. She'd broken out in a sweat.

A hot flash.

Bane didn't want to put weight in that observation, but he did. Hot flashes were another sign that a *Deesha* was primed for a mate. And it went with her unquenchable thirst.

"Here," she said with a soft tone. Then she whimpered and squirmed in his arms while digging into her pocket for the house key.

Bane almost kicked the door down to get her inside. With great effort, he forced the instinct down and used his manners, and key, to open the door. Her house smelled fantastic when he stepped inside. Sweet like candy with a little cinnamon. A cat jumped off the couch and ran over to greet them.

He ignored the feline and headed towards her bedroom, still carrying her. The house was small enough to find it without much hunting. He just followed his nose to where her scent was strongest. "Here we are," he said, carefully laying her down on the bed.

"I'm so sorry. I don't know what's going on with me."

"No worries, Kennedy. Just tell me what to do to make it better for you." He knew one way to ease her—if she was actually a *Deesha*—but offering to fuck her senseless right now seemed like the wrong thing to do.

She rolled over onto her side and looked up at him with glassy eyes. "Can you get me some water?"

"Yeah, absolutely. Hang tight." He rushed out of her bedroom and into the kitchen to get some ice water for her. The inside of her house was lovely. Cute and simple. The interior definitely didn't match the exterior.

He could relate.

When Bane returned with the drink, she was out cold.

Now what should he do?

CHAPTER 10

Kennedy rolled over and sighed. Her bed was so comfortable, it was a struggle to ever leave it. Stretching, she yawned big enough for her jaw to crack aaaaannd then recent events pelted her.

Jake. The motorcycle club. The wolf. Her car.

Bane.

"Oh my God." She rubbed the sleep from her eyes. For real, why did the entire world like to shit on her so much? As if having the worst day in the world wasn't bad enough, her night out turned into a total embarrassment with that hunk, Bane.

And he'd been so nice. Now what did he think of her? He probably slapped a massive red flag on her name and ran for the hills. He should, if he had any sense in him. She was a mess with a lot of baggage. A total disaster.

Kennedy sat up. Hey, where was Molly? She usually stayed right with Kennedy whenever she was home. "Pspspsps." Nothing. Oh well, maybe she was snoozing elsewhere. Groaning, Kennedy rolled out of bed and popped the tension in her shoulders and lower back. Lately, her body seemed to age a decade a week. And as much as she loved her bed, she was starting to wonder if she should get a new mattress. Something wasn't right for her to ache all the time.

Not to mention the hot flashes.

Kennedy stared at the glass of water on her nightstand. "Oh shit."

More of last night came back to her. The ride home. The dizzy spell. Bane carrying her inside.

Bane. There was something familiar about him, and it drove her nuts that she couldn't place it. When they'd talked about her car being stolen, she swore her mind was playing tricks on her. His eyes had changed color as he stared at her, going from amber to almost citrine yellow. Everything went bananas after that though, and, well... she doubted she'd ever hear from him again.

"Way to go, Kennedy." She should have never gone out last night. That way she'd never have known what she was missing. Tears almost formed thinking about Bane, but she wasn't going to let them come. She didn't cry over guys she just met.

Tugging her tank top off, she marched into the bathroom and started up the shower. Still dressed from the night before, she peeled her jeans down and tossed them in the hamper. Then she got a whiff of herself. Oh gross. She smelled like dog, sweat, and greasy burger.

Stepping into the shower, she let the hot water melt the tension in her back. It felt amazing until it got too hot and she started getting nauseous again. Seriously, what the hell was wrong with her lately? Maybe she should see a doctor. Or maybe she should just google it. Whatever. Easing back the water temp to make it colder, she sighed as the cool water soothed her skin. Much better. Even her belly agreed.

She shampooed, shaved, and scrubbed until there was nothing left to do in the shower except...

Eyeing the shower head, she almost went for it. Wouldn't be the first time she used that jet between her thighs, especially when she set the thing on pulse mode. Instead, she shut the waterworks off and got dressed for the day.

Depressed that Bane hadn't even left his number on her nightstand, she figured that picnic wasn't happening now. Why did that have to hurt so much? Ugh.

"Molly!" Entering the kitchen, she grabbed a can of cat food and tapped her nail on the tin top. "Pspspsps."

Still no response. Okay, now she was starting to worry.

Movement outside caught her attention, and she ducked down, grabbed her baseball bat from the corner by the door, and peaked out through the window.

No. Way.

Dropping the bat, she opened the front door and gawked. "What are you doing?"

Okay, so he'd overstayed his welcome, going by the look of horror on Kennedy's face. But he couldn't just leave her to fend for herself when she lived out in the middle of nowhere and there were *Savag-Ri* all over the place. Granted, he doubted any would show up at her doorstep, but that didn't mean he was willing to take the risk. Especially when she'd been vulnerable last night.

The Louisville slugger leaning against her wall by the front door spoke volumes about how safe she felt in her own home. People didn't put a weapon by their door without good reason.

"I uhhh..." How could he explain himself?

Molly, her cat, was perched on his shoulders. The damn thing hadn't left him alone since he'd tucked Kennedy into bed last night. Her fur was frustrating as hell. It kept getting in his nose and making him sneeze. And she wouldn't get off him, no matter what he did. Including when he mowed her grass earlier this morning.

"I didn't want to leave you alone last night, but I can't sit still for long, so I thought I'd make myself useful." Now that he thought about it, he felt like an idiot. "Sorry."

Kennedy's eyes were wide as saucers as she stepped off the porch and gawked at him. Her ears were a lovely crimson again. And the scent of her shampoo perfumed the air between them, filling his nose with a flowery fragrance. "You mowed my lawn."

"Sorry."

"You just... you mowed my lawn."

"Yeah." The way she kept gawking made him feel like he might have overstepped. "The throttle linkage was broken. I fixed it." Great, now he sounded like a total douche. "Your mower works fine now, so I figured I'd just," he paused and looked around the grass, "mow it?"

Kill him now.

Kennedy's gaze swiveled to the mower Bane had put back under the small lean-to. He was just about to split some of the wood that had been dumped under it, but his energy was waning and his leg hurt like a motherfucker. Certain he'd popped a few stitches again, he decided to not go whole hog on her yard today.

"Thank you," Kennedy said. Her brow remained pinched in confusion.

Realizing he might have gone too far, Bane pulled Molly from his shoulders, but the cat dug her claws in, making it impossible to pry the furball off. "Shit, get off, get off, get off!" Molly meowed in protest, her body stiffening as she clung to his shirt. He gave up and let her go. She settled back onto his shoulders. "I don't know how to win with her."

Kennedy stared at him like he had six heads. Cue the awkwardness again.

Bugs zipped around in the yard. Gray clouds loomed overhead. "So..." Bane let some tension leave his shoulders in hopes of not looking as uncomfortable as he felt. "Are you feeling better today?"

She looked good. Nah, scratch that. She looked fantastic.

"Yeah." Kennedy crossed her arms over her ample chest. "I'm... wow. I don't know what to say, Bane."

Okay, so maybe he'd overstepped with the lawn care. And sleeping over without her fully aware of it was probably also crossing boundaries. He jabbed his thumb at his truck parked in the driveway and said, "I'll get going."

At the same time, she asked, "You want to stay for breakfast?"

They laughed awkwardly at each other again.

Look, Bane was a smooth Lycan. He never had trouble with conversation before. But Kennedy wasn't some regular chick he picked up at a bar. Even if that's how it looked to her. She was, or might be, his *Deesha*, and that's what made him so nervous.

Because what if she rejected him in the end?

Shit, he couldn't go there. Not right now. Just the thought of rejection and being forced into his wolf form forever made him queasy. It wasn't just his life depending on her. It was Bowen's too. His twin would make good on his promise and live as a wolf with Bane if it came down to it. Bane didn't want that to happen.

"Breakfast sounds perfect." It was noon.

"It looks like it's going to rain." She tipped her head up and the angles of her lovely face were enhanced by the low light filtering through the clouds. "I don't think we'll be having a picnic today."

71

She still wanted that? Bane's chest puffed up with relief and hope. "Carpet picnics are good too."

Kennedy's grin nearly knocked him over. How the hell could a woman be this stunning?

"Well, okay then." Kennedy turned and headed back inside. He followed. She stopped at the top step. "Thanks for—" She turned and ran smack into his chest. "Ooph!"

Yeah. They sucked at this.

Bane lifted her chin with his finger and stared at her for a few heartbeats. He tucked some wet strands of hair behind her ear. Then he deliberately let his gaze sail, nice and slow, down to her mouth. Leaning forward, he pressed his lips to hers softly.

He pulled back to see her reaction. Kennedy's eyes were heavy lidded. She licked her lips and sucked on the bottom one, as if savoring his taste. Bane flashed her a wolfish grin. "You mentioned something about breakfast?" He was playing with her, keeping it cool, but still testing her out. "You talking about yourself, or pancakes?"

"Both." Kennedy gasped, her eyes widening in horror. "Oh my god, did I just say that out loud?" She cupped her cheeks and groaned.

Bane laughed and wrapped his hands around her waist, driving her backwards and into the house.

CHAPTER 11

Of all the lousy times to get interrupted, it just had to be in the midst of flipping pancakes and crisping bacon. Kennedy wanted to pout about Bane having to leave so suddenly, but she was a grown woman. Grown women didn't pout.

They got even.

Besides, it looked like he was pretty bummed out about not being able to stay. When his brother called, Bane's playful nature morphed into a severe scowl in a blink of an eye. His tone dropped. He even turned away from her while he talked to the caller.

When he came back into a kitchen a few minutes later asking for a raincheck, she was a little surprised. And quite honestly, also a little relieved. Bane was too easy to fall into a comfort-zone with. That was dangerous, considering she didn't know him at all. But his easy-going attitude, playful nature, and adorable awkwardness spoke to her soul.

That was bad news. It meant she could easily get her heart broken and Kennedy had enough on her plate already, no sense in adding emotions to it. Speaking of enough on her plate, she'd made enough batter for a mountain of pancakes, and now it was just her eating them.

"Maybe I'll just feed them to the birds." She sighed, staring down at the platter. *How many of these would Bane have eaten?*

And why the hell couldn't she stop thinking about him?

Molly rubbed against her ankles, meowing loudly. Kennedy frowned at the furball. "You like him too, huh? We're in trouble, girl."

Kennedy stared at the pound of crispy bacon cooling on a

plate. "Fuck it." She snatched both the bacon and maple syrup and brought it to her table. Next, she grabbed the platter of pancakes and a banana. Making herself a plate, she cut the slices of fruit over her pancakes, and couldn't keep Bane's smile out of her head. The way his gaze ate her up when they talked. His laugh still echoed in her skull. Good lord, she swore she could still feel his big, hot hands on her waist.

It made her squirm in her seat.

A loud engine purred from a good distance away. Dread hit her gut. "Great." Kennedy's ears were trained to pick up on the exact roar of her brother's bike. She hated that thing. The rumble of his truck wasn't much better. Any time Jake stopped by, it made her uneasy. How shitty was that? By the time he pulled into her driveway, a knot had formed in the pit of her stomach, leaving very little room for food. This was his third time seeing her in less than a week, which, with Jake's track record, meant he was in trouble. Again.

Jake didn't bother to knock, and Kennedy didn't get up from the table when he walked right into her house. Sending him the stink-eye, she stabbed into her stack of pancakes and took a bite.

"You cut the grass."

She didn't respond.

"Any of those for me?" He pulled off his sunglasses and dropped them on the table before taking a seat across from her.

"Help yourself." He would have anyway. Jake was a garbage disposal. Just like she figured, he didn't get a plate. Instead, he dragged the platter of pancakes over to himself and snagged the syrup. Plucking the knife from her side of the table, he used it to stab hunks of pancake and stuffed it all into his mouth. Kennedy went back to eating. Neither said anything for a full minute. Okay, enough was enough. "What's going on with you now?"

Jake's eyes narrowed. "The fuck do you mean by that?"

She leaned back in her chair. "You only come around this often when there's something you need to tell me and can't nut up to do it."

Jake stopped chewing, swallowed, and rested his elbows on the table as he glowered. "Maybe I'm just being protective of you."

"Because you got me into some shit that's so bad I need a watchdog?"

His slight cringe meant that was a yes. Great. Just fan-fucking-tastic. They both stared at each other with matching expressions. It was one of the very few similarities they had, beyond their eye color and hatred of cilantro.

Jake clenched his jaw and didn't blink as he continued to glare. Kennedy raised her eyebrow and sighed heavily. She lost her appetite and shoved her plate away. It was always the same with him — trouble, trouble, and more trouble.

Someone else in Kennedy's shoes might cut ties from a brother like him and let him burn in his own dumpster fire, but she owed Jake. And at this point, she was beginning to wonder if or when her debt would ever be paid off. Aaaannnnd that made her feel like shit because Jake went to prison for her, and here she was almost wishing to cut and run just to get away from his toxic bullshit. *I'm part of the reason he's in this Hell to begin with.* She would never forget what he did for her, which meant she always caved when he needed something.

Jake dropped his gaze, a look of remorse etched onto his face. He had crow's feet already, and a little salt-and-pepper action in his hair. The mix made him look hard and handsome, but edgy. "You look like Dad," she whispered.

He scoffed. "Thanks for the insult." Jake shoved his food out of the way and crossed his arms, which were both covered in ink.

"How are your stitches holding up?"

"Fine." Their sour moods stretched across the room until it filled the atmosphere and Kennedy had to get up and move around to expel her nervous energy. "Look," Jake said with a bark in his tone. "I need you to hold on to something for me."

"Nope."

"Kennedy."

"No, Jake. Whatever it is, you can't keep it here."

He slammed his fists on the table, rattling the whole piece of furniture. "I could have just hidden it without asking."

As if asking made him a considerate criminal? "No, Jake."

"It's not what you think!" He shot up and his chair screeched across the floor. "Please, Kennedy."

"No!"

His hands balled into fists. It was easy to tell Jake got close to blowing his top. Well, tough shit. His anger, threats, and lash outs

75

didn't impact her in any way. She wasn't changing her mind on this.

Two other motorcycles roared from down the road. Jake paled, his eyes popping wide. "Shit, shit, shit!" He pulled something small out of his pocket and dashed down the hall. He was gone less than ten seconds and was back at her side before the bike engines cut off out front.

"*Jake.*" Kennedy's voice shook with fear. Her brother was scared shitless, and he was never like that.

"Follow my lead and keep your mouth shut as much as possible."

She hated him for this. Whatever Jake was into, how dare he drag her down with him. And now they were at her *house.* Kennedy's breath hitched as two men opened the door without knocking, both sporting menacing grins on their faces while they invited themselves in.

"Leave." Kennedy shot off, grabbing a kitchen knife from the block on her counter. Jake slowly moved to stand between her and the two huge guys glowering from the doorway. "You're not welcome here."

Jake turned on her, his eyes blazing with panic and anger. He grabbed her throat and forced her backwards until she hit the counter. His hold around Kennedy's neck was firm, but gentle. However, his voice dripped in disdain. "Who the *fuck* do you think you're talking to, *bitch*?"

Her chin trembled. Jake knocked the knife out of her hand so fast, the cling of the blade hitting the floor echoed in the too silent kitchen. She met his gaze, pleading for him to stop and go away. Ease off. Leave.

Reluctantly, Jake let her go and Kennedy was half-tempted to pick up the knife and stab him in his other arm for putting her through this. His gaze remained cold, but she saw the set lines in his jaw. The pleading in his eyes. The look that he had when they were younger, and she was forced to play into whatever game he was playing.

Follow my lead, his gaze said. *Trust me.*

She shouldn't do either of them, but... "Why are you here?" Damnit, her voice trembled so much it made her angrier.

"I need morphine," Jake growled. "As much as you can get."

76

She shook her head violently. "I... I don't have morphine. I have no way of getting that stuff."

Jake got all in her face, as if to intimidate her. "Then get us animal tranquilizers."

She wasn't sure if she should cower away or slap him. Instead, she tried dodging him. Kennedy didn't get far before she bumped into another body.

"Skittish, isn't she?" The man with a straggly beard and bright blue eyes grinned down at her. He smelled like cigarette smoke, engine grease, and something so pungent it made her eyes water. "Got a nice rack on her though."

"Acid," Jake growled. "Back off."

Ignoring Jake's commands, Acid dipped his finger between Kennedy's breasts. She smacked him. He stepped back, pretending to play nice. *Oh God.* Terror and humiliation warred within her. Kennedy's gaze volleyed from Jake, to Acid, to Blade, who continued standing at the front door, staring at her. She swallowed the bile rising in her throat. Her hands trembled as she balled them into fists. "All of you need to get out."

"You have three days to get us tranquilizers." Acid jabbed his finger in the air at her. "I'll be back to collect the goods myself." Jake tensed the same time Kennedy did. Acid didn't miss it. And... *oh no...* his smile widened. That couldn't be good. "Your sister's got a hell of an ass, Diesel. Can't wait to tear it open with my dick."

Panic slammed into Kennedy so hard, she grew dizzy. Her immediate reaction was to look over at Jake for help. He knew. Acid knew they were related. Shit, shit, shit!

"Wait in line." Blade sauntered over and by the time he entered the kitchen area, all the air evaporated from Kennedy's lungs. She broke out in a sweat and swayed on her feet, but she couldn't drop her gaze from Blade. He held her captive in terror. "Such a pretty mouth," he cupped her trembling chin and shoved his dirty thumb between her lips, nearly prying her mouth open to do it. This was even worse than Acid shoving his finger between her tits. It was disgusting and violating. Furious, she bit down on him.

He laughed, completely unaffected by it. And the worst part was? She'd held back. She should have bit his whole goddamn finger off for shoving it in her mouth, but instead she gave a warning nip and all it did was humor him.

And humiliate her further.

"Three days," Jake barked, bringing the attention back to him. "She's got three days to get the product."

Blade ignored him, keeping his attention deadlocked on Kennedy's mouth. He shoved his thumb further between her lips, pressing down hard on her tongue, and triggered her gag reflex. It made her eyes water and mouth fill with saliva. Smirking, he slid his thumb out of her mouth, not caring that her teeth scraped his filthy skin, and sucked her spit off his thumb. "Three days, sugar."

Tears welled in her eyes. She hated all of them. Staring at Blade, she imagined gouging his eyes out. Next, her attention swiveled to Acid. He'd figured out she and Jake were related. How? When? And what was he going to with that information? Jake told her when he joined this MC that they would never know he had a sister. It's why he rarely visited, except when big shit hit the fan. And now the jig was up. It shouldn't feel like that big of a deal, but the way they all kept staring at her, and seeing how little power Jake had, Kennedy felt like a rabbit in the center of a cage of tigers.

Acid kept Kennedy's attention for longer than she meant to allow, only because she was panicked in working out the terrifying scenarios in her mind. As she glared at him, he slowly brought his hand up to his face, made a V with his index and middle fingers, and flicked his tongue fast and vulgarly between them.

She looked away and stared at Jake's boots. Letting her eyes slowly rise to meet his, she hoped he got her message loud and clear with the look she sent him. *Leave and never come back. Don't put me through this. I can't do it again.*

In response, she wished he looked back at her with an expression that said, *I'll make this right. I'll leave you alone from now on. I'm sorry. Goodbye.*

Instead, she got nothing. His eyes were dead. His mouth set in a cold frown. His coldness sent ice into her veins.

This was Jake's way of protection now. Shutting down. Turning off his humanity. He learned that in prison. Seeing him sink into that protection mode made her stomach twist. She couldn't depend on him. Not anymore. His self-preservation was too strong, and he'd trained himself to morph into whatever he had to in order to survive the life he was caught up in.

Part of that was all her fault.

"Let's go," Blade ordered. He turned and left the kitchen first, leading the way out.

Acid followed, but not before looming over her one last time and smelling her hair. Something feral flickered in his gaze. His lips peeled back with a sneer, and he stared at her as though her scent offended him.

Kennedy fought the urge to cringe and held her ground. Her cheeks burned even though she didn't say a word. Acid raked his eyes down her body one last time, his jaw clenching, and then he looked over at Jake. "Get the fuck out of here, Diesel."

Jake stayed where he was.

"I said, *move!*" Acid turned his full attention to Jake and went after him. Kennedy realized Jake was luring Acid away by purposefully pissing him off. Otherwise, it could very well have ended with Blade and Jake outside, and Acid alone with her in the kitchen until he saw fit to show himself out. Out of all three men, Acid was the one she feared the most. He was also the one Jake warned her about before.

Blade roared from the doorway, "Acid! Diesel! *Now!*"

Oh thank god, Kennedy thought as they both marched out the door. Blade stared at Kennedy for a long moment. "Get what we want, sugar. You've got three days."

"And..." Kennedy's panic made the edges of her vision darken. "What if I can't get what you want?"

"Then we'll *take* what we want." He flashed her a cold smile. "And we'll start with your mouth and work our way through your holes until we feel your debt is satisfied."

"I owe you nothing."

"Not according to the payment we gave you already."

"Take it back."

"That's not how this works, sugar. If I were you, I'd get a move on and make sure you do as we say." He licked his lips obscenely. "My men are hungry, and you look like a woman they could feast on for a few days. Get the tranquilizers or watch how fast we gentlemen can make a woman turn into a raw piece of meat." He slammed the door shut and their engines roared to life in her driveway.

Kennedy sank to her knees and sobbed.

79

CHAPTER 12

"You can't be serious." Bane wanted nothing more than to punch Bowen in the throat. "You said this was an emergency."

"Not a lie." Bowen's argument was so flimsy, it was insulting. "But it got cleared up."

"Damnit, Bowe. This is bullshit!" Bowen had called him saying Emily, their little sister, had gone missing—one of the very few things that could tear Bane away from his potential mate. He'd left Kennedy mid-pancake flip and raced home only to find out the mystery was solved. He was glad she'd been found. "You could have called and told me that." Bane turned around to head back to his truck.

Bowen stormed behind him and grabbed his shoulder. "Stop, Bane."

"You just pulled me away from my *Deesha*. Fuck off."

"You only *think* that's your *Deesha*. But you don't know for sure. And you spending time with her will only cloud your dreams."

What a crock of shit. "She's mine."

"How do you know?"

"Because I—" Hell, Bane didn't know for sure. But Kennedy had to be the real deal. "She's got to be it. I saw her in my dream. She's the only one who turned her head."

Bowen had the nerve to laugh. "Not good enough. You're wasting time, Bane. Precious little time we have left."

"It's not a waste! I'm—" What? Dating her? Seducing her? He

hadn't done a damned thing but feed her, talk, ice her down after her hot flash, and mow her lawn.

"You're fixating," Bowen said, shoving a finger into Bane's chest. "You're nothing but a dog with a bone. And this time, it could cost you everything."

Not true. Okay, yes, true, but being fixated on what matters wasn't a bad thing. "She's the one."

"You saying that doesn't make it true." Bowen was right. Not that Bane was willing to admit it out loud. His twin sighed heavily and looked down at the ground. "Bane, all because you want her, doesn't make her yours. And the more time you spend with her, the harder the break will be if she's not the one."

She is. She has to be.

But a kernel of doubt landed in the pit of his stomach and embedded itself. Bowen was right. Kennedy could just be a well-placed, perfectly timed distraction that could keep him from discovering his *Deesha* in time if he wasn't cautious.

Or… she really was his fated mate.

"You spent the night there," Bowen accused. "That's a problem."

"She needed help. She had a hot flash." Okay, even as he said it, the excuse sounded stupid. "It was big, brother. And she was thirsty all night."

"How old is she?"

He knew where this was going. "Too young for menopause or even perimenopause."

"Maybe she was dehydrated. Nervous. On drugs."

"No," Bane growled. "She's the real thing, Bowe."

"You hope."

Couldn't argue with that. "Fuck right, I do." Because he was already falling for her. She was fun and sweet and smelled divine. She had a great laugh and loved animals. A body to die for. He had no doubt the more he got to know her, the harder he'd fall in love with her.

"Damn it all to hell," Bowen scoffed. "You're already doing it."

"Doing what?"

"That thing you do when you're into a woman." Bowen rubbed his face with both hands and growled. "You jump in with

81

both feet too soon, man. What did you do with her last night and this morning?"

"Nothing." Now he was offended. "I just mowed her grass!"

"Mowed her—" Bowen groaned like Bane had done something wrong. "And what else? Clean her toilets? Bake her muffins?"

If they weren't twins, Bane would have knocked him out. "Nothing wrong with providing for your mate however she needs."

"By scaring her off? Yeah, way to go, bro." Bowen tossed his hands up. "You go too hard straight out of the gate. You try too hard."

"Unlike you, who never tries at all." Bane couldn't help how he worked. He was hard wired this way. So yeah, he went all in, one-hundred and ten percent, with the things he enjoyed. And when it came to his *Deesha*, there was no limit to his efforts. Kennedy deserved nothing less.

"What's that supposed to mean?"

Bane tipped his head up to the sun and sighed. "You have so many walls, your *Deesha* will never be able to climb over them."

"And you don't know the meaning of the word *boundary*."

Touché. Bane scuffed his boots along the gravel outside their cabin. Neither said a word until someone else drove up the driveway and honked. It was their sister, Emily. So not only had she been located, but she was also coming over? "What's she doing here?"

"No clue," Bowen frowned. "She called me just after I told you she'd gone missing. Said she was headed to us."

"Emerick's gonna be pissed."

"Already is." Bowen ran his thumb along his eyebrow, scratching it. "And this conversation isn't over," Bowen warned him.

Yes, it was. Bane had nothing more to say to Bowen about Kennedy. Not yet, at least.

In unison, they slapped on big smiles to greet their little sister. Bane tapped the hood of her car once she parked. "What's up, Em?"

"I need a break." She turned the engine off and unstrapped her seatbelt. "Emerick's driving me insane."

"Yeah, he'll do that." Emerick was their oldest brother. An alpha destined to take over the Woods' pack, though he hadn't stepped into their father's boots yet. Bane had no clue what he was holding out for. And Emerick had made it his life's mission to watch Emily like a hawk lately. As the only girl in the family, she was precious to them. But she was also an adult, and sometimes Bane wondered if Emerick forgot that. "You coming to stay with us for a bit?"

"If you don't mind."

Bane grinned. "Of course not. Come on in."

"We only have two bedrooms," Bowen argued. As if they didn't all know that?

"She can have my room." Bane could take the couch. Or Kennedy's bed, fate willing.

Emily stuffed her hands in her pockets. "I'm not staying long. I'm headed south."

That got their attention. "Why?" Bowen's gaze narrowed on her. "Who's South from here?"

"Dorian, asshat. I'm sick of the woods." Emily didn't bother getting her duffel from the backseat. Bane got it for her and carried it inside. "I feel like I'm suffocating at home."

"You live alone," Bowen argued. "Emerick's visits can't be that awful."

Of course, he didn't get it. But Bane had a feeling he did. "You're crawling out of your skin, huh?"

Emily sighed heavily as she climbed their steps and went inside. Bane took that as a yes. Ever since Dorian, their adopted brother, had found a mate, Emily had become distant and colder than usual. Their mom called all the brothers about it over the past couple of months with explicit orders to watch her closely. Emerick must have taken that as a sign to turn into a helicopter.

It might sound overbearing, but it was always kind of necessary. Emily was a wanderer. Wanderers were easy pickings for *Savag-Ri*.

If she thought coming here would offer a break from the overbearing routine, she was sadly mistaken. Bowen wasn't going to be much better than Emerick. Emily had to know that.

"I'm only staying one night," she warned and plopped down on the couch. "I feel like I can't stay anywhere longer than that."

"But you're staying with Dorian?" Bane double-checked.

"Yeah. It's time. He rubs off on me in a good way."

Dorian rubbed off on all of them in a good way. Funny, since he was a vampire, which technically made him a Lycan enemy. But the Woods family didn't roll like that. In fact, Dorian was family. Leave it to the Woods to adopt a bloodsucker and raise him as their own kin.

Bane sank down into a chair across from her and leaned forward, resting his elbows on his knees. "What's up, Ems?"

The fact that she wouldn't meet his eyes had his hackles up. Bowen's too. He sat next to her and nudged her with his elbow. "Come on, Emily. What's going on?"

She looked up and tears fell down her cheeks. "I miss him," she said quietly. "I miss Killian."

Fuck.

"Us too," Bane said. Killian was their youngest brother who'd lost himself to his wolf a couple of years ago because he hadn't found his *Deesha* in time. He shifted into a wolf and took off, never to be seen again. And a few months ago, during one of the Lycan ceremonies on the Woods' family property, they'd had a scare. Someone had strung a wolf, completely disemboweled and ribs cracked open like butterfly wings, into a tree on their property. They all thought it was Killian at first. Emily was the first one to stumble on the gruesome scene. She'd lost her shit that night and, by the looks of things, she still wasn't right about it.

"Promise me," she whispered, sniffling. "Promise me you guys aren't going to drink the silver. I can't stand the idea of losing anyone else."

Bane and Bowen looked over at each other. Bane's heart dropped out of his ass. Bowen's gaze burned with regret. Neither said a word. Instead, Bowen put his arm around her shoulder and brought her into his chest for a tight hug.

But his gaze remained pinned on Bane.

CHAPTER 13

Kennedy spent the rest of the day crying, screaming, and hitting her baseball bat against a tree in her backyard. Thank God she didn't have neighbors close by. They might have called the asylum on her. Once exhausted, she stormed inside and tore her bathroom and bedroom apart, looking for whatever Jake might have hidden in that mad dash he did just before Acid and Blade walked in.

Damn him. Damn all of them.

She was sick of crying. Sick of being scared. Sick of everything.

She went to bed and barely slept. Was up long before her alarm went off. Then it was dress in scrubs and sit outside to wait for Risa to pick her up for work.

"Whoa girl." Risa's expression looked as appalled as Kennedy felt frustrated. "What's happened?"

"Nothing."

"That boy from the bar do you dirty? 'Cause I got no morals, a shovel, and an alibi."

Kennedy slid into the passenger seat and buckled up. "No, it's not him."

"Your brother again?"

She clenched her jaw and stared out the window. She regretted ever telling Risa about Jake. It was a slip up one night a couple years ago, and she'd had a guilty feeling about it ever since. Mostly because she hated talking badly about her brother to anyone

85

after what he did for her. But also, because she didn't like others to know about her secret shitshow of a life. The weak moment and lapse in judgement over margaritas and nachos meant Risa knew more than she should now.

And although Risa wasn't a judgy person, she also drank, drugged, and partied too much. Something Kennedy hadn't realized until it was too late. But really, she'd said nothing incriminating. Only that Jake was a fuckup and a half and Kennedy always had to clean up his messes. Honestly? It felt good to vent once in a while to someone other than her cat.

"I know blood is thicker than water and all that," Risa said, "but it's not terrible to set boundaries even with family."

"Noted."

Risa didn't push the subject, and that was one of the many things she loved about that woman. Risa called it what it was and moved on. She didn't hover, push, or kick a dead horse over and over. Had she even tried, Kennedy might have flung herself out of the car.

"Mark's pissed. He said there was an untagged dog in the freezer." Risa side-eyed Kennedy. "You know anything about that?"

Damnit! The damn crematory should have picked those animals up before Mark saw them. This was just her luck. "I hit the dog on my way home," Kennedy lied.

"That's why your car's in the shop?"

"Mmm hmm." It felt awful to lie to Risa. But what choice did she have?

Risa frowned. "The dog looked chewed up, not banged up."

Kennedy was going to puke. Her mind raced to come up with another lie, but none formed. She couldn't see past her fear, worry, and guilt. "It was attacked by another animal."

"Then I guess you might have done the poor thing a favor by putting him out of his misery. Even if it was by accident."

Kennedy teared up as her throat tightened.

Risa hung a left. They were only about five minutes away from work, and the car became eerily quiet. Finally, Risa said, "You sure there isn't more to this story you want to share but think you can't?"

Kennedy's brow pinched. What the hell was she trying to say? "Nope." Risa didn't need to be dragged into Kennedy's shitshow.

She wasn't saying anything more about this.

Kennedy swallowed the lump in her throat. Risa might have her issues, but she was ethical about most things. If she found about a group of men coordinating dog fights in the area, she'd want to report it. And if the cops were alerted about the dog fights, then they might eventually catch Blade's crew. But if they caught the Wolf Pack, they'd catch Jake too. Kennedy was still mad enough at him to have mixed feelings about that. "I don't know anything about anything." She crossed her arms and shriveled a little. Time to deflect and distract. "Did you have fun at the strip club the other night?"

Risa smiled. Mission accomplished. "Girl, I hooked up with one of them backstage." She turned to face her, perking right up. "He had a dick that was—"

"TMI!" Kennedy threw her hand up. "T.M.I."

"This big around!" She used two hands to make the circle. "Fattest cock I've ever seen in my life."

"Wow. That's.... intimidating." They pulled up to the clinic and any remaining tension between them snapped the instant Kennedy opened the door and got out, cutting the conversation short. "Thanks for the ride." She went inside without waiting for Risa to grab her stuff and head in with her.

The workday had been a long one. Double shifts were hell on the back and feet. Add her current family issues, and evading Mark's constant questioning, Kennedy felt tapped out on emotions and energy. Risa was sweet enough to offer to come back and pick Kennedy up to take her home. The kind gesture was balanced with an attitude though. And a cold shoulder. Risa seemed wired and didn't say a word the whole way home. That girl's attitude and energy were so polarized, it sometimes gave Kennedy whiplash. She was too tired to ask her what was wrong. If that made her a shit friend, fine. So be it. She just didn't have the energy right now.

As they pulled onto her road, Kennedy leaned forward, resting on the dashboard, and her jaw dropped. For a second, she thought she was hallucinating from lack of sleep and too much stress.

87

"Hey, your car's fixed!"

Yes. Yes, it was. Kennedy thanked Risa for the ride and slammed the door shut. Then she waved her off while cautiously approaching her vehicle. It was... holy shit! It was completely fixed, cleaned up, and even the old dent in her back bumper had been repaired.

She didn't know if she should laugh, cry, or run into hiding.

This felt personal and weird. The gesture was... creepy.

Who stole a car, then returned it all fixed up and cleaned? She opened the driver's side and sat in it. The keys were in the ignition. No note. Not that she thought the thief would leave one, but still. This was scary. How had the thief known where she lived? Her gaze sailed around the dash and floorboards, over the center console and into the backseat. Maybe he got her info from the registration card in her glove box?

Her heart hammered in her chest. If he knew where she lived, he could come back. Clearly, this guy had issues if he stole a car and returned it in better shape than when he took it. What kind of person did that?

A fucked up one.

Holy shit. She had a stalker. Kennedy scrambled for her cell phone. Shit, shit, shit. She couldn't call the cops and tell them anything, but she could call...

Who? Jake? Fuck him. And fuck her too, for even considering it. But damnit, he was the first one she thought of.

Risa? No. Not after the uncomfortable conversation they had yesterday and her strange attitude today.

Bane? The night they met, they'd exchanged numbers. But calling him for something like this was wrong. Weird. Terrifying. What would he think of her if she explained any of this to him? Maybe she didn't have to explain it. Maybe she could just call and see if he wanted to come over for a movie with the secret agenda of having him there, so she wasn't alone. Was that being too forward? Too selfish? And if he did come, and there just happened to be a bad guy hidden in the closet, then what?

Nope. No way. She wasn't putting Bane in a dangerous situation like that. How horrible of her to even consider it an option. God, her head hurt. She just needed to woman up and go inside her house. Search the area for intruders and take a hot bath.

And that's just what she did.

No one was in her house. All doors and windows were locked. Her trusty baseball bat sat in its corner, like always. As a precaution, Kennedy drew the curtains and turned on every light in the house. She even carried a kitchen knife into the bathroom with her.

This was some b-rated horror movie bullshit right here.

Running a bath, she sank into the hot water and sighed. Every inch of her body ached from staying so tense. Molly nudged the door open and strolled in, meowing. Curling up on the rug, she flicked the tip of her tail and stared at Kennedy as if waiting for a reply.

Her cell rang. Immediately, her mind went to Jake. She almost didn't want to look to see who it was. Because if it wasn't Jake, it was most likely work, and she wasn't going back in tonight, damnit. Mark could kiss her ass. By the third ring, she caved. Curiosity and obligation had her leaning forward to see who it was.

Bane.

Damn if Kennedy's heart didn't skip a beat. She tapped her wet finger on the screen, accepting his call and putting him on speaker. "Hello?"

"*Hey.*" His deep, soft phone voice made goosebumps ripple down her arms. A smile spread across her face. How on earth could one simple word said in that sexy voice be so impactful? That was concerning. Kennedy didn't get like this over men. "You there?" he asked, half laughing.

Shit, she hadn't responded! "Yes," she said, face-palming herself. Water sloshed and her chin dripped with bubbles. She snagged a towel, sloshing more water around. "Sorry, I uh…" she wiped her face off again. "You just surprised me, is all."

"It sounds like you're busy. Want me to call back later?"

"I'm in the tub," she said. Shit, she sounded like a tease.

Bane grunted on the other end of the line. "You're killing me, woman."

She leaned back with a laugh. Of all things to latch onto, she was making Bane her comfort. Closing her eyes, emotions welled up. It wasn't fair to make him her new focal point. But it was hard to deny herself this taste of happiness. His voice soothed her. If he was here right now, his energy would calm her. Hell, even his scent stirred peace in her soul. And those were just a few notable qualities she'd picked up on between the bar and the ride back to her house. She couldn't speak for what happened when he ended up carrying her inside and tucking her in bed while she suffered a horrible hot flash and nausea. And the fact that he fixed her lawn mower and cut her grass wasn't as weird as it was thoughtful. For once, someone was taking care of Kennedy. It was almost always the other way around.

"How was your day?"

Wow. He had an incredibly sexy phone voice. "Long."

"Want me to let you go so you can get some rest?"

"No." She sighed. "I like talking to you. Your voice is..." *making me wetter than this bath,* "soothing."

He lightly chuckled. "Then I'll keep talking."

She smiled at that. Settling back against the tub, she added more hot water by flicking the faucet with her foot.

"Got bubbles in there?"

"Mm hmm," she closed her eyes and focused on his voice. "Just added more heat."

"I could help with that," his tone dropped to an even lower register.

Good God almighty, where did this man come from, a fantasy romance novel? "Oh, yeah?"

He kept his voice deep. "Want me to?"

Was Bane asking permission to have phone sex with her, or was she misreading this? It had been a while for her, and rules changed too much on the dating circuit for Kennedy to know for certain. She needed to play this by ear. "Yes," she whispered.

"Pull the temp back on the faucet for me, *Deesha.*"

Deesha? Instead of asking what that meant, she obeyed him. "How so?"

"Make it warm, but not hot for me."

"Done."

"Now," his voice dropped to an even lower register. "I want you to scoot that fine ass of yours up to the stream and spread your legs as wide as you can for me."

Her mouth dropped.

"I better be on speakerphone," he nearly growled.

"You're on my Bluetooth speaker," she laughed. She'd

90

hooked her phone up to it with the intention of playing music but hadn't done anything but sit in the water and sulk.

"Oh, good." Bane sounded turned on already at the mere mention of his voice taking up the whole bathroom. "Now do as I say and spread those glorious thighs for me."

Blushing, she scooted up and spread her legs as much as she could in the tub. It wasn't easy or comfortable. But it sure was exhilarating. Biting her lip, she couldn't believe she was doing this. Her heart kicked up in pace, making her head spin a little.

"Make sure you put your clit directly under the running water," he said. Jesus, it felt like he was in the room with her. Kennedy's eyebrows went into her hairline, but she did as he told her. The contact made her jolt and want to pull away. "Don't move," he ordered. "Don't you dare pull away from it, *Deesha*."

There he went again, calling her that name. She almost asked what that meant, but the water flow hit her clit just right and the words melted on her tongue. "Oh my God."

"If I was there, I'd be behind you," he said. "I'd have your legs spread so wide you'd barely be able to stand it."

Her breath hitched as the water flow assaulted her pussy. She bit her lip and closed her eyes, gripping the sides of her tub. "And?"

"I'd pinch your nipples and bite your neck."

Her toes curled. Heat bloomed low in her belly.

"Pinch those pretty nipples for me, *Deesha*. Twist them."

She did and sucked in a harsh breath.

"That's a good girl. Imagine my teeth grazing them, pulling them taut, just enough for you to cry out."

Damn, he was good at this.

"I'd lick your tits. Roll my tongue around your nipples. Do you know what I'd want to do next?"

"What?" she felt an orgasm begin building. The faucet's barrage of water pummeling her pussy, the temp setting off her skin, his words buzzing into her bones, her mood lifting until she floated... everything intensified and aimed its focus on her clit. "What, Bane?"

"I'd fuck those pretty tits and come all over you. Give you a pearl necklace with my cum. Would you like that?"

"Mmph." Kennedy's thighs quivered as she struggled to keep them spread. The water was almost too much to bear. His words, too hot for her ears. Sweat trickled down her temples while she arched back. "Oh my God."

"Don't come yet," he barked through her speaker. "Pull back."

"What? No!" She was so close! No way was she pulling back now!

"Pull back, *Deesha*."

Too late. Kennedy's orgasm ripped through her like a hurricane. She bucked against the stream of water and cried out Bane's name. Water went everywhere. Her muscles ached from holding her position long enough to get to this point. She pushed back and leaned against the tub, scissoring her legs as the aftershocks rippled through her.

"You're going to pay for that," Bane growled out of her speaker.

"Oh yeah?" She was out of breath and smiling like the Cheshire cat. "I have no regrets."

"You will."

She didn't believe him for a second. "And how do you plan to make that happen?"

He didn't answer.

"Bane?"

Still no answer.

She sloshed water out of the tub as she leaned forward to grab her phone off the floor and stared, wide eyed, at the screen.

He'd hung up.

CHAPTER 14

Oh, she was going to pay for that, Bane thought as he beelined for his truck. After dreaming of her again last night, he couldn't stop thinking about getting his hands on her or get his dick to soften all fucking day. His sister had left just after dinner, and Bowen was out again, which meant Bane was unsupervised, on borrowed time, and desperate to get back to Kennedy.

He'd called just to feel her out and see if he could sweet talk his way back over to her house. But after that phone call and hearing her come without his hands, tongue, teeth, and dick in her somehow? Fuck that.

He slammed on the gas and soared the forty-five minutes back to her house. The entire ride was spent planning her punishment. Lycan were wild, their imaginations more so. Kennedy wasn't going to walk for a week once he was done with her.

So much for going slow. Bane was all in. Why hold back when he could go full throttle? Either it would scare her off or thrill her. That might be a decent way to figure out if she was his true *Deesha* or just a well-timed, perfectly shaped distraction to keep him from his true fate.

Was it destructive to not care which she was right now?

All Bane could focus on was getting his hands on her.

He pulled into her driveway and smiled at her car. He, Bowen, and Emily worked together to fix the car as much as possible so he could return it. They didn't tell Emily whose car it was, or why they had it, she—like Bane—was all too grateful for a project to focus on for a few hours. After she left their house, Bane dropped Kennedy's car off earlier and hoped she hadn't freaked out too much about it. He was well aware that returning a stolen car was considerate and creepy at the same time. But she didn't need to know the truth about him being the wolf she'd hit, or the man who stole her car to get away and not get caught in the kennel.

That could come later.

First, she was going to come again. And so was he.

His cock pressed tight against his pants, desperate for release and a warm, wet woman to sink into. He hopped out of his truck and stormed up her steps. Just as he was about to knock, she flung the door open, bright eyed and bushy tailed.

And dressed in a robe.

Fuck. Me. Sideways.

Bane nearly turned into a feral animal on her doorstep. His chest puffed out with each ragged breath he sucked in. His eyes burned. Jaw ached. He was close to shifting and wouldn't that be a total mood killer.

"You came," she said, breathless.

"Not yet," he growled, stepping closer and forcing her to back up and get her sweet ass inside. "But you did. Without permission."

Her cheeks turned scarlet. He could see her nipples harden through her robe. They were big. Suckable. He sucked his bottom lip in between his teeth, grazing the flesh as he released it slowly as she watched. He could smell her lust.

But he also smelled something else. It made him pause.

She was scared.

And that changed everything. "What's wrong?" His voice softened when the playfulness vanished. "Kennedy, what's wrong?" Her pulse pounded so rapidly in her throat, he worried she was going to have a stroke. Gripping her arms, he walked her further into the house and kicked the door shut. "Don't be afraid of me. I'd never hurt you. I just—" he let her go and ran a hand through his hair, stepping back. "Shit, I thought you were into it like I was. I—"

"It's not you," she blurted.

Great. The whole, *It's not you, it's me,* bullshit. "I'll go. I'm sorry. I misread this." He turned to leave.

She slammed her hand against the door as if to block him

94

from yanking it open. "Don't," she said in a guttural tone. "I'm not afraid of you. Which," she half- laughed, half-whimpered, "I probably should be since I don't know you, but that's not it."

He calmly faced her again and tried his best to not be as intimidating as he usually got in these situations. "What's going on then?"

"Nothing," she lied. He could tell she was lying to him. *Easy. Go slow and don't spook her.* Someone else had done that already. If she wouldn't tell him, maybe he could figure it out the Lycan way. His nostrils flared as he scented her and the living room. There was a strong flowery fragrance from her bubble bath, but undercurrents of cigarettes, booze, and... something that made his aggression crank all the way up to ten. *Who's been here?* The question perched on the tip of his tongue, but he didn't give it a voice. He had no right to know what company she had. Not yet. Maybe as his *Deesha*, he had the right to ask, but he wasn't sure she was his fated mate yet. And until he confirmed it, Bane needed to be careful he didn't scare her off by being a possessive, jealous, aggressive brute.

His wolf disagreed.

As a shifter, Bane's instincts were to mark his mate. Come on her. Bite her. Lick her. Fuck her and rub all over, so she wore his scent.

Living by the code of *I licked it, it's mine,* was a whole new level for Lycan. The tip of his tongue darted out, and he licked his bottom lip while staring at her mouth. "You okay?" That's all he managed to get out without a full-blown animalistic growl ripping from his throat. As it was, his voice had dropped to a dangerously deep register.

Her eyes lit up at the sound of his voice. The tips of her ears turned red. He could hear her heart pounding, thundering.

"Say yes or no, Kennedy." He couldn't budge an inch without her giving an answer.

"I'm okay," she said with a shaky voice. "I'm better now that you're here."

Some of the tension left his shoulders, but not enough to relax. "Is your safety in jeopardy?"

She swallowed. "No."

Liar.

"Not tonight. Not with you."

Not with me. So, with someone else? His gaze darted to the baseball bat. It had a few new dents in it. Had she split someone's skull or just used it for cathartic reasons?

He'd make sure to find out later. For now, Kennedy was his only priority. "Well," he said cautiously, "I'm happy to stay. Or... take you out. Whatever you want from me, consider it done."

"Stay?" she reached out and played with the hem of his cotton t-shirt. "Please?"

Well, since she asked so nicely. And hell, even if she hadn't, he wasn't leaving. She was in some kind of trouble, and that was unacceptable. As her mate, Bane would protect her from anything and anyone. Fuck the consequences.

Bowen's warning echoed in his skull, *"If she's your Deesha."* The reminder messed with Bane's motives. He closed his eyes and blew out a long, aching breath. When he popped them back open, Kennedy was still staring at him, her gaze begging him to drop the subject and focus on what he originally came here to do.

Or at least he thought that's what she looked like.

If she needed a distraction for a night, he'd oblige. It would only garner him more of her trust in the end. Then he'd figure out what was going on with her personal life and take care of it. His wolf rolled around under his skin, clawing at him from the inside out. It wanted release.

Bane rejected it.

"What would you like to do?" he asked cautiously.

Still toying with the hem of his shirt, she brushed her fingertips across his abs. It made him quiver. "Maybe... continue where we left off when you so rudely hung up on me."

"That was awful of me." Damn, she felt good. Just the slightest touch from her, and he struggled to keep his control tethered. "I should say I'm sorry."

"Yes," she said with a smile brighter than the moon. "But actions speak louder than words, don't they?"

Was he one lucky Lycan or what? Cupping Kennedy's face, he said, "Well then, *Deesha*, you better hurry into your bedroom. Unless you want your punishment here?" Because he could fuck her all over this house and the yard. Hell, he planned to, no matter what.

Her eyes widened. "Punishment? That's not what—"

96

"Did you forget that you disobeyed me first?" he took a predator's step forward. "You came when you weren't supposed to."

Watching her struggle between having the upper hand and giving it over to him was beautiful. As a submissive, at any level, she had all the control… and he'd have her trust. This might just be a playful game to her, but it was more than that to Bane. The stutter in her exhale said she was anxious. The red tips of her ears said she was riled up. The smile she was beaming said she liked this. And when she cocked her eyebrow at him and bit her bottom lip, he knew she was all in with him. "Better hurry," he warned, "or I'll be forced to give you *two* punishments before my apology."

She backed up, sashaying her hips. His mouth watered as she lured him towards her bedroom, their gazes deadlocked on each other the entire trip. As he prowled after her, Bane caught the faint scent of something concerning from the kitchen area, but nowhere else. It set his teeth on edge. His wolf growled, and the rumble lifted out of his chest and slipped through his clenched teeth.

Kennedy's pupils blew wide hearing it. Her lips parted slightly. Her breath hitched.

So… she liked primal sounds. Excellent. Bane's mouth lifted with a hungry smile and made a mental note to go back to the kitchen later. For now… "Get on the bed, *Deesha*. On all fours."

Watching Kennedy do what she was told made his cock jerk in his pants. Her trust and obedience made him feel like the luckiest sonofabitch on earth. She looked over her shoulder at him, waiting, no, *bracing* for punishment.

He calmly approached her from behind, admiring the view. Her robe lay like a silken second skin across her ass. He lifted it slowly, like curtains rising before a spectacular show. Holding the material with one hand, he raised his other and slapped her ass. Not hard enough to make her cry out, but enough to leave a faint red handprint.

She clenched her bedsheets and groaned.

"Do you like that?" He already smelled the answer. She didn't like it. She loved it. He bit his lip and grabbed her ass with both hands, then spread her cheeks, as he squatted down to lick her from the bottom of her sweet cunt all the way to her puckered backdoor.

"Shit!" she squeaked and pitched forward.

As if she could escape him so easily? Not a chance.

His fingers dug into her ass cheeks harder, spread her apart further, and he dove back in to swirl his tongue around and around, teasing her.

"God, Bane!" she rocked forward again.

He repositioned, grabbing her hips to hold her in place. "Don't move." He slipped his fingers along her pussy to test how wet she was already. Her lust filled his nostrils, making him wild. The wolf in him howled. The man in him roared. Bane clenched his jaw to contain his needs and doubled down on doling out Kennedy's punishment. "You think you can come when you want, even when I tell you no?" He spanked once more before standing up. "Answer me."

She looked over her shoulder at him again, her lust-filled eyes sultry. "Yes."

He spanked her again, this third time much harder than the other two. She sucked in a breath, her fingers digging into the bedsheets. He watched her toes curl, so he smacked her one more time. It made her yip and then laugh. "Your ass is so fucking red," he rubbed away the sting.

"Good," she dropped down so only her ass was up and poised for his pleasure.

He slipped his finger inside her sweet pussy and hooked it, hitting her g-spot. Then he cracked her ass again while finger-banging her closer and closer to the edge of oblivion. "You took an orgasm from me," he growled. Pressing his hand on her lower back, he loved how she kept her ass up for him like this. "Now I get to take one from you."

She whimpered. Her thighs shook. A sheen of sweat bloomed across her back. "No," she said, her voice cracking. "Please."

"Please what?" he pumped into her harder, making sure to keep pressure where it was best. "Say it."

"Make me come again."

"Again?" he pulled out and sucked his finger clean. "I didn't get to do it the first time."

Kennedy's body blushed with sexual frustration. It made him smile. "If you want to come, you do it only when I tell you. If you detonate before that, we start all over and I'll make you pay double."

Her mouth dropped open. Her brow pinched together. And then?

Her confidence bloomed, and she grinned at him over her shoulder. "Then I guess you better buckle down, Bane, because I came again after you hung up on me."

Bane's wolf leapt at a chance to bite her, and he clamped down on the urge by dropping to his knees and shoving his face between her legs. "Bad girl." He licked her folds, then hooked her thighs under his arms and flipped her. "Spread your thighs."

She playfully resisted, so he nipped the arch of her foot. She squealed again. He nipped her calf next. "Spread them for me, *Deesha*." He helped her along by pressing his hands down on her inner thighs and parting her legs. The scent of her pussy made him howl inside. "This," he lowered down and dragged his tongue along her cunt, "belongs to me."

Her belly quivered as she panted. He licked her again. The swipe of his tongue along her pussy was as good as downloading everything he needed to know about her. She was heaven sent to bring him out of Hell.

Kennedy raised her head enough to watch him devour her. He made sure to lock gazes and be obscene about it. Her eyes rolled back, and she sank into her mattress with a guttural groan.

"These," he growled, running his hands greedily up and down her thighs, "are mine." He loved making her tremble with need. Spreading her thighs further apart, he lowered down and pulled one of her nipples into his mouth. Sucking on it and using his teeth, Bane twirled his tongue over her hardened nipple, sucking in as much of her breast as he could fit in his mouth, then let it pop out so he could cup and massage them. "These are mine too."

Kennedy's eyes were huge. She hadn't stopped panting.

"Every orgasm, every touch, every lick... all your curves, your taste, your cum, and your groans," he warned, locking gazes with her, "they all belong to me."

She swallowed hard.

"Now, let's try this again. No coming until I say so." Bane dipped down and gave her his undivided attention.

CHAPTER 15

Not gonna last. Not gonna last. Not gonna —

Kennedy's thighs slammed together, clamping Bane's head in a vice grip, and she screamed in unholy ecstasy. Her orgasms unraveled her, making her head spin and lights burst in her vision. Gripping a fistful of Bane's hair, she kept his head steady and gyrated against his face with no shame.

She saw motherfucking stars with that one. Stars!

Kennedy had never been taken so thoroughly or owned so completely before. She liked it. As far as exploring kinks go, she'd never gotten past websites and romance novels to get her fantasy collection in order. Bane was neither of those things. She didn't have to use her imagination. He was a hot-blooded, merciless animal in the bedroom.

She liked how he spoke to her. Liked the kind of threats he slung when she disobeyed. He was huge enough to be intimidating, but his bites, barks, and warnings felt too good to be terrifying. And when he'd called her a good girl? Yeah… some kind of beast inside her perked up at the sound of that. And his orders? Was it weird to obey him so completely and feel amazing doing it?

Her days and nights were spent thinking and fixing and making a million decisions. It was extremely freeing to not have to do that in this environment. She'd never experienced something like this before. And the results were… mind-blowing.

As the last of her orgasm trickled through her, Kennedy relaxed her legs and let Bane breathe. At some point, she'd lost her robe. And as he looked at her, she never wanted to cover up again.

"Bad girl," he nipped her again, just as playful as the other times.

"This is going to take practice," she laughed.

"No complaints on my end," he said, and then licked his lips as if to savor her taste a little longer. "So, now you owe me six orgasms."

"*Six*?" As if that was even possible. And how did that even math out? Didn't matter, she was looking forward to it. "I'll take a raincheck."

"Nope. This doesn't work like that." He spread her legs again and dipped his mouth back down.

She was so damn sensitive! Even his hot breath against her clit made her hips jerk. "Bane! Stop!"

He lifted his gaze but kept suckling on her overstimulated clit. With a cock of his eyebrow, he added two fingers to the party and hit her g-spot with expert precision.

Holy shit! Kennedy broke out in another sweat. Arching her back, her heels dug into the mattress and hands slammed down on Bane's head, holding him steady as another orgasm pummeled her, fast and furious.

Her body was out of control. His tongue was merciless. This was insane!

Too much! Too much! Too much! She was going to stroke out. Her heart couldn't be beating in a healthy rhythm. Her cheeks tingled and she couldn't catch her breath at all. So why did she cling to him, forcing his head to stay still just so she could rub against his mouth and come again? Kennedy had lost her mind. Lost her control. She was practically shameless while riding her orgasm until it faded out and she was able to finally catch her breath. "Wow," she whispered with a raspy voice.

"You're terrible at this." Bane kissed her inner thigh and smiled at her.

"I know," she said with an exhausted grin. "I don't even care. This feels too incredible to care."

Bane shook his head and licked her again, gathering the last drops of her pleasure onto his tongue. She watched him through hooded eyes. Jesus, he was still fully clothed. Bane seemed like the kind of guy who ate pussy for his pleasure, not a woman's. That made him dangerous.

Kennedy's eyes rolled back as he started building her up for another one. How the hell did he know how to do this so well? She didn't think she could stand another orgasm, but damned if she was going to say no to it either.

"Hold back," he instructed. "Keep your pussy tightened."

She clenched her inner muscles for him.

"That's a good girl. Fuck yes, just like that." Bane slowed down with the finger work and licked her again. "I feel you clamping down on my fingers. Makes me want to give my dick a turn."

"What are you waiting for?"

Bane picked up speed again, and Kennedy melted under his infernal touch. "Squeeze," he ordered, putting her back on track.

She obeyed, but it was excruciating and frustrating. And wasn't doing anything to stop the next orgasm from coaxing her closer to another climax. But she liked his praise. Wanted more of it. And really wanted a lot more of him.

"Fuck me, Bane." Kennedy's thighs fell open for him in invitation. "Please."

He let out another growl. Deep and animalistic, it was just the thing to send her over the edge. She came again. Her thighs slammed shut once more, only this time Bane's upper torso was wedged between them. He used his body to keep her spread open and held her pelvis down as he sucked, flicked, and destroyed her all over again.

She broke out into a hot flash that made the room spin. "Stop."

Bane pulled back.

"I... I need a minute."

"Hang on," he said, and rushed out of the room.

Hang on? Hang on to what? Kennedy was half-floating, half-twirling in a zero-gravity situation and considering she was naked, swollen, spent, and exhausted, she didn't have the strength to hold on to shit.

Bane returned a moment later with two glasses of ice water. Holding the back of her neck, he lifted Kennedy so she could sit up. "Drink." He tipped the glass to her mouth. The instant the icy water hit her tongue, she started chugging. Grabbing the glass from him,

Kennedy drained it in four chugs and swiftly reached for the second glass.

Holy shit, why was she like this? She needed to go see a doctor. This wasn't normal.

And now she felt embarrassed because they were in the middle of something great and she'd just ruined it.

"You're really burning up," Bane said, frowning. Pressing his palm to her cheeks, forehead, and neck, he frowned. "We need to lower your temp."

"It'll pass. Just give it a minute." Kennedy wasn't entirely sure that was true though. This was definitely the worst hot flash she'd had to date. And the nausea was way worse, too. "The room keeps spinning." She was going to puke. If she puked, he'd be grossed out and probably leave. She didn't want that to happen, so Kennedy buckled down and tried to hold in her vomit. *Breathe in through the nose, out through the mouth.*

The edges of her vision started to darken. A ringing in her ears intensified. Saliva built up in her mouth and she instinctually grabbed Bane's shoulder to keep steady. Next thing she knew, Kennedy was lifted into the air and carried into the bathroom. Bane placed her on the toilet while starting a fresh bath. Even then, he kept one hand braced on her, the other grappling at the faucet and plunge the stopper.

"In we go," he said in a soft tone. To her embarrassment, he helped her get into the tub as it filled with cool water. Even though she shrieked from the temp, the shock snapped her vision back to crystal clear, and her skin pebbled with goosebumps. It felt incredible. Bane beamed her a big smile. "Better?"

"Yeah," she said, groggily. "This is really embarrassing."

"Nothing to be embarrassed about, *Deesha*. It's just nature."

She didn't have the energy to correct him. This wasn't nature. It was torture. "I think I better make an appointment to see my doctor. I'm too young for hot flashes like this."

Bane grabbed a washcloth from a stack she kept in a basket. Drenching the cloth, he wrang it out on her chest and dabbed her neck and forehead with it.

"You're really good at this," she said.

Bane swept some of her hair back so he could dab her forehead next. "How do you feel now?"

103

"Much, much better."

"Good." He sat back and rubbed his forehead with one hand and sighed. "Had me nervous for a minute."

She wasn't sure if she should apologize or not. "Didn't know you had front row tickets to my shitshow, did you?" She tried to play it off with humor, but really wanted to cry. Kennedy had enough baggage to fill a train station, and who knew what her health issues were. The hot flashes were getting worse and worse. He didn't need to see all that. "You should probably go."

Bane looked at her, dejected. "Do you really want me to leave?"

No. Yes. She didn't know. Suddenly, a motorcycle rumbled outside. Her breath hitched, and body tensed. Plenty of people pulled down her road and turned around when it dead ended. It was a scenic strip of dirt and woods, easy to make a wrong turn to nowhere on. Photographers often parked for hours on the side of the road, taking pictures of wildlife. Sometimes kids would race down the strip, hooting and hollering. Holding her breath, Kennedy listened as the bike kept travelling and disappeared. *Phew.*

"You panic when you hear a bike."

How could he know that? Was she so obvious? Now Kennedy felt exposed and vulnerable. And she was cold. Turning the water off, she climbed out of the tub and snagged a towel to cover herself.

Bane stood up and gave her room to maneuver in the bathroom. "What's going on, Kennedy?"

"Nothing," she lied. It wasn't like he could help her anyway. "Thanks for... you know... everything."

"If you're in trouble, maybe I can help."

"You can't."

Bane glared at her like he took her words personally.

"I'm..." Shit, what should she say? The fact of the matter was, Kennedy didn't want Bane to leave. He made her feel safe, which was completely too soon to say about someone she'd just met. And Kennedy also wanted to get weight off her chest and had no one else to talk to about what was going on in her life.

Should she tell Bane and risk putting him in danger? Probably not. But something in her said to spill the beans. Confide in him. Of all people, this stranger brought her more inner peace with just his presence than she'd felt with a lifetime of people coming in and out of her bubble. Maybe Bane was a temporary escape. Or maybe he'd turn into a forever man.

So, should she chance losing him by telling him her troubles, or did she go on pretending her life was roses and lie to his face about the terrors in her life?

Bane didn't know what was worse—his wolf trying to claw out of him, or the look of fear in Kennedy's eyes. Was she close enough to the peak of transition for all her senses to heighten and sense his wolf? While he attempted to figure her out, the wound in his thigh screamed at him. He thought it was fine until he felt a few of his stitches pop during Kennedy's third orgasm earlier because his muscles tensed too much, and he almost shifted for no good reason other than his wolf wanted out... most likely to bite and claim what was his.

While he worked his girl up, he also had to tame his wolf down. Talk about striking a balance.

Now his wound burned like hell, and it pissed him off that he hadn't healed right or fast. It was a weakness he couldn't afford and could do nothing about.

But his body wasn't his priority. Kennedy was.

She wrapped herself in the towel and looked like she wasn't sure which way to go in her own house. The terror in her eyes faded into relief. Why? What was up with the motorcycles? Bane did a quick inventory of other sounds he might have missed, but her house was eerily quiet. No noise other than the whir of electricity and the dripping of her faucet registered. Outside, the occasional person drove down the road, and twice a dog barked, but none of that should make Kennedy fearful.

He'd already run a perimeter check and made sure the outside was taken care of earlier. He even carved a small symbol under her porch to deter *Savag-Ri*—just in case. But as far as he could tell, there were no threats around her. Only the scent of visitors. And even though he swore he'd picked up the stench of a *Savag-Ri* earlier, it could have been her damn garbage.

Yesterday, he ran a light background check on Kennedy. Didn't find anything on social media except her credentials on the vet clinic's website. Other than that, she was a total mystery to him. And if she was in trouble, he wanted to be there to help her handle it. So again, he asked, "What's going on, Kennedy?"

"Nothing." She was lying. Her eyes gave her away. As well as the sudden spike in her heart rate, which he could hear with perfect clarity. She moved towards the bathroom door, eager to get away. "Thanks for... you know... everything."

Everything? As in all the orgasms? The cold water bath? This woman had no clue what he was about, which was the only reason Bane bit his tongue and kept calm when he really wanted to rip apart anything and anyone who could trigger her panic with just the rev of an engine. Because he was pretty sure that's what made her pulse race. Remembering those men from the Wolf Pack MC having visited her the other day, he figured it had to do with them.

Good. He had a starting point for his hunt. "If you're in trouble, maybe I can help."

"You can't."

I can. He tried to not take it personally, but she was going to find out exactly what lengths he was willing to go to for his *Deesha* soon enough.

"I'm..." Kennedy paused and looked down at the tiled floor.

Bane lifted her chin, forcing her gaze to rise and meet his. "Whatever it is, it'll be okay."

"No, it won't." She pulled away and left the bathroom. He followed behind, keeping his wolf on a tight leash. It wanted to come out and hunt. Kill. Protect. It also wanted to bite the woman wrapped in a towel and turn her. A low growl rumbled out of his chest. It happened before he could stop it. Kennedy whipped around, her eyes wide as she stared at him.

"I don't like being underestimated," Bane said as calmly as possible. "If I ask what's going on, don't assume I can't help and just walk away from me."

She shook her head and went into her room and shut the door. He stood on the other side. *Breathe.* His hands balled into fists. *Breathe!* In through his nose, out through his mouth, Bane tamed his beast and gave Kennedy the privacy she so obviously needed. But he wasn't leaving here without knowing exactly what had her so scared.

And if he had to go after every bike club in the area, so be it.

Everyone in the surrounding six counties would know not to fuck with his woman by the time Bane made his rounds. He was thorough like that.

To his relief, Kennedy came out a minute later in a tank top and sleep shorts. Guess this was his signal to leave? He might have followed through had it not been for the smell of salty tears. She ducked past him, and he let her, putting a few paces between them as he followed his *Deesha* into her living room. Kennedy sat on the couch next to her cat and stared at her coffee table like it was the most interesting thing in the room.

"If you want me to leave," he started to say, shoving his thumb over his shoulder at the front door. "I can g—"

"Are you close with your family?"

Her sudden blurt out made him pause. "Yes, very."

Kennedy nodded and swiped a tear from her cheek. He wished he could have been the one to do it. Instead, he stayed back to give her space, regardless of his instinct to do the opposite.

"I have a brother." Kennedy leaned forward, crossing her arms over her chest. "He's older than me by ten months."

"I have an identical twin brother," he offered in exchange for more trust.

She almost brightened up. "I can't imagine a universe being so cruel as to put you and a clone on this earth. You two probably drove every girl crazy in school."

"We were homeschooled." He came closer and sat on the chair opposite the couch. No matter how much he wanted to sit next to her or pick her up and put her on his lap, he stayed back. She might need a little distance to feel safe, and the last thing he wanted to do was smother her. "Didn't have a lot of friends outside our..." *pack* "...circle."

Kennedy's lips tightened with her smile. "I grew up in a trailer park." He noticed she didn't specify where. Kennedy started picking at her nails. "My brother, Jake, was always in trouble. My parents were too preoccupied with themselves to give a shit. I was the outsider. Too quiet. Too shy. Too easily overwhelmed."

Bane leaned in, desperate to hear more. "Must have been hard."

"It was sometimes. I studied a lot, hellbent on making a better living than my parents did. We didn't have a lot of money, and

107

what we did have came from the drugs they sold."

Wow. That's just… wow. Bane couldn't relate to it. His family was tight-knit, as all packs were, and they supported each other with everything. *Not everything*, he corrected himself. His parents were going to shit a brick when they found out about the silver he drank.

"I went to school and finished my degree in seven years, by fast-tracking it to becoming a veterinarian. Four years up north, then another three down here."

Smart girl. Bane puffed with pride that his *Deesha* was a beautiful, smart, headstrong woman.

"Jake moved here with me just after he got out of prison."

His breath hitched. "Prison?"

"He went there because of me." Kennedy rolled her shoulders back. "That's all I want to say about it."

Okay. Bane leaned back and took in a deep breath. "So how do the motorcycles fit into this? Your brother in a club or something?"

She bit her lip. "He joined one immediately after getting out of prison early. The Wolf Pack is what they're called."

He had to dissect this carefully. "What did he go to prison for?" She didn't answer. "I'm not asking about your involvement. I just want to know what he was charged with." He waited, hating that her silence meant he was getting nowhere. "Hey," he said, getting up and sitting next to her on the couch. Grabbing her hand, he squeezed it. "I'm not saying a word to anyone. I just want to help you and I can't do it well unless I have more information."

"I don't know why I'm telling you any of this." Kennedy's chin quivered and tears filled her eyes. "I'm in over my head right now and," she swiped her cheeks again, "I feel like you're so easy to talk to. I just need to get this off my chest, but now I —"

"I'm not saying a word to anyone, Kennedy. Trust me."

"I do," she said, pulling her hand out of his. "And that freaks me out. I don't know you. And I don't tell *anyone* about my shit. Ever. Except for one other person when I moved into town, and that's a regret I still carry."

"Has your brother ever hurt you?" Was that why Jake got locked up? She said it was because of her, right? It was so hard to maintain his control and keep his tone soft and level. His wolf gnashed its teeth inside, clawing and digging its way out. Bane broke out in a sweat, locking down his urge to shift. "Has he hurt you, Kennedy?"

"No," she finally said. "Never. He'd never hurt me intentionally."

That barely cooled his fury down. *Never hurt me intentionally....* Not that he's never hurt her. That's a slippery slope. "Then what's he gotten you into?"

"His MC wants me to get them animal tranquilizers and I can't. I'm scared of what they'll do when they come back for them, and I don't have any." She curled into herself a little more and started crying harder. "And now I feel like a shithead for telling you all of this. It's just that you make me feel safe and I haven't felt safe before."

I haven't felt safe before. Bane's heart cracked and crumbled. Had Kennedy lived her entire life scared? Now his wolf was ready to tear apart the entire world for frightening her.

"Stay with me," Bane insisted. "Come to my house and stay with me until we can clear this up."

"No," she cried, shaking her head. "I can't put you in danger too. I've already fucked this up. I'm not blaming you one bit for being smart enough to walk away."

"Not happening."

"*Bane.*" She slammed her hands on her thighs. "I need you to leave."

Nope. Not a snowball's chance in Hell. And her fear could morph into anger all night long. He still wasn't budging. "Do you truly want me to go? Because if you think you kicking me out will stop me from protecting you, it won't."

She cried harder, and it made him feel terrible. "Just stop," she said between sobs. "I feel shitty enough without you playing hero."

"I want to help."

"My brother always does this to me. He drags me into things because he has no one else to turn to. And these men he's with are... awful. Scary awful."

"All the more reason to have protection."

"You can't protect me, Bane. That's not realistic or fair to you."

109

"Fuck fair." It's an honor. "I'm not letting something happen to you, Kennedy. That's as realistic as it gets."

"You can't prevent it either. And that's not why I'm telling you all this. I don't want help. I just want someone to listen. It's always been me and Jake. I'm not dragging you into our circus too. I only wanted to get this off my chest."

"Then tell your brother to call them off." He knew it was a wasted suggestion considering if her brother wanted, or could, do such a thing, he would have already. But Bane needed to understand how far her brother would go to protect her before self-preservation kicked in and reigned supreme.

"He tried." Kennedy sniffled. "They didn't even know he had a sister until one of them figured it out the other day when they visited. I'm not even sure how the guy knew. But Jake's trying to protect me and get me out of it. They're just two steps ahead of him all the time. They even followed him to my house and my work the other night."

Bane stiffened. "Why do you think they're following him?"

"He can't be trusted," she said sardonically. "And if you tell me to go to the cops about any of this, you can fuck right off. I'll never turn in my brother or put him in worse danger than he already gets himself in. Jake might do horrible shit, but he's my brother and I owe him and I love him."

The debt remark came before the love one. Bane hadn't missed the prioritization. "What's your brother doing that has them tailing him, do you know?"

She shook her head. "I can't imagine. But he brought me a dog the other night." Her watery eyes flicked to him. "It was in a dogfight and lost."

Bane's next growl came out of its own accord. He couldn't stop it. Didn't even realize it was happening until Kennedy's eyes widened. "And the men came to you and saw you with the dog?"

She shook her head.

Jesus, just imagining Kennedy in a room with a bunch of lowlife criminals who, going off the ones he saw come out of her house the other night, were big men. She must have been scared out of her head. "Did any of them touch you?"

Her silence made him go apeshit. "Where did they touch you, Kennedy?" He was too furious to sit. When she wouldn't answer,

110

he shot to his feet and started pacing. His wolf wanted to eat those men for touching what belonged to Bane. For scaring her. Threatening her.

Touching her.

For every finger they placed on her, he'd break five of their motherfucking bones. Then he'd beat them to a pulp and leave them for the coyotes to feast on.

"They just tried to intimidate me, is all. Nothing I haven't dealt with before."

If she was trying to make him feel less murderous, it wasn't working. She was minimizing whatever they'd done. Why? *Because she's had to do this her whole life.* Bane scrubbed his face with both hands and paused. "Pack your things," he said. "Now."

"I'm not running," she argued. "And I'm not hiding. They'll find me. Jake will find me."

"Good," Bane growled. "And they'll find you're not alone. They'll find you surrounded with enough protection to send them running with their tails between their legs." *So I can hunt and chase them down properly before ripping their throats out.*

The tips of her ears reddened. "Bane, no."

"Pack or I'll pack for you." His patience only lasted so long. He wanted the choice to be hers on whether she went with him or not, but if she refused? Shit, he wasn't sure how far he'd go to make her see things his way. The thoughts rolling in his head were half-man, half-animal, making his imagination run wild.

"Why are you doing this?" She stood slowly, her chin quivering again. "Why are you putting yourself in this position? You don't know me."

"I do," he said calmly and closed the gap between them. Rubbing her arms, he hoped he wasn't coming across too controlling. He also wanted their physical contact to help calm her down. His wolf would have it no other way. "I know you, Kennedy. And deep down, you must feel the same with me or you wouldn't have let me in this far."

So many expressions danced over her beautiful face. She was terrified, yet hopeful. She was stunning. When her features softened, triumph thumped in his chest. "Pack," he said sternly. "I'll go grab your cat."

111

CHAPTER 16

Kennedy stared at Bane like he'd lost his damn mind. "No."

"What do you mean, *No*?"

Shaking her head, she walked around him and plopped back down on her sofa. "I'm not packing. Me and my cat aren't going anywhere." She was staying right where she was because running didn't solve shit.

Too bad she had no clue what would fix her issues though. If running wouldn't, staying wasn't going to be much better. For the first time in a long while, Kennedy wished she could just disappear. Become someone else entirely and vanish into thin air. Turn into a fox or bird and take off.

"You only just came into my life, Bane. And I appreciate all you've done." Okay, now she was cringing, because that sounded terrible. Did she just thank him for eating her pussy? Was she giving him gratitude for the cold bath? The ice cream and conversation the other day?

"Kennedy," Bane growled.

Growled. Her name didn't even sound the same with the rumble he made. Her body responded to it in an embarrassing way. Rubbing the goosebumps on her arms, she said, "I'm not dragging you into this. I appreciate the offer, but I don't want you involved." Her heart settled back into its cave. *Time to end things.* "You need to leave."

This was the end of what could have been a beautiful thing. But Kennedy wasn't letting Bane into her life when it was this bad.

What kind of woman dragged a good man into a train wreck? "I don't think I'm ready for anything serious anyway."

Before Bane could get a word in edgewise, she shut down her emotions and entered the mindset of independence and cold-heartedness. It was her trauma response—her tried-and-true survival tactic. Kennedy had to do everything on her own since she was a kid. And the more she stayed to herself, the better off she felt, because then no one could disappoint her. No one could hurt her. No one could pry her open and laugh at what lay beneath her aloofness. Jake was the only one who ever saw the real Kennedy, and it was staying that way.

Speaking of her brother...

The dick had perfect timing to pull up at this exact moment. Bane stalked over to the window and looked outside. Kennedy didn't bother getting up from the couch. She knew it was her brother by the sound of his bike. She was like a dog with trained hearing, conditioned to his noises. But she watched Bane's reaction. Saw his broad shoulders tense and seem to expand a little.

Bane was a big guy. Built with solid muscle. His skin tone was deep golden brown, he most likely caramelized all summer long, and it lasted through winter. His chestnut hair was clipped short and always out of his face. He was all the colors of the woods and sun—hues of gold, amber, oak, earth. His jeans hugged his ass and the fabric of his pockets were worn down. His boots were scuffed from heavy use outdoors. He was perfection, and she was hellbent on kicking him out.

Jake's engine turned off.

Kennedy's gaze locked on Bane.

Jake's silhouette moved across the lawn.

Bane turned to look at her.

Jake's boots thundered onto her creaky porch. But her attention remained locked on Bane. She wished he wasn't here right now. Wished he wasn't about to meet Jake. But maybe this was a good thing. It would make Bane run faster in three... two... one...

Jake swung open the door without knocking. "You need to get out of here," he said, barreling towards her, paying Bane no mind.

"No."

"God damnit, Kennedy!" Grabbing her upper arms, Jake

jerked her forward and upwards. "Get the fuck out of here!"

"Hey!" Bane hollered. "Get your hands off her."

Jake's hardened grip on her arms ripped away from her in a flash. Before she could blink, Bane had him up against a wall. Holy shitballs! Could this get any worse?

Don't answer that.

"Who the fuck do you think you are?" Jake knocked his arm to break Bane's hold on him. It didn't work. In fact, it seemed to only piss Bane off more and made his hold on Jake tighten.

"Stop it, both of you!" She didn't have time for this machoman bullshit.

"You don't get to touch her like that." Bane ignored Kennedy's scolding and shoved Jake against the wall a second time, like it might rattle some sense into the poor bastard. It wouldn't. She'd tried it several times before.

Jake's face contorted with anger. "Kennedy, who is this asshole?"

"Bane, meet my brother Jake. Jake, this is—" *My boyfriend? My hookup? My mistake?*

"I'm the motherfucker who will not tolerate you putting your hands on Kennedy like that." Bane snarled before she could say more.

Jake laughed. All out *laughed,* as if Bane just made the most hilarious joke he'd ever heard. Okay, enough of this. Kennedy shoved herself between them. "Both of you back off."

Bane eased up first, which ended up being a mistake. Jake took the opportunity to cold cock him in the face. Kennedy gasped when she saw Bane's head snapped back and heard a cracking sound. *Oh my God! Was that Bane's nose breaking?*

It wasn't.

"Gotta hit harder than that to impress me." Bane snarled.

Meanwhile, Jake held his hand like it smarted big time, his face turning sixteen shades of crimson and scarlet.

Did he... did he just break his hand on Bane's *face*? Kennedy couldn't take much more of this. "Leave!" she yelled at both of them.

"You broke my hand!"

Bane flashed him a deadly grin. "Shouldn't touch things you can't handle, motherfucker." There wasn't even a red mark on

Bane's cheek, and she knew damn well Jake's punches were brutal.

"Out!" Kennedy wrenched open her front door and shoved her brother out first.

"Kennedy, God damnit!"

"I can't with you right now, Jake. Just leave."

"No! You need to pack and go!"

Kennedy ignored him and grabbed Bane's arm next. He all but let her lead him out of the house like an escort. If this episode in the Life of Kennedy didn't freak him out and send him running, Bane was as crazy as Jake and that meant bad news. If he hit the road and never looked back, good for him—it meant Bane had some common fucking sense.

"Kennedy!" Jake stood furious in her front yard. The tendons in his neck stood out as he yelled her name a second and third time. She hated his temper, but she also wasn't giving him an inch. Waving him off, she grabbed the side of her door, preparing to slam it shut. Jake hollered, "I'm not through with you."

"Well, I'm through with you! Fix your shit, Jake." Her temper flared. "This night is *over*. Leave. I've busted my ass at work, which I have to go back to soon, and I really need to get some sleep." Nothing like a reminder to Jake that one of them had a fulltime job and adulting to do.

He stormed onto her porch and growled in a low tone, "It's not safe for you to stay here."

Her gaze flicked to Bane, who hadn't budged from the front lawn. Positioned halfway between her house and his truck, he watched Kennedy and her brother argue. Kennedy's embarrassment shot sky high because she was an adult, not a teenager, but her behavior wasn't proving it. "Then make sure you change that, Jake."

It was all she could say in front of Bane. She didn't want him involved, and this was her brother's fault to begin with, so it was his mess to clean up. "I'm not running. So you need to *fix it*."

"Kennedy, I—"

"Bye." She slammed the door with Jake roaring at her from the porch.

She locked the door and leaned against it, then slid down till her ass hit the floor. Muffled sounds of two deep male voices filtered in, but she couldn't make out what they were saying to each other because her heart beat too loud in her ears for much else to penetrate. Soon, Jake's bike roared to life, and he took off again. Bane's truck engine started just after that, but he remained in her driveway for several minutes because finally leaving.

Wow. Just.... Wow. Her life was a dumpster fire.

"Bye, Bane." She figured this was the last time she'd ever see him again.

Kennedy was called into work early. Such bullshit. She'd barely slept and only had time to shove an apple in her mouth before having to hit the road and head back in. All night, she'd thought of Bane. It made her chest ache. Her head throbbed too, and her eyes itched and burned.

How much longer was she willing to go on like this? Work was running her into the ground. Her brother was draining her. And Bane? Well, he'd just given her a glimpse of what she might have if it wasn't for her circus of a life. Stomping her foot on the gas pedal, Kennedy refused to admit her heart hurt in ways it shouldn't over a man she barely knew. Bane was never going to want a relationship with her after this. No man in his right mind would be with a hot mess like her.

Thanks a lot, Jake.

She strangled her steering wheel, pretending it was his neck. Kennedy had control of everything in her life except her brother, and he was the one who needed a tight leash, boundaries, and a muzzle. Why was he in that club? Why couldn't he stay out of trouble for once in his life? And why did he always, always, always bring her down his rabbit holes?

One thing was certain: She wasn't running and hiding.

Not yet, at least.

If Kennedy's mother taught her anything, it was to stand up for herself if she wanted respect from someone. *"Never let them treat you like shit. And never let someone else call the shots in your life."* Her mother should have taken her own advice, but whatever.

The irony of this situation? Kennedy worked hard to travel a different path than her parents had...

Only to land at the exact same destination: In the middle of the circus.

Parking in the back of the vet clinic, Kennedy refused to acknowledge that on top of everything else, she also had a weirdo car thief who suffered stealer's remorse. It's like buyer's remorse, but more illegal than that. She should be more suspicious about how the hell her car was back in her possession, repaired. Sadly, she didn't have the energy to invest in it.

Heading into the back of the building, she stuffed her keys in her pocket and swung open the heavy metal door. Her muscles were so tense, it felt like she had a Charlie horse across her shoulders. And the splitting headache that started in the car was now a raging migraine.

Lovely.

"Hey, Mark." Kennedy set off to keep busy for the next twelve hours. Grabbing the chart for Room 1, she glanced at the notes.

"Hey Kennedy, can I speak with you in my office for a quick sec?"

"Sure." She placed the clipboard back in its holder and followed Mark inside his office, thinking nothing of it, when he closed the door behind them. He sat down behind his desk and gestured for her to do the same in the only chair left. Kennedy eased into the uncomfortable chair, her muscles so tight she winced. "What's up?"

"I did an inventory yesterday of our supplies."

"You need me to place an order or something?"

"We're missing Tramadol and Diazepam."

"Okay, I'll order more," Kennedy said with a shrug. She stood up and got all the way to the door before looking over her shoulder to ask, "Is that all you need?"

"No." Mark got up and calmly stalked over to her. Placing his hand on the door, he barred her exit. The hair on the nape of her neck stood up. "That's not all I need."

Her heart rate elevated. "Let me out, Mark."

"I know what you did." His hot breath tickled the back of her neck. He was too close. Way too fucking close. "I could have your license revoked."

She had no idea what he was talking about. "Back away, Mark."

117

"You stole the meds, Kennedy. That's not going unpunished." He slid the back of his hand down her arm and pressed his body against her backside. "Now sit the fuck down and do as you're told or say goodbye to your career."

Her palms grew sweaty as she clutched the doorknob. A hot flash burned its way across her back and down her chest. "Mark. You do *not* want to do this."

He grabbed her wrist and pulled her arm behind her back before shoving her against the door with a loud thud. "I have you on video, Kennedy."

Her eyes widened. "You're mistaken."

"Am I?" His breath tickled her ear and she could smell the tuna salad he'd eaten earlier. "So that wasn't you with a gang of bikers using the clinic's supplies? That wasn't you stitching up that man's arm? That wasn't you who dragged a dead dog into the freezer, that had clearly been abused and chewed on by other animals?"

Her throat tightened. "It's not what you think."

"Not what I think? Hmm…" Mark's free hand slid down to her waist, and he gripped it tight. "What I think is you better get over to the desk," he whispered in a low tone, "and bend the fuck over."

Kennedy kept her breaths even as she carefully released her hand from the doorknob and reached into her pocket for her keys. Holding them tight between her fingers, she said, "This is your last chance to back up from me, Mark."

"And this is your last chance to save your job."

So be it.

Kennedy pulled her keys out, the tips sticking out through her fingers like a mini set of claws, and she punched him in his thigh. He yelped and hopped back, fury turning his face scarlet. "*Bitch!*" Blood started soaking through his pants and he clutched his thigh.

"Fuck. You." Kennedy swung the door open, hellbent on getting out of his office and into a space with more witnesses. She ran into the main area, her chest heaving with each breath, and looked around. There was no one there. Had they all run off when Mark brought Kennedy into his office? Risa popped her head out of Room 1 and frowned.

Mark swung open his door and glared at Kennedy. *Oh shit.*

Oh shit! She backed away, shaking her head. *What do I do? WHAT DO I DO?* Her thoughts were too scattered. Fight, flight, or freeze.

Kennedy bolted out of the back door and ran straight for her car.

Her career. Her life. Her safe space. Goddamnit! Everything was blowing up, and Kennedy had a dreadful suspicion there was no putting it all back together after this.

Would Mark press charges on her? Had he lied about the drugs going missing just to see if he could take advantage of her? Gripping the steering wheel with white knuckle fever, Kennedy tore out of the parking lot, sobbing.

She didn't know where to go. She didn't have anyone to turn to. No one except...

Pulling her cell out, she dialed her only source of safety, who just happened to also be her biggest risk. "Come on, pick up, Jake."

Her brother's voicemail kicked in. She hung up and threw her phone on the passenger seat and screamed in fury. Slamming the heel of her palms against the steering wheel, she blazed down the country road and nearly threw up. "Not again," she said to herself. "This can't be happening again."

What was she thinking, calling Jake for help? Thank God he hadn't picked up. He'd have gone after Mark and left no piece of him behind to be identified later. Kennedy refused to be the reason Jake went to prison *twice*.

Pulling into her darkened driveway, Kennedy managed to tame her panic and went on autopilot. Shutting off her headlights and engine, she sat in her car and stared at nothing. Her career was over. No place would hire her once Mark made some calls. And it was her word against his. With her track record versus his reputation, it was a no brainer who would be believed or not.

Wiping the tears from her face, Kennedy got out of the car and marched up to her front porch. Unlocking the door, she stepped inside and flicked on the living room lights. "Molly." At least her cat was drama free. She leaned against the door and caught her breath. "Molly! Pspspspsps!"

"She's a little tied up right now."

Terror robbed her of breath. She froze and stared at the bastard standing in her kitchen with her cat trapped in a pillowcase.

CHAPTER 17

Bane kept reminding himself that this was Kennedy's brother. Her. Brother. If Jake was so hellbent on keeping Kennedy safe, he should never have her in a position where she was even close to danger and then promise to make it better. It's like tossing someone in with sharks, then flinging them a life jacket after the fact and saying, "swim faster". It's bullshit.

As stubborn as Jake was about getting her out of the house, Kennedy was more persistent about staying. They were in each other's way. But Kennedy should have listened to Jake and left like he'd told her to. Better yet, she should have listened to Bane and packed her shit to live with him. He'd die to protect her, which was more than he suspected Jake would do.

After that motherfucker stormed away and hopped on his bike, Bane's instincts had torn straight down the middle. Half of him wanted to follow Jake. The other half wanted to kick down Kennedy's front door, grab her and her damn cat, toss them both in his truck and bring them home to his cabin.

Instead, what did he do? Sat in her driveway and practiced his breathing exercises to calm the hell down. His wolf swiped his claws and gnashed his teeth. Rammed into Bane's bones, howling for release.

Setting loose in wolf form around here would raise too many questions with the wildlife experts in town, and he wasn't sure what his wolf would do if Kennedy stepped out of her house. As an animal, catching her scent would likely cause his animal to go into a frenzy, and then what?

Would he eat her? Hump her? Bite her?

Holy shit, Bane was just as dangerous to her as the rest of the men in Kennedy's life.

He'd like to say he'd never hurt her, which was absolutely true, but his wolf had a different view on what hurting was. Bites, scratches, and bumps were playful acts sometimes. Signs of love and affection.

"He'd never hurt me intentionally." Kennedy's words about her brother now bit Bane in the ass.

His wolf would never hurt Kennedy… intentionally. But if provoked, it was hard to say what his wolf might do. Animals were not as predictable as humans. His wolf was already starting to separate its needs from Bane's… a side effect of the liquid silver.

Scrubbing his face with both hands, Bane had backed out of her driveway and headed in the direction he saw Jake go. Too restless to head home, and unwanted at Kennedy's, Bane was a loose cannon with no target to aim for. He was a creature who liked to stay hyper focused on things. Jake was a good start.

With his sensitive hearing, it didn't take much effort to track down Jake's loud bike. The human headed into the main part of town and stopped at a fast-food joint. Bane parked a good distance away and waited, then followed the guy to a house on the other side of town.

It was in a quaint little neighborhood, complete with flowerbeds and a tire swing in the front yard. Jake had parked his bike in the garage and closed it, but not before looking around to make sure no one saw him there.

This guy. Had Jake any sense, he would have noticed he'd been tailed by Bane for miles. It was hard to not eyeroll over Jake's obliviousness. But maybe he figured Bane was a non-issue, because, in Jake's mind, there were worse things than a shifter watching him.

Bane couldn't help but think about the stench of fear that wafted off Jake in Kennedy's house. He was scared shitless for his sister. And his paranoid behavior in the garage led Bane to believe he was scared shitless for himself too.

What was this guy involved in?

Again, Bane felt ripped in two. Should he sit here like a stalker and wait to see where Jake went next, or should he head

121

back to Kennedy and tail her to keep her safe? She mentioned she had to go to work. Bane checked the time and realized an hour and a half had passed already. Kennedy was likely at work by now. The thought eased a little of his anxiety. She'd be completely safe at work. Surrounded by people, animals, in a locked facility that had cameras. No one was going to fuck with her there.

So he had time to go home, shower, eat, and catch some Z's before she got off her shift. He needed to talk with Bowen too. Yeah, he needed to get going. No sense in sitting here. If he needed to tail Jake, he could do it another day, in another way. Or just corner him and beat the information out of him.

Slamming his gear in drive, Bane pulled off and headed back to his cabin. His chest ached the entire way home and his inner wolf howled.

Bane pulled into his long dirt driveway and, by the time he put his truck in park, he could barely catch his breath. Was he having a heart attack? Did shifters even have heart attacks? He might be the first one in history to have one. Holy fuck, this hurt. Rubbing his sternum, he slowly slid out of his truck and stumbled up the porch steps and through the front door. "Bowen!"

His brother peered out through the kitchen, his eyes widening to the size of saucers as Bane crashed to the floor. "Can't... breathe..."

Bowen rushed forward and tried to haul Bane over to the couch. "What's happened?"

"Don't... know..." he squeezed his eyes shut and wheezed as his chest constricted. "Hurts... chest hurts..."

"Shit." Bowen pulled his cell out of his back pocket and hit the screen a few times. Placing his hand on Bane's head, checking for a fever, Bowen's brow knit together in concern. And fear. "Hey, we need you to come to the cabin. Now. Bring your bag." Bowen's gaze looked stricken as he stared at his twin. "Yeah, *that* bag. No. Yeah. Just come now and I'll explain later." He hung up.

Out of nowhere, it felt like he'd been hit by a bus. Bane bowed backwards, roaring in pain. Sweat bloomed across his brow and chest. His vision flashed with white light specs and saliva built in his mouth so fast, he didn't have time to swallow it all, so it flooded between his teeth and dripped off his chin.

Bowen gripped the sides of his head. "Brother," he whispered with a cracked voice. He looked around the cabin, then darted into the kitchen, leaving Bane panting for air. He came back moments later with a bag of frozen peas and another of frozen blueberries. He slapped one on Bane's chest, the other on his forehead. "Breathe," he urged. "Damnit, Bane, *breathe.*"

He couldn't. The tightness in his chest was a vice grinding tighter, clamping down on his bones and compressing his lungs. Bane clawed at him, sinking his fingers into Bowen's t-shirt as his boot heels dug into the couch. A second surge of pain flowed through him and he didn't have air in his lungs to scream with.

"Let it go," Bowen urged. "Turn, Bane. Just turn and let him out."

Bane's head canted back, and he shifted.

He was wolf. The animal in him had finally burst free, but they were less connected now than the last time Bane shifted. He was always self-aware, no matter which form he took. As a human, Bane felt his wolf inside and knew what it felt or needed, always. As a wolf, Bane's humanity remained behind the eyes of the animal, always. His instincts were primal, but his thoughts remained human. He'd feel the dirt on his paws, the burst of flavor on his tongue with a fresh kill, the wind in his fur like a soothing breeze across his very skin. They were the same. They were united.

Until now.

Naked, Bane stood in white space. White as the moon on its brightest nights. But there was no ground, no trees to bring depth perception. No sky to tell which end was up. Gravity was his only clue that he was upright, walked, stumbling, swaying towards more white light. He had no idea what this place was, only that it was terrifyingly lonely here.

Worry and fear were slow to form. His limbs felt weighted down. He couldn't string his thoughts together. *Where...*

Bane squinted against the brightness to look around. His eyes watered and burned. The instinct to move, shout, turn, run, do something… it didn't come. Despair crept into his heart. He put one foot in front of the other, numbly. Stumbled forward. Fell down and crawled. *Where am I?*

No wind on his skin. No moon on his face. No meat in his mouth. No air in his lungs. He was dead and stuck in this bright, blinding emptiness. Bane didn't breathe. He wasn't even sure he blinked. *Where am I?*

A figure stood miles away, their silhouette so dark against the bright white emptiness. *Help,* he wanted to say. He reached out towards the person. *Help me. Help my wolf.*

He should have emotions attached to those words. Should have a voice too. But Bane had nothing.

Was nothing.

He was worse than dead. He didn't exist at all.

The silhouette came closer. And closer. Soon, he was able to make the features out. *It's a woman…*

That was his last thought before… nothing claimed him.

CHAPTER 18

Kennedy's heart hammered in her chest. Could this night get any worse? As Blade stood in her kitchen holding her cat hostage in a pillowcase, her gaze nonchalantly flickered to the corner she kept the baseball bat.

It wasn't there.

Of course, he'd take it. Damnit.

"I don't have the tranquilizers." Kennedy's grip remained on the door handle. She should bolt. Now. Run for her life. But first...

Blade gestured at the kitchen table. "Have a seat."

"I'm good where I am." Because she was going to run, just as soon as she got her cat away from this guy. No way could she leave Molly behind.

"Sit. Down." Blade backed up and dropped the pillowcase hard on her kitchen table and Molly made an awful noise.

Something lurched in Kennedy's chest hearing it. "Please don't hurt my cat."

"Don't make me hurt your cat." Blade pointed to a chair. "Sit."

Defeated, Kennedy did as she was told. Sinking into the chair, she didn't pull her eyes off Blade, no matter how badly she wanted to glance at her cat trapped between them.

"Good girl," he growled. Easing into the chair opposite her, Blade kept a tight grip on the pillowcase.

Molly growled and hissed in the sack. Kennedy swallowed through the growing tightness in her throat. She wanted to snatch the pillowcase but hadn't mustered the courage to go for it yet.

"What do you want?" she finally asked.

"For you to deliver when I give you an order."

"I told you I couldn't get you tranquilizers, and I meant it." It was hard to keep calm, but Kennedy managed. She'd grown up around bullies like Blade all her life. The key was to never show fear. Men like Blade thrived on that kind of thing.

"I told you what would happen if you didn't get what I wanted."

Kennedy's heart flopped in her chest. Her stomach dropped to her knees. Clenching her teeth, she made sure to not break eye contact with him. She didn't know what to say. No rebuttal came. No badass comment formed in her rattled mind. She just stared at him and used all her energy on not crying or running or begging for him to go away and not hurt her.

Damn you, Jake. That's what she thought. *Damn you, Jake!* Her anger was a small spark that kept the heated fury in her gaze burning.

"You're lucky I'm the one who came to collect. I could have sent Acid." Blade leaned forward and pulled the pillowcase closer to his chest. Molly had gone completely still inside it. "He's not as forgiving as I am."

Swallowing the lump in her throat, Kennedy scrambled to figure a way out of this. She couldn't. No escape could be made without saving her cat.

Blade rose from his chair slowly. His smile made Kennedy's thighs clenched together as if already blocking his intrusion before he even got started. She knew that look on a man too well. "No," she said.

"I already told you, sugar..." He tossed the pillowcase across the room and the loud thump and short burst of a cry from Molly cracked Kennedy's heart in half. She couldn't even look to see if her cat was moving because she refused to pull her attention away from the huge monster looming over her. "I have zero respect for that word."

Kennedy lurched out of her chair and dashed to the drawer she kept her knives in. Blade reared up and grabbed her by the hair, pulling it hard enough to make her cry out. His fingernails scraped her scalp as he tugged her by the roots, then his other hand clamped down on the back of her neck. He shoved her face into the counter, bending her over.

She pulled open the drawer, regardless of her position, hellbent on getting armed. Blade kicked the drawer shut with her hand still in it, but her hand wrapped around a handle, and she pulled a weapon out.

A bread knife. A motherfucking bread knife the length of her forearm with a rounded tip. DAMNIT! Regardless, Kennedy swung out with it. Blade smacked it out of her hand easily enough and the stupid weapon clanked onto the floor with a mocking sound of failure.

He'd let go of her neck, but still had a hold of her hair. "Stupid cunt." He shoved her forward again. Grabbing between her legs, he almost shoved his finger inside her as he violently yanked on the fabric of her scrubs, underwear, and tearing dignity right with it. "You ever come at me with a blade, you best aim for my jugular and not miss."

Blade jerked her across the kitchen, away from all the drawers, and he slammed her against the kitchen sink. Dirty dishes looked up at her. The moonlight shone in her backyard, where she saw he'd parked his bike so no one would know he was there. This far out in the country, no one would hear her scream. And no one would find her if she died. Her mind wasn't working fast enough to form a plan out of this. But she didn't have it in her yet to give up the fight.

Kennedy's hips jerked as Blade yanked on her pants, trying to tear them off or pull them down, or make a goddamn hole in the fabric big enough to fit himself into.

Dishes. Moon. Bike. Hands.

Her thoughts slowed, along with her reactions. She was checking out. In what might have been a handful of seconds, felt like an hour in her head. "No," she said, tears finally finding their way down her cheeks. "NO!"

The sound of fabric tearing was as loud as a scream. She felt something hot and rough press against her opening. "Spread, bitch." Blade kicked her legs out. "Or I'll use that blunt tipped knife to help you. The serrated edge might just tickle if I take my time cutting you open."

A surge of... she didn't know what... blasted through her.

Clarity and courage funneled into her system along with a shot of adrenaline. "I said *NO!*" She grabbed a dirty pan from the sink, twisted and smashed it across his head. It didn't knock him out, but made him stumble. She swung again and cracked him in his temple. He took a step back. She swung again, using the Teflon-coated frying pan to try and beat this motherfucker's head in or at the very least knock him out.

She had no such luck, but Kennedy did manage to slow him down and stun him enough to get the hell out of the kitchen, grab the pillowcase with Molly still in it, and run out the front door. Blade didn't make a sound as he stormed after her.

Kennedy ran to her car and panic slammed into her when she realized she'd left her keys in the house. Shit! Clutching Molly, she ran faster than she ever had in her life into the woods and didn't stop until she eventually reached the hill that descended into traffic.

Later, she'd calculate the sprint at nearly three miles of uncharted forestry she'd run through, but for now she just saw an escape route that worked. Blade hadn't chased her through the woods. But she hadn't stopped running to verify it either.

Look, she wasn't a runner. Hated that shit with a passion. And never in her life had she run so fast with energy to spare at the end. But here she was, out of breath, her legs burning, lungs sawing for air, with a boost of adrenaline demanding her to keep going. *Run, run, run!*

Kennedy darted across the main road, with only the moon lighting her way. She'd made it into town. Those woods provided one hell of a shortcut to civilization — one she'd never realized until now. Once across the street, she finally pulled Molly out of the pillowcase. The cat dug her claws into Kennedy's shoulders as she tried to flee, and Kennedy clutched her a little tighter to keep her from running off. Molly's mouth was open, the hair on her back and tail puffed out. She panted in distress but wasn't injured. Thank. God.

"I got you," Kennedy said through a sob. "I got you, Molly."

Cradling the cat, she hurried towards a convenience store and pushed the door open with her ass. "I need help!" she called out.

"What is it, sugar?"

Kennedy froze at being called Sugar. The voice didn't register at first, only the name that Blade kept calling her. But it wasn't that

128

asshole addressing her now. It was a woman who looked to be in her fifties behind the counter. "I need a phone. Please. I need to call someone."

But who the hell was she going to call, the cops?

Any sane person would be smashing 9-1-1 right now and have Blade found and arrested for breaking and entering plus assault. But Jake would be the one to suffer if cops got involved. Kennedy knew how this shit worked. Blade might get arrested, but he wouldn't stay gone long enough to save Jake, or Kennedy, from the Wolf Pack's punishments.

Did she call Jake?

He needed to fix this and make things right. But Jake seemed just as paranoid as Kennedy was about the men he rode with. And Jake would likely kill Blade for attempting to violate Kennedy. She wasn't letting her brother go to jail for murder.

Did she call Bane?

Nope. Not at all.

Risa?

Kennedy swallowed the saliva building in her mouth. Heat bloomed down her back that had nothing to do with running and everything to do with another major hot flash. She sank down into a crouch and huddled while holding Molly close. The cat clawed and meowed so much, Molly ended up twisting out of Kennedy's hold and running away.

She watched her cat dash out the door the instant someone opened it to come inside.

Run.

Kennedy wasn't going to chase her. Tears filled her eyes and sweat poured down her temples and chest. *Run, Molly.*

At least one of them deserved a chance at survival... and it sure as hell didn't look like it was going to be Kennedy.

CHAPTER 19

A heavy weight lifted from Bane's chest lift as if someone pulled an elephant off him. He opened his eyes and blinked a few times before things cleared up. The first face he saw was Bowen's.

"Like looking in a mirror," he joked with a gravelly voice.

"Fuck, Bane," Bowen said, backing up just enough for someone else to step in. "You had me scared shitless."

"How do you feel now, son?"

Oh shit, his father was here? Bane's guilt for secretly taking the liquid silver washed over him like cold water. He instantly felt like a five-year-old caught doing something he knew he shouldn't have done without permission. Considering his age, that said a lot about the guilt he carried over his decision.

Which actually pissed him off and made him defensive.

"Can you hear me?" Alistair's heavy brow pinched together as he waited for Bane to respond.

"Loud and clear, Dad. Yeah." Bane sat up, grunting with the tremendous effort it took to do so. Shit, he felt hungover. "I can't string my thoughts together yet." He noticed his father and Bowen glance at each other. The looks on their faces made Bane's balls tuck in tight. "What?"

"Bowen says you took the silver." Alistair rubbed the back of his neck. "This true?"

Bane cheeks burned. "Yeah. I did." He couldn't put a word to what this emotion was rolling inside him, but it felt like a mix of embarrassment and pride. "I want my *Deesha*. I'm sick of the

130

longing. I have no regrets for what I did, even if I didn't do it the traditional way." *There. Put that in your jaw and crunch on it,* he thought.

His father chuckled. "Leave it to you to break off and try to keep your biggest life change on the down low."

"I don't like audiences." *And I don't like people witnessing my failures.* Bowen liked credit, where credit was due. Bane preferred flying under the radar because he hated attention — good or bad.

"Your mother's going to blow her lid over this."

"Then don't tell her." Even as the words left his mouth, he shrunk back in the couch cushions just imagining his mom, Marie, getting all emotional over one of her babies drinking the silver and potentially damning himself in the process. "I didn't want her or anyone else to worry," Bane confessed. "Not after Killian."

Alistair's golden gaze turned glassy for a moment. He cleared his throat before saying, "I understand, son."

That was as close to being told "you're not in trouble" as it ever got within his family.

"Have you dreamed of her yet?"

Bane's heart split down the middle because now he had something else he really didn't want anyone to know about. "I thought so."

Bowen stepped closer, his arms crossed over his broad chest and face twisted in a hard scowl. "What do you mean, you *thought* so?"

Why did he feel like a kid getting into trouble again? Damnit! Shoving himself up, he swung his legs around and leaned forward with his elbows resting on his knees, and he scrubbed his face with both hands. "I just had another dream."

Shit, shit, shit. The implications of this were huge, and he was scared. That's what this feeling really was. *Confusion.* He wasn't a kid caught with his paw in the cookie jar. He was a man caught between fate and fantasy.

"You going to explain yourself or leave us hanging with our mouths open and stomachs dropped, boy?"

He looked up at his father, not even bothering to hide the emotion in his gaze. "I dreamed of Kennedy the night after she hit me with her car."

Alistair held his breath. His jaw clenched while waiting for

131

Bane to drop the other shoe…

"And just now I dreamt of someone else."

Bowen gripped the sides of his head and walked backwards until his legs hit a chair and he slammed his ass down into it. "Holy Hell."

Alistair's tone stayed steady. "This second woman. Did you see her face?"

Aaaannnd there Bane went, unable to breathe again. He rubbed his chest, feebly attempting to soothe the ache growing with each second that ticked by while he sat on his couch and did nothing to save himself from a fate like his baby brother, Killian. "Yeah, a little."

"A little?" Bowen barked. "How much is a little?"

"She was a silhouette. She had long, dark hair. But her features were… hidden. I feel like…" he scrambled to snag the image of her again. Tall, lithe, long dark hair. There was more. Bane had a feeling if he saw her on the street, he'd be able to pick her out of a crowd, but conjuring her image in his mind was a no go. *Fuck me sideways.* He tipped his head back and rubbed his chest again. "Can I have two *Deeshas*?"

"It's not unheard of, but it's really rare, son." Alistair dropped down next to Bane and rested his arms on his knees. "What else did you see?"

"I can't tell," he confessed. "My head's not right. I can't piece things together fast enough." He sighed and ran the back of his thumb along his bottom lip. "Earlier, I could barely make a sentence form at all—in my head or out of my mouth."

Alistair's shoulders sagged. "It's the ripping," he said solemnly. "Your wolf and man are tearing in two."

Bane's heart bucked in his chest as panicked surged in his veins. "What do I do?"

"Find your *Deesha* and turn her, Bane." Alistair glowered. "You might have until the next full moon to do it, but if you have two women to chase, bite, and turn, you'll need every second of it."

I can't have two, he thought. It didn't feel right that he'd have two. More so, "I only want Kennedy." The words flew out of his mouth as if his instincts took over his voice box. "It's only Kennedy for me."

Bowen stood and jabbed a finger in his direction. "You better hope you're right about this, brother."

"It's a big risk, son."

Didn't feel that way to him. Kennedy was it for Bane. He knew it in his bones. But that other woman? Who was she? *Where* was she? As quickly as her image formed in his mind, it disintegrated again. He couldn't latch onto the vision at all. She had blue eyes. No, wait, brown. Hazel? Why couldn't he grip her image correctly? Something sharp sliced inside him and he doubled over. *The ripping.* "Fuuuck."

"Bowen, do you know where this Kennedy woman lives?" Alistair placed his hand on Bane's nape and started massaging it hard.

"Yeah," Bowen sounded defeated and tired. "I'll get her."

"No, *I'll* get her," Bane argued. But when he tried to stand up, his father's grip tightened, holding him down on the couch. "Let go of me."

"You're not leaving until your wolf has recovered."

"It's fine."

"The fact that you're willing to lie about it proves otherwise."

Damnit, he hated how his father was so perceptive. And Bane's wolf was in distress. He could tell by the way he was breathing. Both he and his wolf were panting. "It'll be okay." Not sure if he was saying that to himself or his family.

"Bowen," Alistair barked, "Go get this woman and bring her here."

"Don't scare her." Bane's gaze lifted to his twin's. "Please. Let me be the one to explain all this to her." He knew his brother well enough to know when that Lycan got scared about something. He got aggressive. If Kennedy didn't go with him willingly, Bowen would likely toss her over his shoulder and carry her off like a Neanderthal. He was also someone who laid out facts, giving zero fucks about how crazy those facts might sound to a human or anyone else.

"I'll do my best," Bowen growled just before he stormed off. Seconds later, the front door slammed shut and the truck's engine roared to life.

"I didn't tell him where to find her." Bane pushed off the couch and ended up tipping over and slamming onto his hands and knees. "Shit!" His body and mind were totally out of whack. "She's at work... or," what time was it? "She could be at home."

"He's good at hunting," Alistair said. "He'll bring her back, no matter where she is." Alistair popped off the sofa and crouched down in front of Bane. "Now turn, son. Your wolf needs help."

But he didn't want to turn. For the first time in his life, Bane was scared to do it. Earlier, he thought he'd shifted, but hadn't. And it landed him in a white space with nothing but the worst case of despair he'd ever suffered.

"I can't," he confessed.

"You must."

But what if the shift was permanent?

CHAPTER 20

Kennedy waited in the convenience store until she'd gathered her courage and a healthy dose of crazy before deciding her next move. She ended up not calling anyone for help and when the store manager asked about it, Kennedy waved her off and lied by saying she was fine.

It's all good. Nothing to see here. Carry on.

It was late at night by the time she left the store and a terrible time to go traipsing around alone, but Kennedy lost her ability to care. Detached and fresh out of fucks, she trudged back home the way she came — through the woods. It was the safest option. She highly doubted the Wolf Pack MC was going to comb the woods looking for her. If Blade went back and told them about their encounter and they decided to collectively hunt her down, they'd do it on their bikes or in their vehicles. They're not going to scour the woods like a pack of wild animals, tracing her scent, for crying out loud. That made this route better and safer than the lit streets of town and the long way home down her dirt road.

Was she worried Blade might still be there when she returned? A little. But it was unlikely he'd stick around. If he did, it was because he was dead and as nice as that sounded, the likelihood of her frying pan being that successful was miniscule.

Slowly trudging through the woods, Kennedy didn't want to think about anything other than putting one foot in front of the other. She was exhausted. And her pants were ripped, which meant half her ass was showing — also not something she wanted shown in public or feel pressured to explain to a stranger.

God, she could still feel Blade's paws on her. And another's…

Kennedy blew out an angry breath, thinking about the last man who tried to attack her. Jake had beaten the sonofabitch nearly to death and went to jail for assault. It could have been worse. Had Kennedy not stopped Jake, he would have killed the bastard. There was no doubt about it.

And that's one of the many reasons Kennedy remained loyal to her brother. No matter what he was into or how bad things got, her devotion to Jake was unshakeable because of what he did for her. And what he suffered for her.

One might think she should call him about this. After all, it was his friend who went after her. But that was only pointing out a problem she already knew he didn't have a solution to. You can't expect a knight in shining armor to show up out of the blue and fix everything. Besides, if she told Jake about what Blade did, she highly doubted a beating would happen this time. Jake would either be forced to let the insult go or put a bullet between Blade's eyes. One would be taking their parent's approach to life, the other could land Jake in prison for life.

Kennedy didn't want to put Jake in that position. Her heart wouldn't survive it. Neither would he.

What a goddamn mess.

To top it all off, Molly was gone. Her one true friend. Molly was the only one Kennedy trusted implicitly.

Risa wasn't a friend. She was a coworker who was fun outside of work. And Kennedy knew damn well Risa stole those fucking meds from work. That might have been a harsh accusation if Kennedy hadn't seen her sneak them before and confronted her about it. Twice.

She should have reported it to Mark and didn't. Now she was taking the blame for Risa's actions. Not that Mark would have done much about it. Risa wasn't just sneaking meds, she was also blowing the boss. And look, all that might make some folks raise their eyebrows, but Kennedy had seen plenty of people do a lot worse to get a lot less and she never judged. The only thing she urged was for Risa to get help.

Besides, Mark was a piece of shit boss. Maybe it was a good thing Kennedy would no longer be employed there. He didn't respect her. He always gave her the shittiest shifts — even though she had more certifications than he did, for crying out loud. Their clients preferred her over him because he wasn't patient with the animals, while Kennedy took her time and worked with each one, no matter how temperamental they got.

"My career's over." She said it out loud, as if voicing the truth could make it more believable. All those years in school, all the college debt, all the time and sleepless nights, double shifts, and energy she put into being a veterinarian and now what?

Gone. Poof. Kablooey.

Mark was a big enough asshole to drag her name through the mud in this small town. And he'd take great pleasure in it too. Asshole.

Damnit! Kennedy hugged herself as she trudged up a hill. Getting out of her head, she looked around and it hit her: This was the dumbest decision she'd made all week. What, the ever-loving *fuck*, was she thinking traipsing through the pitch-black woods, by herself, unarmed, in the dark for? No cell. No weapon. And clearly no common sense.

All so she could do was... what? Go back home to the potential of Blade still being there waiting for her?

She should have killed him when she had the chance because he was going to make sure she paid for her actions.

Oh my God. The consequences began piling up, making her falter. Looking around, Kennedy had no clue where she was. What kind of idiot did something like this? The fact that she'd reached town earlier had been a miracle. These woods had no signs or trails to follow, and she couldn't retrace her steps. What adrenaline fueled her every move when she ran through this place and reached town had finally vaporized. Now, she was running on fumes. Her nerves were shot. Her muscles ached.

Stopping to catch her breath, she dropped down and leaned against a tree. Bending her knees and hugging them, she rocked back and forth.

"What am I going to do now?" Wait out here until daylight and try to navigate back home then? She couldn't turn around and go back to town. She'd already gone too far back into the woods. There was nothing to mark the way. Nothing to light the ground with so she could see better. Her best bet was to sit here until daybreak. And hope she didn't get eaten by a predator.

Her life just kept getting better and better. Kennedy could see the headlines now: Woman found half eaten in the woods. No suspects as of yet, police investigation ongoing.

Jake would set a wildfire in revenge for nature taking Kennedy away from him.

Her eyes stung from unshed tears. Holding herself tighter, she rocked back and forth until she heard a noise. Something rustled in the darkness to her right. She held her breath and didn't move a muscle.

There it was again!

It was getting closer.

This wasn't a squirrel. They were safe in their nests this late at night. It couldn't be a coyote either. They moved so soundlessly, one could creep up on her and she'd never hear it until it was too late. This sounded much, much bigger. And it was getting way too close for Kennedy's comfort.

Shooting up, she scrambled to find a large branch to scare it off with. Swinging a dead tree limb, she felt insane screaming, "Go away! Get! Shoo!"

"You're gonna need a bigger stick if you're trying to scare me off."

Kennedy's heart ran in panicked circles in her chest. "Stay away from me, Blade!" She swung her stick harder, backing up to put more space between her and the large man coming straight towards her. He didn't stop. He reached out, and she cracked him as hard as she could with her stick.

"Ouch! Fuck, woman!"

"I swear to God," she growled with a shaky voice. "I'll kill you. I'll fucking kill you if you come any closer, Blade."

"Who the hell is Blade?"

She froze. In the dark, it was hard to make out anything more than a hulking silhouette. The moon barely shined through the thick trees, so she had to rely on her other senses—all of which were going haywire lately. "Who the hell are you?"

A low growl rose from the man's throat as he snagged her branch clean out of her hand and tossed it. Before she had a chance to spin and run, he grabbed her arms and shoved his face in hers. "Not Blade," he said.

138

"Oh my God, *Bane*?" Relief flooded her system, and she clutched his arms. "Holy shit, what are you doing here?" Kennedy clung to him like a lifeline and wrapped her arms around his neck, holding him close.

Aaaannnd cue the water works. She sobbed in this chest as he held her tightly. Rubbing her back in small circles, he remained tense as she cried her eyes out against him. "Easy," he said calmly. "Easy, Kennedy. Nothing's going to hurt you."

She believed it. Those words from his lips left zero room for doubt. Until he said…

"But I'm not Bane."

Kennedy pushed away and looked up at him again. Okay, was she completely off her rocker? Nope. This guy looked like exactly Bane. He felt like Bane.

But didn't *smell* like Bane.

Swiping her tears away, she sniffled. "You're his twin brother."

"Bowen," he said with a warm smile. "Bane would be here himself, but he's incapacitated at the moment. I came for you instead."

"Came for me?" Kennedy backed up a little more. "I don't understand."

"Seems we both have some explaining to do." Bowen gently grabbed her elbow and started leading her through the woods. "I stopped by your work. They said you were no longer employed there. I came to your house, but you didn't answer your door."

"Then how'd you find me out here?" The hair on the back of her neck stood on end. Yet the comfort she felt having him with her was undeniable. Bane's brother was her safest bet, and he was a complete stranger. Wow, how far had she gone down this rabbit hole? Was there a bottom to it?

"Why don't you tell me why you're out here alone, this deep in the forest, at this time of night first."

She'd really rather not. "What's wrong with Bane?"

Bowen walked several paces in silence before saying, "You're hurt."

It wasn't until he said it that the sting registered. Her ripped scrubs were in worse condition now and she'd managed to scrape her legs and arms while running through the woods like a scared

139

rabbit. "I'll be fine. Just some scratches."

Bowen grunted as if he didn't believe her. She tripped over a root and fumbled. "Ouch! Shit!" His grip on her arm tightened and the next thing she knew, Kennedy's feet were off the ground.

"Is this okay?" he asked while carrying her.

She wasn't sure how to respond. "I can walk on my own."

"You want me to put you down?"

Was it awful if she said no? She was exhausted and everything hurt. Besides, Bowen's strides were twice as big as hers and she'd struggled to keep up with his pace. "Not yet," she finally admitted.

She stared at his profile, watching his jaw clench. Even in the dark, she could appreciate how identical Bane and Bowen were. It made something in her chest warm and tighten. *Bane.* She had no idea what was going on, but the moment she thought Bane was standing in front of her like some kind of savior, a huge weight had lifted off her shoulders. It was preposterous, but that didn't make it any less real. For it to end up being Bowen was kind of a letdown. And a blessing. She wouldn't want Bane to see her like this, so scared and lost.

"Can you take me to him?" she said quietly.

"That's the plan."

Bowen ended up carrying her all the way home. When they stepped into the clearing of her backyard, the illusion of safety vanished. "Put me down, please."

He obeyed immediately, taking great care to place her feet down gently on the grass. Kennedy looked around cautiously. Blade's motorcycle wasn't there anymore. The lights in her house were off. "I umm," she wrung her hands nervously. "I'll just be a minute."

"I'd like to go in with you. If you're okay with that."

She was more than okay with it. She just hadn't wanted to sound like a scaredy cat and ask. "That's fine."

Together, they climbed onto her back porch and she stared at the broken doorjamb and trim. *Fucking Blade.* That's how he'd gotten in earlier. Through her back door. Piece of shit didn't even pick the lock, he just kicked it in.

Bowen noticed the damage. It was hard not to. He cocked his brow and clenched his teeth as he looked over at her. If he was

140

expecting an explanation, he was out of luck. "Lots of repairs to do around here," she said with a nervous smile.

He might be Bane's twin, but she didn't owe Bowen her tragic story. Pushing the door open, she flicked on the kitchen light. Bowen's gaze darkened as his brow furrowed. His nostrils even flared.

Was it any wonder?

Blood spatter decorated the floor. The frying pan she'd used on Blade was cast to the side by the fridge. A chair had tipped over. Clearing her throat, she righted the furniture and said, "Need to clean, too."

"Mmm hmm." Bowen kept his mouth shut as he continued to survey her small house. When she headed down the hall to her bedroom, he stopped her and shook his head. Then he went in first and looked through each room, in closets, and even the behind the shower curtain. Kennedy stayed a short distance behind him, equal parts nervous and grateful to have him scanning her house. He turned around and said, "All clear."

Then it was like she'd turned into a ticking time bomb. Everything sped up—her heartrate, her breathing, her thoughts. She acted like a chicken with her head cut off, racing around with no true direction or focus. She wasn't really sure what the hell to do, but her need to get out of there was driving her towards her closet.

"Pack some bags, Kennedy. I'm taking you home with us."

Us. Him and Bane.

"Okay," she said numbly.

Why she'd feel safe with two men who were basically strangers showed what level of the danger zone she was in. Bowen stood at her doorway with his arms crossed over his chest and a serious scowl on his face while she shoved clothes into a bag. Crawling across her bed to grab the gun she kept in her nightstand, Bowen growled so deeply she half thought a wolf was in the room.

"Put on fresh pants," he ordered.

Her cheeks flooded with embarrassment. So deep in her head, Kennedy completely forgot about Blade ripping her pants at the ass and crotch. She'd just flashed Bowen. And it wouldn't take a detective to figure out what might have happened to her earlier. *Oh. No.*

She shimmied off the bed and held her hands behind her to

shield the view. Choking up, she didn't dare look at him. Snagging a pair of sweatpants from her laundry basket, Kennedy pulled on her scrubs and couldn't seem to make anything work right. The tie was too tight on the waist. *Which was why Blade had to rip them instead of pulling them down.* Trembling, she looked over at Bowen, who was already heading towards her. "I need... help," she whimpered.

"Here." His voice was almost a whisper. "May I?" His fingers hooked on her waistband, and he waited for a response. All Kennedy could manage was a nod as his gaze remained locked on hers and he ripped the waistline, snapping the drawstring. Bowen cautiously pulled her pants down while keeping his eyes locked on hers. Her legs were a bloody mess of bruises and scratches. Chin trembling as bad as her hands, she held onto his shoulders for balance as he helped guide one leg and then the other into a fresh pair of pants.

"I'm so sorry," she said to him. "I'm so sorry."

Bowen rose to his full height and cupped her face. "Nothing to be sorry for."

She fell into another crying fit and buried her face in his chest. She wanted so badly for him to be Bane that her chest hurt with longing for him. Bowen was hard and tense and she knew Bane would have held her tighter and kissed her head and...

"I need him," she said through sniffles. "I need Bane."

"Come on," Bowen pulled her off him and grabbed the half-packed bag. "Let's go."

They entwined their fingers, which gave her something to hold on to. Bowen led the way out of her house, stopping by the cat tree in the living room. "Your cat?"

Kennedy bit her bottom lip and shook her head. Bowen didn't question it, just nodded once and unlocked the front door. Once again, he scanned the yard before tugging her outside and over to his truck.

They drove in silence the whole way, which was about forty-five minutes. Too wrecked to talk, she pressed her head to the window and stared at nothing. She should have asked questions, but knew he'd likely ask her some as well, and she wasn't ready to answer any.

When they pulled onto a dirt road, her heartbeat sped up.

Still, she felt safer with this guy than she had even in her own job with Mark breathing down her back all the time. God, what a fucked-up life she'd been living, right? They pulled up to a gorgeous cabin with warm lights glowing from the porch. A huge woodshed lay off to the right side, all the wood stacked meticulously in rows. Bowen parked the truck and hopped out, grabbing her duffel from the back before opening her door and helping her out.

She expected Bane to come out.

He didn't.

Stupid to think he would bound out of the house and across the driveway to say hi. He wasn't a dog. But still, she wished more than anything for Bane to appear and take Bowen's place. Then she remembered Bowen saying he was "incapacitated."

She was the first through the door. The scent of man and animal and woods assaulted her. It smelled like heaven.

"Bane!" Bowen called out as he kicked the door shut behind them. "Bane!"

"He's in his room," said a man from the kitchen.

This guy was older and built similar to Bowen and Bane. He had a thick beard with a little gray in it and a streak of white that went from the corner of his mouth to his chin. When he flashed a smile at Kennedy, part of her warmed, irrationally. "Hi, I'm Alistair." He came forward with his hand out. "The twins' dad."

This was their *father*? Holy shit, talk about good genes. "K-Kennedy."

The instant her hand slid into his massive one, she felt that familiar warmth she associated with Bane. It caused something else in to unravel. Her composure.

But damned if she was going to cry again. That seemed to be all she'd done over the past week. It was bullshit. Kennedy sucked back her emotions and pulled away from him. "Where is he?"

Alistair's brow knit together. Tossing his thumb over his shoulder, he said, "Upstairs. Second door on the right."

Kennedy held her breath and headed up.

143

CHAPTER 21

Bane felt like he'd been hit by a tank, set on fire, beaten with ball peen hammer, and slapped a few dozen times with a wet noodle. After refusing to shift into wolf form, he bore the most excruciating pain of his entire life until eventually passing out. Still unable to take deep breaths, he worked his way up to filling his lungs, allowing his chest to expand, and exhale through his cracked lips. Mouth breathing was the worst, but his wolf was still attempting to run the show and as the distressed animal panted, Bane did too.

Everything looked blurry once he cracked his eyes open, but Bane could see his dresser and leather chair over by the window. Morning light filtered in through the seam in the drawn curtains. He licked his lips and tried moving his legs, stretching them out until they draped over the end of the bed.

He'd laid in a curled fetal position all night, per his wolf. Now his muscles cramped and ached from holding the tight position for so long. Bane wasn't complaining though. His pain was his fault. Had he shifted to his wolf, things might have gone way smoother and a lot less painful, but he was too scared to try. No way did he want to get stuck in that white space again.

With his face smashed into his pillow, half his body draped off the side of the bed, and his feet dangled over the edge. Everything felt wrong and right at the same time. And, it might sound crazy, but something solid settled deep in his mind, as if fate itself nailed it in place, making whatever it was unmoving… *definite*.

Eventually, he was able to move his limbs and take deeper breaths. Laying on the edge of the bed, he tried to not move much as the last jolts of pain ebbed away and he finally felt normal again. Man, was he glad to have some family with him. What the hell would he have done without them last night?

Thud. Something bumped the back of his thigh.

Bane tensed for a moment, confused and alert. Lifting his head, he turned over…

This had to be a dream. Some kind of very vivid, wild, fever dream. It's the only way to explain why Kennedy was in his bed right now. Carefully, he touched her arm. His breath caught. She felt warm and soft and *real.*

Call him crazy, but the possibility of her actually being in his bed right now lit a spark inside his chest and he burst with new energy and clarity. Even his wolf tipped his head back and howled inside Bane's soul. He sat up, body shaking with the aftershocks of last night and the surprise of seeing his *Deesha* in bed with him. Reaching out again, he traced the length of her arm, dip of her hip, and curve of her thigh with a trembling finger. She was out cold, lightly snoring on top of all his covers.

He caught the scent of salt and blood. Was she hurt? Had she been crying?

Too many possibilities ran through his wild imagination, and none of them good. He pumped the breaks on his protectiveness and growing aggression to think things through. The events of last night pieced themselves together one by one. She was here because Bowen had retrieved her. Kennedy was facing away from him, but as far as he could see from this angle, her cheeks were flushed with a healthy glow and she didn't seem distressed. She looked peaceful. Her breathing was nice and even. Deep.

He was dying to roll her over and bury himself inside her however she'd let him. The urge to fuck was strong. Unwelcome. Alarming and uncalled for. His dick hardened to the point of pain, but he wasn't about to disturb her. Instead, Bane did the next best thing—he slid out of bed and tugged his side of the covers over her to keep her warm and comfy. Walking around to her side of his bed, Bane swept the hair from her face. Even though they were closed and laced with a gorgeous amount of thick, black lashes fanning across her cheeks, her eyes looked puffy and the tip of her nose was

145

pink.

Something was wrong.

He wasn't so full of himself to think she'd cried herself to sleep over him. And what was with the scent of blood? It was super faint, but there. And it wasn't menstrual.

Yes, shifters could smell and know the difference.

Since he wasn't willing to wake his *Deesha — please, fate, say Kennedy was his Deesha, and he wasn't making the biggest mistake of his existence —* he went downstairs to talk with Bowen. Maybe he knew what was up with her.

Quietly leaving his room, the distance between Bane and Kennedy grew with each step he took down the steps, and it woke a weird instinct in him — the one that wanted to crawl inside and claim her. Fuck. Bite. Claw. *Mate.* Biting the urge to make a U-turn, skip the steps two at a time, bust down his bedroom door, rip away the covers and bite, nip, suck, kiss and lick every square inch of her glorious body, Bane headed into the kitchen and poured himself a glass of water.

He chugged it in three swallows. Refill. Repeat. With the faucet still running, he cupped his hands and splashed some on his face. Splash, splash, splash.

Bowen kept quiet over by the stove, studiously making bacon, eggs, and potatoes with his back to Bane on purpose.

"Where's..." he had to clear the gravel and glass shards out of his throat, "where's dad?"

"Left about two hours ago."

Bane eased into a chair at the kitchen table. Shame tried to crawl across his skin, but he didn't give it much space. "Did something happen to her?"

Bowen's silence was nails on a chalkboard. Bane slammed his fist on the table. "Did something happen?"

"Yeah," Bowen answered in a gravelly tone. He turned around with two full plates of food and dropped one in front of Bane. "You need protein. Eat this and this." He shoved the second plate at him.

"Bowe..."

"*Eat,*" his twin snarled. "And I'll tell you all I know while you do."

This was total and utter bullshit. So why was he picking up a

146

fork and stuffing eggs into his piehole? Because his wolf needed the protein and he was starved and knew damn well Bowen wasn't going to say a word until Bane did this. *Fucker.* And the fact of the matter was, Bane needed to be at a hundred percent so he could take care of Kennedy and be there for her.

She wasn't going to want a mate who ran on an empty tank.

He cleaned one plate in record time and shoved it aside. Chugging another glass of water, he slammed it down on the table, wiped his mouth with the back of his hand, and pulled the second plate over. "Start talking. I smelled salt and blood on her. She was crying and I want to know why." *So I can kill whoever upset or hurt her.*

Bowen blew out a tired exhale. "I found her in the woods behind her house."

Bane's eyebrows rose to his hairline.

"I went to her work first. They said she no longer worked there. Then I went to her house and saw the back door had been... altered."

A growl flew out of Bane's mouth deep enough to rattle the plates on the table.

Bowen leaned in and dropped his voice to a mere whisper. "There was blood on the floor and the scent of a man. I've no clue who. There was obviously a struggle. I searched her property, hoping to pick up a scent trail. Ended up hearing her stomp through the woods like sasquatch. Followed the sound and picked up her scent soon after. Found her crying against a tree."

Bane's breakfast turned to a lump of lead in his belly. *I should have been the one to find her. I should have been there for her, not my brother.* But damn, was he grateful Bowen was there to get her. If he had to choose someone to take his place, it would always be Bowen. "The blood I smelled?"

"She scraped herself up in all the brush and thorn bushes. Nothing too serious on that front."

Well, that was slightly comforting. At least whoever broke into her home—someone from the Wolf Pack MC, he'd wager—hadn't hurt her. If any of those pieces of shit laid a hand on his *Deesha*, Bane would set their club on fire with everyone in it. Or worse.

"Your girl's a strong one, brother." Bowen tugged his shirt

sleeve up and showed a wicked bruise already beginning to fade on his arm. "She got a swing in before she realized who I was."

Bane's gaze locked onto his twin's. "She was scared. What else was she supposed to do, cower and whimper?" Not his Kennedy. That woman was a fighter.

He loved her already.

"There's something else..." Bowen rubbed his chin. "Whoever was in her house, she got a few blows in. Saw a frying pan on the floor, which I'm assuming was her weapon of choice. The blood was definitely the male's and not hers."

Pride swelled in Bane's chest along with resentment for not being there to defend her himself. These Wolf Pack cocksuckers would pay for trying to fuck with Bane's *Deesha*. Bane was almost looking forward to it.

But that wasn't all that happened to Kennedy last night. He could tell Bowen was holding something back. It made Bane's wolf growl and hackles raise. "What else?" Because it better not be something along the lines of where Bane's imagination now headed...

"Her pants were ripped. Not her panties, but..."

Bane didn't want to hear more. He shoved himself away from the table, hellbent on racing back to Kennedy to hold her. Whatever she'd been through was too much. Especially knowing he could have prevented all of it had he gone caveman on her and carried her out of her house and brought her home like he'd wanted to when she'd kicked him and Jake off her property.

"Bane!" Bowed barked as he gripped his arm to halt him. "She's rattled, but nothing happened that can't be overcome."

"I don't need you to tell me how to handle my *Deesha*."

"Your wolf is what I'm worried about, brother. If her fear spikes, the animal in you will sense it."

Bane ripped his arm out of Bowen's grip. "Did he... they... do you know if..."

"I don't think it got that far, but..." Bowen's expression softened, "she put her problems aside the instant she heard you were in trouble. She's displacing her issues to focus on yours. Cried when you wouldn't wake up. Then she held you tight while you whimpered like a pup in your sleep."

Bane's knees nearly buckled. *I don't deserve her.* That was the first thought to pop into his head. The second was, *But I'll earn her.*

"You need to get to the bottom of this, Bane."

Didn't have to tell him twice. "Have the pack on standby?"

"Already done. That's why Dad left as soon as he did."

Climbing the steps, he clamped down his aggression and caged his beast. Bane wanted to hear the entire story from Kennedy and no other. But that was going to take some coaxing, he'd wager. And it might still be too fresh for her to talk about.

The worst part?

Bane feared he was going to hurt her more than the Wolf Pack MC could, because Kennedy still had no idea she was sleeping in a den of wolves.

CHAPTER 22

Kennedy ran for her life. Deep in the woods, a path lay out before her, clear and flat. Trees loomed overhead, everything glowing with a particular brightness that was too vivid to be real. It reminded her of the way grass and flowers seemed brighter in color after a thunderstorm. The forest felt busy but remained dead silent.

Until a low, rumbling growl rippled through the air, sliding ice down her spine. It's back, *she thought.* It's coming for me again! *Whenever this thing chased her, no matter how fast she ran, her legs couldn't move quick enough. Kennedy picked up pace, feet pounding hard on the earth, arms pumping for more momentum.* Go! Go! Go! *Her survival instincts screamed at her. And she tried. God, how she tried to go faster than a snail stuck in molasses. But even at the pace she was able to sprint, this thing was faster. She couldn't outrun it. And maybe she didn't want to anymore. She halted again, looking around the landscape, trying to figure out where it was, where she should dash next. There was no place to hide. No limb to climb up on. Only the path before her. Kennedy felt its hot breath on the back of her neck. Its heat licked her skin as it got closer, closer, closer. The icy feeling she had a moment ago now burned like a blazing inferno.*

She broke out in a sweat. Her legs grew heavy. The air became thick. Her pace slowed.

What started as a mad dash through the woods decelerated as her body felt heavier and heavier. Kennedy panted, staring at a cleared path with nothing that could stop or slow her down. Yet, it felt like she was stuck, waist-deep, in mud as she grunted with the tremendous effort it took to move even one step forward.

Exhausting herself, she stopped. The beast, she knew in her soul, was right behind her. Watching her. Kennedy had no clue what it was or what it might do… but she knew exactly what it wanted. Her.

I can't get away from this thing. *The craziest part about it? A part of her wanted to get caught. Morbid curiosity slowed her down until she came to a complete stop. Staring at the vast path before her, she caught her breath and felt the thing approach from behind. Something hot and rough caressed the back of her arm, her hip, and outer thigh, leaving a burning sensation in its wake.* It touched me. Oh God… what do I do? *She turned around and —*

Kennedy's eyes popped open, and she yelped. Holy shit, that dream felt real. Every time she had it, the beast chasing her got closer and closer. This was the first time it touched her though. Hand-to-the-man, she could still feel his heat lingering on her skin.

But that was only a dream and with her eyes wide open, reality set it. She wasn't being chased; she was at Bane's house. Kennedy stared at the wall next to his bed as she reeled in her confusing emotions. A symbol of some kind was painted on the wood. It looked oddly familiar, but hell if she could bring herself to care enough to investigate it further. Next, Kennedy inhaled and got a nose-full of Bane's glorious scent. He was a mix of all the good things a man should smell like, with a shot of extra spice. Rolling over, she—

Bane flashed her a tremendous smile. "You're awake."

His voice, coupled with his glorious grin, gave Kennedy an irrational comfort. She didn't know this guy. Yet, here she was, in his bed, feeling like she'd been with him for centuries. The rest of her awful night tried to claw her illusion of safety to ribbons, but she didn't allow it. Kennedy was a pro at deflecting and evasion. It was part of her trauma response when shit went sideways in her life. That, and always insisting on recovering by herself.

Snap out of it, she bristled. Rolling all the way over to face him head on, she looked into Bane's amber eyes and couldn't stop the cheesy grin from sliding across her face. Man, he looked great. So much better than he had last night when he wouldn't even wake up for her. "How are you feeling?" She cupped the side of his face, loving how he seemed to almost crave her touch.

Bane leaned into her touch, much like a dog would when she

pet it. *Okay, stop comparing Bane to a dog, asshole.* He wrapped his hand around her wrist, pulled her hand off him, and kissed her palm. Weird, right? But it felt nice. Special. Kennedy closed her hand and tucked it between their bodies. The heat radiating off him made her scooch closer.

"I like waking up to you in my bed," he said. His voice was extra gravelly and sleepy.

"I like waking to you in your bed too." And that was also weird.

In the back of her mind, Kennedy knew she was deflecting again. Getting wrapped up in a man who was too good for her. Too innocent for her. Too genuinely nice and wonderful. And though she might deserve a guy like Bane, he didn't deserve to be with a woman like her when she was at this crossroad in her life. She didn't want to drag him into her circus.

Yet she couldn't deny the comfort she felt being here. The instant Bowen brought her inside last night, something awful clicked into place. She'd call it belonging. That's exactly what it felt like. She *belonged* here. Except it wasn't true, and deluding herself right now was a disservice to them both. And when she came upstairs last night and saw Bane whimpering, curled on his side, feverish and shaking, she'd gone into medical mode. Iced him down, held him close. Whispered things to him she had no business saying or admitting. Cried over it because she wished for things she couldn't have, and Bane was a reminder that they were from different worlds.

His house was safe. His family was obviously tight. His brother was wonderful. They had good, big hearts. The longer she stuck around, the more she'd taint them with her toxic family and all that came with it.

"I should probably get going," she suddenly said.

Bane's brow dug in. "You're not leaving here, Kennedy." He shook his head and added, "I mean, you're not a hostage, but... I don't want you to go. Stay."

"I can't."

"Why not?"

Good question. "Because I—" *Because I have to go back to my house and wait for Blade and the rest of the Wolf Pack MC to finish what he started. Because I have to go out and find a new job. Because I have to*

152

fix my busted back door and go grocery shopping. Because I have to go look for my cat... The last made her throat tighten. *Molly*. Tears sprung to her eyes, stinging like a bitch. "My cat ran off," she said.

Hurray for deflecting.

"She's a clever cat." Bane smiled. "I'm sure she'll find her way home."

But home is dangerous, Kennedy wanted to say. But she didn't.

"How about something to eat?" Bane slid off the bed and held out his hand for her. "And a hot shower. Then we can go look for Molly?"

Her throat tightened again. Nodding, she had no words for his kindness. And damn her for wanting so badly to cling to this guy. Sitting up, she swung her legs out, and they hit the hardwood floor. By the time she stood up, she was in productive mode. That gave her some semblance of control. Eat. Shower. Find cat. All three were doable. Yes. This was good.

As she walked across his room, she pointed at the painted symbol. "What is that?"

"It's for protection." Bane shrugged.

"From ghosts?" Hard to believe Bane would be a believer. Then again, she needed to remember she didn't know him as well as she kept thinking she did.

"From lots of bad things." His head tipped to the side. "I put one on your porch. It's small, but..." he stopped talking and shrugged. "Size doesn't matter. Only intent works."

That should weird her out. He just admitted to painting some kind of magic woo-woo-juju thing on her porch. Without her permission. Instead, she felt precious again. And taken care of. Annnd protected. Bane kept doing that. Kept making her feel safe, even while doing things she knew nothing about. "Thanks."

"You're welcome."

They stared at each other, both of them with stupid, super-sized grins on their faces.

"Come on." He grabbed her hand. "You have to be starving."

Kennedy followed him down the steps and into the kitchen. She expected to see Bowen, but he wasn't there. Thank God. She didn't think she'd have the nerve to look him in the eyes after everything that happened last night. But she wanted to thank him.

"What are you in the mood for?" Bane swung open the fridge.

153

Not food.

Kennedy found herself closing the gap between them. She pushed the fridge door shut, and kept her gaze locked on his while she did so. "I don't think I want food." *I want comfort. I want to feel safe.* She didn't say it out loud because it wasn't Bane's job to make her feel safe. The fact that she felt any level of protected under his watchful eyes was strange enough. The last thing she wanted was to get used to it. Start to depend on it.

I shouldn't be here, risking Bane like this. But he and his brother offered her their home, and she wasn't foolish enough to turn it down twice. Not after—

She inhaled a shaky breath. "A shower might be good."

Bane's features softened, as did his tone. "Okay." He rubbed the back of his neck and looked around the kitchen. "How about while you shower, I make some pancakes?"

Carbs cured most heartaches, right? "Okay." If he really wanted to do all the things, she'd let him. This one time. Kennedy wasn't used to people taking care of her. It was usually the opposite. Didn't mean she wasn't above liking or needing the kindness. "I'll umm..." She pointed back at the steps. "I'll go back up then."

"I'll get you fresh towels."

Neither made a move towards the steps. And there were about six feet of floorboards between them, which felt like fifty yards. His gaze dropped to her mouth. She wickedly licked her bottom lip before biting it, enticing him to make the first move.

He stepped closer, reaching out to collar her throat with his large hand. It made it feel caught and wanted. Secure.

Hot.

His thumb rubbed alongside her throat, soothing, lulling. Bane leaned in and sealed his mouth to hers with a slow, drawn out, torturous kiss. He had all day to do this. That's what his mouth said with the way he pressed, nipped, pecked, and slid his tongue across her seam, asking for more. She opened, inviting him in. His tongue was hot velvet. He tasted like bad decisions and glorious promises. Sweet, bold, and addictive.

His other hand slid around her waist, his hand gripping her hip as he deepened the kiss, driving her backwards until her ass hit the fridge. "Fuck the pancakes," he said against her lips. "I just want

154

this." His hand slid up her side, up her back and to the nape of her neck. The one collaring her throat loosened until he cupped the side of her face. Keeping her head cradled, Bane dipped down and kissed her harder this time. Stealing the breath from her lungs.

Kennedy gripped his shoulders, digging her nails into his muscles until she was sure she'd leave little half-moon prints on him. And that pleased her to no end. She wanted to leave her mark on this man. Put a piece of her in him so he'd remember her always.

Bane groaned as he sucked in her bottom lip, teasing and grazing it with his teeth before kissing her again. Deeply. Hungrily. His lips were hot and full. Tongue, dominating. She threaded her fingers through his thick hair, scratching his scalp. He groaned into her mouth again, making her toes curl.

It was getting crazy hot in here.

. He pressed her against the fridge and lifted her arms up over her head. Holding her in place, he kissed along her jaw, neck, and collarbone before biting down on the meaty part between her neck and shoulder.

Kennedy's knees buckled. All medical training, common sense, and human language failed her. He must have realized he'd found a sensitive button on her body because he tugged her shirt down to expose more of her shoulder and bit again. Not enough to break the skin, but—*fuck me now right on this please*—definitely enough to open the floodgates between her thighs.

The room started spinning. The floor went wobbly on her. Heat ignited, growing, expanding, melting everything in its path and oozed out of her pores in a horrendous hot flash.

No! No! No! Her cheeks blazed along with her back, chest, and neck. Bane pulled back, his gaze hardening, while he watched her turn into a wet hot sponge of embarrassment and pent-up sexual frustration. His Adam's apple bobbed when he swallowed. Then a low, deep, rumbling growl vibrated her bones.

It was coming from Bane.

Okay, wow. This was just… yeah. She needed to simmer down. "Shower," she said nervously. They'd gotten too carried away, and seeing that hungry look in his eyes, Kennedy wasn't sure if she should drop on her knees or run for the hills. But that growl? That growl was the scariest, deadliest thing she'd ever heard in real life. It sounded like the thing that haunts her dreams. And it sounded like the wolf that she hit with her car. It was both a turn on and a red flag. But it always served as a reminder of what she had going on right now.

She wanted Bane more than anything, but making selfish decisions at a time like this would only make things worse for both of them. She'd allowed herself to forget that just now. Diverted her attention so successfully, Kennedy nearly collapsed on the kitchen floor in a heap of limbs, orgasms, and… "I'm gonna shower."

"I'll…" Bane cleared his throat as he backed off. "I guess I'll make the pancakes then."

Desperate to get a grip, she hurried out of the kitchen, feeling like it was the opposite of what she should be doing. By the time she reached the bathroom, sweat was pouring off her in rivulets. It was disgusting.

Locking the door, she leaned against it to catch her breath and caught a good look at herself in the mirror. Hair a tangled rat's nest on her head, sweat soaking her shirt, face pale, cheeks bright red, and her eyes were swollen from crying so much during the night. Downstairs, Bane stared at her like she was a Goddess of Lust and Fertility. Seeing the truth, put things in perspective. She was a train wreck.

Getting undressed, Kennedy noticed a bunch of bloody scratches on her legs. And now that she saw them, of course, they all started to sting at the same time. Bruises decorated her upper arms and between her thighs. Kennedy's chin trembled. It took her a full minute to gain enough composure to push away from the locked door, step over her heap of discarded clothes to start the shower.

As she sat on the tub floor, hugging her knees with the water cascading over her head, Kennedy realized she didn't feel like herself anymore. She felt…well, she felt like she did the day Jake went after Lucky…

"What the fuck is going on here?" Jake spoke with his jaw clenched, forcing the anger to slip from between his teeth. His chest heaved with controlled breaths, his hands already fists at his side.

Kennedy was on the floor, too paralyzed with fear to think straight. Her knuckles stung and cheeks tingled as she gawked up at her brother. Words failed her. Fear stole her breath.

156

"What. The fuck. Is going on here, Kennedy?"

"Chill man, we were just – "

Jake clocked Lucky in the jaw, sending him backwards. "I wasn't asking you. I was talking to my sister."

"He... he..." Kennedy couldn't get the words out. "He..."

Lucky was their parent's drug dealer and had come to collect payment.

Their parents weren't home.

It didn't take a detective to put two and two together. Kennedy's biology book lay on the floor, opened face-down. Her can of root beer had spilled all over the coffee table, soaking her notes. She was on the floor, having crab-crawled until her back hit the TV stand. Lucky's face was bloody with scratches and a swollen left eye.

Jake filled in the blanks. "He hurt you." Not a question. A verification.

"He tried," she finally spat out.

That's all it took – two words, one truth – to set Jake off. "You piece of shit!" He shot forward, grabbed Lucky by the shirt collar to hold him steady, then thrust his fist in Lucky's face over and over in quick jabs. Jake was built lean and muscular, his moves fueled with enough anger and resentment to never lose a fight he started.

Kennedy clamped her hands over her ears and curled into a ball on the floor while Jake tore into Lucky. The dealer didn't stand a chance. As the thuds and grunts and sounds of wet gurgles slowed down and stopped all together, she snapped out of her stupor and screamed, "Stop! Enough!"

Jake dropped the unconscious drug dealer onto the floor and turned to Kennedy. He looked wild. Unhinged. Droplets of blood dotted his face. His eyes peeled wide with fury and adrenaline. His fists remained clenched at his side, and he stepped on top of the coffee table, swiftly making his way to her. Squatting down, he said in a dead-calm tone, "Did he get too far?"

Too far? What was too far? He'd grabbed her boob, cupped her crotch and tried to force her to her knees. But... "No."

She felt like she'd told a lie, saying that. Lucky had gone too far. But not as far as Jake so obviously feared. Not nearly as far as it could have gone. Her stomach clenched, realizing what she'd just done. Kennedy had drawn a line for herself. Identified a level of tolerance and survivability when it came to her mind and body.

Jake's tolerance bar was much lower than hers.

"I hate them," he said. "I fucking hate them so much."

Kennedy wished she hated her parents too. It would make her heart

157

stop hurting all the time if she just hated them and walked out. Ran away. But someone needed to take care of them. Someone needed to make sure things stayed okay around here and the bills got paid. She and Jake took that responsibility, and with Jake's track record and reputation, she feared he was going down a road she wouldn't be able to follow.

All because he was their golden child didn't mean he should stay that way. If they were smart, they'd both leave together. Leave their parents to fend for themselves. Let the drugs, cops, or enemies take care of things, so Jake and Kennedy wouldn't be stuck like this anymore.

"Here," he held his hands out and she slipped her cold fingers into his palms. Jake hoisted her up and inspected her arms, neck, and knees first. Then he stared at her hands, noticing the redness on her knuckles. "You get some punches in?"

She nodded, feeling sick to her stomach.

"Good."

"Scratched him too."

"I saw," Jake said before a smirk appeared on his blood-stained face. "You did really good, Kennedy."

She didn't agree. "I didn't realize it was him," she said quietly. "I was studying for my biology test and heard the door open. Thought it was you, so I didn't even look up."

"Not your fault."

"I should have had the door locked."

"Not your fault."

"I should have looked up."

"Not. Your. Fault." Jake grabbed her shoulders, shaking her a little. "Hey, look at me. That piece of shit had this coming to him. And none of it is your fault."

Her chest tightened. Swinging her attention over to the unconscious drug dealer on the couch, it felt like it was all her fault. She'd left the door unlocked. She didn't stay guarded. She'd assumed she was safe in her house.

Sirens went off. Her heart slammed into her chest and gawked at Jake. The blood drained from both their faces.

"Fuck!" Jake panicked. "Fuck, fuck, fuck!"

"Run!" Kennedy all but shoved him out the door, but it was no use. Not in the end.

The cops caught Jake before he made it three trailers down. With his blood-spattered face, busted knuckles, and panicked sprint, he looked every bit as guilty as they accused him of. When they shoved him on the ground,

158

Kennedy screamed for them to stop. She tried to say they didn't understand. Screamed that they were arresting the wrong guy. But Jake was put in the back of a cop car, cuffed and arrested for assault, anyway. Kennedy ran towards him just as they slammed the car door shut. Another officer held her back as she cried and begged for them to not do this.

"Not your fault." Jake said loud enough for her to hear when they cuffed him. He repeated it when they escorted him to the car. Even after the door shut. With the lights flashing, the neighbors all watching, Kennedy crying, Jake stared at her with dead eyes – as if he knew he was going away for a long time already – and he said it again. "Not your fault."

But it was her fault. If she'd been more careful, more aware and alert, Lucky wouldn't have gotten into their house. Had she stayed locked in her room and remained quiet as a mouse, like normal, he might have come in and left without ever even seeing her.

It was her fault the cops had been called. Her screams had attracted attention and concern. If she'd kept her mouth shut, the cops wouldn't have come so fast, and Jake would have had time to get away.

It was her fault Jake beat Lucky to a pulp. She should have lied to him and worked around it. Told him something else instead, because she knew he would never let Lucky get away with touching her. Jake was super protective, and she knew that. She knew he'd beat Lucky up. She said the truth, wanting him to beat Lucky up.

Oh God, this is all my fault. Jake, I'm so sorry.

An ambulance pulled in and eventually the paramedics rolled Lucky out of the trailer on a stretcher. Kennedy wanted to strangle the bastard with his IV tubes and bash his head in with the medical kit. The cops took Kennedy's statement, but even as she told them everything about Lucky...

All they cared about was Jake.

They wanted him locked away. He had priors already, and even if it was small, stupid stuff, his fate was sealed. She knew it. He knew it. The lawyers couldn't work an angle that didn't paint Jake guilty for assault. And judges don't care if you have a good reason to beat the piss out of someone. They saw a drug dealer, a delinquent, and a teenage girl all in a house with no parental supervision. The fact that mom and dad were two club members with drug problems remained hidden because if they were put away too, Kennedy would spend her senior year in the foster care system, which Jake didn't want happening.

So, when he was sentenced to seven years in prison, Kennedy felt like it was All. Her. Fault.

Kennedy crawled out of her head and locked her past back up in its cage. Ice cold water sluiced down her face and body. Holy crap, how long had she been sitting here wasting water and time? A noise made her perk up. Scrambling to turn the water off, she listened for it again. "Hello?"

"Hey," Bane said from the other side of the door. "You okay in there?"

"Yeah." Embarrassment flooded her cheeks. "Be out in a minute!"

"Take your time. Just wanted to check on you."

Was that sweet or overbearing? *Get a grip, you're in his house and likely just used up every drop of his hot water.* She turned the water back on and took a cold shower. It felt like Heaven, even as her nipples hardened into tiny pebbles and her skin was nothing but goosebumps. She sudsed up, rinsed off and hopped out in record time. Snagging a towel from a rack, she was impressed at how neat and tidy the towels were arranged in here. They smelled really good too. Wrapping one towel around her head and another around her body, she clutched it tight and popped her head out of the door. Bane wasn't in there, but a tray of food sat on the bed. Complete with a tiny flower in a shot glass.

Ohhhh this guy! Seriously, they just didn't make men like Bane anymore. He was too good to be true.

Ding! Her cell chimed from her duffel bag, reminding her there were things going on outside this lovely cabin that she needed to stop ignoring. Aggravated about it, she refused to check the message. They could wait.

Bane knocked on the bedroom door. "It's me," he said from the other side. "Can I come in?"

"Yes." She clutched her towel tighter as he opened the door and popped his head in. The concern on his face melted into a playful smile when he saw her. "Brought refreshments." He pushed the door open all the way and carried in another tray of coffee, water, and juice. "Had to use a cookie sheet," he joked. "We only have the one fancy tray and it's not big enough to hold everything I wanted for you."

She looked over at her stack of pancakes and fresh cut fruit displayed on the "fancy tray" sitting on the bed while Bane put the drinks down on his dresser. Her phone dinged again. Then again.

160

Kennedy bit her lip, her heart thudding fast in her throat. She wasn't popping this bubble yet. *Fuck that*, she thought, making her way over to the clothes in her duffel bag. She grabbed what she needed and said, "I'll be right back," and changed in the bathroom. Except she didn't lock the door this time.

Stupidity must be in the air to be this trusting of a man she didn't know, when she couldn't even trust the people she did know and had been around her entire life. Her parents were awful. Her boss was awful. Her "friends" weren't friends. And now she had actual enemies to boot.

As for Jake? She hated to think what category to put him in lately. His actions went against everything he was... *because prison changed him*. Kennedy yanked on a shirt and leggings, feeling too sick to eat the pancakes waiting for her. Brushing past Bane, she snagged her phone from her bag. Bane remained quiet and out of her way. Part of her fantasized chucking the phone out the window. Another part of her wanted to put out all the fires in her life so she could give Bane nothing but the best of her and leave her baggage behind. Yet another part of her ached to be someone else entirely, so this life would end and another could begin. *With Bane.*

If Bane was her forever or her for now, she didn't care. Kennedy just knew he made her feel some kind of way, and it was wonderful.

To see how far things would go with him, she couldn't stand here all day clutching her cell phone. *Handle your shit or ignore it.* If she wanted to spend any time with Bane, Kennedy wanted it to be drama and tension free. Okay... time for a painful reality check. She pulled the cell away from her chest and looked down.

The phone was dead.

For the first time in her life... Kennedy didn't care. That should be a red flag, right?

CHAPTER 23

Bane held his breath when Kennedy glanced at her phone. Whoever was blowing her up was likely going to give her one more hit of anxiety she didn't need. If Bane had his way, he'd fix her life for her. Toss that cell right out his window and offer her a new life right here, right now.

With him.

Instead, like a chump, he asked, "Everything okay?" The worry lines etched into her brow and mouth had eased up when she'd stared down at her phone. Then... a blank expression took over. It made him nervous. In his experience, when a woman made a face like that, it was bad news. It meant their last fuck just flew away, never to be seen again.

"Cell's dead," she answered calmly.

"I have a charger." When she didn't respond, he pressed, "Want me to charge it for you?" Surprisingly, Kennedy handed her phone over to him to plug it in. Seemed silly, but that was a small extension of trust with a personal item. Regardless of her being in his house and all they've done so far, this little thing was still notable. He plugged it in and set it carefully on the table. "How about you eat while it charges?"

Kennedy sat on the edge of the bed and picked up the tray. Not bothering with a fork and knife, or even the syrup, she rolled a pancake up and chomped on it. As if Bane needed another reason to fall in love with her? A woman with a voracious appetite was sexy as hell.

Stifling a hungry growl of desire, he handed over a glass of orange juice. Their fingers brushed as she took the glass from him and chugged it. Handing it back empty, Kennedy wiped her mouth with the back of her hand. "I'm suddenly starving."

She should be, he thought as he sat next to her on his bed. As a primed *Deesha*, she was going through lots of changes. Her metabolism would be shifting...

If she was a *Deesha*.

He couldn't forget his dream. That woman might have been blurry, and Kennedy might also be showing all the significant signs of a Lycan mate, but that didn't mean she was one... or that she was *his*.

The idea of someone else feeding her pancakes, touching her, protecting her, and loving her made Bane want to shred the universe to ribbons. The growl he swallowed moments ago unleashed with a primal edge that made Kennedy's eyes round with terror. She stopped chewing. Swallowed. Gawked at him with a spectacular blush across her cheeks.

She leaned over and kissed him.

Oh. Hells. Yes.

Bane let her lead and set the pace, not wanting to spook her or pop this fantasy bubble. But damn, did his balls tighten and dick harden when she swept her tongue across the seam of his mouth, tempting him to open up and let her in. He did. Threading one hand through her wet hair, he got a good grip and tilted her head back so he could deepen the kiss. She might be setting the pace, but he was setting the bar. Bane wasn't here for tiny pets and little nibbles. He was a Lycan who craved the whole meal and sank his teeth into what he wanted and didn't let go.

Taking charge of the kiss, he let her know his intentions.

With his free hand, he slipped the tray of food off her lap and maneuvered it behind him. At the same time, she twisted and moved until she was standing between his open legs. Bent down, Kennedy braced herself on his shoulders and damn if he didn't grunt with pleasure when her nails bit into his skin.

"Bane," she said against his mouth. Then his sexy *Deesha* made a little noise that set his blood on fire.

Bane pulled back just enough for her to get a good look at what his name on her lips did to him. He knew his eyes were

163

glowing a little. All that Lycan magic burning just below the surface wanted to show itself. He also knew his muscles were tense, making his body harder than granite. And his scent? Yeah, she'd fucking smell it. It permeated the air, calling her into his arms. It's a trifecta of Lycan power that would turn her on and leave her breathless.

And that made two of them.

Kennedy wasn't without an arsenal to overpower his good senses too. Her touch, her taste, her scent, all those little noises she kept making in the back of her throat. It was a miracle the heat between them didn't set the room ablaze.

She stared at him, biting her bottom lip before exhaling a shaky little breath. And that blush in her cheeks started creeping down her neck and below the collar of her t-shirt. Damn, she was stunning.

Bane played with the hem of her shirt, testing how far she might like to go this time. His fingertips barely graced her belly before her breath hitched. Smiling, she pulled her shirt off for him, giving Bane the best view of her hefty cleavage.

He wanted to fuck her tits so bad he almost begged.

Licking his lips, he leaned back on the bed and braced on his elbows, hoping like hell she'd crawl on top of him. Shoving the tray of food clean off the bed, neither of them flinched when it crashed to the floor. She was already between his legs, leaning in and making her way back to his mouth. *Hells. Yes.* Kennedy had so many layers to her, and he was learning and loving each one — her sensitivity, her confidence, her nervousness, and now her lust. He couldn't wait to find out how many more parts of Kennedy he'd get to see.

"Bane," she said against his mouth again.

Might as well be a beast, because she was absolutely his master. "Tell me what you want." *I'll make sure you get it. I'll spend every day making sure you have everything you want and need.*

"I want comfort."

Their gazes locked. He swallowed, unclear on what her comfort levels were. Then he took a chance on what Lycan considered comfort and hoped she was on board.

Running his hands down her arms, along her ribcage, he settled on her generous hips. Running his thumbs back and forth, he loved how soft her skin was. How supple. How divine. With a quick shift of positions, he rolled her over and smiled in triumph. Having her under him did wild things to his system. His wolf howled in his soul. His blood pumped faster in his veins. His gaze latched onto her mouth, and he rubbed his pants-covered-cock along her legging-lined-pussy as he kissed her again.

There was no fight for dominance. She submitted immediately. "I want to be inside you," Bane confessed. "Let me in."

She hooked her legs around his waist and rolled him over so she was once again on top. Talk about a head spinner. This woman owned his ass, dominated in all the right ways for a Lycan like him. He groaned when she raked her nails down his chest. Swallowed hard as he watched her unbuckle his belt.

Silently, they both worked together to pull his jeans off. Next, she pulled his boxers down enough to spring his cock free. "Mmph." She bit her lip and stared at it.

Bane cocked his eyebrow. "You'll give me a complex if you keep looking at it like that."

"I'm going to give myself a complex if I can't at least fit half of you down my throat."

"Shiiit," he whispered when she swirled her tongue along his fat tipped cock. Bane knew he was a big guy. Never expected anyone to try to take him all down. But the way Kennedy went at him, she was hellbent on attempting it.

And he was dying for her to try.

"Fuck, that's hot," he growled, still watching her wet his head and wrap that plump mouth of hers around him. She clutched him with both hands, then lowered her head down to take more of him. Her tongue was hot velvet. She groaned, sending a shiver straight up his dick and through his veins.

Kennedy made it halfway before gagging. And instead of pulling off, she held steady and breathed through her nose. Bane watched, enthralled. Just when he thought the sight couldn't get hotter, she looked up at him, eyes watering.

He tipped his head back in ecstasy. "Fuuuuuck." Gripping his bedspread, Bane nearly ripped the fabric when she bit down and scraped her teeth along his shaft next.

Popping off him and gasping, she flashed him a killer smile. "You taste good."

Bane didn't have time to take a breath or say a word before she sucked him down again. His goddamn eyes crossed. *Holyyyy shiiitt.*

Holding onto his thighs, Kennedy took more of him into her hot mouth. When he hit the back of her throat, she tilted into a different angle to keep going.

"Fucking hell." When he heard her gag again, Bane tore in half. He loved and hated it. Wanted and rejected it. He didn't trust himself to put his hand on the crown of her head. But damn how he wanted to. Imagining grabbing a fist full of her hair, raising his hips, and fucking her mouth would ruin any sliver of control he still owned. And he might hurt her if he unleashed his wild side. So instead of tugging her hair, he gripped the bedding harder. When she popped off him a second time, his vision was blurry and cheeks were numb. His dick was so hard, it was veiny and angry. Desperate to penetrate her wherever she'd allow him in.

Mouth, tits, pussy, ass… in that order would be Heaven.

The mattress moved and next thing he knew, her leggings and shirt somehow gone, as well as her panties, and she straddled his face to sixty-nine him.

Where. The hell. Had this woman been all his life?

Holy mother of all things unholy! With her pussy in his face and her thighs around his ears, Bane's toes curled. Like a starved animal, he shoved his nose and tongue into her wet heat as she started to suck him off again. One taste of her and Bane turned into a greedy, wild animal.

Craziest part was — so had Kennedy.

She sucked him down and took all of him. All. Ten. Inches. Down her goddamn throat.

Bane wasn't going to last. Holding out as long as he could, he slipped two fingers into her pussy and sucked her clit. He was fucking merciless about it. Slamming into her at the perfect angle to hit her g-spot. She came so hard and fast that he didn't even get to use any of his tricks. And when she ground her sweet pussy into his face, riding her orgasm and creaming all over his tongue, nose, and chin like a good girl, his balls tightened, and an orgasm barreled out of him like an out-of-control freight train that went off the rails. Kennedy groaned with her mouth still wrapped around him. *Oh shiiit.* The vibration sent him over the edge. Bane bucked into her mouth just enough to make her clutch his thighs and hold him steady.

"I'm coming," he warned.

It got messy. She pulled back, keeping only the tip in her mouth just as he started shooting hot jets of cum. His cock pumped hard into her mouth too. Throbbing while she used her hands to stroke him. He watched her eyes water. He could hear her swallowing and groaning like she needed his cum in her more than anything else.

And when he was spent, she kept sucking him, tonguing his head until another orgasm threatened to rip through him. Bane shoved his face back between her thighs and inhaled deeply. Hooking her thighs with his arms, he tipped her over and slipped out of her mouth.

Quick as a flash, he stood up and pumped his cock with his hand. Kennedy lay on her back, her legs spread as she played with herself with her head nearly hanging off the side of the bed... right between his legs.

"Greedy girl," he growled playfully. Her lust-filled laugh gave him goosebumps as she lifted her head slightly to take one of his heavy balls into her mouth. He spread his legs wider to give her room. "Fuck, Kennedy." He jerked himself harder while she sucked, pulling his skin taut and making things extra sensitive for him. "Such a good girl."

She groaned again, gripping his thigh with one hand, and grabbed the other. Leaning in, he sucked her fingers, getting them good and wet. "Show me," he grunted, pumping himself harder. "Show me how you like to touch yourself. Let me watch you come."

Kennedy sucked his ball harder, sending a jolt of excitement down his limbs. He watched through hooded eyes as she took her wet fingers and dove between her thighs.

"That's it, Deesha. Give yourself what you want."

He loved that she wasn't shy. Loved that she gave him a show. And he couldn't drag his gaze away from the curves of her hips and softness of her belly as it fluttered with each pant she made. Her little strokes turned into fast flicks. Her thighs spread wider, wider, wider and started quivering.

Bane spit on his hand for extra lube and started pumping himself faster, in time with her strokes. "You're so damn gorgeous.

167

Don't stop, Kennedy. Fuck yourself for me."

She released his balls to let out a gasp. Thighs slamming tight together, her hand lost between them as she bucked through her next orgasm. Bane lost control at the sight of her coming undone. But he wasn't giving in yet. Kennedy's body blushed. A fine sheen of sweat covered her. When she pulled her fingers away from her swollen, wet cunt, he caught her wrist. Bringing her slickened fingers to his lips, he sucked her cream off and shot his load all over her luscious tits and collarbone.

He drenched her in his scent, his essence. His mark. And there was plenty more where that came from. Bane could unload at least six more rounds on, and in her, if she let him.

"Holy shit," Kennedy said, all out of breath. "I had no idea how badly I needed that."

Bane huffed a laugh, torn between cleaning her up and staying enthralled with her on his bed, naked, slobbery, and covered in his come.

It was a serious dilemma — to be a gentleman or be an animal.

Before he could decide, Kennedy dipped her finger in his come and spread it across her chest, then licked her finger. "Jesus, you taste good."

He would to her. As mates, they would taste divine to each other. Was it awful that he almost pouted when she got up and went into the bathroom to wash her chest and face off with a wet towel? Bane followed her in, without even realizing he'd done so. Leaning against the doorjamb, he watched her grab a washcloth from the shelf and wet it. Then she swiped her mouth and neck.

"I almost hate to waste it," she said in the mirror. Her smile was huge.

He was still hard. His hand itching to grip his shaft again.

"You want a fresh one?" she asked, pointing at the stack of towels and washcloths folded on the shelf.

"I'm not washing this off." He licked bottom lip, savoring her taste. "Fuck that noise. I'm *never* washing this off."

She giggled and her cheeks got all rosy again.

How the hell she went from hot, to cold, to scared, to happy, to lost, to comfortable so seamlessly was beyond him. Bane was just happy to see her happy. It looked incredible on her. But now that she was naked and his vision was a lusty haze, he saw things he'd missed before.

Like the bruises on her arms and legs. All the scratches. Yeah, the cuts were from running in the woods—he was accustomed to those since he got them too. But the bruises?

"Who did that?" He couldn't help that his voice dropped to a deadly tone. "Who fucking touched you, Kennedy?"

And just like that, the bubble burst.

"It's nothing," she said, now cleaning his cum off her chest as if it burned her skin to be there at all. "It's totally fine."

He wasn't buying it for a penny. Bane moved closer and when she suddenly took a step back and rammed her ass into his counter and winced, he realized she needed him to move slower or she'd spook.

This woman was an enigma. The way she could take what she wanted one minute and then cower the next was confusing. Then again, humans were complicated creatures with too many emotions always trying to be in the driver's seat.

"I want you to..." Bane bit back his words and rethought them. "I know you're in some kind of trouble," he started to say. "Bowen said he found you in the woods. That someone had been in your house."

Was that jealousy creeping around in his heart because his twin had been there for his girl when he couldn't be? Maybe. He'd get over it.

"I want you safe, Kennedy. You can stay here as long as you'd like, but I want you to also feel safe enough... *comfortable* enough... to tell me what we're up against."

Her shoulders rolled back as she went on defense. "*We're* not up against anything," she said. "And I'm not staying. I can't."

Now he got mad. "Why not?"

"Because I don't know you, Bane!" Her eyes blazed with her rising temper. Tossing her hands in the air, she added, "I shouldn't have come here. This was so stupid."

When Kennedy tried to leave the bathroom, he blocked her way, not caring if it made him an asshole. "I'm just asking you to trust me."

"We're nowhere near that level yet." She tossed the washcloth into the open hamper and crossed her arms. "Wow, I jump out of the frying pan and into the fire every fucking time."

Bane didn't take the bait. "Who gave you the bruises? Was it Jake?"

Worst accusation he ever made. Kennedy reared up on him so fast, he actually backed up. If any Lycan saw him do that, they'd hand him his balls. But he wasn't dealing with another Lycan. He was dealing with a fated *Deesha*. That meant he backed up and gave her some dominance.

Kennedy's mouth opened and closed like a fish. Her eyes shined with unshed tears.

His heart fractured that she was still trying to fight her battles by herself. He was in her life now, which meant she'd never be alone again.

But she didn't know that yet.

"God, Kennedy," he whispered, coaxing her to come to him with a gentle tug of her hand. She allowed it.

By the time he had both arms wrapped around her, she was crying in his chest. "My brother is a good guy, but he's with some bad people. One of them attacked me at home and I bashed his head with a frying pan. He had Molly in a pillowcase."

Bane's heart thundered in rage.

"And then I ran out of my house but didn't have anywhere to go and no one to call. My cell and everything were left behind. I waited until I thought it was safe enough to go back to my house, but it was so dark, and I have no idea how I even ran that far through the woods to begin with. I figured it must have been a short distance, and I'd be able to find my way back, but I couldn't. And I was too scared and tired to keep trying. Then your brother just appeared out of nowhere and — "

The rest was history.

"Thank you," he said, kissing the top of her head. "Thank you so much for trusting me enough to tell me all that."

"Bowen told you all that already," she hiccupped in his chest.

"He really didn't tell me much. Just that he found you in the woods and your clothes were ripped."

She pulled back and wiped under her eyes. "He tried to get me," she said.

"Who?"

"Blade. He tried to..." she shook her head, "I got him with the frying pan before he could rip my underwear too."

170

It took every ounce of control Bane possessed to not shift immediately and hunt this motherfucker down this instant. He physically shook with rage. Clutched his *Deesha* tighter. His muscles tensed and nostrils flared while he worked to contain his anger. He needed to keep a lid on his aggression because he didn't want to scare Kennedy.

His wolf, however, was another beast entirely. He clawed and gnashed and howled and snapped his teeth. A growl tore out of Bane's mouth and Kennedy hugged him tighter, as if she needed to hear the animal rise out of him. She had no idea how close she was to seeing that happen.

"I didn't want you to be part of this," she said quickly. "I didn't want you to know what a shitshow my life is. But then Bowen said you were hurt, and I was already in danger and when he insisted on bringing me here to you, I packed my shit and came. I don't even know why! I don't know you. I can't just do things like this. And I did it anyway."

His vision hazed red. His wolf howled. The marrow in his bones boiled. Inhaling her scent, Bane kissed the top of her head again and rubbed her back. "I'm glad," he said with an impossibly deep voice. "I want to protect you. You should be here with me. And I know you don't know me well, but you will. Trust when I say I'll never let anything or anyone hurt you ever again."

His wolf attacked him from the inside. Bane's knees nearly buckled. If he shifted now, he'd lose her for good. Clinging to his fraying control, Bane swallowed the lump in his throat.

Kennedy pushed away and said, "Jake's in this stupid Wolf Pack MC. Has been since he got out of prison. They wanted something from me, and I couldn't get it. I refused. Blade came back to make good on his threat."

"And now I'm going to make good on mine." Bane cupped her face. "I mean it when I say I'll do anything to protect you, Kennedy."

Her relief was palpable, even though she tried to fight him on it. "You don't know me."

"I do."

"How can you say —"

"And you know me too." Bane's wolf howled, rattling his teeth as he clamped his mouth shut to keep his beast silent. Taking

171

in a few measured breaths, he finally said, "We're in this together, okay? No matter what."

She shook her head. "I don't want you involved."

"Too late."

"I can't let you—"

"I'm asking you to trust me. I'm asking you to let me keep you safe. Going back to your house and waiting for another attack is *not* an option." Bane tipped her chin up, so she'd look him in the eyes. "And you can't go to work always looking over your shoulder."

Her brow pinched together. "I don't even have a job anymore." Her temper rose to a new heat level, and she shoved him back. "God, I feel like a train wreck admitting all this to you. Just stop!"

"Not happening." He stepped forward, forcing her to either stand her ground or back up. She backed up, damnit. "I'm going to protect you, whether you want me to or not."

"Why?"

"Because you're mine." It slipped out. That totally, one hundred percent slipped out. He meant to say *"because it's the right thing to do"* but his mind and mouth were short-circuiting. "And you know it," he added, because why not go for gold?

Kennedy bit her bottom lip and swiped her tears away again. "This is crazy."

"Doesn't mean it's not true."

"We don't know each other well enough for this level of nuts."

"We might have just met but..." at the risk of sounding like an over-the-top whacko he said, "we know each other well enough to want one another. For keeps." If she rejected him now, he wasn't sure what he'd do. Holding his breath, he watched a million emotions dance in her eyes, one after another. "Do you feel it?" he whispered. "Do you feel our connection?"

Please say yes. Please say yes. Please say—

"I'm... I'm not sure what I feel," she whispered.

"Do you feel safe with me?"

"Yes," she said without hesitation.

Okay, that's one win for Bane. How many more could he get? "Do you want to stay here, with me?"

172

Kennedy hesitated. "Yes," she finally said, though her voice small and laced with disappointment. "And that's my hang-up. I don't know you. I don't want you to know me like this. And I can't depend on you to keep me safe. I'm not a bunny rabbit in a wolf den, Bane. I'm a grown ass woman."

Wow. Okay. Think before you speak, Bane. Think before you... "And you're incredible at handling things on your own. I'm not trying to take your independence away, nor am I trying to make you dependent on me. But I can't just sit here and watch someone need help and not offer it, especially you. I *want* to help you. I want to help *protect* you." *More than anything in the world.* "And I want you to feel like you can come to me when you need help." *But you are a bunny in a wolf den. At least until I make you a wolf like me.* "What kind of man would I be if I took you back to your house and dropped you off, knowing there's someone out there who might try to attack you again?"

"Someone who minds his own business," she said while crossing her arms. But then her eyes filled with tears again and her cheeks turned red. "I feel like..."

He swallowed the lump lodged in his throat. Pushing down his wolf's howl, Bane waited for her to gather the courage to say exactly what was on her mind. Risking rejection, he reached out and rubbed her upper arms. Lycan craved touch. The animal in them enjoyed nuzzling, cuddling, nipping and rubbing bodies. With her naked, and the scent of her pussy still lingering on him, Bane struggled to not grab her and sling her back on the bed to love her thoroughly and properly. "What do you feel like?"

"I don't know how to do this," she finally confessed. Her shoulders bunched, but she didn't pull away from him, even as he brought her in closer.

"What can't you do?" Because he was pretty certain she could do anything she put her mind to.

"I can't depend on you." She looked up at him with guilt-filled eyes. "But I can't walk away from you either. I don't want to."

His chest puffed out with pride. "Good."

"It's not good!" she shoved away and stormed out of the bathroom to grab her clothes and get dressed. "This is going to end horribly."

"Or maybe it won't end at all."

Kennedy shoved her head through her shirt and tugged it down. "Like you want to get involved with a shitshow like me? My life is a mess right now, Bane."

"I don't mind messes."

"I do."

"That's on you then, Kennedy. I'll take you however you are. Raw, independent, feisty, busy, upset, mad, confused, exhausted, happy... the only thing I won't tolerate is you being scared."

She slumped on the edge of his bed and ran her hands through her dark hair. "You say the right things. But you'll run. And I won't blame you when you do."

"How about you ease up on assuming you know what I'll do, okay? Like you said already, a dozen times, you don't know me." Bane leaned against the doorjamb still naked. "Do I look like I'm ready to run?"

Kennedy stared at his face, then let her gaze sail down his body, nice and slow. She swallowed hard. Her hands trembled a little in her lap. But he stood stock-still and allowed her to have her fill of the view he offered. He wasn't going anywhere, and they both knew it.

This was as vulnerable as he'd ever been... and the most confident too.

He knew his heart—she was sitting on his bed, confused by her feelings.

Maybe Kennedy never had someone like him in her life before. Maybe she was scared to let a permanent man into her one-person salt circle. Kennedy might think her brother was the only person who truly cared about her, but she was wrong. Bane cared. Shit, Bane more than cared. And her life wasn't a shitshow, it was just difficult right now. But that would soon change when he turned her into a Lycan.

"Your leg." She pointed at his upper thigh. "How'd you get that scar?"

Oh. Shit. The damn scar still hadn't completely faded from the other night. "Accident."

"Must have been a doozy."

"Nothing that couldn't heal," he shrugged.

"What happened?"

She's deflecting, he thought. Or trying to pull out any

174

vulnerability or imperfection she could about in order to put them on even ground in her head. He'd asked about her cuts and bruises, now she was asking about his. He didn't mind in the slightest.

Didn't mean he wasn't going to evade the hell out of it though.

No way would he lie to her and make up some bullshit story about how he got injured. And no way was he going to tell her the truth yet.

Fortunately, fate stepped in before he could open his mouth. Her cell charged enough to resume dinging like crazy and she crawled across the bed and snatched the thing, leaving Bane and her unanswered questions behind.

He watched her face drain of color as she read her text messages. Started walking around the bed, towards her, when he heard her breathing pick up. He even knelt and rubbed her thighs to offer comfort as she started to tremble.

"It's Jake," she said, looking up at Bane with an apologetic gaze. "I have to go."

CHAPTER 24

When was she going to learn? Kennedy was up to her tits in danger and would drown before she could get herself out of it. Dragging Bane in with her was the worst decision she could make, but damn if she could find it in her to go see her brother alone. "Can you take me to him?"

"Absolutely."

"He might have others with him," she warned.

"All the more reason to stay by your side.

What was with this guy? Did he have some kind of hero complex? She'd heard of men who were genuinely good guys — the ones who gave you the shirt off their back and all that — but never actually met one for real.

In her experience, people acted like the good guy until their true colors showed.

What were Bane's true colors?

As he quickly grabbed his clothes and got dressed, she tried to figure him out. He was calm and collected. Seemed rock solid with his emotions. But there was something he was hiding from her. This might sound so mean and shitty, but Bane reminded her of a dog who dug up the garden out back but came inside with a guilty conscience, tail not wagging, and acted just a little off... until you went out back and saw what he did.

For the love of Kibbles and Bits, this was the second time she'd referred to Bane as a dog. God, she was such a bitch.

No pun intended.

As Bane got dressed and put on his shoes, Kennedy ran through Jake's texts again.

Jake: Where are you?

Jake: Are you okay?

Jake: Answer your phone.

Jake: Call me back.

Jake: Kennedy answer me.

Jake: NOW KENNEDY

Jake: WHERE ARE YOU?

Jake: FUCKING DAMNIT K. CALL ME BACK.

Jake: I'm coming over.

Jake: Where are you?

Jake: KENNEDY WHERE ARE YOU?

Jake: Jesus fucking Christ K call me. I can't find you anywhere.

Jake: Come home. I'll wait.

He also left two voicemails and called an additional six times. She didn't even bother listening to his voice messages. They'd just be him screaming and cussing at her because he was mad and scared, too. He must have found out about Blade. And if he went to her house, he'd see the shamble in her kitchen and the bloodstains on the floor.

Good. She wanted Jake to see it all. Needed him to get slapped in the face with the reality of their situation and understand exactly what happened when he put her in the center of his firing squad of "friends".

But she hated that Bane was going to see it too. And now that he was dressed and standing in front of her, ready to go, she found herself scrambling for an excuse to make him stay here while she went to meet Jake alone.

God, the thought of being alone though? It made her stomach twist. Jake might not be the only one waiting for her. And he might not be able to protect her by himself if that was the case.

"I know I shouldn't go," she said out loud. "But I can't not go."

"He's your brother." Bane shrugged. "I get it. Got a twin, remember? We sometimes do things we normally wouldn't when our family's involved."

"It's more complicated than that. He went to prison for me, Bane." There. It's out. Let it be one more step for him to take down

177

her little rabbit hole. "Back in my senior year of high school, our parent's dealer came to the house and tried to take payment from me. Jake came in just as Lucky got started. He beat him within an inch of his life and went to prison for it. For me."

Something in Bane changed at that moment. His head tilted with an eyebrow cocked. "I might end up actually liking your brother after all."

She almost smiled. Jake and Bane would make great friends if it wasn't for one thing. "He's in this motorcycle club that's... into shit. I don't even know what all they're doing, but I know they're into dog fights. Jake brought me one of their animals to try and save. I couldn't. Whatever attacked it was..." she shivered at the memory. "It tore it all to pieces."

"Jesus."

"Mmm hmm." Kennedy might as well go all in seeing how hellbent Bane was to be with her. If she told him everything, he'd at least be able to make an educated decision on whether she was worth the trouble or not. "Jake's always kept me separate from the rest of his life. They didn't even know he had a sister until that night with the dog. I guess they tailed him. And when they pulled up on their bikes at my clinic, I saw Jake scared for the first time in my life. He wasn't even scared when they sentenced him in court. Never flinched in a fight. But that night? He was fucking terrified."

"What happened when they saw you guys?"

"Long story short? They tossed money on the table and said I was on retainer to help stitch them up on an as needed basis. And then two of them said I had three days to get animal tranquilizers or else."

Bane's gaze flitted to her crotch. It was such a slight move, but it felt like a major shift between them. "I'm going to kill them."

"Jake might have already," she warned. "If Blade came back and everyone saw what I did to him with that frying pan, and Jake was there? He'll murder Blade."

"I'm starting to really love your brother."

"This isn't a joke, Bane." Kennedy slapped her thigh in frustration. "Damnit. Do you not hear what I'm fucking telling you? Dog fights. Illegal shit everywhere. Murder. Do you understand that if you stay in my life, I'll end up dragging you down with me? You might think you're a life raft for me, but I'll poke holes in you

178

somehow and you'll sink with me."

"Good thing I'm more buoyant than I look."

God damnit! He wasn't getting this! "Bane!" Now she was pissed off. "Are you crazy? *Listen* to me!"

"*I am listening to you!*" he roared. His voice boomed in the room and caused her heartrate to escalate. She froze as he roared, "I hear you're in trouble. I hear someone's threatened you. I hear someone's already tried to attack you and you had to fight them off by yourself! *I hear you, Kennedy!*" His chest heaved with heavy, angry breaths. Even his eyes looked like they were on fire. "Now *you* need to listen to *me*. If I say I want to protect you, I mean it. If I say I'm going with you to make sure you stay safe, I mean it. When I tell you I don't care how bad it gets because I'm gonna always be there to protect you, *I fucking mean it*. This isn't some boy scout bleeding heart bullshit, Kennedy. There's nothing I wouldn't do for you. You're my —"

He stopped himself.

"What?" she asked, urging him to finish his last sentence. Kennedy stepped closer to him. "I'm your what?"

"You're my *Deesha*."

He couldn't lie. Not to her. It felt like the worse thing in the world to say it like this. She wouldn't understand what he meant, and now wasn't the time to explain.

"You've called me that before," she said calmly. Too calmly. "What's it mean?"

"It means," he said with a sigh. "It means..." *fuck, fuck, fuckity fuck.* "It means we need to get going, okay? Call Jake and tell him we'll meet him in town. At the convenience store on Buckleberry and Anderson."

"He's at my house," she argued. "We can just go there."

"And risk walking into a trap?"

Kennedy got good and pissed. "Jake wouldn't trick me."

"Jake wouldn't, but what if that's not Jake who texted?" Bane cocked his brow, letting that sink in. "Or what if Jake's there with some of the others? You said it yourself. He fears them. He's not the Alpha there. He's a Hunter at best, but I'm betting nothing more

179

than an Omega."

She shook her head, this cute little crinkle forming between her eyes as she thought it through. "You've taken the Wolf part of the Wolf Pack a little too far."

No, he hadn't. MC clubs worked similarly to packs.

"Either way," Bane argued. "He's not in charge. And if they know you're his sister, Kennedy, they now know his weakness. We'll meet him someplace in broad daylight with lots of cameras and witnesses. At best, he's alone and you two can have a private conversation. At worst, we'll have the public eye on our side and whoever is with Jake won't be able to do shit to you." Not that Bane would let anyone touch her ever again, but humans have some common sense — usually — so if Jake came with "friends" they would have a harder time acting on their impulses this way.

And Bane would have trouble acting on his.

Make no mistake, he would take Blade and anyone else who threatened Kennedy down. Just not today. Bane couldn't shift in daylight and attack these assholes on the street without being seen. And he wasn't calling for backup yet either. Let's face it, Bowen would jump at the chance to fight, and hell, so would a bunch of other local Lycan, but Bane wasn't going that far yet. If it was just Jake who showed up, Bane would have plenty of opportunities to go after the rest of the Wolf Pack MC later.

He'd make sure of it.

Kennedy texted Jake back, telling him she was safe and that she'd meet him at the Gas and Go in an hour. When they pulled up, Jake wasn't there, and Kennedy's tension was tight enough to snap like a rubber band.

They waited ten minutes before she called him. He didn't answer his phone.

"Wait a little longer," she said quietly.

"Not going anywhere until you say so." Bane reached over and rubbed his hand on her knee.

Finally, they saw him pull up in a pickup truck on the other side of the gas station. Kennedy blew out a relieved exhale, fumbling with the door handle. "Finally."

"Want me to go with you?"

"No," she said fast. "It's fine."

"If you need me, just whistle."

She nodded and hopped out of his truck, then walked over to meet her brother halfway in the parking lot. Jake's face was bruised and swollen. Enough to see it from fifty feet away and make Bane suck in a hiss between his teeth. Someone did a job on him. Didn't take a genius to figure out who.

What had Bane's hackles raised was that he was here alone. Beaten and scared... *and set loose.*

As wily as Jake might think he was, his crew was smarter and stronger. They didn't let him go out of mercy. This was far from over.

Bane split his attention between his *Deesha* and the public. Ears perked to count the engines running, eyes flicking all over the lot, he made sure no one new pulled in without him seeing. Hand hovered on the doorhandle, he was prepared to lunge out and attack in the blink of an eye, if the need arose.

So far, so good.

Kennedy's hands were flying all over the place, her voice loud enough for Bane to hear just fine with his Lycan sensitivities. She was crying. Worried sick about him. Jake matched her energy. They were like a diabolical pair of animals who bounced off each other aggressively, but in the end hugged.

Jake gestured towards his truck. Kennedy gripped the sides of her head and made a mad dash for it.

Bane's heart leapt in his throat. Was she taking off with him? He gripped the door handle tighter, preparing to jump out of his truck when he froze. If she wanted to run... he couldn't chase her like a predator. It wasn't right.

It was necessary.

No, it was stalkerish.

No, it was the best thing for her.

No, it was—

Kennedy swung open the passenger side door to Jake's truck, leaned in, and pulled out her cat. Sobbing, she clung to Molly with all her might as Jake rubbed her arm and then escorted her back to Bane's truck.

Jesus, the closer he got, the worse he looked. Bane hopped out of his truck and tossed Kennedy a smile. *Keep calm. Don't be aggressive. Stay chill.* "Got your cat back, huh?"

"Can you believe it? Jake found her on the roof of my house.

She made it home."

To see the expression on his *Deesha's* face while she held the one piece of stability she owned, made something in Bane crack into pieces. He reached out and scratched under Molly's neck. "We'll stop at the store and pick her up a new litter box, food and whatever she needs."

Kennedy swayed with relief. "Thank you."

No clue if she was thanking him or Jake.

"She's staying with *you*?" Jake asked, tilting his head to the side.

"Yeah." Bane had a good sixty pounds of muscle on Jake. And nearly six inches of height. He used every bit of it when he glowered at the human.

Jake wasn't intimidated. "And you are?"

Her mate. Her protector. Her lover. "Bane."

"*Bane*," Jake repeated like he didn't believe it. "How long have you been seeing my sister?"

"Long enough to know she's in trouble and needs help and protection." The energy between them was charged enough to hotshot a battery with. "She was attacked in her home," Bane growled. "She won't be attacked in mine."

Jake actually dropped his gaze. A submission. Glad to see this guy knew who held more power between them. Maybe he wasn't as stupid as Bane thought.

"Keep her there," Jake ordered. "Don't let her go back home for any reason until I say so."

Little did this guy know, Kennedy wasn't going home ever again. She was staying with Bane forever. "Whatever your little biker boy band is up to?" Bane seethed as he shoved his finger in Jake's direction. "It's not touching Kennedy ever again. Understood?"

"It won't." He didn't even try to be the tough guy.

Bane almost felt bad about it. Not enough to give him a pep talk, but… damn, this guy was likely in his mid-thirties and looked like he was pushing fifty. His life hadn't been kind to him, and it showed. Bane didn't want Kennedy anywhere near that level of danger.

"Handle your shit," Bane said before swinging his gaze to his *Deesha*. "You ready to get out of here?"

182

"Yes," Kennedy said.

"Remember what I told you," Jake warned her. "I fucking mean it, okay?"

She bit her lip and nodded. Holding Molly close, she climbed into Bane's truck and slammed the door shut without saying goodbye.

Jake stared at her through the windshield. His jaw clenching while he ground his molars. Bane took the opportunity to study the guy further. He was cold, angry, and resentful. His scent carried fear, booze, and a sweet perfume leftover from a woman. When his gaze swerved and locked onto Bane's, he didn't blink. His bloodshot eyes were hard even though they were swollen, and his mouth set in a scowl. But even with his razor-sharp edges and bruising, he looked a lot like Kennedy. It made Bane want to help the bastard despite his better judgement.

Jake gave him a once over. "You hurt her and I'll kill you."

I'd love to see you try. "Worry about your boys. I'll take care of my girl."

They turned and walked away from each other.

"Hey!" Jake called out, halfway back to his truck, walking backwards. "Don't let her give you whiplash with her emotions. She's had to be on her own since we were kids. She lashes out a lot. Deflects. Evades. She'll distract you so you don't focus on what matters."

Been there, done that, Bane thought. Kennedy had used those tactics from night one.

"Don't let her scare you off," Jake said.

"I don't spook easily."

Jake wasn't as bad as he thought... but he wasn't good enough for Kennedy either. As Bane watched him walk off, another fissure spread through his cracked heart. "Hold up." He stormed over, a little pissed that Jake would let his sister go off with a mere stranger. Didn't matter if Kennedy was a grown ass woman or not, she was already in danger with other guys in Jake's life. How could Jake just let her go off with Bane? "You don't want to know where she's staying?"

Jake's teeth clenched. Squinting against the sun, he looked over Bane's shoulder to where Kennedy sat waiting in the truck. "The less I know, the better at this point." He scratched his neck and

183

said, "That goes both ways." He swallowed, his brow pinching together. "Take care of her for me."

Something squeezed Bane's heart. *Take care of her for me.* It wasn't an order. It was a goodbye.

Jake hopped in his truck and took off.

CHAPTER 25

Three hours later, they pulled back up to Bane's cabin and Kennedy was so tired she could barely keep her eyes open. Stress made her sleepy. Naps were a great escape from reality, and she needed one right now. Holding Molly, she went up the porch steps without saying a word and left Bane to carry all the new cat stuff he insisted on buying instead of just getting from her house. The worst part was, she was glad for the pseudo-fresh start—even if it was just a litter box and food bowls.

I can't stay here, though. Not forever. This isn't a fresh start, it's temporary housing. She'd be parasite if she stayed. A plague upon Bane's house. Holding Molly close, she kissed her cat's head and asked Bane, "Are you sure Bowen won't mind Molly?"

"It's fine," Bane smiled. "Bowen can adjust to a damn cat."

Once inside, she set Molly down. The cat dashed off under the sofa in the living room. Kennedy didn't have the energy to try to coax her out. But she needed to do *something*. Feeling useless made this situation worse. "I can take those." She reached out to snag the box of litter and bag of food from Bane.

"It's fine."

"I said I've got it!" *Okay, stop snapping. He doesn't deserve your attitude. Calm your tits.* "Sorry, I just..." Just what? She had no excuse for herself.

"Here." Bane handed her a bag. "How about you take this and get Molly's food set up. I'll find a spot for the litter."

She took the bag and went into the kitchen to make up a little food and water station in the corner by the fridge. It took a whopping five minutes, then she was twiddling her thumbs and feeling shitty again. Sitting at the kitchen table, Kennedy held her head in her hands and went over the conversation she'd had with Jake earlier.

God, his face. Jake didn't mention who beat the piss out of him, but she didn't need to hear Blade's name to know it was him. *I should have bashed Blade's head in and not stopped until he was dead.* Because once again, Jake was suffering on behalf of Kennedy.

She couldn't help but think Bane would be next.

If she had any courage at all, she'd cut and run. Except Jake stressed the fact that she couldn't go back home. Not now, at least. It was something she'd yet to tell Bane, so when he said he didn't think it was a good idea to go back for the cat stuff, she didn't make a peep about it.

And going by the look of fear on Jake's battered face, this was going to get worse before it got better. Shit. Kennedy might have to leave town entirely and change her name. *Damnit, Jake!* She scrubbed her face with both hands, fighting back her tears. She hadn't cried this much since she was a teenager. It pissed her off. Wolf Pack MC her ass. They were more like Monsters R Us.

And they had Jake under their boot.

"Litter box is in the laundry room," Bane said from across the kitchen. "Not sure if it'll work since it's a tight space in there, but we can try it and see."

"Why are you doing all this?" Kennedy stopped rubbing her temples and looked over at him. "Why, Bane?"

"I told you already." He sat down across from her at the table.

"This is too much, too soon."

"You don't have much of a choice right now, Kennedy." Bane clenched his jaw a few times before adding, "And as for what I can handle, that's up to me."

It's not your threshold I'm approaching, she thought. "I'm not sure how much I can handle."

"Good thing you don't have to do any of it alone, huh?"

"That's not what I—"

Bane leaned over the table and kissed her, shutting her up in a very effective way. "Come on. Let's lay down for a bit."

She let him lure her out of the kitchen and up the steps. By the time they were halfway to his room, her feet were dragging. He opened the door, ushering her in, and even pulled the covers down for her. "I feel like it's been days since we were in this bed." When it had only been a few hours.

"All the more reason to catch some Z's." Bane patted the mattress. "Come on."

She was too defeated to fight him about it. Laying on her side, she faced the windows and sighed when he big spooned her. "I don't deserve this," she said quietly. "None of it. Not what Mark did. Not what Blade did. Not what Jake's done. And… not you."

"Shh," Bane kissed the back of her shoulder, and she felt it zoom through her entire body. "Rest, Kennedy."

She closed her eyes and passed out.

Never thought the world could fit in his hands, but here she was. His world, all tucked up good and close to him so he could shield her while she slept. There was something insanely satisfying about having a woman fall asleep in one's arms. A hefty amount of trust and dependency came with such a thing. Bane remained Kennedy's harness, shield, radiator, and second skin while she snored, sighed, and breathed heavily for hours. The longer he held her, the more he wanted to mark her.

It was a test of wills between him and his wolf.

Kennedy probably thought she was tired from stress, and that might be part of it. But her body was preparing itself. As a fated *Deesha*, she would experience a myriad of symptoms like insatiable hunger, hot flashes, exhaustion, body aches, and her scent would strengthen from pheromones kicking into high gear to match his.

That meant others would be attracted to her, which put her at risk of sexual assault. Only gentlemen had control and morals. Bane had lived long enough to know there were few gentlemen left in this world, and counted himself among those remaining.

It pissed him off that her sexuality could jeopardize her safety. Women had a hard enough time as it was out in the big, cruel world. A primed *Deesha* was even more vulnerable to attack. A low growl rumbled in his chest when he thought about other predators trying to take a bite of his girl.

At least she was equipped to defend herself. Kennedy's strength, agility, and stamina were all perks of a *Deesha*.

She could run for miles, pack one helluva punch, and likely heal fast. She would also be able to fuck for hours. Just like Bane.

Her perfume wafted into his nose, as if her body sensed how close he was to unleashing. It taunted him. Teased him. Boosted and bewildered him. Bane couldn't wait to sink his teeth into her. Bury his cock in every hole she allowed him to and come everywhere he could.

Down boy.

His wolf howled, the sensation not its normal thrill down his spine, but more of an ear-piercing, chest vibrating high-pitched tone that made him flinch. Shit. Bane kept forgetting he was in danger himself. Staying worried about Kennedy meant he'd let his fate simmer on the back burner. He'd yet to turn. Too scared to do it and not be able to shift back, Bane knew his wolf was suffering, and it killed him. They were the same, he and his wolf. There was never a dividing distinction between man and animal. Hell, he was more a twin to his wolf than he was with his identical twin, Bowen. But ever since he drank the silver…

There was now a tear at the seam of his soul and it was starting to rip them in two.

He needed to work faster. He had about three weeks left to make Kennedy his mate. Twenty days to woo her and make her fall in love with him. Four-hundred and eighty hours — give or take — to bite and turn her into a Lycan. And that was if he even had his days straight, which he wasn't confident in. All the nights since he drank the silver had melted into one another. He didn't know if it was Tuesday or Sunday or…

Holy shit. His heart pounded like a ticking timebomb.

He had roughly twenty-eight thousand, eight hundred minutes to make the mating happen, or all was lost. Every second, every heartbeat that thumped by, was another step closer to his doom. Was this really enough time to make the shift?

Hollyyyy fuuuuuck. Her shift. Bane's heart dropped to his balls. What if she didn't survive her first shift? I'll talk her through it. We'll go slow and steady. She could handle it. God, just look at her. Bane kissed her temple. She was the strongest woman he'd ever met in his life. She could absolutely survive the turn and first shift.

Only then would he be saved. Only then would his wolf be under control. Only then would this nightmare be over for both of them.

But...

Rolling onto his back, he let Kennedy go and scrubbed his face with both hands. *But what about that other woman I dreamt of?* It was easy to forget it wasn't just Kennedy he'd dreamed of after taking the silver. And that could very well be his downfall. Kennedy might not be his *Deesha*. And if she wasn't, Bane was well on his way to damning her soul to live a cursed life as a Lycan until she found her mate.

And he'd be lost to his wolf—unable to protect and love her as she was meant to be loved.

Make no mistake, the blood curse transferred.

It was one of the many reasons Lycan didn't go around turning everyone they caught feelings for into creatures like them. They were as close to immortal as it got and gifting that magic to another wasn't generous. It was selfish. Those who "infected" humans in the past to be with them longer were assholes and punished accordingly. No matter how badly you want someone to be with you for eternity, biting and turning them shouldn't be an option unless you know it's your *Deesha*.

If he was wrong about Kennedy, there'd be no time to punish Bane for it. His wolf would take over at the next full moon and his worst nightmare would become reality. For the ten billionth time, Bane's thoughts wandered to Killian. His little brother hadn't found his *Deesha* in time. That night, when he made his final shift, Bowen, Emerick and Bane had been there to see it.

It was gruesome and soul shattering.

Bowen still had nightmares about it. Bane still woke up some nights screaming Killian's name. They'd lost their younger brother over two years ago, yet the pain was still a fresh wound the entire Woods family felt daily.

Bane might be next.

Would his parents survive losing two of their kids? No, not two, *three*. Because Bowen would insist on shifting to stay with Bane until the bitter end. Bowen was too Alpha for someone to change his mind—stubborn asshole—but his wolf was just as powerful, which could mean once Bowen stayed a wolf for a long period of

189

time, his wolf could very well take over and never let the man free again.

Lycan were aggressive creatures. Pack-minded. Voracious, protective, and stubborn as hell. Their wolves had a lot to do with that.

A door slammed downstairs, snapping Bane out of his thoughts. *Bowen's home.* The relief was short-lived. Bane heard Bowen stomp across the hardwood floor into the kitchen. Next, the fridge door opened and slammed closed. Bane's ears perked at the sound of a water bottle cracking open. The plastic crackled under his brother's fist as he drained the thing and tossed the crushed-up trash in recycling.

Any minute now, Bane thought, holding his breath. *Any —*

Bowen growled long and slow. Next came a hiss. "You've got to be fucking kidding me."

Bowen just found the cat.

"Bane!"

Damnit. He was going to wake Kennedy yelling like that. Bane slid out of bed as careful as he could then headed downstairs. Molly was rubbing against Bowen's leg, leaving white and brown fur all over his dark jeans. Bowen's scowl was comical. "No."

"It's her cat."

"Nope. Nuh uh. Not happening."

"It's a damn cat, not a hippo."

"Do you remember the time you brought in the skunks and the mess they made?" Bowen tried to step back to get Molly off him, but she just twirled between his legs in a figure eight.

"That was different. Those skunks were defenseless." Not his fault they were learning how to work their spray glands when Bane brought them home. "Besides, that wasn't here. It was at Mom's."

"You always bring in strays."

"This isn't a stray. It's Molly, Kennedy's cat. It's the only thing she has that's stable in her life."

"And if one of our wolves eats it?" Bowen jiggled his leg to get Molly off. She purred loudly and climbed his leg like a tree. Undeterred by his growls, she snagged his shirt with her claws and kept climbing until she reached his shoulders. Bowen deadpanned Bane, "This animal has zero survival instincts."

"She likes you." Bane laughed. "In cat speak, this..." he

twirled his finger at Bowen and Molly, who just draped herself across the back of his shoulder, forcing him to hold her backend like an infant, "means you're the chosen one. Feel special."

Bowen snarled.

"Come on, brother. It's a cat."

"It's dinner if our wolves get to it." Bowen peeled the cat away from him. She snagged his t-shirt and ripped two holes in it. "Damnit, get off me!"

Bane gently peeled Molly away. She was easy to maneuver, especially when she realized Bane was the one to do it. She curled into his arms like a baby, and he cradled her, scratching her head and behind the ears. He had a terrible feeling he was going to enjoy spoiling this furball as much as he was going to love spoiling his *Deesha*.

Bowen stepped back from the two of them. "Have you told her yet?"

"No." There hadn't been time to discuss the whole, *Oh hey, I'm a Lycan and you're my fated mate* talk yet. "We met her brother and spoke with him. He knows she's staying with me."

"And does he know where we live?" Of course, Bowen was going into defense. He didn't like anyone knowing where they lived, and given the situation, it was wise to be cautious.

"No, and he didn't follow us home. Didn't ask anything about me either."

Bowen cocked an eyebrow. "He was totally fine with a strange man taking his sister for the foreseeable future."

"She's a grown woman."

"Emily is too. Doesn't mean any of us would be okay with her going off with some stranger."

Facts. "Emily's different."

Bowen shook his head, obviously not happy with any of this. "Did Kennedy tell you everything?"

"She told me what you told me."

"And what about her job? What happened that made her lose it?"

Okay, Bane hadn't found out about that part yet. *"I don't deserve this,"* she'd said before falling asleep. *"None of it. Not what Mark did..."* Mark was her boss, that much he knew because he looked up the clinic online. What had her boss done to her? Maybe he fired her for something stupid. *Nope.* His gut said it was something way worse than that.

Jesus, how much could one woman go through in a week?

Bane placed Molly on the floor and brushed the fur off his clothes. "I'm not doing any of this right."

"I doubt there's a right or wrong way to handle this shit."

"She's scared to death. Honestly, so am I. And my wolf is…" Bane's breath caught. Just mentioning his wolf had it snarling and clawing at his insides. "He's angry."

"Let him out, brother. He needs to be unleashed."

"*I can't*," Bane whispered angrily.

"You have to, or it'll get worse. This isn't only about you. Your wolf is just as eager to be relieved of the curse as you are. It's been in longing too. It suffers with you. Silencing and caging him will only put more pain between you. That's not something you can afford right now."

Bowen was right, but with Kennedy sleeping peacefully upstairs and Molly scratching the couch with her claws, Bane still wasn't ready to take the risk. His wolf was a big one. A strong one. He might be a beta, but he was just as aggressive as an alpha, and that meant he had to be careful. Not just with Kennedy and her damn cat, but with Bowen too.

Bane loved being Beta. But his wolf was so aggressive lately, he feared what it would try to accomplish. Would it challenge Bowen? They weren't a pack. At least not a complete one. But in this house, order and control were two things both twins demanded. Bane easily let Bowen take the lead as alpha because his wolf submitted to Bowen's long ago. Didn't mean things couldn't change.

Bane didn't want a challenge with his twin on top of everything else. It was too much to handle right now.

"What if shit goes sideways?" he asked quietly.

"We'll handle it together. It's what we do." Bowen's deep, even tone gave Bane hope. He wasn't alone in this. He had a huge support system if he chose to utilize it. "So help me, Bane, if you don't shift, I'll fucking force it."

Bowen never made an empty threat.

And… it was time. "Take me into the woods," Bane whispered. "Stay by me until I say otherwise."

192

Bowen's expression morphed from furious to relieved. "Always, brother. *Always*."

They left the house together and once they arrived in the middle of their property, they both shifted and took off for a run.

Leaving Kennedy alone and unarmed.

CHAPTER 26

Kennedy was in her chasing dream again. Only this time, she was doing the chasing. Running in the woods with someone at her side, she couldn't tell how she was running. It didn't feel like she was using her feet. Her speed was the fastest it had ever been, too. Everything around her a flash of blurry greens and whites and browns. The path was laid out before her, completely cleared of all obstacles. And she wasn't alone, even though she didn't see anyone with her.

I'm not afraid.

That single fact fueled her speed. The freedom and light-footedness lasted until she heard a howl rip through the air. The song, the call of the wild, struck her heart, piercing her soul...

It jolted her awake.

Startled, Kennedy sat up, catching her breath.

Another howl echoed outside. *Wait, what?* Kennedy peeled the sheets off and padded over to the window. It was nearing sunset. The woods around the cabin were crisp and vibrant as the sun sank down, basking everything in a warm glow.

Another howl tore through the air. A second one joined in chorus.

The hair on Kennedy's arms stood on end, and her nipples hardened. *Maybe it's a pack of wild dogs*, she thought. But no, there was something to the sound of a wolf's call that couldn't be mistaken for a coyote or dog. It was a lament. A song of longing. The sound carried on until the two animals ran out of breath.

She ran down the steps and out the front door, desperate to

hear it again.

A wolf. And since she hit one with her car a few days ago, it wasn't too far-fetched to assume the one she was hearing was the one she'd hit.

It has a friend. Kennedy smiled, warmed at the possibility that the wolf wasn't as alone as... her.

Was there a pack of wolves traveling? The possibility made her excited in a geeked out way. When she was in school, there was a wolf sanctuary a couple hours away from where she lived, and she'd go to every full moon event they had when she could afford a ticket. Sometimes the wolves howled in unison. Sometimes they didn't make a peep all night. Elusive, shy, lonely — Kennedy related to them in ways she never cared to admit. And as she ran out the front door, she hoped she heard them sing again.

Where was Bane? Bowen? Could they hear the wolves too?

A rustling behind her made her breath catch. Bane came around the side of the cabin, tugging on his shirt. His cheeks were flushed, and hair tussled. He looked out of breath. Wild. The man was a stunner. He stopped dead in his tracks when he saw her standing on the porch steps. "Kennedy..."

"Do you hear them?" she whispered excitedly. "Did you hear the wolves?"

Bane looked as if he was about to puke. "Uhh."

"They must be moving territories," she went on. "I'm not sure how that works for them, but I heard two howling just now."

"Probably coyotes."

"No. It's wolves. I..." she almost slipped and said that she hit one with her car. But then she'd have to explain why she didn't report it and confess that it also somehow got away at the vet clinic. Bane wouldn't believe her if she told him the animal somehow bent the bars and got out, disappearing somehow right out of the building *and* how her car was then stolen by a naked man at the same time.

Some crazy shit needed to stay in the lockbox.

Bane pointed to the front door. "Wanna come inside and get some — "

"Shhh!" she held her hand out. "I want to hear if they come closer."

Bane swallowed, his brow furrowing. "I'm sure if it's wolves, they've run off. They don't normally get close to humans."

Still, she was hopeful to at least hear their song again. "They make the most beautiful music, don't they?" She sat on the steps and gazed towards the edge of the woods. "Something about their howls hits me here," she tapped her heart. Bane came over and sat next to her. He smelled like pine and sweat and a masculine scent that admittedly drove her wild with lust. He was also incredibly tense. Kennedy's breath caught when she spotted movement at the tree line. "Oh my god."

A huge wolf prowled forward, his gaze locked on her.

"Holy shit," she whispered. Dizziness threatened to take hold, but she breathed through it as the animal came even closer. Kennedy started to sweat. Holy shit was right. This was her wolf. His coloring was the exact same and there was no way she'd mistake him for another. It was absolutely identical to the one she'd hit with her car and had to stitch up.

Except... this wolf walked with no injury. Not even a limp.

Before she could analyze anything else, the beast stalked closer and stopped fifteen feet away from her. A low growl sounded from....

Bane.

The wolf growled back without taking his gaze off Kennedy.

The animal, with its magnificent auburn, gold, and black coloring, approached her with his head dipped down. His tail wagged. And like a fool, Kennedy instinctively reached out for him to sniff her hand. Bane stiffened beside her. She could almost hear his tendons snapping and something crunching, as if he was grinding his teeth too hard. But she didn't speak or look at him. Didn't bother to tell him to calm down because animals sensed fear. No, her attention remained glued on the wolf before her.

The minute it bumped his muzzle to her hand, Kennedy let out a shaky exhale and went for gold. She ran her hand up his head and scratched behind his ear. The wolf pushed into her until he was sideways so she could pet his back and flank.

This was... wow... this was the single most incredible moment of her entire life.

She teared up. So in awe, Kennedy made a strangled noise as the wolf turned to stare at her again. It tipped his head to the side. The air shifted around her. What felt curious and exciting just a

196

second ago now had a heaviness to it. The wolf went from warm and inviting to —

It dipped his head and growled. His hackles raised. Standing this close to Kennedy, one leap and she was done for. She froze in absolute terror.

A loud, animalistic growl ripped through the air — not from the wolf, but from the man next to her. "Bane, don't move." If he threatened this animal, it would attack.

It might attack anyway.

The wolf snarled, revealing perfectly sharp teeth. *Oh shit. Oh shit. Oh shit!* The beast lunged. Kennedy put her hands up in front of her face on instinct and shut her eyes. She screamed.

And then all hell broke loose.

Wind swept her skin. There was a bump and jostle on the porch. Kennedy curled into a ball to protect herself from an animal attack. Snarls, barks, nasty noises. She uncovered her face and scrambled up the porch when she saw two wolves attacking each other.

And the second one had a limp.

They were identical in color and size. But the one that was injured was far more ferocious than the one she had petted.

They growled, snarled, gnashed their teeth, and bit at each other. The limping one tackled the other on the ground, pinning it with its teeth at the neck of the other.

Annnd then Kennedy really lost her shit.

The wolf pinned down shifted into a naked man. A triumphant smile spread across his face as he gripped the wolf by the ears and said, "There, brother. It's done."

WHAT?

In the next blink, the second wolf's fur rippled, and Bane was suddenly kneeling over his twin, his mouth no longer latched onto his neck. The twins were both naked, covered in dirt, glaring at each other. "You *asshole!*"

Shock rendered Kennedy speechless. She ran inside the house, slammed and locked the door, and dodged into the kitchen for a knife.

They came into the house, Bane first, and held their hands out, "We can explain."

She brandished a chef's knife in one hand and a cast iron

frying pan in the other.

"Oh my god," she squeaked. "What... what is this? What are you?" She couldn't grasp this. Not even a little. But that didn't mean she wouldn't try. Her eyes traveled down the length of Bane's naked body and landed on a pink line at his thigh. The truth—as far-fetched as it was—hit her like a lightning strike. "You're the wolf... you're the one I hit with my car." Annnnd then the memory of the man who stole her car flashed in her skull. She felt the blood drain from her face, and she swayed. "You're the man who stole my car."

"Kennedy, I—"

"Stay back," she swung the pan at him. "Both of you stay back."

Bowen walked over and took a seat at the kitchen table and plucked some of the dried leaves out of his hair. "She's handling this better than I thought."

"Shut the fuck up!" Bane and Kennedy both said at the same time. Then they looked at each other again and Bane's gaze looked apologetic and scared. "Kennedy."

"I trusted you," she whispered, her voice laced with anger. Tears spilled down her cheeks, hot and angry. "You said you'd keep me safe."

"And I mean it, *Deesha*. I'd die to protect you."

"He shifted because I pretended to threaten you." Bowen explained, leaning back in his chair and folding his hands behind his head. "Even though he knew I wouldn't lay a paw on you, his wolf couldn't stand the idea of even a mere harmless threat. Lycan are aggressive, protective, and territorial to a fault, Kennedy. Welcome to the pack."

"I..." her gaze volleyed from Bane to Bowen, back to Bane again. "*Lycan?*"

Bane closed his eyes and tipped his head back as he sighed. "I didn't know how to tell you any of this."

"So, I did it for him." Bowen stood and winked at her before slapping Bane on the back. "You're welcome, brother." He walked away with confidence and a bare ass.

Once they were alone in the kitchen, Kennedy set the frying pan down on the counter. Still gripping the handle of the knife, she asked herself if she'd really cut Bane. The answer was... no. So, she

198

put that down too.

Her survival instincts must have a goddamn glitch in the system if she'd unarm herself like this.

Lycan. Actual *Lycan*! This was too wild to be real.

"I've never lied to you," he said quietly, staring at the floor. "And I never will. I just couldn't tell you everything from the start because..." His chest raised as he drew in breath. "*Fuck.*"

"Shift."

His gaze snapped to hers, his brow furrowing. "What?"

"Shift." Kennedy crossed her arms over her chest and glared at him. "If I'm not crazy, and I saw what I saw, I want to see it again. Shift." Because she had to have hallucinated this on some level, right? Otherwise... "Shift, Bane."

"I didn't want it to be like this," he said, shaking his head. Then he rotated his neck, slammed down on all fours, and shifted.

CHAPTER 27

A ripple of muscle, jerk of his head, and *boom* a wolf stood in the kitchen, facing Kennedy off. He remained still as a statue, his gold eyes pinning hers as he tracked her movements. Kennedy cupped her mouth to stifle her gasp. Then she cautiously took a small step closer to him.

"C-c-can you hear me? Understand me?"

The wolf responded with a tail wag and sat down. He was *massive*. Healthy looking. He watched her as intensely as she studied him. Jesus, her heart was pounding fast. It made her feel dizzy and hot. The wolf—Bane—stretched out and laid on the floor with his tail and front legs stretched out. She got a great view of all his angles like this. Sinking to the floor, she, too, crawled on all fours to get closer to him. Their gazes remained locked the whole time.

"Your leg," she said nervously. Reaching out to inspect the injured flank, Kennedy froze mid-way when the wolf growled at her. "It's okay," she said calmly. "I just want to see if it's—"

The wolf's flank muscles twitched when she touched it. "Easy," she said calmly. This might be Bane she was talking to, but it didn't feel that way. The qualities Bane possessed were different as a wolf. He was wild and unpredictable.

Yet she felt completely safe with him.

Kennedy stretched forward and ran her hand down his back, all the way to where she'd sewn him up only days ago. The fur was already growing over where there'd once been stitches. "Looks good." She ran her hand down his back. She couldn't stop touching him. Wow, he was huge. And healthy. Solid muscles and thick fur with phenomenal bone structure.

Lycan.

Not wolf. Not man. Both. Was Bane like the Lycan in movies and books? Was she actually analyzing all this right now while sitting five inches away from a set of huge jaws filled with sharp teeth?

Yup.

He wasn't like the Lycan in the Underworld movies. He was all animal. Intelligent and dominant.

Gorgeous.

The wolf's bone structure was breathtaking. Much larger than a dog's, his face was chiseled, and body built for survival in the wild. "You heal fast," she said to him. The wolf didn't respond. Was she expecting it to?

He pushed his muzzle into her hand. Tears welled in her eyes. This was strange and scary and...

Meant to be.

The thought landed in her mind like an anchor hitting the ocean floor. *Meant to be.*

Kennedy's throat tightened. She didn't understand what any of this meant, and of all things, the fact that she had no desire to study Lycanthropy on this creature to further her career stood out to her. She didn't want to study him. She wanted to be like him.

To run free. Wild. Strong. Fierce.

Closing her eyes, she pulled back from the wolf and attempted to pull herself together. "All the dreams," she whispered. "All the times I was running in the woods being chased, then running alongside something..." *It was you,* she almost said, but didn't. Her words were stolen along with all her senses because Bane had shifted back into a man and suddenly was kissing her.

His hot hand cupped her cheek, just under the ear, and he pressed his mouth to hers as if they belonged locked together. His tongue delved into her mouth, dominating her and seeking approval at the same time. He groaned against lips, and she leaned backwards, hoping he'd follow her.

He did.

Bane crawled on top of her, naked, hard, and hungry for what she had to offer. This was ludicrous. She knew it. But still, she wanted him. This. All things Bane.

For the first time in her life, Kennedy wanted to believe she'd finally found a place to belong. There was a reason she was a solitary person. There was a reason she only liked being around animals. There was a reason she hadn't called and reported hitting that wolf—hitting *Bane*—with her car. There was a reason she bought an old house at the end of a road, surrounded by woods. There was a reason she was hot and hungry all the time. Her speed and stamina the other night in the woods hadn't been a fluke. Her dreams, and this, they weren't hallucinations.

"*Deesha*," Bane growled against her lips.

Meant to be. That thudding fact hit her again, settling in her bones. "W-what's a *Deesha*?"

"In the old language, it means fated mate."

Ummm okaaay. "And… as your fated mate, what do I do?"

Bane swept the hair from her face and kissed down her neck. "Break my curse."

Her thighs clenched, and a wave of heat spilled down her back. "Your curse?"

"Mmm hmm." He palmed her tit and licked down her throat.

She smacked the top of his head. "Stop, stop, stop." She couldn't think straight when he kissed and touched her like that. And this was serious. "Back away for a minute."

Bane obeyed instantly. Sitting with one leg up, the other down, he blocked her view of his massive cock with his thigh and gave her space. Kennedy stared at the faint pink line on his thigh—all that was left of his wound—and watched it fade until there was no trace of him getting hit by a car at all. The breath whooshed out of her. It completely vanished. "This is crazy."

"This is fate."

"I…" she crab-crawled away from him. "I can't process any of this. It's too much to—"

"How about we go upstairs and talk it out?"

"No." She didn't want to go upstairs. She wouldn't behave at all if there was a bed and a naked Bane all in the same room. She was having a hard time behaving with a naked Bane on the floor of the kitchen, for crying out loud. Even with all that's happened, her

202

dirty mind kept flashing to him fucking her on the counter, the floor, on the kitchen table. Even against the fridge. As if some spell was infiltrating her common sense and overwriting her instinct to do anything but *fuck him,* she couldn't stop imagining it.

Bane chuckled in a deep register that made her toes curl hearing it. "Your hormones are peaking," he said. "I smell it on you. That lust. That need to get railed harder than you ever have in your life. It's because you're primed for a Lycan."

She balled her hands into fists. "That's..." *Not your business. Not possible. Not true.* "Not what needs to be talked about right now."

"You'll think more clearly if you let me ease your needs, *Deesha.*" Bane sounded convincing, but he didn't come closer either. Even as he stood up—his muscles rippling and tensing, showing off sinew and abs for days—the man didn't take a step towards her. "Trust me, Kennedy."

"Trust you?" Now she grew angry. She moved to put more space between them. Kennedy stepped back, guided by the rim of the kitchen table until it was a buffer between them. "You... I... this isn't..."

"Isn't what?" he prowled around the table. "Isn't real? Isn't what you want?" Before she realized it, he was already in front of her, sucking up all the air in the room. "I've never lied to you, and I never will." His fingers grazed along her jawline, down her throat, and between her breasts. "I'm your mate, Kennedy. And I know exactly what you need, when you need it, and how to give it to you."

God, that sounded so good.

It also sounded like a cheap porn skit.

"I want the truth," she practically moaned, which totally ruined her badassness.

"I can give you that too." Bane ran his thumb along her bottom lip, staring at it for way longer than necessary. "Okay... you win."

The instant he backed off, she had to fight the urge to close the gap between them and climb that man like a tree. It was the biggest contradiction of her life. Kennedy watched, her mouth slowly opening, as Bane turned away from her. He picked up his tattered clothes from the floor and disappeared out of sight.

Should she follow him? No. Better wait in the kitchen for him to come back. Wait, would he come back? And holy shit, he was ripped. Had he gotten bigger in the past hour? Sexier? Heat pooled between her legs, forcing Kennedy to stifle another groan.

God damnit, what was her problem?

She felt feverish. Confused. Excited. "I'm a mess," she whispered to herself. Beelining for the sink, she splashed cold water on her face.

"Here," Bane said, handing her a small towel to dry off with. He was wearing pants now. Part of Kennedy mourned over it. Another part of her was relieved. Then she noticed they were gray sweatpants, and she wanted to kill him for the audacity.

He knew what he was doing wearing the world's comfiest thirst trap.

"Curse," she snipped. "What's this curse about?" It was going to take time to work up to a convo about Lycanthropy.

Sighing, Bane pulled out a chair for her to sit in and then slumped into the one across from her again. "Not sure where to start, but..." he rubbed the back of his neck and leaned forward with his elbows on the table. "Lycan are hunted by these creatures called *Savag-Ri*. We were almost killed to extinction once. Legend has it, one of us bedded a woman who ended up with twins."

"Twins run in the Lycanthropes?"

Bane shrugged. "Not this time. This particular woman ended up with superfecundation twins. Do you know what that is?"

Kennedy's eyebrows popped up to her hairline. Finally, something she was familiar with. "Two dads," she nodded. "It's common with dogs to have hetero paternal superfecundation litters where each pup is from a different sire."

"Damn, I love your brain, woman."

She waved his compliment off. "Go on, please."

He frowned before continuing and she wondered if he was trying to find a way to sugar-coat whatever came out of his mouth next. "The Lycan and other guy didn't stick with her while she was pregnant. Some say they were detained at war. Others say they were selfish assholes. I don't think anyone really knows the truth, but she ended up isolated and alone, pining for both of them the entire time their babies grew inside her."

Kennedy felt her stomach twist at the idea of such a thing. She couldn't help imagining her belly swollen with Bane's child and him vanishing on her. "What happened then?"

"She wrote them all the time. Begged them to come back."

"Were the men lovers?"

"Uh, no. Definitely not. They didn't even know about each other until they came back while she was in labor."

"Convenient timing."

"Very," he agreed. "There's been tons of theories on that as well. But for the purpose of this story, I'll skip them all and get to the point." He blew out a long breath and dropped his volume a little more. "She was filled with rage and resentment while she pushed the twins out."

Who wouldn't be in those circumstances?

"She cursed the children with her last breath as she bled out on the birthing table," Bane said. "Damned her own babies. Said they would live in constant longing forever. That curse was infused in their blood—pumped right into them from her."

Wow. He was dead serious and looked angry as hell about it. "Constant longing for what?"

"Love. Satisfaction. Completion here," he said, tapping his chest. "We live a half-life until we tempt fate to show us our mate. Only once we find our *Deesha* does the curse lift."

He was leaving something out. Don't know how she knew that, but Kennedy felt it in her bones. "And… if you tempt fate and don't find your mate, what then?"

Bane licked his lips and dropped his gaze. "Well, the rest of the story…" He cleared his throat. "The Lycan took his son and lived in agony over what happened to the mother. He bayed at the moon, crying his apology and regret to the woman's soul every night. He raised his son and wooed many women, promising to care for, and do better than he had with the mother of his firstborn. He never succeeded. There was no love in his heart anymore. Maybe there never had been to begin with. Not all Lycan back then were lovers, many were just animals with big appetites for pleasure of all kinds." Bane closed his eyes and took in a few deep breaths. "Anyway, his son fell in love with a girl. Married her and kept his wolf form a secret. They had a ton of kids—all of which were Lycan, unbeknownst to the mother—but when another woman came into the tribe as a bride for someone else, he felt immediately protective

205

and possessive of her."

Kennedy swallowed the lump in her throat. "Like how you feel with me?"

"*Exactly* how I feel with you." Bane let that sink in for a second before continuing. "But he stayed faithful to his wife and drank heavily to dull his instincts. No manmade drink was strong enough to obliterate his senses. Lycan have fast metabolisms, so he went to a witch for something stronger and started drinking a form of liquid silver he got from her in exchange for a year's worth of fur and meat. Rumor had it, he drank the silver and dreamed of the other woman every night until it drove him wild and restless. As the full moon grew closer, his desires for this other woman got stronger and stronger."

"And... what did his wife think about that?" Kennedy's heart was in her lap at this point. She found herself leaning in, hanging onto every word Bane spoke.

"She killed the other woman." Bane's eyes were laden with sorrow. "When that happened, the Lycan turned into a wolf and stayed in his animal form forever. He never saw his family again. He was never human again either."

That weight in her chest? That anchor wedged on the ocean floor feeling? Well, it just cracked open a pit in her belly and sank to her toes. "W-what's that mean... for you? Did you drink the silver as well? Do you have to do that to break the curse?"

"Drinking a form of silver water is a practice Lycan have done for thousands of years."

That wasn't answering her question. "Bane... did you drink it?" He stared at her for so long, she felt ill with dread. Kennedy slammed her palm on the table. "*Did you drink it?*"

"Yes."

The bottom fell out of her reality then. As wild as this story sounded, she didn't think he was lying about any of it. Kennedy pushed up from the table, the wooden chair grinding across the floor. "What's this mean?"

"You're smart enough to put two and two together, Kennedy."

He was at risk of turning wolf forever.

Her mind scrambled to figure out the time remaining until the next full moon, but her panic made everything jumble together in her head. Shit, shit, shit! "How long do you have?"

"A little less than three weeks."

Three. Weeks?

"And..." her heart fluttered frantically in her throat, "You found me, so you're cured, right?"

"There's more to it than that."

"How much more?" Because she didn't think she could handle anything else tonight. Jesus fucking Roosevelt Christ, how was any of this possible? Sweat bloomed down her back and she caught a whiff of stink, cringing, knowing it was coming from her.

It was the smell of fear.

How she knew that's what it was bent all rules of reason, but there you have it. Fear smelled bitter, pungent, and disgusting. Kennedy raced back to the sink and splashed more cold water on her face. It did nothing to wash away her feelings or fix her situation. "What else has to happen, Bane?" She couldn't even look at him. Staring in the reflection of the kitchen window was as close to making eye contact as she could get with him right now. "What. Else. Bane?"

"You have to become Lycan yourself."

Her knees buckled. She wasn't sure if she was terrified or elated. Seemed Kennedy was one big, curvy contradiction of feelings lately. "How?"

"I fuck you. I bite you. I mate and bond with you. I turn you."

That... that... *hollyyy shhiiitt.*

Again, she was torn in half. Part of her wanted what he was offering—as crazy as that sounded—while the other half of her wanted to run away screaming.

"Your hot flashes, cravings for meat, your stamina in the woods, even your dreams... Kennedy, they're all part of your body priming to become Lycan."

She crouched on the floor and put her head between her legs. *Inhale, exhale. Inhale, exhale.* "Don't touch me," she barked when Bane approached.

"Let me help you," he said quietly. "You don't have to suffer alone, Kennedy. We can do all this together. That's what a mate does..."

But suffering alone was all she knew how to do. Her independency was born from a lack of socializing, a healthy dose of

207

parental neglect, and a side of constant bully threats. She didn't know how to let someone else into her bubble to help. She didn't know how to react other than curl into herself, shutdown, and cut the threads tying her to things that scared her.

"If I say no?" Kennedy almost hurled from her empty threat, but she had to understand all the possible outcomes. "If I say I don't want to be a Lycan?"

"Then it's a no," Bane answered with a voice full of shredded glass. "I'll leave you alone, set up an account so you can move away from here and the Wolf Pack MC, and you'll never hear from me again."

Because you'll have turned into a wolf... forever. Kennedy squeezed her eyes shut and forced her emotions down her throat. She didn't want such a dismal fate for Bane. It might be nice to be a wolf temporarily, but forever? To go from man to animal with no return? Her heart cringed at the idea of Bane living like that.

But did she really want to change herself?

"How long do I have to decide?"

"Until the next full moon."

Not long enough, she thought. She had less than three weeks to decide not only her fate, but to deliver Bane his. That wasn't enough time. It wasn't fair.

To make it worse, there was something else Bane was keeping from her. Kennedy could *feel* it. "What else?" She started rocking back and forth on the floor. Her pent-up escape-to-survive energy needed to be spent, and she wasn't willing to sprint out the front door just yet. She also desperately wanted comfort. Fighting back the temptation to ask Bane to hold her, Kennedy bit her bottom lip and squeezed her eyes shut. She feared if he touched her, she'd never want him to let go and that was unacceptable. She needed to think this through without distractions or impulses. And she needed to know all the facts if she was actually considering what it meant for their future. "What else aren't you telling me, Bane?"

His loud exhale was all the admission her heart needed to shrivel up. *Oh shit, what is it? What else could there be?*

"I dreamt of you the night you hit me with your car." He swiped his hand across his mouth nervously. "I was running in the woods, lost in my head, trying to escape the consequences of my actions. But..."

"But. What."
"I've dreamt of someone else too."
Kennedy's vision tunneled and her world hazed red.

CHAPTER 28

Bane's wolf nearly did a back flip when Kennedy's rage exploded in the kitchen. And as a man on the cusp of either having or losing everything—and it all hinging on the decision of the woman going ape-shit in front of him—well, it warmed his moon loving heart.

"Who is she?" Kennedy's voice was carefully controlled and low, but it shook with her unraveled rage, regardless.

"*She* is a faceless creature I don't know. And *she* is not who I want."

Kennedy ran her hands through her hair angrily. When Bane tried to reach out and soothe her, she smacked his hand away. "Don't touch me."

Okaaayyy. He held his hands up in surrender, smiling all the way. Lycan weren't usually jealous creatures. But they were possessive. Kennedy, acting jealous of a faceless, nameless woman in Bane's dream, only solidified that she was his *Deesha* and not the other woman.

Call him crazy, but he had to risk it. The little bit of time he'd spent with Kennedy so far had him sinking deeper and deeper into a bond with her. His instincts to protect her, care for her, bite her were too real and deep-seated. He couldn't fathom feeling such need for anyone other than her.

And Kennedy's jealousy would end once they bonded and mated. Lycan were so loyal, even if death took their partner, they never moved on. Hell, most died soon after their mate because to breathe without them seemed impossible. Jealousy didn't have space in a wolf's heart. They knew where they stood, in a pack and in their relationship. And they'd die protecting it if they must.

Kennedy started pacing. "This is too much. I can't even…. This is too much all at once."

Again, Bane wanted to touch her. Comfort and ease her. He balled his hands into fists and kept them at his side. "I know," he whispered. "But time is short and…" He felt like a dick bringing his fate up and placing it into her hands like this. "You're taking it all really well." What else could he say? How on earth could he make this better?

Fucking Bowen. If his brother hadn't shifted and come at Kennedy, Bane could have found a better way to bring all this up.

Yeah, right. There was no way this wasn't going to go badly. Time was running out. She needed to be bitten, and her human life had to be altered. The sooner, the better.

The only positive thing about this was that Bane had found her so fast. Fate was on his side this time. *Unlike Killian…*

Bane's heart fell out of his ass. Killian. If Kennedy rejected Bane and walked away for good, Bane meant what he said. He'd respect her wishes and not chase her. It would kill him to do it, but he would. And then he'd end up just like Killian.

And would take Bowen with him.

Bane wasn't telling Kennedy any of that yet. Putting that level of responsibility on her shoulders wasn't fair. Ultimately, it was his choice to respect her decision or not. And it was up to Bowen if he wanted to shift and stay with Bane until he died. None of that was on Kennedy's shoulders, and Bane intended to keep it that way.

"I want to rip this kitchen apart," she blurted. She braced against the counter with her back turned to him. "I want to rip this world and everyone in it apart."

Bane noticed her grip tighten on the granite surface.

"I don't understand how I can feel this way." She whispered angrily. "This isn't like me."

He moved in close enough to brush against her back. Damn, she was beautiful, and her heart was too big and felt too much — even rage made her lovely. "You've been through a lot lately."

"I hit you with my car."

The switch in subject jarred him. "I survived."

Kennedy spun around to face him with tears welling in her eyes. "But what if you hadn't?"

Her voice cracking put fissures in his heart. "Then all this wouldn't be happening."

"Would I no longer be your *Deesha*?"

Was she planning on killing him? Hell, he wouldn't blame her if she wanted to. Becoming a Lycan, if she chose to, wasn't a slap and tickle for a night. It was going to break her and rebuild her into something else entirely. Then she'd have to eventually walk away from her human life and begin a new one with him.

If someone told Bane he'd have to break away and never see Bowen or his family ever again? Shit, he didn't think he could do it. That meant he wasn't putting all his hope in this connection with Kennedy. He couldn't ask her to give up everything for him, even if he knew damn well he could offer her an eternity of love and joy and safety.

Bane stumbled back at the thought. Safety? What safety was there in being a Lycan? None. *Savag-Ri* were always hunting them down. And other Lycan packs had territory wars all the time. And then there were the vampires. Plus, the occasionally vengeful witches.

He hadn't even mentioned anything about those yet to her.

"What?" Kennedy growled. "What else is there?"

He shook his head, refusing to say another word. Kennedy was most likely at her limit and if he opened his fat mouth to say one more thing, she'd likely run for the hills. "I just keep thinking of how I want to make you safe and keep you forever. It's a little overwhelming."

"Gee, ya think?" She hugged herself, her shoulders bunching up.

Bane no longer controlled his urges. Gently grabbing her hands, he unfolded her arms and kissed the back of her hands before tugging her into him. "I wish it was different."

"You mean you wish I was different?"

"What? No."

"Look at me, Bane. I'm not exactly wolf material."

Oh, he was looking alright, and he and his wolf both agreed she was the most perfect creature to ever cross their path. "You'd make an amazing Lycan, Kennedy." Her gaze dropped to the floor.

Not in an embarrassed way, but in a *I can't stand to look at you* way. It frustrated him. "I wish the laws among my kind were different. That's what I meant." Bane placed his finger under her chin and lifted so she met his gaze. "And I wish I had a way to be with you that wasn't so..." he didn't have a clue what word to pick here.

"So permanent? So life-altering? So terrifying?"

"All that, but..." he shook his head, unable to pinpoint exactly how he wanted to say what he felt. "Look, why not come meet my family. See what a pack of Lycan are like. Let's start there and move forward with what time we have left. You met my dad already, right? Might as well meet my mom, brothers, and sister too."

"You have a big family?"

"Including me and Bowe? There's five boys and one girl. We're part of a bigger pack and my dad's the alpha." It felt strange to talk about his family like this.

"I thought you said Bowen was an alpha?"

"He is. Hasn't formed a pack on his own yet, though. Emerick, the oldest, will likely take over for dad once he steps down."

"And... you?"

"I go where Bowen goes." Shit. "I mean... I'd like to. If you're good with that. I wouldn't join a pack, even with Bowen as the Alpha, unless you were ready to commit to it too. It's something we'll discuss when the time comes."

Kennedy shook her head and looked away again. "This is... weird."

Tell me about it, he wanted to say.

"I feel..." she rubbed her chest and cringed, "I feel this tightness. And I'm so mixed up inside, Bane. I feel like I should be more freaked out than I am."

"I mean, you did swing a knife and frying pan at me, so it's not like you weren't a little freaked out." He was shooting for humorous. Pretty sure he just sounded like a complete douche though. Damnit. "Hey," his voice dropped to a soft whisper. Coaxing her with his tone as much as his touch, Bane slid his hand to the back of her head and lightly massaged her scalp as he pressed his mouth to hers. "I'll make it good for you," he promised. "All of it. I can give you a loving, wonderful life, Kennedy."

"I can't think about that right now." She pressed her hands on

213

his chest and he immediately hardened. Even a simple touch like this set him off and made him crave more. "I just want to be in this moment with you, Bane." She tipped her head back to look at him again. "I think what scares me the most is walking away from you."

"Then don't." His hand covered hers on his chest. "Stay with me." *Forever. For always.*

"I'm not sure I can."

"Then give me one week," he begged. "One week to show you my life and what could potentially be your life. Then, if you want to leave, I won't stop you."

Bane feared he just told his first lie.

CHAPTER 29

One week. Kennedy could handle one week. Sure. No problem. Except one week was seven days longer than she needed to make up her mind. Turning into a Lycan? Actually, being able to shift into a wolf? Yeah... no.

She needed to check herself into a mental institution pronto.

If she hadn't seen Bane burst into fur and a tail with her own eyes, she'd never have believed it. Hell, she was still struggling to grasp it. Maybe it had been a sleep deprived, stress induced hallucination. Really, as a medical professional, there were more practical explanations for what she saw other than *Lycanthropy*.

Right? *Right?*

Damnit! Kennedy needed to get a grip. Think about this carefully. Thoroughly.

Seeing a grown ass man turn into a massive wolf was one thing. But the real fear driving her to Insanityville was how she felt about Bane. Kennedy didn't know him enough to be making life-changing decisions yet. So why on earth did every time he called her his mate or *Deesha* make her feel all warm and calm inside? She could live her whole life happily being called *Deesha*. And that was dumb of her. Desperate of her.

Why did she run up those steps when she was first brought to this house? Why did she ever agree to come here and stay for even a night? Why couldn't she pull her hand away from his chest right now? Why did she see red when Bane said he dreamt of someone else? Jealousy didn't live in her veins. She'd never felt such a thing in her life. But something awful and snarly inside her wanted to eat that other woman's blurry face off.

And how horrible was that?

Bane wasn't good for her if she got this vicious about him even *dreaming* of someone else. Some people brought out your worst, others brought out your best. Bane yanked out Kennedy's non-existent-until-this-moment bucket of fucks, and she didn't appreciate it one bit.

You got jealous because you wanted him to only dream of you. You want to be his mate. You want to belong... to him. To something bigger. You want this to be meant to be.

Meant. To. Be.

Meant to be. Meant-to-be. Kennedy gasped when she heard the words ricochet in her skull. That nagging little voice struck her in the pit of her stomach. *Meant to be.* What the hell? Was this some twisted Jack and Sally Halloweentown bullshit or what? She should get out of here right this very minute. Cut loose from Bane and never look back. Curses and shifters and fated mates, her ass.

Meant to be.

Kennedy squeezed her eyes shut. She'd lost her damn mind. "I don't feel good." The possibility of keeping or losing Bane simultaneously poured ice water in her veins as well as set her soul on fire. She shivered through a hellacious hot flash. Great. Just fabulous.

"Do you trust me?" Bane asked when she doubled over with nausea. Sweat trickled down her spine. "Kennedy," he said a little louder when her knees buckled. "Do you trust me to take care of you?"

What kind of question was that? Did he not see her ship sinking right now? "Yes," she muttered through clenched teeth. If he had some magical way to take care of her in this condition, she'd welcome it. Her stomach clenched so tight, it robbed her of breath.

The floor fell through. She started to float. Flicking her eyes open, Kennedy realized she was being carried away, out of the cabin. "I've got you, *Deesha.*"

Hearing him call her that made Kennedy want to cry. *Deesha.* It sounded too lovely and wild to be true. Good things didn't happen to Kennedy. She always got the scraps tossed to her when she looked pathetic enough—the apathetic smiles, the last guy left at the bar, the worst shifts at work. Hell, she even ate more leftovers than fresh-made meals. For Bane to come at her with this fated mate stuff and say all these things to her didn't sit well on her chest. Kennedy was already waiting for the anvil to drop. It made moments like this precious and painful. He was taking care of her. Holding her like a precious treasure, close to his chest and everything he said, he meant.

Heat flared up her spine again, making her groan. How the hell can so much sweat come out of one person at once?

"Here we go," Bane announced, picking up his pace. She'd buried her face between his neck and shoulder, breathing in his scent to ground her a little. Crunchy noises filled her ears. "Almost there," he cooed to her. "You're doing great, Kennedy."

Doing great? She wasn't doing anything but radiating enough heat to sizzle a steak on her back and water the grass with the sweat dripping off her and soaking her clothes.

Face still buried, she relied on her hearing to give her clues on where he was taking her. Crunchy ground turned into rushing water. She felt them descend. *Splash, splash, splash.* "Here we go, *Deesha.*"

Relief washed over her skin as Kennedy submerged into water. It was cold, but she almost wished it was colder. Sighing, her eyes rolled back and she let go of Bane's neck as he dipped her into the river. Propping her up with one arm under her thighs, the other across her back, Bane suspended her in the slow current. "Hold your breath. One, two, three." He dunked her completely, and it felt incredible. Pulling her back up, Bane held her tight to his chest again.

"You can let me go," she said, feeling so much better. "I'm sure I can stand on my own."

"I'm sure you can too." Bane frowned, brow crinkling. "But I don't want to let you go."

They stared at each other for several heartbeats. Then Bane let her go, looking like he was giving up the only thing that mattered to him. She pressed her hands on his chest again. Could feel his heart pounding beneath his muscles. His skin was nearly as hot as hers, she realized. And his gaze blazed with a mixture that she was certain contained sorrow and lust. Or maybe that was her reflection.

"This is really real," she whispered.

"You tell me." Bane pulled on the hem of her shirt and tugged the drenched thing off. Tossing it to the bank, it landed on the rocks with a splat. "Does this feel real enough to you?" He played with her bra strap for a moment before pulling the cup down to capture her nipple in his mouth.

"Shit," she squeaked. His tongue was hot velvet on her. His licks, long and lazy. She had this wild notion it would be amazing to spend all day being licked by him. "You feel so good."

"I'm about to feel a whole lot better." He toyed with the waistband of her leggings before sliding them down her legs. They were waist deep in the water. It felt like the current was picking up, but that might have just been her heartbeat and adrenaline. Bane crouched down and pulled her leggings off.

Later, she'd notice the lanterns hanging on the tree limbs. The chairs set up at the riverbank. The fire pit and stack of wood. But for now, all she noticed was how Bane's body brushed against hers. He flashed a devilish grin and tossed her leggings over his shoulder and onto the bank with her shirt.

"Float," he said, standing up, so the water sluiced off him. "Float with the current, *Deesha*."

There he went again, calling her that. And there her body went, lighting up at the sound of it. "Why?"

"Just do it."

Kennedy wanted to fuck, not float down some river. "How deep is it?"

"I won't let you drown. Just float. Let me come to you."

This was confusing and weird. So why was she doing it? Because when Bane stared at her like a predator in the water, she realized how badly she wanted to be chased.

He wanted to hunt her through the woods. Tackle and mount her. Fuck her senseless amidst the dirt and leaves. But no way could he allow that much of himself out to play today. He and his wolf fought for dominance the second he stepped into the woods. If he chased Kennedy like he wanted, his wolf would force a shift.

That would likely terrify her.

But he needed the hunt. Needed the chase. Needed the

capture.

So, floating downriver until he was certain her body temp had lowered again was the best way to satisfy everyone.

"Float," he ordered, knowing he must sound crazy to her. *Float so I can snag you halfway down the bend and fuck you on the flat rocks there. Float so I can expel my pent-up energy before I get to you. Float so I can have the pleasure of watching you get wetter before I make you drenched.* "Float with the current, Deesha."

Look how her eyes light up every time I call her that. Bane would never tire of seeing that look on her face. Such a simple name, with a profound effect. She wanted to be a *Deesha*.

And she wanted to be fucked. He could smell her lust even with the wind sending her pheromones East.

After a little back-and-forth playfulness, Kennedy finally succumbed and floated on her back. Her tits bobbed like big buoys. Water trickled across her belly and legs. Her little unpainted toes pointed towards the sky. She tipped her head back, closed her eyes, and slowly floated away from him.

He heard her giggle when she was about ten feet away and already picking up a little speed.

There was nothing in this part of the river that could hurt her. No rocks to bump against. No broken bottles or fallen trees. Animals didn't usually come through here, but those that did were harmless.

Bane let her get about fifty feet downriver before he swam towards her. The current was stronger in the middle, which was where she now was. The cold temps barely soothed his burn for her. In the middle, the river deepened to about fifteen feet. He took advantage of it and dove down to the bottom. The water was a little murky, but not impossible to see in. Lycan sight was great in daylight, okay under water, and best in the dark, though colors weren't nearly as bright.

Swimming under water, he felt his wolf just below his skin. It was curious. Waiting to see what Bane would do. Holding his breath, he swam strong and fast until he caught up with her. Pushing up from the bottom, he rocketed to the surface and watched her float a little further away from him.

This chase wasn't good enough. Not thrilling enough to satisfy him or his wolf. But damn, did she look like perfection

219

amidst nature.

The sky's pink tint complemented Kennedy's coloring. The water's dark gray hues, accompanied by the trees just starting to change colors, made her a vision of perfection. Her pale skin, unpainted nails, no makeup, saturated dark hair, and red lips were so enthralling. He should call her a siren, not a *Deesha*. For he knew he'd follow Kennedy into the ocean's darkest abyss, happily.

Bane let the current sweep him away for a moment as he tracked her. She remained calm and still. Her arms floated out at her sides, feet pointed forward, head tipped back a little—she was a sacrifice to the water gods.

An offering to a Lycan.

Licking his lips, Bane growled with hunger and submerged again. Swimming directly beneath her, he pushed up from the bottom and blew bubbles along her backside. Heard her squeal as she lost her balance. Her feet sank, and she kicked him while trying to right herself and lay flat on the surface again. He popped his head up to take another breath. Now he was in front of her. Kennedy's hair spread through the water like paint, spilling in waves of mahogany, auburn, and a few prematurely gray strands. He ran his fingers through her silky tendrils before dipping back down again. He needed to cool off. Slow down. Changing direction, Bane pushed hard against the current and swam directly under her for a fantastic view of her ass.

To see prey so vulnerable, and within in his reach, was enough to make his wolf shift underwater. He felt a swell in his chest. His cock hardened and balls tightened. Popping up out of the water again, he swam behind her with her feet in front of him.

"This is scary and fun," she said loudly.

He smiled. Kennedy had sensed him there without looking. That was good. And not a hint of fear came from her either. Not even when the river narrowed, and the current grew rougher. It splashed down her face and jostled her along, but she didn't fight it one bit. That was good too. Letting go like this would come in handy later.

No longer able to stand not touching her, Bane slipped his arms under her and guided her carefully towards the bank. Once in shallower water, he picked Kennedy up, and she immediately wrapped her legs around his waist. Her eyes were blazing with adrenaline and lust.

"That was incredible," she said breathlessly.

His jaw clenched as he climbed out of the river and carried her over to the flat boulders. Naked, wet, and alive from her little adventure, Kennedy was ripe with need. "I want to be inside you," he confessed, unable to stand it much longer. "Now."

"Took you long enough."

His smile went a mile wide.

After setting her down on the flattest stone, Bane tensed with anticipation as Kennedy spread her thighs in invitation. Hells. Yes. He gripped his cock, giving it a few pumps before coming closer. He'd shed his sweatpants off in the river already. He ran a hand along her inner thigh, "Do you have any idea how gorgeous you are?"

Bet she didn't.

Kennedy looked like a Greek goddess leaning on that boulder. All soft curves, long hair, plump lips, wide hips, and a hunger in her gaze that was best told through legends. And she was all his. Crushing his mouth to hers, Bane ate her moans and pressed the tip of his cock to her opening. He loved foreplay, could do it for hours, but this time he needed to bury himself as deep as he could get inside her and didn't want to wait any longer to do it.

Teasingly, he rubbed the crown of his cock along her wet seam. Kennedy's skin was covered in goosebumps, her nipples tight and pebbled, perfect for sucking. Bending over, he captured one in his mouth, flicking his tongue over it while sinking two fingers in her pussy. He might be starved for her, but he didn't want to hurt her by getting too rough too fast.

"I don't want your fingers," she said with her fingers threading his short-cropped hair. "I want your dick."

"Can't hurt you," he said against her breast. Switching to her other nipple, he added a third finger to the action. "I'm too big."

"Bane," she arched into his mouth, giving him more flesh to feast on. "I want it."

He popped her nipple out of his mouth and cocked his brow. "You sure about that?" he wrapped her hand around his cock, reminding her that his girth mattered as much as length.

"Absolutely," she said, then bit her bottom lip.

Smiling, he pushed the tip in. Pulled out. Pushed the tip and an inch in. Pulled out. Looking down, he watched her take more, and more, and more of him. Then they both groaned when he sank balls deep into her.

"You feel so good." She clutched his shoulders, and he pulled out nice and slow, letting them both watch his shaft slide out before plunging back in again. "Look so good too." Her eyes lit up as she watched him pump in and out of her.

"You take all of me." He thrusted into her again. "Such a good girl." He felt her inner channel squeeze, and she groaned against his skin. Kennedy was built for him. Made for him. "So perfect," he said before kissing her again. "Every damn inch of you is perfection."

He pressed his thumb to her clit, rubbing in slow circles while he worked her over with his kisses and cock. In no time at all, her thighs started shaking. Kennedy's tits bounced with each of his thrusts, tempting him to bite.

"More," she said, hooking her ankles behind him. "More, Bane."

He happily complied. Rubbing her clit and sucking her nipples while fucking her sweet, hot pussy, Bane felt every bit like a starved animal at a banquet for the first time in his life. He couldn't get enough of any one part of her. He wanted it all. Every inch. Every breath. Every moan and touch and orgasm. He wanted everything she was made of.

The wolf in him howled with delight and Bane's goddamn toes curled when she bit down on his shoulder. "That's right, *Deesha*. Bite me harder. Leave your mark."

Kennedy doubled the pleasure by adding her nails, scratching them down his back.

Squeezing his eyes shut, Bane nearly blew his load as sensations tore through him—each one more intense than the last.

He felt her inner walls clench again. Her breaths turned to pants. Bane picked up pace and hooked his arms under Kennedy's thighs to keep her close. The heat between them was intoxicating. Both slick from the river, drenched in lust, and hard from unspent energy, they unraveled together.

"More," she said again. "Give me more."

His wolf wanted to give her everything and Bane was inclined to the do the same. Picking her up, he spun them around and sank to the ground. "Ride me."

She shocked the hell out of him when she squatted down on his dick and bounced. It had to hurt. She was taking all of him. But the look on her face was pure ecstasy. He let her ride until he felt her inner walls quiver again. Then he rolled them over and pulled out before she had the chance to come again. "Spread 'em."

Kennedy's ass went up in the air like a goddamn offering. He smacked it hard enough to leave a bright red handprint. "This ass is mine."

"Yes."

He palmed her ass cheeks before sinking into her from behind. "This pretty little pussy is mine."

"Mmm hmm."

Holding her hips, he rocked into her, awestruck by how much her cream coated his length. She was *drenched* — *her* lust saturating not just his cock, but his balls too. Time to return the favor. "You want me to come inside you?"

"Yes," she grunted, rocking backwards to force him deeper inside.

"You want me to fill you up, *Deesha*?"

"Yes." She looked over her shoulder and met his gaze. "Give me everything."

She had no idea how much he wanted to grant her wish. He'd spend his life giving her everything she ever wanted. They could fuck like this every day. Chase each other every night. Shift, sleep, laugh, play, and live, side by side, forever in love and riding the highs of pleasure day and night.

"Don't stop," she said and looked behind her again. "Don't stop, Bane."

Bane's world fell off its axis. *Don't stop, Bane.* Kennedy's husky, lust-induce tone, coupled with her pose and intensified by those words? It was his dream come reality. *Don't stop, Bane.* She was his *Deesha*. Any doubt hidden in his mind that she wasn't the one for him vanished.

His hips turned to pistons as he chased his release. At the last minute, he pulled out and jerked himself until he unloaded all over her ass. Thick ropes of cum jetted out of him, his muscles pumping hard as he grunted her name over and over. Bane's orgasm went on and on. By the end, his goddamn ears were ringing.

Kennedy, still panting, crawled across the ground, towards the flat boulder again.

"Where do you think you're going?" he asked in a deep, animalistic tone. "I'm not finished with you yet."

He dragged her back by her ankle, spread her cum-slicked ass cheeks and licked her.

"Oh my God." Kennedy clawed the ground, sticking her ass out to give him better access. "Oh my God, *oh my God.*"

He sank two fingers into her pussy and hooked them to hit her g-spot, then feasted on her from behind until she squirmed so much he couldn't keep his hold on her. Bane smacked her ass again, saying, "Stay still till I finish."

Kennedy's next grunt was absolutely undignified and just the thing he wanted to hear when he doubled down on his efforts.

She gushed around his fingers in the most satisfying way. "Bane, stop!"

He didn't want to stop. He wanted her to squirt again. Call out his name again. Come harder. Bite him harder. Claw him and own him. Instead, he playfully licked her again, testing to see if she'd push into him or tip forward in an attempt to escape.

"Give me more," he growled before nipping her ass cheek. "You taste too good to stop eating, Kennedy. And I've starved for way too long while waiting for you."

Kennedy managed to squirm her way over to a boulder and got on her knees. He fingered her again. Made her come again. Catching her breath, she managed to make in onto her feet. No problem. Bane ate her in every position she went into. Finally, Kennedy rose up on her tiptoes and bent over the boulder, giving his penetrating tongue even more access. On his knees, he made it almost impossible for her to stay upright with her next orgasm. Then he spun her around and remained on his knees so he was face-to-face with the apex of her thighs. "Every angle you go in gives me one hell of a view, *Deesha.*"

"I think I'm going to stroke out. My heart's beating so fast and my ears are ringing."

"You'll be fine. Promise."

"I can't breathe."

"Try harder." He flicked his tongue out with no mercy and assaulted her clit, proving that she indeed have air left in her lungs.

He pulled back long enough to say, "Anyone who can scream like that certainly has to draw breath to do it." He made her call out his name with her next orgasm. They were becoming quick and easy to catch. He'd rather her orgasms be long and prolonged, but these short-fired ones were fun too. "Still want more?"

She'd begged for *more, more, more* this whole time. Was she sated yet? He hoped the fuck not.

Looking up at Kennedy, he waited for her answer. Cocked his brow to show a little impatience. She bit her lip and nodded.

"Good girl." He chuckled low in his throat and lifted her by the ass, so her legs draped over his shoulders and her back pressed to the boulder. He ate her until her voice was hoarse and she started yanking on his hair to pry him off. He pulled back and licked her juices from his lips. Holy hell, she looked lovely and wrecked. "You're so damn beautiful." Untangling himself from her, Bane leaned in and said, "Lick your pleasure from my mouth."

Kennedy groaned, her lashes fluttering at his command. She obeyed without pause, dragging her tongue across the seam of his lips until he opened his mouth and kissed her back. She pulled away, breathless, and he laughed. "Wild girl."

"I've never been fucked like that in my life," she said, still catching her breath. "I'm ruined now."

Ruined for all others but him. Yeah. He knew that already. That was part of the plan. "Gotta make you want me forever, don't I?" He nipped her throat playfully. "Can't do that with shit bedroom skills."

"Wow." Kennedy stepped back and ran her hands down her sides. "I feel… I don't know what I feel."

"It's called worshipped, *Deesha*. You feel worshipped because you are. Get used to it." He grabbed her hand and yanked her into his chest to kiss her again. "You'll be getting a lot more where that came from."

CHAPTER 30

Two blissful days later, Bane was still making her feel like a Goddess. Between his bed, the woods, the river and twice in the kitchen, Kennedy was blissfully sore and slept so hard she didn't even dream. Bane couldn't take his eyes or hands off of her. Not that she was complaining one bit. And Bowen even spent a little time with them last night at the bonfire by the river. Seeing the twins together, the way they joked around, finished each other's sentences, and made the exact same facial expressions was hilarious. They even laughed at the same pitch, with their heads tipped back and shoulders bunched.

Kennedy could get used to this.

And tonight, she was going to meet the rest of their family. To say she was nervous was an understatement. "What if they don't like me?"

"What's not to like?" Bane spooned her in bed. Running his fingers lazily down her thigh, he said, "Everyone's going to love you, Kennedy. Trust me."

She wasn't convinced. Kennedy looked like she had her shit together on the outside, but inside, she was a hot mess. What if they thought she wasn't good enough for him? What if they asked about her family? She wouldn't lie to them, which meant telling the truth could end up with her booted out of the pack before she fully made it in.

Wait, was she really considering being a member of a pack?

Maybe. Kind of. Okay, yes. It was just so nice with Bane. Even the air was fresher around him. And his cuddles? Please, she'd turn into a jellyfish if she had to for one more night in this man's arms.

Meeting his family would allow her to understand how he grew up, show her a little of their dynamics, and she hoped would ease some of the curiosity and concerns she had about Lycan. Again... she couldn't believe she was even considering Lycanthropy being a thing outside of Hollywood and novels.

How was this her life?

"I have a confession," she said, sleepily. Turning to face him, Kennedy ran her fingers through Bane's tussled hair. "I felt homesick without you."

Bane's brow furrowed.

"When I kicked you out and went to work the other day?" Putting a timeline on this might have been helpful. "The minute you pulled away, I felt sick. At the time, I thought it was my nerves and anger, but... when I think of us being apart, I have the same feeling." She placed her hand on her belly. "It almost hurts."

Bane leaned down and kissed her ribs, then belly, and playfully nipped her fingers. "Well, you won't have to feel that anymore. I'm not going anywhere."

She bit her lip. How did she tell him she was scared to do this? To be a Lycan? To be a mate? Kennedy was going to suck at it. She wasn't wife material, which, in her mind, was what a mate equated to. She was too independent and closed off to be someone's other half.

And yet she really, *really* wanted it.

"This is crazy." She covered her face with both hands to hide her expression. It was a mix of happy and terrified, and honestly, she was also a little sad. Her life experiences taught her good things never lasted long and to balance out the joy, the universe always tossed her a buttload of misery.

When was the misery going to come?

"We better get going." Bane pulled her hands off her face to kiss her. "We have a long drive ahead of us."

Right. The family dinner. "How far away do they live?"

"Just a few hours."

That's a hike for dinner. "Will we spend the night?"

"Most likely." Bane slipped into a pair of jeans. "If it's nice, we can tent it outside."

"Camping?" She hadn't done that in ages.

"You call it camping. I call it fucking under the moon."

Winking at her, he shrugged on a t-shirt next. When he pulled it over his head, it rumpled his hair even more. The man looked wild and happy. Excited. Flashing her a wolfish grin, he jabbed a finger in her direction and playfully growled, "Don't you dare go there thinking you're getting any sleep."

"It's your parent's house."

"So?" He raked a hand through his hair, making it worse. "Lycan are different. Think Bowen hasn't heard us for the past two days?"

"Holy crap." She pressed her hands to her cheeks. "I was that loud?"

"Woman, your screams can be heard by any animal within a thirty-mile radius."

Kill her now. "This is humiliating."

"Shouldn't be. Lycan are sexual beasts. Besides, the family house has legit soundproof walls. Nobody wants to hear what anyone else is doing. Just wait till you come to a ceremony."

She loved how he talked about them and the future. "What kind of ceremony?"

"My parents throw huge dinners during the full moon four times a year. Other Lycan packs come too because they're epic. Lots of naked bodies and wolves running around."

That should skeez her out, right? A massive orgy... at his parent's house. Soooo, why was she suddenly excited about seeing this?

Because she needed therapy.

"My parents start the show and after the formalities of the ceremony are over, they usually leave and hide up in their room for the rest of the weekend with the curtains drawn and bedroom door locked."

"This kind of sounds like a massive frat party when the 'rents go on vacation."

"Yes, and no. It's..." Bane frowned, pensively. "It's just different. We're animals on the inside. Modesty isn't in us. We're too primal and carnal for it."

Hence why her limbs ached just right, and her pussy was a little sore. Bane was absolutely insatiable. If he wasn't pleasuring her, he was thinking about it. She wasn't sure what she loved more—his tongue, his fingers, or his massive cock.

Her secret goal was to get at least three-quarters of his dick down her throat. She doubted she'd ever get the entire thing. So far, she'd managed a little more than half. Bane kept giving her credit for deep throating, but that's only because she was good at making it messy and using her hands, tongue, and teeth well enough to keep his brains scrambled. If she could actually swallow his ten-inch monster, she'd feel like the goddess he kept treating her like.

"What should I wear?" She needed to change the subject before she ended up on her knees, taking him into her mouth again.

"Whatever's comfy." Bane sat on the bed and started putting on his socks. "Full warning though. My mother's cooking is phenomenal, so definitely wear something with an elastic waist."

"I can't meet your family looking like a slumpadink. I should at least wear a dress."

But she didn't have any to wear. All she'd packed was comfort clothing. Shit.

"Don't you dare wear a dress. That's just cruel and unusual punishment."

"For who?"

"ME!" Bane turned around and crawled on top of her. "I don't have the self-control it would take to keep my hands off you if you wore a dress, *Deesha*. That's just... nope. Don't be mean to me."

Could this man be any more perfect? He said things that made her heart get all swoony. "Sweatpants and a baggie t-shirt it is."

Bane groaned, like that was an even hotter choice than a dress. She couldn't help but laugh at him. "Okay, big guy. You pick out what I wear. How's that?"

"Really?" He got this devilish grin on his face that made her thighs quiver. "Whatever I want?"

"Sure."

How bad could it be?

She should have never given him the opportunity to pick out her clothing. Bane was too much Lycan to turn down the chance to dress her in his clothes so she'd be covered in his scent. As if fucking her senseless for the past forty-eight hours wasn't enough to penetrate her pores and smother her with his pheromones. But he hadn't planned on her looking so damn delicious in a set of leggings—that were hers, thank you very much—and one of his flannel button-down shirts.

Kennedy looked like a snack.

Holy Hounds of Glory, he was starving...

Bane couldn't wait to rip that black and red checkered monstrosity off her later and fuck her tits. What? Have you seen those things? They were perfect. All supple and soft and full and heavy and—

This drive to family dinner was a true test in self-control. He kept wanting to pull over and do bad things to her. Reaching over the console, Bane placed his hand on her thigh, needing that touch, but also trying to not yank her pants down to fingerbang her.

His libido was out of control.

And now his dick was too hard and losing blood flow. *Thanks, jeans.* At least Bowen had come up separately. He left earlier this morning to head home, leaving Bane and Kennedy to have a nice private drive together.

But it felt weird to be without Bowen. Twinning was confusing sometimes. Bane was so used to doing everything with Bowen, that lately it felt like he was missing a piece of himself since he was spending so much time getting to know his *Deesha*. But he needed to get used to it. No matter the outcome—whether Kennedy became his mate or not—things were going to change between him and Bowen.

Bane pulled away from Kennedy and put both hands on the wheel. For the rest of the drive, she asked a ton of questions. He answered them as best he could. Then they talked about dumb movies, concerts, and what was better—pie or cake.

Clearly the answer was pie.

Then they fell into an electrified silence. It was obvious they were both deep in thought about the future and weren't willing to discuss it. While Bane imagined turning into a wolf and having the same fate as Killian, he wondered if Kennedy was thinking about her brother, Jake.

They finally pulled onto a dirt road and a weight lifted from his shoulders. Being home, on pack land, always brought Bane a sense of belonging and warmth. His parents had overseen their pack for centuries and did a damned good job of ensuring safety and comfort to anyone who made it onto their land.

The sound of ATVs could be heard in the distance. Bane smiled, eager to see his family and have some fun. "My brother Emerick is a showoff. He acts like he's in charge just because he's the oldest, but don't let his bossiness fool you. He'll turn into a puppy if you so much as giggle at one of his jokes." Bane slowed down and carefully navigated up the narrow drive. "Emily's a spitfire. I'm not sure if she'll be here or not, but if she is, she'll drill you on everything. Not that she's nosy, she's protective."

"That seems to run thick in your family, huh?"

"All Lycan are this way." He honked the horn as the house came into view. "She's probably going to be pissed at me about this," he blurted. "Emily's on an *I-don't-need-a-mate* kick and she's already lost Dorian to a mate. He was the one who taught her living in longing was better than chancing fate." He didn't say more about it, and Kennedy didn't ask. Probably because she was too awestruck at the size of the house and property.

It was a beauty.

Bane put the truck in park, hopped out, and howled. He got two responses from the woods just as the front door swung wide open with his father, Emerick, and Marie coming out to greet them.

"Kennedy!" Bane's mom beamed. "I'm Marie. It's so wonderful to meet you!" She charged right towards Kennedy with her arms wide open and crushed her with a hug.

"Don't squeeze the life out of her, Marie." Alistair said. "She needs air to breathe."

Marie let go and smacked Alistair's arm. "Is it so wrong to be excited?"

Kennedy looked shell-shocked and nervous. Bane grabbed her hand and kissed it. "This is my mom, Marie. And you met my dad, Alistair, already."

"Hi." Kennedy's awkward wave was adorable.

"This ugly motherfucker is Emerick."

Emerick narrowed his eyes. "At least I've never had fleas."

"Hey!" Bane gawked, acting offended. "That was *one* time!"

"Come on," Marie said, swatting away their conversation, "Let's go inside. I've made your favorite."

That got Bane's attention. "Apple?"

231

"Of course, and I made two, so your *Deesha* can have her own."

"Oh my god, you made me a pie I don't have to share?" Kennedy looked positively giddy. To see her fall into the Woods family so easily with just intros was amazing. "I think I love you," she said to Bane's mom.

"Come on. You better stake your claim before the others come in and make a mess of the house." Marie led Kennedy up the stairs, and Alistair and Emerick held Bane back for a minute.

"Dorian brought Emily back." Alistair said. "They're in the woods with Bowen right now."

"Shit, so she knows?"

"Yeah, and it went as well as you'd expect." Emerick's lecturing tone was thick. "Bowen got here early and worked with Dorian to break the news to her."

Well now Bane felt like shit. And that pissed him off. "It's not like I did something wrong," he snarled. And fuck Emily if she was going to be selfish and pissed off about Bane wanting happiness.

"She's still dealing with Dorian having a mate, bro. And she's been so edgy lately, I'm about ready to pull my hair out dealing with her."

Bane glowered at Emerick. "She's our *sister*, not something you deal with. And she's a grown ass woman. Leave her alone and let her navigate her own life."

"And risk losing our only female in the family besides mom? What is wrong with you, Bane?"

"Enough, you two," Alistair growled. "Emily will get over herself, eventually. That's not what this dinner is about. Bane, go inside and be with your *Deesha*. Your mother's likely hovering and asking too many questions as it is. Emerick, go stack logs for a bon fire later. We're going to make sure Kennedy feels every bit as welcome and safe as possible while with us. Arguing isn't going to accomplish that. Neither is barking at each other over things you can't control… like your sister. Now go."

Bane stomped up the steps and went inside the house, immediately hearing laughter in the kitchen. Storming into the room, he found Kennedy and Marie sitting at the massive kitchen table, four pies in front of them and five more on the counter.

" —swear it was the worst smell in the world." Marie went on like Bane wasn't there at all. "But he didn't even care. He just took them up to his room, and that was that. The house stunk for *months* afterwards."

Kennedy leaned back in her chair, laughing so hard her eyes squeezed shut. "Guess you can't spray tomato sauce like room spray."

"Oh, believe me, I tried everything. We've never let him live it down."

Bane eased into a seat beside Kennedy and pulled an apple pie over to him, then grabbed a fork from the center of the table. "Are you still going on about those baby skunks?"

"I'll always go on about those baby skunks. I swear, every time I smell one in the woods, I get PTSD." Marie started laughing again. "But truly, Bane is a gentle giant with a big heart. He was always scooping up defenseless animals and bringing them inside when he was little."

Kennedy glanced over at him with a big, warm smile. "Same."

Okay, he felt like a marshmallow—all squishy and sweet. Not a good look on a Lycan. But he was a sap for innocent creatures, and everyone knew it. "Admit it, Mom. They were cute, and you were sad to see them go."

"Never," Marie said with a wink. "Now… should we eat inside or out this evening? Kennedy, you pick."

Bane locked gazes with his *Deesha* and smiled. She belonged here. She looked good here. She fit here. Did she feel it? Did she realize she hadn't smiled this big in all the time they'd been together until she was surrounded by Lycan? Shit, she'd even lost some of the tension in her shoulders in the few minutes they'd been sitting here talking. And her face wasn't as flushed anymore either.

That's the magic of pack land. That's the result of a strong pack with positive energy covering everything they owned. The protection symbols painted on the doorway, windows, and all four corners of the property helped too. Made from *Savag-Ri* bone and Lycan magic, it was all they had to repel the fuckers with.

"Outside," Kennedy said.

"You heard your *Deesha*." Marie turned her gaze to Bane. "Let's give her what she wants."

Oh, he planned to. Bane was absolutely, one hundred percent, on board with that. Now and always.

CHAPTER 31

Kennedy never laughed so hard in her life. After meeting the rest of the family while setting up for dinner, she sat between Bane and Emily—who remained quiet for the most part but seemed friendly enough—and they ate outside at a massive wooden table in a barn nearly the size of her former vet clinic. Lanterns and twinkle lights hung around the perimeter and across the ceiling. There was even an upstairs area that had cushions and hammocks.

Dinner was a mix of bad jokes, embarrassing sibling stories, and asking Kennedy about her life. It didn't feel intruding. It honestly felt like they each wanted to get to know her as best they could in the time they had. Marie loved that she was a veterinarian. That much was obvious in how she held her chest and smiled.

Emerick was interested in where she'd traveled to. Alistair asked about her family, which, wasn't as hard to talk about as she'd thought. Not that Kennedy went into great detail about what a dumpster fire her family was or anything.

Dorian, who turned out to be the adopted brother, asked about her house in Georgia and how long she'd lived there. Said his mate was from Georgia too, and what a coincidence that was. "Wish she could have come up for dinner this time, but she needed time in the ring."

Bane's eyes rounded. "And you let her go alone? I'm impressed."

"I fear for them more than for her. And Victoria's with her."

"Oh shit." Bane pretended to look shaken. "The club will

never be the same now."

Okay, Kennedy was a little lost. "The club?"

"Underground fighting ring." Bane said, grinning big time.

Her eyebrows shot into her hairline. "And here I thought the first rule of Fight Club was—"

"Shhh." Bane held a fork loaded with baked potato on it in front of her, feeding her as he winked. "I usually never miss one, but I've been a little preoccupied." He leaned over and nipped her shoulder playfully.

"I can't wait to join the fun." Emily grinned. "Dorian's just taught me a new move and I'm dying to try out."

Bane scowled. "You're not going to a fight, Emily. And you sure as shit aren't competing."

"So you can, but I can't." She glanced over at Marie and eyerolled. "I love the double standards with the men in this family."

"Em," Dorian hissed. "We talked about this. Those moves aren't for clubs, only defense during an enemy hunt."

Swear to God, Kennedy thought Emily was going to stab Dorian with her fork. Instead, she put it down and wiped her mouth with a napkin, flipping him the middle finger.

"Aww, you're number one in her book, Reaper." Bane held his glass out in salute before taking a sip. When Emily flipped him the bird too, he said, "Hey! I'm right up there with you."

"Will any of you ever grow up?" Emerick reached for the bowl of peas. "Seriously, guys."

"Someone pull the stick out of Emerick's ass," Bowen teased.

"Yeah." Emily grinned. "Maybe we can get him to play fetch with it."

"Oh, you're gonna pay for that." Emerick threw a roll at her. Emily caught it easily enough and stuffed the entire thing into her mouth. Everyone started laughing again.

Kennedy stabbed another piece of steak and counted the family members while she chewed. "Are we missing a brother? I thought Bane said there were five boys and one girl. Where's the fifth brother?"

Emily dropped her fork with a loud clank. Marie paled and glared at her daughter.

"He's off running around somewhere," Emerick said with a tight smile. "He doesn't come to dinners anymore."

Oh. Maybe he was the black sheep in the family? That was relatable. Hopefully she'd get to meet him someday.

"So," Emily said, taking the spotlight again. "Are you turning Lycan now or waiting until the last minute, so my brother stays suspended in torture for as long as possible?"

The table went silent. Kennedy placed her utensils down and wiped her mouth. "I have to figure some things out first," she answered.

"Tick tock." Emily stabbed her steak and shoved it into her mouth.

Okay, what the hell was up with this woman? Emily had enough pent-up rage to blow the Smoky Mountains to rubble. Kennedy didn't think she should push the conversation though. It was obvious Emily was struggling with her life. Not that Kennedy had any advice to offer because she was too new to all this. But, damn... attitude much?

"Let's get dessert! Emily, help me with the ice cream." Marie glowered at her daughter.

Kennedy pretended to not notice. "This meal was wonderful, Marie. I've never had steak cooked so perfectly before. I usually just char it until it's rubber."

"My wife's an incredible cook," Alistair said with a proud smile. "And an even better baker. Which leads me to ask, why the hell are we having ice cream for dinner?"

"Because the pies were the appetizers, dear." Marie winked at Kennedy. "And temperature control is important right now for her."

Kennedy looked from Marie to Bane to Emily, who just shoved away from the table and grumbled about pathetic, weak human systems.

"Trust me, it's a new experience," Marie said before following Emily out of the barn and back into the house.

"Your body temps fluctuating," Bane explained. "Remember how good the ice cream was on our first date? It's about to get way better. And this stuff's homemade with fresh fruit."

Temperature regulation. Weak human systems. Kennedy leaned back in her seat and rubbed her belly. "Well, this weak human system will always have room for ice cream."

Alistair laughed. "Melts in and fills all the nooks and crannies, am I right?"

She couldn't help but laugh too. "Exactly!"

The tension in the air lifted on that note and Kennedy noticed Bowen hadn't spoken much all night. He seemed content though. Maybe he was just the quiet one of the bunch when they were all together.

Marie and Emily came out moments later with trays of sundaes. "Here we go!" Marie placed her tray down on the table next to Emily's and Bane passed a bowl to over to Kennedy, serving her first.

"Life is really good here," she said quietly while staring at the filled-to-the-brim bowl of homemade ice cream, whipped topping, sprinkles. It even had a cherry on top. "Life is... it's really good here, isn't it?"

She didn't know what the responses were. Kennedy sank into the deepest corner of her mind and stayed there until dessert was over.

CHAPTER 32

After dinner, they started a bonfire. Music pumped in through strategically placed, all-weather speakers. Bowen and Emily went behind the barn to shift, agreeing they both needed to go for a run. Kennedy tried to hide her shock when they prowled around the fire pit and took off through the woods in wolf form. It hadn't worked. Her accelerated heartbeat gave her away.

Marie was still inside to clean up from dinner and though Kennedy kept insisting on helping, none of them would have it. With great effort, Bane finally coaxed her to relax by the fire. Alistair and Emerick sat across from them, talking quietly together.

"I'll never get used to this," Kennedy said as she tucked herself under Bane's arm.

He kissed the top of her head. "Get used to what? The shifting or..."

"All of it." Kennedy pulled away from him and it felt like she took a piece of his soul with her. "You guys. This place. The laughing and being together." Kennedy wrapped her arms around herself in a tight hug. "I've never had this."

Alistair and Emerick stopped their private conversation and gave her their full attention.

"You read about these things, you know? You see it in movies and maybe get to go home with someone else for Thanksgiving break in college. You get a glimpse of what life is like for other people. But then you have to go home to your shit-tastic life and it's nothing like... *this*."

They were fixated on her now. Dead silent and focused, hanging on Kennedy's every word.

"This can be yours too," Bane cautiously reminded her.

Kennedy guffawed. "Until when? Until you wake up and realize you mated a hot mess? I'm a train wreck, Bane. And my brother..." She bit back her words and shot up from the log they sat on. Bane rose with her.

Would he chase her if she ran right now? Most likely. Did she want that? She wasn't even sure anymore. Kennedy was too confused to know the difference between want and need. But she couldn't run from her life anymore than she could run from her fate, so her feet remained planted on the ground.

"Good things don't happen to me," she said to all of them. "And you? Your family? This all feels like a good thing."

"It's okay to want better things for yourself, Kennedy." Alistair's gaze locked onto hers. He had these crinkles in his eyes from years of laughter and seeing them shattered something in Kennedy.

"I don't know how to live a good life." Kennedy started to back away. "I only know how to make do. How to... how to stay down until the storm passes."

"Then let us teach you how to run in the rain." Bane said to her, gesturing around him. "You can be part of this life. We *want* you to be part of it."

"But at what cost, Bane?" she barked back. "You have this great relationship with your brothers and sister. *And* your parents! I can't even fathom what your childhood was like."

"Don't do this," Bane warned. "Don't try to twist this into being something other than it is."

"And what's that?" Now she was good and furious. She wished he'd kiss her hurt away and hold her tight. Instead, he stayed back.

"This," he growled, "is what you deserve, Kennedy. You deserve happiness and safety and comfort. You deserve a man who will treat you like the most important thing in his life and love you like you're the reason his soul was created to begin with. Whether it's me or someone else."

She hated to even think of being with anyone other than Bane. How was it possible to feel this invested so soon? *Meant to be.* She

239

took a step back, shaking her head.

Bane closed the space between them again, undeterred. "You deserve stability and normalcy. Love and safety."

To think she'd not really had the basic fundamentals of a family made the concept of what Bane offered her seem foreign. She didn't know what to do with any of it.

"I never thought I'd want or get those things," she whispered. "I've always made do and tried to never compare my situation to others, but..." Kennedy's chin trembled. She looked away from him.

"Fuck this noise." Bane closed the gap between them and wrapped her in a tight hold. "Let me love you how you're meant to be loved, *Deesha*."

She shook her head, shoulders bunching with her next cringe. "I know what I deserve. I just don't think I have the capacity to not destroy it in the end."

Bane's brow furrowed. "You're smart, talented, strong-willed, compassionate —"

"Please don't list my qualities. I know what I am, Bane. I'm a woman in her thirties who had to grow up faster than most. I did well enough in school to get a scholarship, made it through vet training and got two degrees, can speak fluently in Spanish and German, am well-read, and independent."

"Perfect package."

"No," she barked, holding her hand up. "I know what I'm worth. And I know what I cost." Her heart slammed into her chest as her temper rose. "I know that to grow up fast, it was because I had to fend for myself by the age of six. My parents weren't around and if they were, they didn't acknowledge that they had children to care for. Jake and I were on our own too young. And I did well in school because I was the outsider in my house. It wasn't that I wanted a better life... shit, I didn't even know what that would have looked like! I never left our trailer except to run to a neighbor's house once when Jake said our dad wouldn't wake up and my mom was gone. I started school late because they didn't register us. And when I was old enough to see that most of the world didn't live in empty beer cans and powder on their kitchen counter, I finally smartened up with my eyes wide open. I stole clothes from other kids because I didn't have a winter coat. Jake would sneak into

240

other trailers to grab us food in the middle of the night. And I knew the only way to get out of my life was to be better than them." She choked out a heartless laugh. "But that scholarship cost me Jake. My nose always in a book, my mind staying focused on classes and work..." she swallowed the lump in her throat. "I didn't see Lucky until it was too late. My need to be better than them cost me Jake."

"Kennedy —"

"I'm not done," she said, cutting him off. "While he was in prison, serving a sentence for defending me, I went on without him. Without our parents. I still thought I needed to be better than them. I worked hard, graduated top of my class. And guess what?"

Bane stared at her, his throat bobbing as he swallowed.

"In the seven years it took me to get my degrees, I had to bail my parents out of jail seven times. Seven. They had no one else to ask. Their club didn't help them. Their son was locked up already. I was all they had to turn to. So my responsible, compassionate side? It put me in debt up to my ears. I lost my scholarship mid-way through getting my degree because I'd lost time running back and forth to get my parents in rehab and shit. So, on top of bail, I was drowning in tuition debt." Her voice shook, and she wasn't sure if it was from anger or sorrow. Maybe both. "I couldn't escape my life, no matter how much I tried to rise above my circumstances. Jake and I moved here, and it's like we're steeped in our parent's legacy. Jake's in the thick of too much wrong. I'm on the fringes with his hand around my ankle as his lifeline. And I can't make it stop. So, you say I'm smart, talented, strong-willed and compassionate..." she tossed her hands up, "But what you're not saying is that I'm a fool who's vulnerable, incapable of walking away, lonely, stubborn, and hateful too."

"You're not —"

"I am," she seethed. "I foolishly thought I'd be better than my parents. Better than anyone in my life back then. The bar was so low, it shouldn't have been difficult. But I failed. I'm right back where I started. Jake, the MC, drugs and fights, and... Blade was just another Lucky."

"No family's perfect," Bane argued. "Just look at us."

She'd been looking all night. "Yeah, poor you. Your family is a circus full of monkeys."

"One night of us on good behavior," Emerick said from the

241

back, "Doesn't mean we aren't without a lot of fuckups and pain too."

Bane crossed his arms and glared at her. "Does it matter?"

"Does *what* matter?"

"Any of it. You're past. My past. Our current situation. Does any of it matter in here?" He tapped his chest. "Does any of it matter for tomorrow, or the next day, or the day after that?"

It should, but...

Her cell rang, cutting off what she was about to say. Great, speak of the devil. "It's my brother," she warned, pushing away from Bane. She had a ringtone set for just him. One more way to alarm her of incoming bad news. And just like when she heard motorcycles rev by, this ringtone also triggered her panic.

"Answer it," Bane ordered.

She didn't appreciate his tone. But he was right. Kennedy needed to get through this shit with her brother so she could focus on doing things for herself. It was clear she put Jake above herself. Hell, she put everyone and everything above herself. She was raised to treat herself no other way.

"See what he wants, Kennedy."

It was going to be trouble. She could feel it in her bones. It made her all the madder that Jake's reach was this far when it came to Kennedy's life. And she felt like shit for being mad about it too, because what if things had been different back then? What if Lucky had never come through their door? Would Jake have been a better person had he not gone to prison? Would Jake be someone else entirely?

No. She didn't think so. Jake was always trouble, long before he went behind bars. His love for her didn't change the fact that he was trouble for her, too. Angrier than a bear, she tapped her screen and snarled, "What?"

"Where are you?"

"With Bane. Why?" Her grip tightened on her cell. "What is it now?"

"Where is it?"

"Where's what?"

"Kennedy, stop fucking with me. Where did you put it?"

She had no clue what he was talking about. "I didn't put anything anywhere."

"It's not here!" He screamed into the phone.

Annnd that was it. She was done. This was over. Brother or not, she wasn't going to be part of his disaster of a life a moment longer. "I can't do this anymore." She turned her back to the Lycan watching her and hissed, "I'm done with your bullshit."

"Kennedy, listen to me! I *have* to have—"

"No! *You* listen to *me*! I'm not helping you anymore, Jake. You got yourself into this, get yourself out! I have no clue where you hid your shit in my house, nor am I going to help you look for it. And I'm not handing over meds or tranquilizers to those assholes you run with either. Nor will I be stitching any of you up when you get hurt. I'm *out*. Do you hear me? And if you have any sense left in you, you'd get out too."

"K-Kennedy. I—"

"Fuck off. I deserve better than this, and so do you. Goodbye." She hung up and tossed her phone into a bush. It started ringing again. "Ignore it," she hollered to the Lycan watching her. Her cheeks heated with anger and embarrassment. Her one nice night with a happy family doing happy family things and Jake had to shit all over it by being his typical self.

"Is everything okay?" Emerick asked cautiously.

"No, nothing is okay," she snapped. Then she felt like shit because Emerick didn't deserve her attitude. "Sorry, I'm just... my brother is a piece of work."

"He sounded desperate," Bane said, his brow pinched together. "What was he looking for?"

She shook her head, disgusted, and hugged herself again. "He *always* sounds like that. And I'm always a sucker for it. I'm done. I have no clue what he's looking for. I suspected he hid something in my house a few days ago, but I couldn't find it." She wanted to crawl into a hole and hide just admitting that much. Bane's family was now seeing exactly what they were inviting into their pack.

She looked each of the men in the eyes. "I swear I'm nothing like him."

"Hey, whoa." Bane got all defensive. "No one's throwing stones, Kennedy."

She stared at the ground, her throat tightening as she fought back tears. Bane tipped her chin up so she met his gaze, his eyes warm and understanding. No judgment lurked behind those amber peepers. No disappointment twisted his mouth into a frown. He was a solid mass of confidence and security.

"Turn me." Kennedy blurted. "Turn me Lycan. I want to be a Lycan."

CHAPTER 33

Bane didn't know the right thing to say, so naturally, he said the first thing that popped into his mind. "You're mad and being impulsive."

Shit. Wait. He'd like a do-over. Shit, shit, shit. If he had a tail, it would be tucked under his ass. Kennedy's fury practically made her foam at the mouth. A pissed off woman was a hell of a dangerous thing. He would not recommend being the reason for their anger.

"*What?*" That one word crawled out of her mouth with such viciousness, Bane's balls did the tuck and hide. "Are you..." She backed up. Her eyes narrowed. "Are you changing your mind about me now?"

"Hell no," he said without hesitation. "But you need to be sure about this, Kennedy. Being a Lycan will change *everything*."

"No more, brother," Bowen said from the sidelines, flushed from his run. He must have been listening from the edge of the woods. Buckling his belt, he stomped forward and added, "No more life as you've built it for yourself."

Bane watched her face pale as she stuttered, "I-I-I'd have to say goodbye to Jake *forever*?"

This was not how he wanted to have this conversation..

"You just said you were done with him." Bowen pushed when Bane went rigid. "You better mean it if you're asking to be turned. If not..." He shrugged and fell silent.

Bane wanted to rip his twin's throat out. It wasn't his place to

245

step in and say all this. But Bane found himself in lip-stall. What a nightmare. He didn't want to crush Kennedy's heart. Didn't want to hurt her. Didn't want to admit this was going to be a major shift in her existence and DNA. The elation he felt when she said *Turn me Lycan* had the lifespan of a sparkler in a thunderstorm. It lit him up, crackled for a hot second, then fizzled with the truth.

"I want nothing more than to turn you, Kennedy." Bane grabbed her hands and squeezed them. Damn near fell onto his knees for her too. "But you need to be absolutely sure you're ready for this."

Which, clearly, she wasn't.

"You said I was your *Deesha*."

His heart was shriveling. Her voice breaking gobbled up his confidence and he could see she was on the verge of tears. "*You are*." He squeezed her hands again, giving them a little shake. "You are, Kennedy."

"Then turn me. Bite me and make me like you."

"You need time to think this over." What. The fuck. Was he saying? Bane's wolf grew so furious with him, it slashed his insides and barked. He almost doubled over at the painful sensation of his wolf trying to dig its way out of Bane's soul. Instead, he held his shit together and added, "You've seen what we have to offer, but you need to know it comes at a price. This life isn't perfect either, *Deesha*. Lycan know full well what they're worth and what they cost. Same as you."

Kennedy's lips formed a thin line. She swallowed hard.

Bane squeezed her hands. "After I turn you, there's no going back. No more being human. We might have a good life, but it's not without danger. And ours is next level. The *Savag-Ri* will always hunt you. Vampire wars are prevalent. And your first shift could —"

"Stop," Kennedy ripped her hands out of his. "Stop, stop, stop." Taking two steps back, Bane made up for the space by putting one foot forward. "Is this all some kind of… I don't know… a trick?"

"How is this a trick?" Bane didn't bother keeping his temper under control. For her to accuse him of doing something untrustworthy set him off. "I've been honest with you this entire time. And what the hell would a trick get me?"

"You're keeping something from me." She jabbed his chest

246

with her finger. "I can *feel* it. You're not telling me everything I need to know about turning. And now you're hesitating when I'm asking you to deliver. You said I was your *Deesha*. You said this was meant to be. You said all my symptoms—"

"I never said it was meant to be."

Her eyes rounded, cheeks reddening with emotions. "W-what?"

Bane's heart thrashed like a two-year-old having a temper tantrum in his chest. "I never said the words 'meant to be'." He grabbed her shoulders. "Did you hear that somewhere else?"

She gawked at him.

"Did you hear those words somewhere else?" When she didn't reply, he turned to look at Bowen, and then Emerick and his dad. "Where'd you hear it, Kennedy?"

"In... in my head. I keep hearing it in my head."

He crushed his mouth to hers so fast she stumbled back and had to hold on to him for support. His fear of going after the wrong woman vanished when his tongue stroked hers. That was, until she bit it.

"Ow! Shit!" He jerked back tasted the blood welling in his mouth from her chomping on the damned thing.

"Don't you come at me with your hot mouth now, asshole." Kennedy held her hand up and said, "*No.* You just... pump the brakes and back the fuck up. I can't think with you like this."

His tongue healed in the time it took her to say all that. Bane respectfully licked his lips and shoved his hands in his pockets. Then he took a step back. "Better?"

"Not hardly." Kennedy looked down at the ground and started pacing. "I think you're right. I'm being impulsive and crazy. Maybe I need time away."

"We can go anywhere you want. Name it and I'll set it up."

"No," she said impatiently. "I mean time away from you."

Bane's heart fell out of his ass. No. No, no, no. He didn't have much time left. "Okay," he heard himself say.

"Give me a couple days on my own, Bane. Then... we'll see where things stand."

"Okay," he said again, this time with a deeper, softer voice.

"Take me home now, please."

As Bane drove her home, the silence between them was awful. It made her stomach clench and hands shake. Kennedy wanted to simultaneously jump out the window and crawl into his lap. A thousand thoughts swarmed in her mind, none of them making her feel the least bit better about anything.

I've been manipulated before. I don't know what a healthy relationship is, so why do I think Bane could give me something close to happiness forever? He's not even human. Do I want to be not human? What is a Savag-Ri *and why are they always after Lycan? Vampires. Do I really want to add that to my list of what the fucks? What will I do for a job? How would I ever say goodbye to Jake?*

Is this really my life? Who has problems like this? What would Jake say if I told him? What would happen if I told him, since I'm not supposed to say anything about Lycan at all? What did Jake hide in my house? What fresh hell has he landed in and will ultimately drag me into?

Is Bane no better? Did I go from one co-dependent relationship into another? Am I willing to sacrifice everything I have — which is basically nothing at all now — to see how this all plays out? Am I being duped somehow?

Am I willing to believe Bane, and actually get bitten and turned because I feel bad for him?

That was a biggie. It cut a little too deep into her heart, making it constantly leak.

Kennedy always took in stray animals and did what she could to save them. Glancing over at Bane, she realized that's how she was starting to see him. A wounded animal in need of care.

Her stomach clenched so fiercely, she bent forward from the pain.

"You okay?" Bane asked with both hands on the wheel. She wished he'd reach over and touch her. Wow, she was a headcase tonight.

"I'm fine."

No, she wasn't. Far from it. But the last thing Kennedy wanted to do was hurt Bane, and saying she kept comparing him to an injured dog in need of compassion and treatment would definitely hurt his feelings.

Punching all the right buttons and aiming the vents, she took in slow, even, deep breaths. Why, why, why, why was her body crapping out on her all the time?

Because I'm fated for a Lycan.

If it's fate, why hesitate? Why didn't Bane just bite her and be done with it? If his life depended on her being his mate, why hadn't he just attacked and turned her by now? "Pull over."

Bane swerved off the road and turned his hazards on. Kennedy barely waited for the truck to come to a full-stop before shoving the door open and retching all over the tall grass. Her heart pounded erratically, giving dizziness a chance to make things worse. She leaned forward, heaving, and didn't even notice Bane at her back, holding her hair out of the way. She swayed on her feet, determined to stay upright. The tightness in her chest had nothing to do with her sorrow and everything to do with the forcefulness of her dinner leaving her body.

She was so fed up. So tired. So sick of feeling out of control.

And she didn't want to be alone anymore.

As she emptied the contents of her stomach onto the side of the road, Kennedy's mind was made up. She wanted Bane. It didn't have to make sense to still be true. And if being with Bane meant leaving her old life behind, so be it, because the very idea of going a day without him...

She heaved again.

Her eyes watered and the amount of saliva building in her mouth was overkill. It dribbled down her chin, and she swiped it away with a trembling hand. "I'm sorry," she said with a hoarse voice.

"Nothing to be sorry for." Bane repositioned himself to be more at her side and still hold her hair out of the way. "Never, ever apologize for feeling your feelings, or thinking your thoughts."

"That a wolf thing?"

"Yeah, kind of. More like a Woods thing. We're unapologetic creatures."

Once she thought the worst was over, she took in a deep breath and turned to him. "I'm just so confused."

"I know."

His whispered words, coupled with how soft his touch was when he swept the stray hairs out of her face, were her downfall. "How can I love you?" It didn't make sense. Nothing made a lick of sense. "How can I feel torn in half and get sick at just the thought of not being with you?"

"Because we're meant to be." Bane looked down the road when they both heard a vehicle approach. Putting himself between Kennedy and the moving car, he watched it speed past them and vanish before saying, "Come on. Let's get you home."

The rest of the drive was torture for them both.

And then it got way worse.

CHAPTER 34

Bane's wolf was feral. In the marrow of his bones, in the heat coursing through his veins, in the depths of his tortured soul, his wolf was suffering. Trapped and anguished, both man and wolf were on a short leash and their collar was tightening around their throats, choking the life from them.

It started the instant Kennedy shoved away from him at the bonfire. It continued when they hopped in the truck and drove home in eerie silence. And now it reached a level of agony that caused sweat to roll down his back, soaking his t-shirt and making it hard to see straight.

As they pulled onto her road, Bane fought for breath. *This isn't the end. She's not leaving for good. It's just a temporary pause.*

She'd left her cat, Molly, at his cabin. Surely if she was going to cut and run, she'd have asked to go back for her things and especially her cat, right? Not just asked to be brought directly home?

His wolf paced, switching between growls and whimpers. It was strange to feel his animal like this. They were always very aware of each other, but lately, a rift in their soul's seam was tearing at an alarming rate. His wolf no longer felt empathy for things. It was in survival mode.

And it was trapped.

No way would Bane shift now. His wolf might never let him have control again.

So, if he bit Kennedy...

Holy shit, the repercussions could be catastrophic.

There were rules about wolves biting when they weren't in their right minds. Bane never thought he'd be one of them though. But this feeling? This gut-wrenching, soul-shredding awfulness was forcing his wolf into fight mode.

He knew his animal would never hurt her on purpose. That's not what Bane worried about. His fear was that he'd bite Kennedy and infect her with feral tendencies that would change her for the worse. Would he still love her? Hell yeah. But she might not like what she turned into, and it would be all his fault.

That's not an issue for today. *You have time, man. You have a couple days to get your head straight while she gets her affairs in order and either makes you the happiest sonofabitch in the world and says yes to you… or seals your fate, turning you wolf forever.*

Bane ground his molars together. Was this how Killian felt as he tore the world apart, searching for his *Deesha*? Did his wolf eat him from the inside out? Bane's throat tightened with the thought of his younger brother feeling even a smidgeon of what rocked Bane's system. Knowing it got worse… that it could be a million times more agonizing… was heartbreaking.

I'm so sorry, brother.

So much for Woods family members being unapologetic.

Killian's fate shook the foundation of his family. As the first and only member to have not found their mate in time, the reality that no one was truly safe hit home and blew shit up. Emily wasn't the same—not that she ever mentioned wanting to find love to begin with. Emerick and Bowen had lost some of their compassion and started keeping people at arm's length and focused on pack business instead of living happily and carefree. Alistair and Marie would likely never recover from the holes in their chests created by never saying goodbye to their baby boy. And Bane? Bane was the worst of them all. He'd secretly chugged the liquid silver and was heading down the same path Killian journeyed on. The finish line was in sight.

And it didn't look victorious.

He pulled into her driveway and felt his stomach bottom out by his boots. "I want to search the place and perimeters before you go in."

If she didn't like that idea, she didn't say so. Kennedy nodded quietly and got out of the truck, following him up the porch steps. Scenting the air, he couldn't trace a damned thing. His legs felt heavy. His body slower. His eyes darted all over the place while he scented the air. Nothing triggered his defenses. No threats detected so far.

Why was he disappointed about that? Hmm. Maybe because he was a sack of skin filled with pent-up aggression. Gee, what on earth could have caused that?

Annnd this was another reason he needed to be careful if — and hopefully when — he turned Kennedy. Bane was a violent creature. It's why he loved the underground fight clubs so much. He could test his skills, practice commanding his inner beast, and burn off his energy in a controlled environment. He went to fights regularly to keep himself in check. And he hadn't been to one since dreaming of Kennedy.

As she unlocked things and opened the door, Bane's hands itched to hold her waist and kiss the back of her neck. If he couldn't fight, he liked to fuck. Neither was happening any time soon. As Kennedy moved to the side and let him go in first, his nostrils flared.

He smelled men. Jake, definitely. But others too. "Stay here." His fingers fanned out as he held his hand up, forcing Kennedy to stay back. When she didn't budge, he stalked forward, taking note of everything.

Her house wasn't torn apart, but it felt off. The drawers of her dresser weren't shut all the way. Her couch cushions were a little askew. "Your house was tampered with."

"Jake was here," she said behind him. "He has a key. He came here looking for something he'd hidden."

"I smell a woman who's not you." Not looking to see her reaction, he continued, "And cigarettes. Tide detergent. Fake perfumes... like an air freshener." He sniffed again. "And something bitter..."

Kennedy let out an exhale. "You can actually pick up all of that in one whiff?"

"Two, if we're counting. But..." he cautiously turned and headed for the kitchen. "It's... something's covered up a lot of it." Bane's brow furrowed. Marching over to the counter, he picked up a can of Febreze and shook it. "Empty."

His hackles raised. "Someone's purposefully covered their scent."

"Why? What would be the point of doing that?"

Bane deadpanned her. "Because they know I'm a Lycan." The *Savag-Ri* knew Bane had been with Kennedy. It was enough to put her on another kind of radar. The worst one. "One of the MC members is a *Savag-Ri*. I picked up his scent last time I was here but wasn't certain and had no way to verify it. This," he gestured towards the room freshener again, "is a quick, temporary way to cover their tracks with us." Baking soda was another. "They mask or neutralize odors in a room, which can confuse us if we're not suspecting it."

Swiping his mouth, more repercussions began stacking up. If Kennedy rejected him, he'd need to put security in place to keep her safe until she died. He wouldn't be able to do it himself. Bowen... shit, Bowen wouldn't leave Bane and would likely hate Kennedy for denying him. Emerick? Could he ask him to watch over Kennedy until she was old and dead?

Seemed dramatic, but it wasn't. *Savag-Ri* were petty enough to still go after *Deeshas* even if their mate no longer roamed the earth. The mere fact that fate made them Lycan mates—whether acted upon or not—was still a good reason to kill them. Or use them. Some of those bastards didn't just torture a *Deesha* for fun. They experimented on them. Always trying to level up in their fight against the war of Lycan and vampires.

Bane damn near chipped a tooth grinding his teeth so hard as he stalked through her house checking room, after room, after room. Her clothes were ruffled in their drawers and her bed was a little rumpled, but that was all that looked out of place. "Is anything missing that you can tell?"

"No," she said in a tiny voice. "Bane, what does this mean? How much danger am I in now?"

He squeezed his eyes shut and kept his back to her, unable to find the words he should say. The last thing he wanted was for Kennedy to lump him in with her brother. Both loved her. Both wanted to protect her.

And both had dragged her into dangerous rabbit holes.

"Bane," she barked, getting angry when he wouldn't answer.

He opened his mouth. Shut it. Opened it again and turned

254

around.

Kennedy's cell rang in her pocket. It was a video call from Jake. Kennedy stared at the screen, hesitating to answer it. Then she looked up at Bane, beseeching answers he wasn't ready to give. Bane never felt so vile in his whole life as he did then. "Answer it."

Now who's deflecting?

Kennedy's eyes hardened. She broke her gaze from his and hit the answer button. "What now, Jake?"

Kennedy's eyes widened with horror when another man's face showed on the screen. "How about you shut your dirty mouth and get that pretty ass over here."

CHAPTER 35

Dogs barked loudly in the background. Jake started screaming—the godawful sound made the blood rush out of Kennedy's face. "Oh my god." Her cheeks went numb from fear.

Her brother screamed again. Coughing and grunting, he yelled, "Stop! Please! FUUUCK! Don't do this!" The sound of metal links clanking as dogs barked even louder overpowered all other noises. The screen jostled. Acid's ugly face came back into view. "Got your attention now, don't I, little sister?" He dragged his tongue across his teeth. "Maybe this will pull you away from your puppy and his pack."

The screen flipped to face Jake.

"No." Kennedy couldn't process what she was seeing. "No, no, nonononono."

Bound with chains and rope, Jake was bleeding all over the place. The camera swept around, giving Kennedy a three-hundred-and-sixty-degree angle of Blade slicing her brother over and over. Slowly. Jake barely looked human with how severely he'd been beaten. He didn't even try to fight back.

But Kennedy would.

"I'm going to kill you," she growled into the phone. "I'm going to fucking kill all of you."

"Relax, sugar." Blade's face popped onto the screen. "He took your punishment for what you did to me. We're even now." He licked the blood from his blade and smiled at her.

Acid turned the camera back to him. She could hear Blade

256

laughing though, just a heartbeat before Jake yelled again.

"Why are you doing this?" Kennedy hated how hot her tears felt as they slid down her face. She didn't want to look weak. Despised how she cried whenever she was infuriated. *"Why are you fucking doing this to us!"*

"Jake's getting what he deserves," Acid shot back. "He wanted to play both sides and got caught. This is what happens to heroes."

Jake screamed again, all gurgled and choking.

Kennedy's heart plummeted to its death. "Don't... don't do more. I'll get you the tranquilizers. I have them." She flat out lied. "I'll come now." She'd say and do anything to get Jake out of this. She'd rob her old vet clinic of everything and bring it to them if that's what it took to get her brother out of there.

So much for being done. So much for walking away. So much for thinking she could have something great in her life.

She was going to either die saving her brother or go to prison for murder over this.

"I'm coming," she growled at him, her teeth clenched with rage and heartache. "I'll bring whatever you want me to bring. Just... stop hurting him."

"That's a good little bitch," Acid teased.

"Where..." Kennedy cleared her dry throat. "Where do I have to go?"

"We're at the old Finnick Farm. Off 16."

Jake screamed, "No! Kennedy, don't—"

Acid disconnected the call.

"What do I do?" Kennedy panicked. "What do I do? What-do-I-do? WHATDOIDO?"

Bane gripped her shoulders and squeezed. Shoving his face in hers, he said, "We'll find him."

God, how she wanted to believe him. "He's... they stabbed him. And the dogs. Oh my god, what was that? And how did he... how did Acid know about you? He..." *Maybe this will pull you away from your puppy and his pack.* Kennedy reared up on Bane with a fresh wave of anger. "What the *fuck* is going on, Bane? Do you know Acid?"

"No more than you do," he said in a flat tone. "But he's a *Savag-Ri*."

"How do you know that?"

"I don't, for sure. But him saying that isn't a coincidence. He knows I've been here. Knows I'll be back. I'm positive he's the one who came here and sprayed the air neutralizer to hide his scent from me. This," Bane stumbled on his words and scrubbed his face hard with both hands. "Fucking Hell, Kennedy. This might all be my fault."

"No," her voice shook. "Jake was in this MC long before I met you. Whatever else there is going on, this started because Jake got caught up in shit he shouldn't have. You and I are in the fallout."

Bane looked around her house, his jaw clenching. "We need backup."

"*We* don't need anything. You're not coming with me, I..." Kennedy's words caught in her throat when Bane's chest heaved with ragged breaths. Hand-to-the-man, she thought he was going to shift in front of her and... Lose. His. Shit. His eyes blazed with fury and hands balled into fists.

"Not. Negotiable." His voice was no longer human. It was too deep. Too gravelly.

"Bane." She couldn't ask him to do this. But she also didn't want to go alone. "How can I possibly drag you into this shitshow with me?"

"You're not dragging me anywhere, *Deesha*. I'll crawl into any trouble you find yourself in. You're mine. Mine to protect. Mine to cherish. Mine no matter what."

She hated herself for this. "Then we have to go. Now."

Dashing out to her tool shed — because she'd yet to find where Blade had hidden her baseball bat — Kennedy grabbed a shovel and crowbar. "This isn't my slugger, but I'm sure I can fuck a man's night up with it." She glared up at Bane and felt her spine morph into steel. "We do this *together*. Everything we do, from this moment on, we do together. Got it?"

"Yeah." He cleared his throat, "Yeah, *Deesha*. Always."

Fine time for him to stare at her like she was the loveliest animal on the planet.

She almost kissed him. Almost. But he stormed away before she had the chance. As they headed for Bane's truck, a million screaming scenarios flew through her mind until she wasn't sure which end was up anymore.

258

Bane started the engine. "I called for backup."

Jesus, she hadn't even heard him talk on the phone. He peeled out of the driveway and headed towards Route 16. Kennedy's grip tightened on her crowbar. Was she really doing this? Was she actually going after an entire crew of monsters with a crowbar and a Lycan?

You bet your ass she was.

Bane glanced over at her. "This isn't in our territory."

As if that mattered? Kennedy didn't give a shit about Lycan territories. She just wanted her brother safe. The road stretched for miles. A cloud of dust streamed behind them as they pushed well beyond the speed limit.

"When this is done, turn me. Promise me you'll do it, Bane."

"You'll no longer live a normal life," he warned again.

"Does this look normal to you?" She shook the crowbar sitting between her legs. "I've never had normal. Why try for it now? I'd rather be stronger. Better able to defend myself. *Happier.*" She looked over at him and stared at the veins and tendons tensing in his neck. "I didn't know happy until you."

"Fuck me sideways." He flicked his gaze to her for a heartbeat. "You won't regret it."

"I know that. How can I possibly regret anything that involves you?"

Something lamentable and worrisome danced across his face. It vanished fast enough to make her wonder if she'd imagined it. As they raced towards disaster at eighty-five miles per hour, Kennedy chewed on her bottom lip. "I wonder what kind of fur I'll have."

She was deflecting so she could deal. And wouldn't you know, Bane indulged her.

"It'll be the shades of your hair." He half-smiled. "You'll be stunning as a wolf, just as you're stunning now."

"Can I eat all the carbs I want since my metabolism will be faster?"

"You can eat all the carbs you want no matter what."

Bane knew all the right things to say, didn't he? Kennedy pressed her head to the passenger side window. She needed to keep talking about things that had nothing to do with what they were about to jump into. Distract herself with anything. Because if she sat in silence too long, her head would explode with fear and fury.

"What was the other man from the twins?" she asked.

"Huh?"

"In the story about your curse. You said one of the lovers was a Lycan. What was the other? Just a simple pain-in-the-ass human or what?"

Oh boy. She noticed Bane gripped the wheel a little tighter. "He was a vampire."

She didn't laugh. Didn't even blink or show any surprise when she said, "Oh."

"Oh?" he looked over at her. "That's all? Just *Oh*?"

"I feel like I should have guessed that." She tugged on her flannel shirt—his flannel shirt—and unbuttoned the top ones to let cool air in. "So do you know any?"

"Vampires? Yeah. So do you." He looked back in his rearview mirror before changing lanes. "Dorian's a vampire."

"Dorian from dinner tonight? Your brother?"

"Yyyup," he popped the p when he answered her. "They have the curse too, but theirs is a little different."

"How so?"

"Vampires see their mates in reflections."

"And you see them after drinking liquid silver."

"Mmm hmm."

"Interesting," she wrung her hands nervously. Shouldn't she be a little bit more mind-blown over all this? Instead, she felt... numb. "So silver is a property for both. Looking glass and liquid."

"Yes, and no." Bane turned down another road. "Vampires can use any reflective surface. Lycan can only dream of their *Deesha* after drinking the silver water. I've never heard of any other way for us to find our mates."

Radio silence.

Kennedy stared straight ahead, chewing on her bottom lip. She noticed Bane glance over at her again and figured she couldn't hide behind distractions anymore. Tears welled in her eyes. Kennedy trapped them there and refused to set them loose. Next, her stomach flip-flopped, and she grew dizzy. "I don't feel so good."

Bane smacked a bunch of buttons and flicked the vents, so they all pointed at her, blasting icy air in her face. When she closed her eyes, he brushed a tear from her cheek before putting his attention back on the road.

Cold air blasted her face, but the chill didn't penetrate deep enough. Kennedy squeezed her eyes shut and prayed...

Please God, Oh Great Spirit in the Sky, Creator of life, Odin, Freya, or anyone who's listening right now... I beg you, get us through this. Please. Help us. I'm not ready to give up. I'm not ready to sink. But I can't let those I love die for something they shouldn't be part of. Not Bane. Not whoever he's called for backup. Not the dogs. And not... not Jake. I know it's crazy to ask for help in a situation like this. I know I should call the cops. But... please just... if it's fate that I be with Bane, then allow fate to take the reins with this. Is fate a person? If so, then I hope you're listening because... Thank you. Thank you for bringing Bane into my life. And if fate's a thing, keep it hanging over us like a cloud, a shield. Stretch it to cover all of us. Protect us. Help us get through this. Whatever happens here, I'll accept it. Whatever is meant to be... is... is meant to be...

Kennedy's heartrate skyrocketed when they reached the old farm. Bane had needed directions at a certain point, but she knew the old place only because she'd once worked on a horse there when she first moved into town a few years back. The owners no longer lived there, and she thought the place had been abandoned or put in foreclosure.

The farmhouse's front windows were bordered up. A dead plant hanging on the side porch. The instant Bane cut the engine, Kennedy heard the dogs barking in the barn.

What horrific things had they done to Jake in the time it took to get here? She couldn't bear to imagine.

"Stay close," Bane whispered.

No lie, if she thought she could climb onto his back, she would. Kennedy was terrified to go in the barn. Scared of what she would see. Gripping her crowbar, she headed towards it with her courage in one hand, and fate in the other.

Ba-bum. Her heartrate plummeted, and the world slowed down. *Ba-bum.* Kennedy's thoughts skipped around in a panic. *Ba-bum.* What did the *Savag-Ri* look like? How would she ever spot another one? *Ba-bum.* Acid looked like every other man in the MC— leather clad, angry, and dirty. *Ba-bum.* Did they have a different smell? Give off a certain energy? *Ba-bum.* Did they shift into animals too? *Ba-bum.* Were they going to turn Jake into one of them?

Sounds rushed back into her ears and her heartrate kicked

back into high gear when Bane touched her shoulder. She looked up at him, her mouth parted as she panted. "Stay behind me," he ordered.

Kennedy nodded and gripped her crowbar until the iron bit into her hand. She was going in there. Jake had saved her countless times. Tonight, she'd return the favor.

I can do this. She *had* to do this. It was her final goodbye. After Jake was safe, she was leaving. Turning Lycan and never going back to any of this. Jake would have to live without her. And he'd be okay with that. Her safety and happiness were always important to him. He'd understand her need to sever ties and go.

They just had to save him first.

CHAPTER 36

The first thing to hit Bane's nose when he stepped out of the truck was the pungent, sour stench of fear. Next was canine, which had an overwhelming amount of health issues attached to them. On the tail end of his inhale was the scent of cigarettes, sweat, blood, and a hint of piss.

Not the finest combo, but certainly not the worst.

Thank fuck this wasn't a *Savag-Ri* nest. As far as he could tell, Acid was the only *Savag-Ri* in the crew, but that wasn't confirmed yet. However, the stink was faint, so overpowered by everything else, Bane was ninety-nine percent certain there was only one there.

And the asshole would bank on Bane showing up.

Present and packing.

It was a smart move. Jake was enough to coerce his sister in for Blade. And Kennedy was all Acid needed to lure Bane in too. This asshole thought he was getting a BOGO deal today. They'd soon find out they'd barked up the wrong tree. Fucked with the wrong Lycan.

And pissed off the wrong woman.

Dog barks echoed from the old barn. It was go time.

In the back of his mind, Bane's human side screamed for Kennedy to stay back. Run. Get as far away as possible. But his wolf? Hate to say it, but his wolf loved that she was here and wanted to see what she was made of.

Nothing said love to a wolf like a hunt and kill. Their prey was just beyond those red wooden doors. As Bane stood between

263

Kennedy and the bastards in that barn, he was a mix of proud and petrified of how this was going to end.

Only one way to find out.

He gave a signal and kicked open the barn door. No sense in pussyfooting around. The MC knew they were there. Bane had seen a scout dash behind the building as they'd pulled in. *Dipshit.* Humans weren't as sneaky or cunning as they thought. Not when up against a Lycan. And if the MC was mostly human, this would be a cakewalk. All Bane had to do was fight these losers, destroy the *Savag-Ri*, and get Jacked Up Jake out of there as fast as possible, all while keeping Kennedy safe.

Easy peasy.

Bane kicked open the barn door, keeping Kennedy behind him in case they pulled guns. His eyes rounded when he saw Jake kneeling, bound and gagged, in the center of what had to have been the MC's dog fight pit. Eight canines, all ranging in breed, weight, and stages of health, were tethered around him, barking and snapping their jaws, straining against their chains to attack the defenseless prey whimpering in the center.

Oh. Shit.

Kennedy rushed forward, crowbar in hand. Bane caught her arm. Put himself in front of her as a shield again.

"Run!" Jake screamed through his gag. Wheezing, drooling, bleeding out, he wasn't going to last much longer.

Bane could hear his heart struggling to beat and the amount of blood running from his gruesome wounds suggested he wasn't going to survive what they'd done to him.

Jake coughed up more blood, gasping, "R-r-run!"

"Shut." *Pop*! "The fuck" *Pop*! "Up!" *Pop*! Acid came forward, his gun still pointing in Jake's direction.

Each bullet had hit Jake in the shoulders, forcing him to jerk back and scream again. He slumped forward, the chains barely giving him a few inches of leeway.

Kennedy roared in fury, swinging her crowbar like it was the Excalibur, and ran, full tilt, at the first man to come close to them.

Gotta admit, it was a little hot. And when she swung her weapon like a bat and clocked the fucker across the face, his head spun sideways to the right, and blood and spit sprayed out of his mouth.

And his *Deesha* didn't stop there. Without breaking stride, Kennedy came at Acid next.

That's when Bane took charge. He was on Kennedy faster than she could reach her target and put himself in front of her again. "No. He's mine."

"He just shot my brother!"

Blade came out from the back with two other men still wearing their cuts. One was rubbing his busted knuckles, the other had Kennedy's baseball bat.

"Kennedy!" Jake cried out.

All around them, the dogs barked and gnashed at anyone who got too close.

"What did I tell you?" Blade snarled at Jake. "I said if you spoke again, I was cutting out your tongue."

As Bane held Kennedy back, Blade went after Jake. Straight through the dogs, he marched over to where Jake knelt and pulled out his knife. Acid's gaze, however, didn't waver from Kennedy's. "What's he worth?"

Jake screamed and thrashed against the blade held to his mouth.

Acid repeated, "What's he worth to you?"

"He's not worth shit! Her and her traitor brother need to die!" Blade hollered, already cutting into Jake's mouth.

Acid pulled the trigger and shot Blade between the eyes without looking. The president of the Wolf Pack MC dropped like a sack of bricks.

Kennedy screamed. Bane's wolf tried to take over.

"I'll ask again." Acid tipped his head while backing into the throng of foaming at the mouth dogs. "What's he worth to you?"

Kennedy stepped forward. "What do you want?"

Kennedy couldn't stand this. The noise. The fear. Her dying brother gasping for air. It was too much. With Blade dead, Kennedy deluded herself into thinking she might have a chance of winning this war. "What do you want?" she asked, skirting around Bane.

Acid didn't take his gaze off her mate, which she took as a good sign. So long as Acid was focused on Bane, Kennedy might be able to—

"We asked you for a very simple thing," Acid said. "All you had to do was get tranquilizers and obey like a good little bitch."

"I brought them," she lied. "Just... just release my brother."

Jake leaned back, off balance, and slumped. "Run," he gurgled. "It's too late. She... she already got it. It's... over."

Nothing Jake said made sense. Who got what?

"I'm so sorry," Kennedy heard a familiar voice say from the old tack room. She almost dropped her crowbar when Risa came forward. "I had to. I didn't have a choice."

Her gaze volleyed between Acid and Risa. "How... how did..." She shook her head. Of course, now would be a great time for a hot flash to start up. Her head got foggy the harder she tried to piece things together. "What are you doing? What's all this about?"

"We gave your brother two chances," Acid said.

Bane, for whatever reason, wasn't attacking the son-of-a-bitch while he flapped his jaws. It was like he'd frozen in terror himself and she didn't know why.

The animals fought against their chains, some whimpering, others snarling. No one was acting right.

"Risa?"

"Your brother was working with the Feds." Acid said. "Had enough dirt on us to put the entire chapter away for life."

No. This... what?

"He hid the evidence in your house. When we suspected he was up to something..." Acid stalked forward a little, and grabbed Risa by the throat, pressing his body to her back while talking to Kennedy. "We had him tailed. Found him meeting a bunch of pigs on the east side of town in a hideout they used in a fancy little development. Also noticed he came by the vet clinic too often for someone without a pet. And then your house. Had a key and stayed long hours at your place. Took me a minute to catch the resemblance though."

"K-Kennedy," Jake said from the ground. "*Run.*"

But she couldn't move. Like Bane, she was frozen in place. Hanging on every word Acid spat out.

"Thought we could set him straight," Acid's hand tightened around Risa's throat. Her eyes were red-rimmed, face turning shades of purple as Acid kept her collared with his hand. "Thought bringing you in would give him a lesson in priorities. But rats don't have loyalty, do they, Jake?"

Jake said nothing.

Acid clucked his tongue. "We gave him protection in prison. We owned him from the minute he came to us asking for help. And this is what we get in return?" He let go of Risa and pulled a USB stick out of his pocket. "He captured enough evidence to put our entire crew away for life. But he was too chickenshit to turn it in when he had the chance. Too much of a pussy to seal his deal with the cops for that shortened sentence they gave him." He stomped on the USB stick, destroying it with the heel of his heavy boot.

The guy Kennedy had knocked out with the crowbar, slowly came to on the ground. Groaning, he rolled over and held his split open temple. "Fucking Hell."

Acid snatched Risa again and lifted her into the air with impossible strength. She kicked and sputtered while trying to fight free. "What do we do to chicken shit traitors, cunt?"

Risa opened her mouth, her feet still kicking wildly in the air. "Feed... feed to the... dogs."

Acid tossed her to the side, pulled the trigger, and shot her between the eyes. "You heard the lady. Unleash the dogs!"

Chains dropped from a pulley system they'd rigged, and the dogs attacked.

Jake screamed in unholy terror as they went after him first. The pack came at him from all sides, biting down on his ankles and arms, tugging him in several directions at once. Jake's terror ripped through the air until another dog chomped down on his throat.

A high-pitched shriek made Kennedy cup her ears. Later, she'd learn that scream came from her throat.

Bane grabbed her by the waist and spun her around, shoving her towards the barn doors when shots fired again. Bane jerked forward, his back arching as a bullet went through his back and clean through his pec, clipping Kennedy in the cheek.

As her brother's cries died out, Kennedy had no idea how she and Bane were getting out of this alive.

267

CHAPTER 37

The chaos, the danger, the sounds of a human being torn to pieces — they were all things Bane could handle.

Kennedy being attacked, however, was in-fucking-sufferable.

Bane had to get her out of here, *now.*

"Can't lose you," he said, His breaths became labored. That bullet might have hit his lung before exiting. Fuck. Gauging the distance between here and the truck, he surveyed where the other shooters were. Tree? House porch? Second-story window? Meanwhile, his wolf kept clawing its way out, trying to force Bane to shift. This was about to get really fucking messy. He didn't want Kennedy to see it. "You have to run."

"Not without you."

"You don't understand." Her safety was paramount. Another shot fired behind him. Bane grunted, his eyes squeezing shut as he worked through the pain of a second bullet burying itself in his shoulder. "I have to get you out of here."

"Not. Without. You." The look in her eyes said she'd lost her brother already and wasn't losing Bane too.

Behind him, the dogs tore Jake to pieces, fighting over scraps of his meat. He couldn't let Kennedy see it. But behind her, four men were already coming out of their hiding places, each with a cocky grin on their faces.

Okay, the odds were in his favor. "Stay low."

Acid was the only *Savag-Ri* so far, so the odds weren't awful. These fuckers coming closer were only an inconvenience.

Kennedy gripped his biceps, using him like a lifeline. "Bane," she whispered when she caught onto what they were attempting. They were trying to corral Bane and Kennedy back into the barn.

He lurched to put himself between her and the three bastards closing in on them. But not in time. *Pop!* Kennedy yelped as her leg gave out and she stumbled into Bane's arms. Blood seeped through her pants leg.

Bane. Lost. His. Shit.

All that aggression he'd kept pent-up over these past couple of weeks ripped out of him in a roar. His vision crisped with his wolf eyes, the rest of him vibrating under the pressure of not shifting. He wanted his hands, not paws, on these men before he tore their throats out with his teeth.

He shoved Kennedy aside, praying she only had a flesh wound, and charged towards the three fuckfaces coming his way. The one in the middle had his gun aimed right at him. Popped off two rounds that hit Bane in the pec and shoulder. It didn't even slow his infuriated ass down.

Bane snatched the piece of shit by his throat and made fist-to-face contact in three short, hard jabs that crushed his human face in like a paper bag. His two buddies didn't do shit as Bane dropped the fucker on the ground and twisted his neck, snapping it for good measure.

"Kennedy!" He kicked the gun over to her that had fallen out of Crushed Face Man's hands. She scrambled to get it. But so did one of the other men.

Bane kicked him in the face when he bent down. "Not for you," he growled. His boot smashed into the second man's chest, sending him airborne. Kennedy got the gun, aimed, and pulled the trigger.

The chamber was empty.

She screamed at the gun as if it personally assaulted her.

Bane dragged the one he'd kicked in the gut over to the last man standing. Grabbing him by his cut, Bane tossed him to the ground like a sack of trash. The last one standing bolted.

He wouldn't get far.

Kennedy ran towards the truck. Thank fuck. Bane wanted her to haul ass out of here as fast as possible.

The air felt like fire in his lungs. He sawed air, his muscles ripping as his wolf tried to force him to shift again. His bullet wounds stung like a bitch. His vision went wonky for a half-second and he stumbled backwards, tripping over the man who'd just grabbed him by the ankle.

Bane sailed backwards and smacked his head on the dirt ground.

But when he popped up, he'd shifted to his wolf.

The Tripper's eyes bulged. "Oh Fuck," he said with a shaky voice.

Oh fuck, was right. Bane's lips peeled to reveal his sharp teeth, his paws digging into the ground for leverage just before he attacked. No circling the prey. No warning snaps or growls. He just reared back and lunged.

The man's throat vibrated with his scream as Bane ripped it clean out. The heels of the man's bike boots dug divots into the dirt as he clutched his neck, gurgling while bleeding out.

An engine roared to life. Bane looked with wolf eyes towards the rumble and watched Kennedy slam his truck in gear and take off towards the man still running towards the overgrown field. Bane tore off after both of them. The blood in his mouth and the aggression pumping in his veins took precedent over the fire burning from the bullet wounds. The injuries slowed him down, but not enough to lose his target. Snarling with every leap made towards his next target, he found the man zig-zagging through the weeds, ducking down so Kennedy would have a harder time seeing him. But Bane followed his stink of fear and cologne with no problem.

Tackling from behind, Bane slammed his massive paws on the bastard's back, driving him face-first into the soil. The truck ground to a halt behind them.

Bane shifted back into human form, grabbed the fucker by the head and… *Twist, pull, c-c-c-crack….* broke his neck in less than two seconds.

He looked over his shoulder at Kennedy. Panting and in pain, he held her gaze, still poised over his kill like a wild, feral monster with no regard for humankind whatsoever.

Was she afraid of him? Would she change her mind about turning Lycan now? Drenched in sweat, blood, and drool, Bane was wild and unhinged. Kennedy hopped out of the truck, her eyes huge as she came closer to him.

"Is he dead?" she asked.

He nodded, too caught up in the moment to speak human words.

She visibly relaxed, her shoulders drooping as she let out a long exhale. "Okay," she said. "Okay." Kennedy looked around the field. "Okay." Her voice trembled. "Okay."

Bane forced his wolf to back the down, and he stood up slowly. His body hurt. His head throbbed. But as he made his way to his *Deesha*, nothing else mattered but her. "Your leg," he said. He wanted to cup her face. Kiss her. Scoop her up and drive her out of this hell and never return. Instead, he crouched down to inspect the damage done to his mate.

"It doesn't hurt," she said.

She was in shock, then. "I need to get you out of here." His voice morphed, growing deeper and gravelly.

"We're not finished," she argued. "I need to get Jake."

Bane looked up at her, his brow pinching with concern. Did she not get it? Did she not see what happened to her brother? Was she in denial or —

"I have to bury him," she cried. "I can't leave him in the barn like that."

Bane nodded. Closure would be good. He wished he could have had it with his own brother, but providing it for Kennedy was an honor he wouldn't refuse.

"The *Savag-Ri* is still in there," Bane warned.

"Two of us, one of him." Kennedy limped as she headed back to the truck. "And we can probably use this truck as a tank. Run him down?"

He preferred to be more hands on. He also didn't want Kennedy to live with murder on her hands. She might think she was okay with it now because her mind was stuck on revenge, but that might not always be the case. "I want him," Bane growled. "I'm taking him out myself."

She looked like she was going to argue at first. But in the end, she only nodded. Bane climbed in the truck, wincing at his weakened shoulder. Lycan's were fast healers, but given all that was going on with him, the holes weren't closing as fast as they should. He felt dizzy and sick.

271

Kennedy kept looking over at him, sweat pouring down her temples while her hands strangled the steering wheel. "You're hurt."

"I'll be fine."

"I can't lose you."

"You won't."

As she tore out of the field, the truck hit every ditch, hole, lump and bump on earth. Straight ahead was the barn. "I can drive right through it," she said, wiggling in her seat. "Should I drive right through it? I... I don't know what to do."

Bang!

Kennedy lost control of the truck as one of the wheels blew out. Bane slammed his hands on the dash when Kennedy hit the brakes, and he didn't waste another second. Jumping out of the truck, he ran straight towards the *Savag-Ri* who stood in the back of the barn.

"Thanks for taking care of my loose ends," Acid taunted from the second floor. The *Savag-Ri* jumped down, landing on the ground like a cat. "Imagine my delight when I was in the market for a new wolf and your scent was all over this bitch," his gaze flicked to Kennedy, and he winked. "Gotta say, I didn't think you'd actually let her come here, Lycan. Thought you animals were more protective than that. But, hey, if you want her to watch you become my pet... I'm cool with it."

Bane growled as the *Savag-Ri* sauntered closer. The dogs didn't attack him — making Acid their true master. Blood covered their muzzles and paws. Some had streaks across their bodies and flanks. They started attacking each other, the cacophony of their violence setting Bane's wolf on edge, as they fought over a severed body part.

"It's just you and me," Bane said, rolling his shoulders back. fighting naked wasn't his favorite hobby, but his clothes were shredded and useless. Modesty wasn't even a blip on his radar now that he was face-to-face with a Lycan killer.

"And the beast makes three." Acid let go of something he'd been holding — a chain — and it flew into the air as something loud crashed down on the ground level. Bane watched in horror as another animal was set loose on them.

A deep, wet, deadly growl rippled through the air.

No. Bane's breath hitched. *No. No. NO.* "Kennedy," he said as calmly as possible. "Do as I say. Get back in the truck *now*. Call Bowen." Bane kept his gaze deadlocked on the animal as he took a step back towards Kennedy. "Go. Slow."

"Is… is that…. W-w-what is that?"

The animal's hair was in patches. Scars and wounds, infected and fresh, disfigured his muzzle and flanks. His jet-black hair stood on end, its head dipped and mouth open to reveal sharp teeth and white foam. The shock collar around its neck was too tight. The floorboards rattled with the weight of his prowling steps, his claws scraping the wood as he crept closer.

Bane needed Kennedy to get out of there *now*. No human. No Lycan. No *Savag-Ri* could survive an attack by this animal.

Its next growl wasn't a warning. It was a promise.

Bane's heart shattered into a million shards. Standing before him, foaming at the mouth, was his brother, Killian.

CHAPTER 38

Adrenaline coursed through Kennedy's veins, rooting her to the spot. She wasn't backing down. She wasn't running. And she wasn't afraid.

But seeing Bane's expression when that monstrous creature who looked like an abused, pissed off, feral wolf came out of its cage, freaked her out more than anything.

Not once had Bane stalled or hesitated. He'd just killed three men, for fuck's sake! But something about this animal made him freeze in absolute terror. And that vibe slammed right into her.

This battered wolf must be a Lycan.

That was a good thing, right? Was there a bro-code or some kind of pack loyalty law thing? Was this wolf on their side or Acid's? The collar on his neck made Kennedy believe the wolf didn't have a choice. And the dogs... *oh God...* they were circling now. Closing in.

Shit, shit, shit!

Acid laughed from the back of the barn. "Bet you wished you had tranquilizers now."

Her calf began to burn from where she'd been shot. Bane still hadn't moved from being directly between her and this wolf. Now wasn't the time to sit still or make any sudden moves. Kennedy's gaze volleyed between Acid and each of the dogs. Two were limping horribly. Acid pulled something out of his pocket and Kennedy ducked behind Bane.

It was automatic. Using this man as a shield made her feel

equal parts safe and guilty. But he could take a bullet — or more than one — and keep walking. If Kennedy got shot in the chest, she wasn't getting up.

Acid held a remote in his hand. She saw him press a button.

The wolf in front of Bane went ballistic and attacked Bane. Her mate stumbled back, catching the animal and nearly taking Kennedy out with them as he slammed on the ground with the wolf gnashing his teeth.

Bane roared. Then shifted.

The two animals tumbled across the floor, biting and fighting each other.

Kennedy scrambled out of the way and a dog rushed forward to attack. She jerked her arm away just before getting bit and slammed into a barrel. It rocked back, causing the contents to splash out of it. When the liquid hit the barn floor, it ate right through the rotting wood.

Oh my God.

There was acid in the barrels. Her eyes widened as she looked over at Bane again. The closest dog skirted around the spill and snapped its teeth at her. Should she stay by the barrel or make a run for a weapon? The crowbar she'd dropped earlier rested about fifteen feet away. If she could reach it, she'd have a better chance of survival.

Kennedy took a quick step to the left. Another dog rushed at her. She barely had time to put her arm up and block his bite when the animal chomped down on her forearm. Kennedy shut her eyes and screamed as its teeth sank into her. The animal pulled hard, tugging enough to rip her skin.

Then the dog was ripped off her. She watched it sail through the air and landed about fifteen feet away. Bane, still in wolf form, crouched down and growled. His teeth were blood-soaked as he poised to defend and attack anything that got too close to them. Kennedy looked over to see the other wolf stumbling.

Acid, however, stood back at a distance, watching the show.

Mother. Fucker.

He was going to let them all kill each other and walk out of here unscathed. She still hadn't looked over at what was left of her brother. But she knew he was unsavable. Jake had always been unsavable.

Growling, Bane put himself between her and the animals creeping closer. Her heart hammered in her chest, making her dizzy. No matter what, Bane kept putting her first and defended her. Protected her.

In some tragic, morbidly fucked up way, it made all the difference. When he said he would always protect her and had her back, it felt real. Absolute and unshakeable. She believed him with all her heart and soul that, no matter how bad things got, he wouldn't back down or cut and run. He would protect her at all costs.

It meant...

It meant that even if she didn't come out of this alive and got killed by Acid or the animals, she wouldn't die terrified and alone because Bane would go to any lengths necessary to save her. There was a strange level of peace that came with fully believing he meant every word when he said he'd always protect her.

Dying alone was terrifying. Dying alone and helpless was far worse.

But to know that someone would at least try to save her at all costs made her next steps bearable.

Sucking in a breath, Kennedy ran as fast as she could...

And headed straight for Acid.

What was she doing! Bane, still in wolf form, tracked her movements and simultaneously kept Killian at bay. His brother. His fucking baby brother didn't even recognize him. His wolf was too far gone from trauma and having its soul ripped and severed made him unpredictable now.

Killian bit and fought as if he had no other option, which meant Bane's choices on how to handle him were limited.

Head dipped down, Bane's lips peeled back as he snarled at Killian. The wolf hesitated. Not with recognition of his brother, but from dominance being established.

The problem was, Bane was a beta, so even though he could assert dominance, this wolf could very well challenge him. And possibly win. Killian was a strong tracker, but had his separation and curse made him alpha material? If so, Bane was in for a hell of a

276

fight.

A dog jumped onto Bane's back. Growling and thrashing, he knocked the canine off, bit down on its neck and jerked it away. He'd feel bad about it later. For now, fuck that dog. All he cared about was protecting Kennedy and saving Killian.

Bane chuffed. Paced back and forth.

Killian tracked his movements. Reared back. Lunged.

They tumbled hard and fast across the ground again, and Bane lost track of Kennedy. He wasn't sure which was the most dangerous animal at this point—the *Savag-Ri*, himself, Killian, or what was left of the dogs. Kennedy hollered as another dog attacked her and Bane sprang into action. With Killian on top of him, he took a chance and shifted into human form long enough to kick him into the air. Shifting back into a wolf, he charged at the dog and rammed his head into the animal's side. It went airborne, yelping when it landed next to the barrel filled with acid.

Yeah, he hadn't missed that part earlier. The bitter scent of the liquid burned the inside of his nostrils. And now he knew how Acid liked to play. There was no doubt in Bane's mind—that guy would dip every corpse in the barn in that shit to get rid of the evidence.

Kennedy crawled across the floor as fast as she could and snagged the crowbar. Acid, unfortunately, met her there. He kicked her in the mouth.

He. Kicked. Her. In. The. Mouth.

It happened in slow motion. Kennedy's head tipped back. Bloody spit misted the air. Her body canted backwards, and she landed on her back, smacking her head.

Bane leapt into the air.

Killian did too.

His little brother put himself between Bane and Acid. Or at least that's what he thought at first. But no, he was protecting his master. Confirmation came when Killian knocked Bane back and gnashed his teeth. Then Killian yelped, tucking his head and tail in. The scent of burning fur and flesh filled the space between them. Killian shook his head, desperate to get the collar off. He backed away, switching between snarls and yips. The other dogs all stopped and laid down on their ground, each facing him in total submission.

And Kennedy? Well, she was a blur of movement again. And

she had the crowbar in her hand.

Holding it like a baseball bat, she screamed and ran at Acid.

He lifted his arm. A gun in his hand.

She swung out with the crowbar.

Killian leapt just as Acid pulled the trigger.

Bane caught Kennedy's leg in his teeth and yanked just as gun shots rang out.

The scent of fresh blood permeated the air.

CHAPTER 39

With the wind knocked out of her, Kennedy laid on the ground stunned with nothing but fur in her face. Bane covered her, shielding her body with his. Beyond the loud thuds of her heart, she picked up whimpers and laughter. "Let me up," she whispered, gripping the crowbar.

Bane growled. Legs planted on both sides of her, he kept her down and covered.

"We have to finish this," she said to her wolf. "I'm okay."

She was pretty sure a few teeth had been knocked loose and the blood in her mouth tasted coppery and disgusting, but it could have been way worse. In her experience, it *would* get way worse. She'd be damned if she was going to take it lying on her back.

"Bane." She gripped his fur and tugged it. He nuzzled her face, licking her cheek. "The wolf," she said. "Go for the animal and I'll go for the asshole."

Bane growled. Snagging the crowbar from her with his teeth, he whipped around and shifted into a human before she was able to sit up. The sheer size of him seemed to have expanded. His muscles tensed and bulged. His labored breathing was the only sign that he was seriously hurt. Blood oozed from several bites and claw marks. He'd been shot too. He was a mess.

Kennedy crab-crawled away, looking for the other animals. All the surviving dogs cowered. Behind her, an engine rumbled.

Oh god. Not more Wolf Pack members.

Beyond Bane, the wolf listed, barely able to stand.

279

"Good timing," Acid chuckled. "This wolf was on his last fight anyway. And don't worry, I gotta bitch on payroll who can stitch you right up before I put you in your place, dog. Isn't that right, Kennedy?" He licked his lips and grinned. "I'm going to make a lot of fucking money off you, pup."

Kennedy watched in horror as Bane attacked the *Savag-Ri*.

Swinging the crowbar, he managed two hits that would have taken any human down. But Acid remained standing. The gun had been knocked out of his grip. So had the remote to the wolf's collar.

Maybe Acid thought he was invincible when the animals were on his side. But his wolf was too injured to fight on his behalf. The poor thing was shaking and staggering, letting out horrible whining noises. The other dogs kept whimpering and had their tails tucked under them.

"Kennedy," said a voice from behind her. "Take two steps back, sister."

Her heart lurched into her throat. It wasn't Jake talking. It was *Bowen*.

"Come on," he said in a gravelly tone. "Step back for us."

Bane remained in front of her, throwing punches as he went fist-to-fist with Acid.

"The w-wolf," she said. Her calf now screamed at her. "The animals."

"We'll take care of it." Bowen's body heat hit her first. She stepped back until she hit his chest. "Good girl. Now, get to my truck."

"Can't... can't leave Bane. I won't leave him here. This is my fight. Our fight. Not tucking tail and running." Her thoughts raced. Her body ached. Her heart fractured.

"He's got this." Bowen said. "He'll get finished faster if you at least back up and get to safety."

She nodded, too exhausted to argue. But she wasn't leaving this barn without Bane. Flicking her gaze all over the place to keep track of the remaining animals, she made it to the door and held her breath.

Bane was a beast. Now that Acid was without his animals, his MC members, and his weapons, he was no match for Bane. Her mate had that piece of shit on the ground in mere minutes, pummeling him until he was raw meat and busted bones.

280

Bowen stayed over by the wolf, staring at it with an expression Kennedy couldn't place. The wolf collapsed. Bowen scooped him up and hurried towards her, his eyes wide and fearful. "In the truck. *In the truck!*"

Bane threw Acid's limp body against the barrel. It tipped over and poured all over his corpse.

Gross. Kennedy looked away, unable to stand the gruesome scene a minute longer.

"Kennedy, get in the fucking truck!" Bowen yelled.

She didn't obey until Bane grabbed her hand and pulled her along. "We have to hurry. We have to try to save him."

"Save who?"

"Our brother, Killian." Bane scooped Kennedy into his arms and ran. They hopped in the bed of the pickup truck and Bowen got in the driver's seat. "Where can we take him?" he roared in panic.

"To my clinic!" Kennedy hollered back. The truck bounced and jostled them all over the place as they kicked up dust and flew down the lane.

"Can he not shift back?" she asked, inspecting the gunshot wounds.

"No," Bane gritted out. Gripping the shock collar, he ripped it off Killian's neck.

Kennedy hissed at the raw, burnt, infected flesh underneath. She didn't think she could save him.

But she was going to try…

Killian. Holy fucking shit, Killian!

Bane couldn't get a goddamn grip long enough to explain any of this to Kennedy. As Bowen tore down the lane, he spent all his energy praying and holding his shit together while simultaneously putting pressure on two of the three bullet wounds.

"I'm so sorry," he said to his baby brother. "I'm sorry we failed you. I'm sorry you were used." His voice cracked as emotions spilled out. "We're almost there, okay? Kennedy's going to fix you. She's going to…" He looked over at his *Deesha*, letting the promises he had no business making die on his tongue.

"When we drink the silver," he said to her, "we start our

clock. We have until the full moon to find our mate and turn them. Killian didn't find his *Deesha* in time. He's lost to his wolf. Lost... to us."

Her eyes welled with tears as they held the wolf down. "I'll do all I can to save him."

He knew she would. His *Deesha* had a heart too big and good for this world. She was the most compassionate human being he'd ever met. And soon, she would be his forever.

If she hadn't changed her mind after all this.

Her promise to do all she could to save Killian landed in Bane's gut with a thud. The reassurance, the confidence in her tone, that look in her eyes all gave him peace—something he had no clue he'd needed until now.

Whatever happened with Killian, Bane would know that they tried all they could for him. He couldn't ask for anything more than that.

Killian volleyed between whimpering and snapping his teeth. Bane held his muzzle shut to keep him from accidentally clipping Kennedy. He felt like shit doing it but had no choice. Occasionally Killian kicked his legs and attempted to get up, but they held him down.

Kennedy kept pressure on the third and worst bullet wound and talked to him in a calm tone. "That's it, Killian. You're doing great. Almost there, okay? You're safe. We've got you."

We've got you.

Bane unraveled one heartbeat at a time.

We've got you.

"Tell stories," Kennedy said. It took Bane a hot minute to realize she was talking to him. "Tell stories about you guys growing up."

Bane's throat tightened, as did his hands on Killian. "We always used to go salmon fishing every year at Lake Ontario." The memory was crystal clear, as if it happened yesterday. "Me, Bowen, and Killian would go camping for a week every September and fish, drink, and run on this other Lycan pack's land. This one time, we borrowed a boat and rigged Killian's line. He was scared of the ocean, so we only ever fished in lakes and streams. But..." Bane half-laughed, "we got him out on the boat and halfway through the day, Bowen slipped into the water, swam to our lines, and attached a

282

rubber shark to it. Then he tugged on the line hard. Like, really heard. Killian got all excited to have a fish on, and started reeling it in. I hyped him all up. Bowen stayed underwater, making the struggle remarkable. Killian was the youngest, and we always seemed to do that with him—make a big deal out of the smallest things. Hype shit up that didn't really matter. And he fed into it every time. Everything with Killian was exciting and loud and... big. Including his imagination."

And his heart.

Bane's chest hurt thinking about how wonderful of a man Killian was. "So there Bowen was, remember Kill? Bowen was thirty feet down in this freezing cold water, yanking on a line with a five-foot rubber shark on it, while I'm on the back of the boat talking about how this must be a huge fish. Too strong to be a salmon." He choked on his laugh and released Kilian's muzzle. Stroking Killian's head, he said, "He reeled the thing up onto the boat and screamed when he saw it was a shark. All his rational thinking about it being impossible for a shark to be in a lake went overboard. Killian backed up so fast, he tripped over our cooler and..." Bane laugh-cried with a painful smile as he looked down at Killian. "Remember you went ass over elbow into the water, Kill?"

The wolf's panting slowed. His eyes remained open and set on Bane.

"Then Bowen snagged him by his feet and pulled him under water. He kicked Bowen in the face and broke his nose instantly. The blood in the water had Killian nearly jumping out of the lake and back into the boat, all the while screaming about sharks." He scratched behind Killian's ears. "Never saw my baby brother swim so fast in my life. He climbed back onto the boat so mad at us, he beat Bowen with the rubber shark and wrestled me across the deck of the boat until we were all wheezing with laughter."

It was one of their favorite memories that always made them laugh until their sides hurt, even years later. Bane had the fleas and baby skunks, Killian had the rubber lake shark. And the stories never got old.

The truck slowed down when Bowen pulled into the vet clinic. Killian gnashed his teeth again and whimpered as they carefully picked up him. Kennedy ran to the back door. Shit, Bane realized he wasn't wearing a stitch of clothing.

And it was mid-day.

Carrying Killian inside, Bowen held the door for him while talking to someone on his cell. Bane only caught a few worlds of the convo but knew he must be telling the family. Bane carried Killian over to the surgical table in the middle of the large room. "What do I do? What do you need?" He didn't have a clue how to use half the stuff in here, but could follow orders.

"Keep talking to him," Kennedy said.

"What the hell is going on here?" boomed a male from the doorway.

"You're going to keep your mouth shut and let me handle this," Kennedy snarled, "or I'll sue you for sexual harassment, Mark."

Say what now? Bane's gaze narrowed on the human in a white coat. Did his *Deesha* just say sexual harassment?

She shoved a finger in Bane's face. "Not necessary. We've got him by the balls and we will use every piece of equipment and supply available. Mark isn't going to do a thing about it." She turned to face this Mark motherfucker. "Isn't that right?"

Since Bane was holding a massive, injured wolf down on the table, Bowen stepped in on his behalf. "How about you and I have a little talk outside." He grabbed Mark by the nape and frog-marched his ass out the back door.

"I need assistance!" she yelled. No one came. "Shit, what day is it?"

Took Bane a minute to figure that out himself. "Wednesday. I think."

"No one's here then. Wednesdays they're closed. Mark uses the day for paperwork and billing." She rushed over and started opening cabinets and rolled over two machines.

Killian's fur rippled under Bane's hands.

He looked down, his mouth drying up at what he saw.

Killian switched between whimpers and... groans. His muscles bunched. Rippled. His teeth flattened.

A door slammed shut and Bowen said, "Mark won't be an issue any—"

They all held their breath as Killian panted on this back. In human form. Scars crisscrossed his limbs. Teeth marks, slashes, bullet holes and gashes bled everywhere. "B-b-bane," Killian cried.

"I'm… I-I-I-I…" his body seized and he bit down on his lip so hard, blood dripped down his chin.

"Shh. Don't talk, brother. We've got you. We're here. Kennedy's going to work on you, okay? I love you, brother. We love you so fucking much."

Killian cried out, his back bowing, hands clawing the air as they morphed back into paws. "Tell…" he panted so hard his throat vibrated. "Tell everyone… tell 'em I love them. Tell 'em…" he screamed in pain as the wolf side shredded this miracle to pieces before their eyes. "Good… bye."

Bane gripped the edge of the table as they all watched Killian shift back to wolf form. His body stilled. The light faded from his eyes.

"No," Kennedy cried out. "No, no, no!" She ripped the IV line and started a drip. "No!"

Bane grabbed her from behind, and gently pulled her back from the table.

"No!" she yelled, fighting to free herself. "I can save him. I can do it!" She stomped on Bane's foot and jerked out of his arms, lunging towards Killian. "I can save him. I have to try and—"

"He's gone," Bane said softly. Gently pulling her back again, he wrapped her in a tight embrace and pressed his mouth to her temple. "He's gone, Kennedy."

CHAPTER 40

He's gone.

The arteries in Kennedy's heart broke loose and sprayed like hoses in her chest.

He's gone.

She couldn't feel her feet.

He's gone.

Jake was gone. Killian was gone.

A sad, high-pitched howl echoed in the room. She could feel it in her chest, bone deep. It reached into her soul and squeezed it. Bane and Bowen howled a second time, their voices harmonized so perfectly she felt something crack in her.

Kennedy swayed, sobbing.

Crack. Her bad leg gave out when she fell. *Crack, crack.*

Pain shot up her legs, making her stomach roil. "Something's wrong." *Crack- crack-crack!* Sharp jolts of electrified agony zipped up her spine. Her back bowed. Her lungs compressed. "Bane!"

His eyes widened, and he caught her before she fully collapsed.

What was happening?

"Shit!" Bane slid his arms under her and he lifted her from the floor. "She's turning!"

"What?" Bowen barked. "You bit her?"

Kennedy's stomach clenched. Heat licked her skin, forcing an immediate hot flash.

Bane's gaze danced across her face. He shook his head. "I

286

can't remember. Things happened so fast."

"You don't fucking remember if you bit your goddamn *Deesha*?" Bowen rushed forward and pressed his hand to her face.

"I bit her," Bane said. "Yeah... I... as a wolf. I bit her ankle when I dragged her out of Acid's way."

Kennedy clawed at Bane, desperate to catch her breath. She could hear everything, as if someone had turned the volume all the way up. "Bitten," she panted. "Bitten more than once."

"Fuck." Bane's eyes were wild with panic. "Check her legs."

"Three bites, one deep enough for stitches," he said.

Bane trembled. "Her arm was ravaged too."

"Dog," she panted. Kennedy's vision narrowed, blackness eating away the edges. "Dog bites."

"Did Killian bite you?" Bane held her tighter. "Kennedy, do you know if Killian bit you too?"

"No," she moaned, trying to stay conscious. Her heart rate dipped, as did her head.

"No, you don't know, or no, he didn't?"

Kennedy passed out before she could answer.

"If Killian bit her before you did, Bane, she's—"

"I know!" Bane roared at Bowen. He knew what it would do and refused to allow that possibility to enter his mind. She'd have to be put down. A bite from a Lycan lost to his wolf was a death sentence. "I have to get her out of here."

"I'll take Killian." Bowen reassured him. "Just get your *Deesha* someplace safe."

Kennedy was deadweight in Bane's arms when he kicked open the back door and ran towards Bowen's truck. Bowen followed with Killian draped over his shoulder. Mark stood over by the dumpsters with a swollen eye and busted lip. "Is she..."

"She's fine," Bowen growled. "But you won't be if you breathe a word of this to anyone." He used his dominance to intimidate Mark, sending him back behind the dumpsters to hide again. For good measure, Bane glowered at Mark and growled low enough to make the human piss his pants. That should do the trick. They would have to bring Derek in to erase his mind ASAP. Until then, rely on fear to keep Mark's mouth shut.

Kennedy started to convulse in Bane's arms. "I got you," he said to her. "You're going to be just fine." He climbed in the bed of the truck and cradled Kennedy in his lap. Bowen placed Killian's body on the other side of him. "Let's go!"

Bowen didn't need to be told twice.

The entire ride home, Bane cooed in Kennedy's ears. This was going to hurt. Change was never without pain. *But if Killian bit her first...* He squeezed his eyes shut. No. Not thinking about it. "You're doing great, *Deesha*. Keep breathing."

"Hurts," she whimpered.

If she was still able to talk, that was a good thing. It meant she'd gained some consciousness back.

"You're so strong. So damn amazing." He kissed the crown of her head. "You're a miracle, you know that? You're a goddamn miracle and I'm going to love you so hard every day."

She grunted, her body wracking with tremors. "Too... hot."

"I know," he combed her hair with his fingers, smoothing it out of her face. "Just keep breathing nice and slow for me." Heat radiated off her skin. The temp surge was from her cells evolving at a rapid pace. Her body tensed, brow pinching together as she curled in his lap. She went into a seizure.

Please, he prayed. *Please don't take her away from me. Don't let her suffer after all she's been through.* He wasn't sure who the hell he was even praying to. *Please help me guide her through his. Give her grace. Peace. All the love she's needed.... All that she's given to others... let it bounce back and blanket her now.*

The ride home went by in a blink. Focusing so hard on Kennedy, Bane lost time. It wasn't just her clock ticking now. It was both of theirs. Bowen stopped the truck and climbed out, grabbing Killian while Bane scooped Kennedy up again. "Everyone will be here soon."

Bane didn't care. "Gotta get her to the woods. Go get her brother and—"

"I'll take care of everything," Bowen assured. The twins stared at each other for a heartbeat, then Bowen ran his hand down Kennedy's cheek. "She's incredible, brother. She'll pull through just fine."

From his lips to the fate's ears.

Kennedy's skin felt too tight. Was it splitting? It felt like it was tearing into ribbons. *Holy shit, this hurts.* She had a horrible vision of herself writhing on the ground as her skin, tissue, and muscles tore off her bones and fell like rags on the ground.

Next came a hot flash unlike any other she'd endured. Had she fallen into lava? Was she melting? Her ears popped. Blood seeped into her mouth and her gums stung. She tried to cry out, but her jaw popped and dislocated.

Terror took hold. She was going to die. Her limbs wouldn't work. Her lungs compressed. A soundless scream morphed into a high-pitched howl. Her throat bulged, swelling with something lodged inside it.

Bane was above her. Cupping her face, holding her steady, he said, "Run."

Run? She couldn't even move! What did he mean *run*? Kennedy kicked her legs out, digging her heels into the dirt. Did she grow extra joints? She was afraid to look down. Afraid of what she was becoming. This wasn't supposed to happen like this. Didn't the full moon have a significant role in shifting?

Guess not.

She rolled over onto her hands and knees, coughing up blood and spit and bile. "Help."

"*Run,*" Bane urged again. "Hit the ground in time with your heartbeat. Trust me."

She shook her head. She didn't have the strength to run. This ungodly pain robbed her of breath and exhausted her. She squeezed her eyes shut, and the vision of Jake being ripped apart by those dogs came to mind. His screams. His inability to fight or escape. It pissed her off. It broke her heart. It made her scream. Shoving the heels of her palms against her eyes, she rubbed them hard enough to see stars.

Her skin began to break again. Her bones snapped and popped, shattering all her pretenses on how bad this could really get.

"Run!" Bane tugged Kennedy up to her feet and propped her against his chest. Pressing a hard, fast kiss to her temple, he shoved her forward. "Run with the beat of your heart. Trust me. I've got you."

I've got you.

Run.

Run, run, run!

Kennedy took off. Her feet slammed on the forest floor, her breaths punching out of her.

Run with the beat of your heart.

She felt a presence quickly approach from behind. She was being chased. Instinct demanded Kennedy pick up speed. Using her arms to gain momentum, tears sprung from her eyes and panic slammed into her. She'd dreamed of being chased. Never once got a look at the thing that always came for her. But as she ran for her life now, in pain and scared out of her mind, she didn't look back at the beast sprinting behind her. She heard the steady pounding of his paws. Smelled his fur. Felt his presence even before Bane came into her peripheral vision.

Kennedy kept running. Sweat dripped down her back. Her thighs ached. Her bullet wound no longer registered because the burning in her body demanded all her attention. She. Kept. Running.

Her feet hit the dirt, she jumped over a fallen tree. *Ba-bum*. She sprinted up a steep hill. *Ba-bum, ba-bum*. Taking a sharp left, she lost traction and slid. Bane bumped her leg, giving her foot purchase enough to right herself and not lose momentum. *Ba-bum-ba-bum-ba-bum*. Kennedy started to feel lighter. Faster. Freer.

Ba-bum-babumbabumbabum.

The forest shifted, trees grew taller, colors morphed, the rich scent of pine and earth filled her nose.

Babumbabumbabumbabum!

Her speed kicked up ten more notches. She could breathe. The burning stopped. The pain ebbed. She smiled and her mouth felt out of whack. Kennedy looked over and saw Bane running beside her, at the same eye level. His head barely moved as the rest of him shot off through the woods, keeping pace with her.

Kennedy slowed down. Bane did too.

She wasn't as out of breath as she anticipated. Then again, she wasn't in the same position she'd started this run in, either.

Kennedy was on all fours. Her heart pounded fiercely in her

ribs. She looked over at Bane, because she was too scared to look down and see if she had feet or paws. Bane sat with his tail wagging. He let out a bark.

She flinched.

Bane barked again.

She flinched more and backed away.

She was... she was a wolf. Staring at the ground, she got an eyeful of massive paws with long black nails. Her fur was exactly how Bane said it would be. *How do I get back to human?* Kennedy skittered backwards, whining and panting. *How to do I shift back to human?*

She couldn't even ask because wolves didn't use words.

Bane shifted and crouched down. "Shh," he ran his hand over her muzzle.

Oh my god, this is the weirdest feeling in all the world. She hated that it felt good. Hated that she wanted him to pet her more. What if she was stuck like this forever? Freaked, Kennedy snapped her teeth and nipped his forearm.

"Breathe, *Deesha.*"

Breathe? What was that going to get her? She needed to get *human* again, damnit!

"Let your body settle for a minute and then melt into yourself."

This guy. Kennedy nipped him again, too scared to listen. Melt into yourself? What the fuck did he think she was, a bowl of ice cream? She began to cry. It came out in whimpers and whines.

Holy shit. She was an animal. A fucking *animal.*

"I've got you." Bane didn't relent. "Just follow my lead." He held her to his chest. She snorted and tried to pull away, but he wouldn't let her. She wanted to run. Get out. Dash out of her body.

And that's exactly what she did.

Kennedy maneuvered out of Bane's hold and shot off again. She was scared and mad and everything felt foreign and exhilarating and her head was all over the place about it. Jake. Jake was dead. Fucking Jake and his bullshit would never affect her again. No more guilt trips, no more obligations.

He'd been ripped apart by a pack of dogs.

And in turn, those men had been fed to the wolves.

Her wolf. Her mate.

Kennedy darted through the forest, letting herself feel a million awful, terrible things. She was so mad at Jake for a lifetime of toxic co-dependency, and was pissed at herself for being part of it. She was mad that she moved down here. Mad that she hadn't done better for herself. Mad that she never put boundaries up between her and her brother.

He's gone.

She'd never have to deal with it again. Shouldn't she feel better about that? Why did it hurt so much? She was free! It was over. But she didn't feel free, and it didn't feel over. She wished she could piece her brother back together and scream at him. Hit him. Call him names and hug him. Thank him for saving her. Say she was sorry he had such a shit life. Tell him she understood how he did what he thought was his only option, even if he might have been wrong. She wanted to tell him that they had shit parents and he was a product of his environment and neglect and abuse. Let him know he was worth more to Kennedy than he'd ever know. Make sure he understood that he was loved.

They'd both sacrificed so much for each other. Almost too much. And now it was over. He had peace.

Kennedy needed to hunt her peace down.

She slowed her sprint to a jog, panting heavily and growing dizzier. A half a mile later, she was running on fumes and had to stop and lay on the ground. Tears streaked the dirt on her face as she allowed herself to have the ugliest cry in history.

She didn't realize Bane was with her until he scooped her into his lap. They were both naked, drenched in sweat and salty tears. His solid body, soft touch, warm skin, and strong heartbeat leeched into her, calming her down after a while.

"I feel too much," she hiccuped. "I'm scared."

"You're the bravest woman I've ever met in my life," he said, sweeping the hair out of her face. "Fuck, Kennedy. You just…" he kissed her forehead and began rocking her. "You're incredible."

She didn't feel incredible. She felt worn out and gross. "Will it always be like that?"

"The shift?"

She nodded.

"No. But for that being your first time, and not having an education or warning on what to look for, you knocked it out of the park." His arms caged her in a tighter hug. "I nearly fainted when I saw your wolf break out of you. It was... flawless."

"Didn't feel flawless."

"No, I bet it didn't. But you handled it beautifully, *Deesha*. How do you feel now?"

"Like hell."

The low rumble of Bane's chuckle vibrated right into Kennedy's bones. Something stirred inside her, making her breath hitch.

"She's strong," Bane said with a grin. "My wolf is howling for her."

Kennedy's brow pinched. It was too much to dissect and process. But she needed to try. "I still felt human. As I ran in wolf form, my thoughts were still all mine."

"That will change a little bit as you and your wolf learn each other."

"Are we different entities?"

"No, only if the curse takes you are you different and completely separated. When that happens, it tears you down the middle, dividing you completely." He cupped her face and smiled. "But that won't happen. You don't have the curse because we found each other. You and your wolf share the same spirit and thoughts. Only your instincts and cravings will be a little different. She'll want fresh kills and your human side will want grilled steak."

Her mouth watered automatically. "This is weird."

"You'll get used to it." Bane lifted her hips, giving a cue to stand. "Let me see you so I can check for injuries."

Kennedy stood on wobbly legs and felt like a newborn faun. "You smell good," she blurted. Her cheeks reddened instantly.

"I sure hope so, *Deesha*. My pheromones are kicking out big time right now."

Heat pooled between her legs, and she clenched her thighs together. Bane groaned, as if he'd already caught the scent of her lust. Slowly, he walked around her, inspecting every inch of her body. "No injuries. Even your bullet wound healed perfectly."

"Strong like bull." She giggled nervously. "And your bullet wounds are healed too." She worried one of them might have lodged in his muscle and cause infection.

"Lycan are fast healers. We reject most metals outside of

silver. So bullets either slide right through or our muscles will force them out."

"Ohhh very handy."

He stopped in front of her and cupped her face again. "I'm so sorry about your brother."

Her heart drooped a little. "I'm sorry about yours too." She wished she could have saved Killian. Kennedy figured she'd live with that guilt for the rest of her life now.

"Come on," Bane grabbed her hand. "Let's get you cleaned up."

"Where are we going?" Because she was fairly certain the cabin was in the opposite direction of where Bane was leading her. "Hey! Where are we going?!"

CHAPTER 41

"I should have thought this through," Bane growled as Kennedy stepped out of the river, soaking wet and dripping with pleasure. They'd fucked both in and out of the river for the better part of an hour.

"What are you talking about?"

"I should have brought down some clothes." He hadn't had the time to prepare for her sudden shift or he'd have set lots of things up differently for her. "If my brother sees you naked, I'll be forced to carve his fucking eyes out."

Kennedy laughed.

He was only half joking.

"At least then you'll be easier to tell apart," she said.

Bane cocked an eyebrow. "You find it hard to tell us apart?"

"No," she said. "But other people probably do. You're identical in every way."

"Not *every* way." He grabbed his cock and gave it a tug.

"I'm not even going to imagine your brother's dick."

"Good," he growled. "Because this is the only one you're getting. No twin sandwiches for you."

"And how many of those have you two served?"

Was that jealousy in her tone? Let's find out. "Only a few."

Kennedy stopped walking and glowered. Her lips peeled back as her throat expanded with a vicious growl.

He hardened instantly.

"Names. Addresses." She narrowed her eyes and jabbed a

295

finger at him. "I'm getting a new baseball bat."

His laughter startled the birds in the trees, and they shot out from everywhere. "I'm joking," he said. "Swear."

Her shoulders relaxed as she walked up to him and smacked his arm. "Not funny."

"A little funny."

"Nope."

Damn, what a woman. He gripped her hips and spun her around, pressing her back against a tree. "I like you wild and vicious."

"Good, because I don't plan to change." She ran her hands through his wet hair.

He couldn't wait another minute to be inside her again. "Too sore?"

"No." She grinned, playfully.

Bane nudged her thighs apart with his knee and reached between them to see how wet she was already. Bringing his finger up, he licked it clean and groaned with her taste on his tongue.

"Take me from behind this time?"

Fuck. Yes. He spun her around and Kennedy planted her hands on the trunk of the tree for support. Shoving that luscious ass of hers out like an offering, Bane cracked it hard enough to leave a lovely handprint. "I can't believe this is all mine."

"Mark it better then," she teased.

His next growl was all wolf. Kennedy laughed and then pressed her hand to her chest. "Oh my god, my wolf just got all excited."

Bane bit his bottom lip to keep from laughing. He squatted down and bit her right ass cheek, making her yip and giggle. Her laugh was a drug he'd stay addicted to forever. He loved that she was happy. Running his hands up her backside, Bane gripped her phenomenal hips and gyrated against her ass with his cock. "Which hole."

"All of them," she said breathlessly. "But… maybe for now…" She spread her legs wider and reached between them, grabbing his length and guiding it towards her wet pussy. "Here."

Bane bit her shoulder as he pushed inside a little at a time. He felt her clench around his length every time he went to retreat, like her body was trying to keep him inside.

Kennedy braced herself with one hand on the tree, the other she bent around her back for Bane to lace his fingers with hers. She was strong. Resilient.

Perfect.

Bane's thrusts deepened until they were both grunting like animals during rutting season. He didn't pull out either. After he made sure she came twice around his fat cock, Bane let her hand go, grabbed her waist, and slammed into her harder, harder, harder. His balls slapped against her skin. Sweat trickled down their joined bodies. He tipped his head back, squeezed his eyes shut, and just as his orgasm barreled out of him, he howled. Thighs tensing, tendons snapping, he filled her to the brim. When he pulled out, Bane shoved two of his fingers inside her pussy, keeping his cum inside her a little longer.

Kennedy's cheeks were flushed, the tips of her ears bright red, and she had the most spectacular smile on her beautiful face that lit him up inside. Christ, if his heart swelled any more, it would likely explode.

"Thank you," she whispered.

"For what?" Because if it was for the mind-blowing orgasms, it was he who should be thanking her.

"You protected me. You said you'd keep me safe, and you did."

Her words held more weight than she let on with that light tone of hers. But he knew what she meant. He'd been a beast in that barn. Taken bullets for her, killed for her, shielded her as best he could. "Always," he said, pressing a kiss on her collarbone, and another on her throat. "Always, *Deesha*."

The sound of car doors slamming popped their bubble.

Reality was back.

Kennedy could barely walk. As they headed up the trail towards the house, a horrible burning sensation settled in her gut. She needed some time to process all that happened, but as voices rose in the distance, her guilt for what she did and didn't do settled into her belly. Seeking comfort, she tightened her grip on Bane's.

He tossed her a reassuring smile.

"Is it your family?" she asked nervously.

"I'm sure."

Oh God. How could she face them? What would she say?

"Hang on a sec." Bane let go of her hand and jogged over to a shed at the back of the property. Kennedy hugged herself and looked down at her dirty feet. Her need to run away was back. She didn't want to face reality. Too many emotions assaulted her at once and she began shivering.

"Here." Bane reappeared with a shirt and boxers for her. After handing them over, he slipped into a set of jeans. "We usually keep a few things in the back just in case of unexpected company."

Kennedy swallowed the rock in her throat. It settled in her belly with a bunch of other heavy stones. Silently, she followed Bane around the cabin to the front yard. Alistair and Emerick were talking with Bowen on the porch. Emily was over by a black mound under a tree. Marie was beside her, on her knees, her body shaking as she held her face in her hands.

Yeah... Kennedy needed to run. Get away.

They would hate her for this. Her brother was part of the MC who'd used Killian as a fight animal. And she hadn't been able to save him in the end. If it hadn't been for Jake's crew or Kennedy's failure, Killian might still be alive.

She took a step back. Aaaannnd bumped right into Bane.

"You can't outrun your fate," he said quietly. Wrapping his arms around her middle, he said, "Shh, I've got you."

But she didn't want him to get her. She wanted him to let her go. Yell at her. Call her a coward and a failure and a horrible woman. Her body trembled from head to toe. Her breath hitched as she watched Marie turn to look over at her.

Kennedy tried to back up some more, but Bane was a solid wall she couldn't break through.

Marie came over, wiping her face as she closed the distance between them.

Kennedy's head spun with panic and regret. "I'm sorry," she blurted out. "I'm so sorry for everything. I'm sorry."

Marie's brow furrowed. She looked exhausted and heartbroken, and it was all Kennedy's fault. "Why?" she asked, cupping Kennedy's face to hold her hostage. "Why on earth are you sorry, sweetheart? You brought my boy home. Never be sorry for bringing Killian back to us."

A wail bubbled out of Kennedy and her legs gave out. Bane held her up and Marie gathered her into an embrace she'd never gotten from her own mother. "Thank you, Kennedy," Marie rocked her gently. "Thank you for making our family whole again." She held Kennedy in a hug that was warm and safe and filled with the kind of love only a good mother had for her babies. As the rest of the Woods family crowded around them, they surrounded Kennedy in a love so profound, she doubted there was a word for it.

Unshakeable came to mind.

Before long, someone let out a long, beautiful, make-the-hair-on-your-nape-stand-up howl, and the others joined in, one-by-one. Kennedy was the last to unite the chorus, but once she did, another piece of her soul set free.

It was the last bit of regret she carried for far too long.

"Come on," Bane said, luring her out of the pack circle and up the steps. Crossing the threshold felt like coming into a new world… and leaving all her tragedy behind.

"Is it over?" Her voice was still a little shaky. "Are you safe… is the curse completely broken?" She couldn't stand the thought of Bane being in the same position as Killian had been in.

"Yes, *Deesha*." He tipped her chin with his finger. "And yours is too. We're free. We're safe."

"And we're together, no matter what."

"Forever," he kissed her slowly. "For always…"

"Meant to be."

EPILOGUE

They had a burial ritual for Killian, and Bowen had collected some of Jake's remains to give him a burial too. The closure was needed for everyone, and Kennedy was able to put to rest so much of her past. It was like a tremendous weight had lifted from her shoulders. She would miss Jake, always, but... some things were meant to be and not all of it ended happily.

She hoped he found peace.

Over the course of a week, Bowen and Bane cleaned up their tracks. The bodies, including some of Jake's remains, were left inside and the barn was set on fire. Cops labeled it a turf war. The surviving dogs were taken to an emergency vet, and from there a rescue center. Mark, her former boss, had his memory erased — too bad he couldn't have his personality erased and replaced with a better one.

"I need to start looking for another job." She rolled onto her side and ran her hands down Bane's torso. They'd slept down by the river, under the stars, last night. They ran for miles under the moon and then worshipped each other until dawn. Life with Bane was incredible.

"Start your own vet clinic. You can be a traveling one."

Kennedy chewed on her bottom lip. "That'll take a ton of money in supplies and stuff. I'd also possibly need a trailer."

Bane merely shrugged. "Spare no expense. Get whatever you need, top of the line."

She arched a brow. "And where is that money going to come

from?" The last thing she wanted was dive into deep debt.

"You don't live as long as we do and not have a bankroll to show for it. Although..." he pursed his lips, "we keep most of it outside of traceable accounts."

Live as long as they do? Traceable accounts? "Wait." She propped up on her elbow. "How old are you?"

"Meh." Bane waved her off. "Age is just a number."

"No. Uh-uh. How old are you?"

"Close to three hundred?"

"Is that a question or a statement?"

"A tester-outer answer?"

Again, his answer came out as a question. She smacked his arm playfully. "For real, how old are you?"

He rolled her over until Kennedy was straddling his hips. His cock wedged between her ass cheeks, and she reached down to reposition it so he was at her opening. Playfully rubbing the head of his cock along her slick folds, she asked again. "How old are you?"

Bane's eyes rolled as he grunted. Pushing his hips up, he tried to shove inside, but she wouldn't let him. "Fuck, I can't math it out when you feel this good."

"Math it out?" She popped up and stood over him, her legs on either side of his body. Bane laughed, tucking his arms under his head, and stared up at her. "If this is supposed to make me math, you're definitely in the wrong position."

Ohhh, this man! "Bane!"

He laughed again and propped up on his elbows. It made his abs flex, and her instinct was to lick all eight of them. She held her ground though. "Answer me."

"I'm three-hundred and eleven. I think. Wait..." He frowned and actually looked like he was calculating it. "Yeah. Three-eleven. Shit. No. Maybe three-twenty-one?" He had the audacity to shrug and lay back down again with his arms as a pillow under his head. "Birthdays got boring after two centuries. I really never kept track. Ask my mom, she knows."

Kennedy gawked. Her mouth opened. Closed. Opened again. "You're serious?"

"I keep telling you, I'll never lie to you. Start believing it."

Holy shit. "Am I going to age slower now?"

"I doubt you'll age at all for the first few centuries." He ran his hand up her calf. "All this perfection is mine for *forevahhh*."

No. Way. Was he *serious*?

"I'm legit, the luckiest Lycan alive. You know how happy me and my wolf are that these thighs get to be our earmuffs for eternity?" He leaned up and stroked her legs. "You should take a seat. I'm dying for breakfast." Bane knocked the back of her knees, making her legs give out and she crashed on top of him. With a wolfish grin, he tapped the corner of his mouth and said, "Crawl up here and have a seat, *Deesha*."

Kennedy made a guttural groan and obeyed.

His tongue was diabolical.

After her first orgasm of the morning, she leaned forward, begging for a minute to catch her breath. Bane laughed and indulged. That's when they both heard a shuffling in the bushes behind them.

Kennedy hopped up, paranoid. She'd yet to have full control over her instincts and still struggled to distinguish certain sounds and smells. Bane moved slowly. Pressing a finger to his glossy, lust-coated lips, he said, "Shh."

Her heart pounded. "It's probably Molly."

"Want me to check?"

"Can't you just sniff her out?"

He licked his mouth obscenely. "I can only smell you. You've smothered me in cream and pheromones."

Sorry, not sorry, she thought.

Bane crept closer to the bushes, halting a second too late. "Oh shit!" He backed away, choking and gagging.

Oh nooooo! Kennedy stumbled out of the way, but the mist caught her too. Gagging, her eyes watered, and she couldn't get out of there fast enough.

Bane grabbed her hand, and they ran into the river together. Not that it made a lick of difference, but at least the skunk wouldn't follow them into the water.

They were both covered in skunk spray.

"Oh my god, this is awful." She couldn't escape the smell. It was in her nostrils, her hair, her skin, the back of her throat.

Bane laughed so hard he was wheezing. She couldn't help but join him. "Welcome to Lycan life," he said, just before dunking her under the water.

302

They swam downstream, chasing, kissing, and laughing while covered in skunk musk.

Kennedy couldn't ask for a better beginning to the life she always wished for.

For information on this book and other future releases, please visit my website: **www.BrianaMichaels.com**

If you liked this book, please help spread the word by leaving a review on the site you purchased your copy, or on a reader site such as Goodreads.

I'd love to hear from readers too, so feel free to send me an email at: sinsofthesidhe@gmail.com or visit me on Facebook: www.facebook.com/BrianaMichaelsAuthor

Thank you!

ABOUT THE AUTHOR

Briana Michaels grew up and still lives on the East Coast. When taking a break from the crazy adventures in her head, she enjoys running around with her two children. If there is time to spare, she loves to read, cook, hike in the woods, and sit outside by a roaring fire. She does all of this with the love and support of her amazing husband who always has her back, encouraging her to go for her dreams.

Made in United States
North Haven, CT
30 September 2024

58141858R00173